White

'A story full of passion, heroism and all those things that will keep you reading long after bedtime'
New Woman

'Outstanding . . . tensions and challenges on every page and breathtaking descriptions of the Himalayan landscape'
The Good Book Guide

'Rosie Thomas continues to justify her reputation as a superb storyteller . . . an epic mix of passion and drama . . . truly a gripping read'
Hampstead & Highgate Express

'Danger, adventure and love . . . terrific stuff . . . a real weepy'
Sunday Times

'Compelling . . . a master storyteller'
Cosmospolitan

'Hugely enjoyable . . . Rosie Thomas writes with beautiful, effortless prose, she shows a rare compassion and a real understanding of the nature of love'
The Times

'Honest and absorbing, Rosie Thomas mixes the bitter and t[illegible] with the knowledge that the huma[illegible]d th[illegible]

Rosie Thomas is the author of a number of celebrated novels, including *Bad Girls, Good Women, A Simple Life* and the Top Ten bestsellers *Every Woman Knows a Secret* and *Moon Island*. She lives in north London, and when not writing fiction spends her time travelling and mountaineering.

Other titles by Rosie Thomas

Celebration
Follies
Sunrise
The White Dove
Strangers
Bad Girls, Good Women
A Woman of Our Times
All My Sins Remembered
Other People's Marriages
A Simple Life
Every Woman Knows a Secret
Moon Island

White

Rosie Thomas

Published by Arrow Books in 2001

5 7 9 10 8 6

First published in the United Kingdom in 2000 by William Heinemann

Arrow Books Limited
20 Vauxhall Bridge Road, London, SW1V 2SA

Random House Australia (Pty) Limited
20 Alfred Street, Milsons Point, Sydney,
New South Wales 2061, Australia

Random House New Zealand Limited
18 Poland Road, Glenfield
Auckland 10, New Zealand

Random House (Pty) Limited
Endulini, 5a Jubilee Road, Parktown 2193, South Africa

The Random House Group Limited Reg. No. 954009
www.randomhouse.co.uk

A CIP catalogue record for this book
is available from the British Library

Papers used by Random House are natural, recyclable products made from wood grown in sustainable forests. The manufacturing processes conform to the environmental regulations of the country of origin

ISBN 0 09 941524 0

Typeset by SX Composing DTP, Rayleigh, Essex
Printed and bound in Great Britain by
Bookmarque Ltd, Croydon, Surrey

for Graeme and Judith

For editorial help, insight and endless encouragement in the various stages of writing this book I am grateful to Mark Lucas, Lynne Drew and Gail Rebuck. Dr Andrew Peacock and Dr Huw Alban Davies provided medical details, and the real Mark Mason allowed me the use of his excellent name. Numerous people shared their knowledge and love of the mountains with me, including Phil Bowen, Nick Evans, Katie James, Adrian Morris and Rebecca Stephens. Barry Franklin, Jean-Claude Charlet and Sandy Allan patiently encouraged me out of the armchair and into the first steps as a novice mountaineer, and I am indebted to each of them.

Charlie and Flora King provided the stimulus and the impetus, for everything.

The sun was overhead, a solid white eye in a harsh sky. As midday approached, the glare and the heat became unbearable and she stopped near a jumble of rocks that offered a narrow margin of shade. She held up her hand to Saddiq, her guide, and when he halted the two porters who followed in their tracks obediently shuffled to a stop as well. The older one immediately rolled the pack off his back and rummaged in the pouch around his waist for tobacco to fill his thin clay pipe.

'I'd like to rest now, Saddiq. Maybe drink and eat something?' she said.

The guide nodded. He had led the young American lady for two weeks, into the amphitheatre contained by the high peaks on the border between China and Pakistan. The solitary white massif of K2 stood out hard and brilliant against the sky, directly behind them.

The doctor lady had barely faltered in twelve days of walking. It was hardly suitable that a young, unmarried Western woman should be making her way alone in such places, Saddiq thought, even under the impeccable guidance and protection of a man such as himself, but he could find no fault with her strength or stamina. She had been as tough as any man and she had won his respect. If the lady wanted to call a rest stop now, high up here on the glacier and barely a morning's walk down from K2 Base Camp, then she had earned the right to do so.

The woman took off her own pack and sat down in the band of shade offered by the rocks. The glacier was a jumble of bare rocks, dirty ice, grit and wind-flayed snow. She stretched out her legs and rested her head against the stone, sighing as luxuriously as if it were a feather pillow.

Her eyes fixed on the high peak. K2. Only the second highest, but a far tougher and more brutal climb than Everest. She had been as close to it, now, as she would ever get but it still drew her eyes and her imagination.

She didn't hear the porters murmuring together as they lit the stove to boil a pan of water. She was daydreaming as Saddiq supervised the brewing of tea in a billycan and the pouring into her tin mug.

But she heard the man's voice so clearly that it cut into her head and settled into the chambers of her skull. Afterwards, long after he had finished, not only the words but the pure sound, the separate notes, vibrated minutely in her inner ear.

He asked the abrupt question as if these were the first words he had uttered for long days.

'Can I have some of that?'

It was a British voice, with a faint unplaceable secondary accent.

In the following instant she looked to see where the voice came from and saw him with his back to the ring of mountains, and with the sun hard over his head. Her first impression was of a black beard masking a gaunt face with skin flayed raw by the weather. Saddiq straightened up and moved protectively in front of her. The porters stepped closer to the discarded packs.

He saw their suspicious reaction. 'I only want a drink. I'm thirsty.'

'Here.'

She scrambled to her feet. She held out her untasted tea.

He took the tin mug in both hands, apparently warming them in spite of the sun's heat. Then he drank, finishing the tea in a single long swallow. The tendons in his neck strained. She saw that he was very thin, almost emaciated.

The man handed back the empty mug. 'Thank you.'

'Would you like some more? Something to eat?'

Saddiq's mouth pinched in a thin line.

'What have you got to spare?'

'Dried fruit. Crackers. Canned and packet stuff. Not a big choice. We're on our way out.'

The man passed one hand over his face. He was exhausted, she realised. She motioned to

Saddiq to refill the mug.

'Thank you,' the man said again. His mouth was painfully cracked.

'We can share,' she said. Showing their disapproval with every movement, her companions went back to preparing food. The kerosene burner hissed at their feet.

The man was carrying a huge pack on his back. She pointed to it. 'Take it off. Sit down and rest.'

He did as he was told, absently, as if his whole attention was elsewhere. He sat down at a little distance, his back against a rock and his face turned to the mountains. He didn't gaze at the high peak in the way that she had done, with awe and fascination. He stared at it blankly, as if he would look anywhere else if he could, knowing that his eyes would be dragged back to it whenever he tried to turn away.

'Are you a climber?' she attempted.

'I was,' the man said curtly. Nothing in him invited conversation and she made no more attempts. He took the plate of tinned tuna and reconstituted mashed potato that Saddiq passed to him via his client and ate. He cleaned the dish mechanically, without visible relish, eating because he knew that he must rather than with the pleasure of appetite.

'Thank you,' he said for the last time when he had finished everything. He drank another mug of black tea and accepted the fistful of dried apricots that she gave him. He tucked the fruit into a side pocket of his pack, then lifted the load once again.

'Can we help you with anything else?' she asked.

'No. I have to get out, that's all. I'm just getting out of here.'

He turned away, the pack tipping briefly sideways on his back before he wearily shrugged it upright and secured the straps. She watched him go. For a man who was clearly close to his physical limits he moved very fast. Before Saddiq and his porters had cleared the remnants of the meal and dismantled the tiny stove, the man was no more than a speck on the blinding expanse of the glacier.

'Dangerous fellow,' Saddiq muttered.

'No, I don't think so. Desperate maybe, but not dangerous.'

One

So many weddings, Finch Buchanan thought.

Weddings under awnings in summer gardens. Weddings in Toronto or New York, out on the coast, in white-walled Presbyterian churches, in flower-decorated homes or smart hotels. One at a ski lodge up in the Cariboo mountains and another at sunset on a Caribbean beach. Long-planned or recklessly impromptu, wherever or however they happened they all seemed the same and this one was no different. Except more so.

This time it was her dearest friend Finch was watching, standing beside an urn of white lilies and stephanotis, and shape-changing from Suzy Shepherd into Mrs Jeffery Sutton of Medford, Oregon. Suzy was about the last of their group to be married, except for Finch herself.

The bride was wearing an ivory satin Donna Karan suit and the groom had been coaxed into navy-blue Armani. As bridesmaid, Finch was wearing a little suit too, hyacinth-blue, of a cut that made her stand with her ankles together and her hands meekly clasped.

I'm too old to be got up as a fucking bridesmaid, she was thinking.

Suzy and Finch were both thirty-two years old. They had been room-mates in their first year at med school at the University of British Columbia and they had gone all the way through training together. Now Suzy was in paediatrics and had moved down to Oregon to be with Jeff, while Finch had stayed on in Vancouver as a medical practitioner. They called each other often, and e-mailed gossip and jokes and medical titbits almost every day, and they met whenever they could. But still Finch missed her friend and ally, and Suzy's marriage could only move her a further step out of reach.

They were exchanging rings. Watching and blinking away embarrassing tears, Finch was in no doubt that the two of them were happy. They were woozy with it, as dopey as a pair of Suzy's neonates after a six-ounce feed. Finch didn't feel envious, exactly; what she did feel was faintly baffled. She had never worked out the secret of connubiality herself. There had been men, of course there had. Both short-term and longer. But lately, not that many.

The short civil ceremony was over. Suzy and Jeff walked arm in arm between the rows of their beaming friends and out under an awning. Beyond it the March rain was ribbed with sleet. A photographer busied around with his Nikon.

After she had kissed her mother and her aunts and her new in-laws, Suzy opened an umbrella to exclude the rest of the audience and whispered to Finch, 'Jesus, did you see that? I did it. I married someone.'

'You married Jeff.'

'Yeah. I love him.'

'I know you do.'

Suzy laughed, showing the gap between her top front teeth. She didn't come from orthodontically obsessive stock, which was one of the reasons why Finch had loved her right from the start – for her difference from and indifference to everything Finch herself was accustomed to and thought she valued. The first time they met, Suzy marched into their room on campus, dropped a duffel bag and an armful of supermarket carriers, and eyed the matching luggage and K2 ski bags that two of Finch's three older brothers had carried up the stairs for her.

'I suppose you're some Vancouver princess?'

'You can suppose whatever you like.'

'Well, I'm po' white trash. My mom lives in a rented two-room and I haven't seen my dad for twelve years.'

It was true. And it was also true that Suzy was by far the cleverest student in their year.

She twirled her umbrella now, sending icy droplets centrifugally spinning. 'Shit, I'm a married woman. You better lead me straight to the drink, help me get over the shock,' Mrs Jeffery Sutton said.

The reception was in a new restaurant and bar that had been designed and fitted by Jeff's company. 'Like it?' he asked Finch.

There were snug booths and wood floors and tricksy mirrors and halogen lighting. It wasn't original but it was well done.

'Very much,' Finch said.

'Well, I guess you don't need me to introduce you to people,' Jeff said. His silk tie was already loosened and his top button undone.

'No.' Finch smiled. Most of Suzy's friends who had

travelled to Oregon were hers too. 'Go on, enjoy the party.'

She slid into the nearest booth with her glass of French champagne and found that Taylor Buckaby and his wife were already sitting there. Taylor had dated Suzy for a while, in the very early days, but in the end he had settled for the secretary to the Dean of Faculty who was a svelte blonde. She was a plump blonde now, but otherwise nothing had changed. Taylor was an orthopaedic surgeon. Finch could imagine just how happy he would be among his bone saws and glinting titanium joints.

'Hello, Taylor, Maddie.'

'Ah, Finch. Hello there.'

They chatted for a while, about friends and work and the Buckabys' children.

'No plans to settle down yourself, Finch?' Maddie asked.

'No, none.'

'Finch goes in for bigger challenges than a husband and kids,' Taylor explained jovially, puffing out his already rounded cheeks. 'Last year she went up to Alaska and climbed McKinley.'

Maddie focused her pale-blue eyes. She looked as if she was used to putting away plenty of champagne, or whatever else might be going.

'*Why*?'

There were a couple of beats of silence while Finch considered her answer. It was not quite the first time she had heard the question, it was just unusual to encounter such dazed incredulity in the asking. She remembered the temperatures on the mountain of forty below, and the avalanching ice, and the risk of cerebral or pulmonary oedema, and the blade-thin ridge that ran up from 16,000 feet with a drop of 2000 feet on either side of it.

'Uh . . .'

She also remembered the easy comradeship and the gallows humour of the group of climbers she had done it with – only by the West Buttress route, 'The Butt', nothing fancy. Most sharply of all she recalled the hit of euphoria that had wiped everything else from her mind as she hauled herself to the summit.

'Because I thought I would enjoy it,' she said equably. 'And I did.'

Maddie blinked and ran her tongue over her lipstick. 'Each to her own, I guess.'

The dancing was starting up. Jeff and Suzy began by spinning slow circles in each other's arms, to cheers and clapping. Finch sat with the Buckabys for five more minutes, so as not to look as if she wanted to get away from them, then eased herself out of the booth. She ate some sushi from the buffet and had a half-dozen more conversations with people she was pleased to see. After that she danced with Jeff, until Jeff's father cut in on them. Jim Sutton was a spry seventy-year-old with hands like snow shovels and a seamed brown face from a lifetime's work in the construction industry. Jeff and Suzy shared the distinction of having travelled a long way from their backgrounds without feeling the need to shake off any of the ties.

Jim did an enthusiastic lindy-hop that left Finch panting for breath. 'You're too much for me,' she protested.

'C'mon, doc. Gimme one more.'

Finch could see that it was past 6 p.m. and she had a plane to catch. Dennis Frame, her medical partner, was covering her busy clinics for her and she had already taken three days off.

'Next time.' She grinned. 'If I'm lucky.'

She went in search of Suzy and found her in one of the back booths. She had dribbled what looked like mayo down one Donna lapel and seemed set in for a serious night.

'Hey, you got out of Jim's clutches with one leap.'

'Baby, I've got to go.'

Suzy frowned. 'It's so early. Don't miss my party.' It was a routine protest, however. As soon as she had promised to come to the wedding, Finch had warned her that she couldn't stay long afterwards because she had to work the next day. And Suzy knew of old how exasperatingly rigid her friend could be about time and her professional responsibilities. They were different, but they understood each other and their friendship had rarely faltered.

Finch said, 'I know, I know. But I've got clinics tomorrow, remember? For Dennis's sake I can't take too many more days off before the expedition.'

Suzy launched herself out of the booth and locked her arms around her friend. Her face turned serious at the last word.

'Listen. I want you to take care. I want you to be safe and to come back down from there in one piece. Who'll be Sutton Junior's godmother, if you're not around?'

'*Suze*. You're not?'

Suzy winked. 'Not quite yet. But I'm planning on it.'

'Well. That's great. And I'll be fine. I'm only the expedition doctor, remember, dosing the d and v, not one of the summit glory boys.'

'Okay, just so long as you remember that. C'mon, I'll see you off.'

They weaved their way in and out of the crowd. Suzy stopped short and peeled away towards the bar. 'Hey, almost forgot.'

She leaned over behind the counter, exposing the tops of her tanned thighs. Jeff caught her and ran his hands over her hips until Suzy straightened up with what she had been searching for grasped in one hand. 'Later,' she admonished him. And she held out her bridal bouquet and stuffed it firmly into Finch's arms.

'Not me,' Finch protested. 'Find someone more deserving. Someone eager for a husband.'

'There is no one else, kid. You are the last remaining authentic unmarried woman. Pretty soon they're going to slap a heritage order on you.'

'You just want me to join the club. You want me to get married because you've gone and done it.'

Suzy smiled, a lovely hazy smile of pure happiness and contentment. 'Sure I do.'

'Forget it, pal.'

They eased their way through the crowd to the door. The party was hotting up, in the way that weddings could do.

'Finch has got to fly home up to Vancouver tonight,' Suzy explained to the last group.

'Weather's turned pretty nasty,' one of Jim Sutton's cronies observed.

'Finch has seen worse,' Suzy said proudly.

Finch put her arm around her. 'Go on, go back to your guests. I'll call you. Have a great honeymoon.'

The newlyweds were going to the Caribbean. Suzy liked beaches.

They kissed each other.

'Remember what I said. About coming back.'

'I will,' Finch promised. 'Be happy, Mrs Sutton.'

'I will,' she echoed. 'Thanks for being here, Finch. And for everything else, all the times we've had. I love you, you know? Plus you were a ripper bridesmaid.'

'I wouldn't have missed it. I love you too.'

She blew a last kiss from the doorway. As soon as she stepped outside, the cold and wind hit Finch like an axe blow. She ducked her head and teetered on high heels to the parking lot where she had left the rental car. The moment she was inside it, with the radio tuned in to some rock station and the heater beginning to do its work, Finch pushed her head hard back against the seat rest and let out a yodel of relief.

One more wedding.

She put her foot down and hightailed it for the airport until a twitch from the rear wheels gave warning of how icy the road was. She slowed at once and watched for the glow of tail lamps ahead of her.

At the airport she nosed the car into one of the Alamo slots and dropped the keys and the paperwork into the box at the closed booth at the end of the lot. The wind had strengthened and there were airborne needles of ice in it. Her thin coat over the pale-blue suit was no protection and there was a long hike to the doors of the departure hall. She dropped her bag and crouched to rummage inside it. From the bottom she pulled out her Gore-tex ski parka and pulled it on with a grunt of relief. She'd brought it with her on her three-day trip to Oregon thinking there might be a chance of some hiking, if not cross-country skiing. As it turned out there had been no time at all, but at least the faithful Patagonia was good for something now. Insulated from her hood to the middle of her thighs, Finch put her head back and marched through the wind. She carried her bag hitched over one shoulder and from the other fist trailed Suzy's wedding bouquet. She had almost left it in the car, but had decided that she could hardly abandon her best friend's flowers to wither on the passenger seat of a rented Nova.

Inside the sliding doors the warmth was a blessing but the concourse was packed. One glance at the departures board told her the worst and the clerk at the Air Canada desk confirmed it.

'I'm sorry, ma'am, the airport's closed. No flights until the weather eases. Tomorrow morning, I'd say.'

Sam McGrath was out running. It was more than a habit, this daily pushing himself through the barriers of disinclination and fatigue to achieve a rhythm and finally the synchrony of muscle and breath and mind that made it all worthwhile. It was a mainstay of his existence. Sometimes, in the blacker moments, he feared it was the only one.

He was skirting the shores of a little lake, and there was ice crusting the dead reeds along the margins and skinning the deeper water. The track wound between trees and bushes with their spring buds blackened by the return of winter; the dirt underfoot was greasy with earlier sleet but Sam knew the route so well that his pace never slackened. He was warm, now, and going at full stretch, his steady breathing making clouds in the bitter air and his footfalls pounding a drumbeat in his head.

He liked this solitude. Mostly his daily running was hemmed in by the city and there were always people within sight.

His father used to bring him fishing for brook trout down here, Sam remembered. Once they had camped somewhere back up in the trees in the old green tent and had fried their catch over a smoky fire. He would have been about ten years old. It must have been some holiday weekend when Michael hadn't swung it to go climbing.

Memories shivered and stirred in his head.

He was eight years old and standing with his father at the foot of a cliff. The face stretched up so high over Sam's head that it blotted out the sun. He reached up his hands, palms flat and raised, and rested them against the sandstone. Mike had ceremoniously dusted them with chalk. Particles of grit scraped minutely against his skin. Slowly, tasting nausea in the back of his throat, he lifted his eyes and searched for holds. Then he bent one knee and pressed the tip and side of his sneaker into a crack.

Up.

His fingers bent and hooked. The crevices were too tiny, but still he forced himself to entrust his weight to them. Sweat burst through the skim of chalk dust.

Up.

The grass, sweet and sappy, was a long way

beneath him. The rock was close to his face and the air behind and below hummed and expanded, and played tricks with gravity. One minute he was a feather, hardly anchored to the boulder, the next a sack of soaking clothes, too heavy to hold up.

Up one more foothold.

He couldn't look up or down.

'Sammy, you're fine. I'm here to catch you.'

He couldn't work out if his father's hands were huge, a great cradle waiting for him, or a tiny cup that he would smash under his weight. He hung on for a moment longer, desperation knocking inside him, then his legs liquefied and his fingers slid from their holds.

He was falling through space. There was a white flash of relief, resignation, before his father's arms caught him and lifted him at once in a great flourish of triumph and strength and pride, and then they were both laughing in delight, and Michael swung his son through a loop of blue infinity before setting his two feet back on the ground again. He kissed him on the nape of his neck, under the wet curl of his hair.

'That's my boy. You'll climb the Cap before you're twenty, just like your old man. And then some.'

Sam let him tug his ear and pummel his shoulder, after the kiss, but he knew that he wouldn't do what his father expected. Wouldn't, couldn't, whatever the Cap might be.

Twenty years later, he made himself concentrate on the length of his stride and keeping his breathing even. Running was good for that, always. You could go for miles, lost in your thoughts and memories, if that was what you wanted. And if you didn't want to think you could edit everything else out of your mind, everything except legs and lungs, and the way ahead.

The track brought him to the tip of the lake, then rose steeply through a belt of Douglas firs to meet the blacktop where it followed the crest of the ridge. With his head up and his breathing still steady even after the hill climb, Sam ran easily along the roadside. One pick-up truck came by, travelling in the opposite direction, but there was no other traffic. It was less than two miles to the turning to his father's house.

The McGrath place lay back from the road, hunched up against the black trees as if it would disappear among them if it could. The white paint on the window frames was faded to grey and it was peeling in places, and the curtains at three of the four windows were drawn tight, with that dead look of never being opened whatever the time of day. Mike McGrath's old station wagon stood on a patch of scrubby ground, with Sam's rental car beside it. Sam had slowed to a walk as soon as he reached the mailbox on its splintered post and the cold wind immediately skewered between his ribs. The sleet had started up again. Sam pulled up the hood of his fleece jacket and skirted the two cars on his way to the door.

His mother used to grow flowers just here. Cosmos and marigolds and goldenrod, he remembered. She loved bright colours. In spite of the cold he loitered deliberately where the margin of her garden used to be, thinking of the way she used to come out here on summer evenings to snap off the heads of fading blooms or pull up tufty clumps of grass from between the clods of earth. The house faced west and the sun would still be colouring the front of it when the woods behind had turned dark.

Sam took one deeper breath. He couldn't linger out here, he told himself. He would have to go in now and tell him.

He pushed open the front door, putting his shoulder to it because damp had warped it and given it a tendency to stick.

Mike was sitting in his chair, watching daytime TV. There was a pot of coffee on the stove and an unwrapped loaf of pre-sliced bread spilling like a soft pack of cards on the counter. Sam pushed back his hood again as his father looked up at him.

'Good one?' the old man asked, without much interest.

'Yeah. I went along past the Bowmans' place and round the lake.'

'Quite a way, then.'

'Not bad. It's cold out there.'

'Coffee's made.'

'Thanks.'

Sam poured himself a cup and drank a couple of mouthfuls, remembering not to wince at the taste.

'Do you want to watch this?' he asked pointedly. The yammering faces of some talk show filled the screen with stories of outrage, attended by resentment and rancour. Although it was appropriate enough, he thought. There was always disappointment here, in this house. A rich deposit of it, seamed with the ore of anger. So why not on the box as well? Maybe it was why Mike liked all these programmes. He felt at home with them.

'I thought maybe we could talk,' Sam added.

He moved his father's stick from beside his chair so that he could pull his own seat closer, partly blocking out the TV screen. The result was that they sat almost knee to knee. Sam could have reached and taken Mike's hand between his own, but he didn't. They had never gone in for touching, not since Sam was a little boy.

Mike's response was to aim the remote and lower the volume by a couple of decibels. Then he turned to look his son in the face.

'I didn't qualify,' Sam said.

There were two, three beats of silence.

Mike rubbed the corner of his mouth with a horny thumb. 'Huh?'

'I ran in Pittsburgh last week. It was the 2000 Trials.'

Sam had been training for the City of Pittsburgh Marathon ever since the USA Track & Field international competition committee had announced that the Olympic men's marathon team would once again be decided, as it had been for more than thirty years, by a single race. And for Sam it had been one of those days when the running machine had kept stalling and finally quit. He didn't suffer many of them, but when the machinery did let him down it was usually to do with the weight of expectation binding and snagging. His father's expectations, specifically. Sam was fully aware of the dynamic between them, but awareness didn't change it or diminish the effects. Even now.

'I didn't know.'

The old man's face didn't give much away. He just

went on looking at Sam, waiting for him to explain himself.

It was so characteristic, Sam thought, that he wouldn't have known or found out about the run in advance even though his son was a contender for the US Olympic team. Mike lived a life that was defined by his own ever-narrowing interests. He watched TV, he read a little, mostly outdoors magazines, he saw a neighbour once in a while and drank a beer.

But it was equally characteristic, Sam acknowledged, that he hadn't told his father about Pittsburgh. He had qualified for the Trials by running a time better than two hours twenty in a national championship race and he had called Mike immediately afterwards to tell him so.

'That's pretty good,' had been the entire response.

In adulthood, Sam had trained himself not to resent or rise to his father's lack of enthusiasm. It's the way he is, he reasoned. He wanted me to do one thing and I did another.

But even so, this time Mike had seemed particularly grudging. And so he had not told him anything more about the big race beforehand, or called him with the bad news once it was over. Instead, he had waited a week and then come down to visit the old man. He had played various versions of this scene in his head, giving Mike lines to express commiseration, or encouragement for next time, or plain sympathy – but the most cheerless scenario had been closest to reality. Mike was neither surprised nor sympathetic, he was just disappointed. As he had been plenty of times before. The pattern was set now.

'So what happened?' Mike asked at last.

Sam caught himself shrugging and tried to stop it. 'I was fit enough and I felt good on the start. I don't know. I just couldn't make it work.'

'What time did you do?'

'Not good. Two twenty-eight. I've done plenty better than that, beat all the other guys who came in ahead of me – Petersen, Okwezi, Lund. But not on the day it counted.'

Mike went on looking at him, saying nothing.

'There's always 2004.' Sam smiled, thinking within himself: It should be the other way round. You should be saying that to me.

'You're twenty-eight, twenty-nine, aren't you?'

You know how old I am. 'Long-distance running isn't a kids' game, luckily. You can stay in the front rank over long-distance well into your thirties.'

'I was looking forward to you bringing home that gold.' Mike nodded to the mantel, as if there were a space there, among the pictures of mountains and bearded men, that was bereaved of his son's Olympic medal.

'I'd have been happy enough just to go to Sydney and represent my country. It never was just about winning, Dad,' Sam said patiently.

'No.'

The monosyllable was a taunt, expertly flicked, that dug into Sam like the barb of a fish-hook.

It's the way he is, Sam reminded himself. It's because he's bitter about his own life. And he's entitled to a grouse this time. He would have been proud of me if I'd made it, so it's understandable that he should feel the opposite way now.

'I'm sorry I didn't make it this time. It was tough

for me as well. But I won't stop running. It means a lot to me.'

'Keep at it while you still can,' Mike agreed. 'You're lucky.'

Do you want me to say I'm sorry for that, as well? Sam wondered.

Mike had already turned his gaze over his son's shoulder, back towards the jeering audience on the television. The volume went up again.

Sitting in this house, with its fading wallpaper and the same old sofa and chairs, and the blandishing blue-sky covers of his father's magazines – he still subscribed to *Climber* and *Outside* and the rest – it was hard for Sam to head off the memories. They lined up in the kitchen space and in the closets, and behind the curtains, waiting to ambush him. Where he lived now, up in Seattle with work to do, and Frannie and friends for company and distraction, he could keep out of their way. But not here, not even most of the time. He supposed it was the same for everyone going home. Whether or not you enjoyed your visit depended on the quality of the memories.

They had moved to this house when Sam was six. Before that, Mike and Mary McGrath had lived on the Oregon coast near Newport, but then Mike had started up a rental cabin and backwoods vacation tour business, with a partner, and had brought his family to the little town of Wilding. The business had only survived a year or two, and the partner had made off with most of the liquid assets and none of the burden of debt, but the McGraths had stayed on.

They had put money into this house, a couple of miles out of town, and Mary had dug a garden out front and started to make some friends. Sam was in school and seemed happy enough, and in any case Mike was as willing to stay where he was as to move on. He took a job as a transport manager with a logging company. Mike didn't reckon much on where he lived or what he did for a living, just so long as he could feed and house his wife and child, and get to Yosemite and the Tetons whenever possible, and to plenty of big boulders for climbing when his budget didn't stretch to proper expeditions.

Other kids had plenty worse things to deal with, Sam knew, but he found the climbing hard.

He went on the camping trips, and while his father solo-climbed he played softball with the other boys and swam in icy streams, and hiked and rode his bike, always in fear of the moment when his father would call him.

'Come on, Sammy. It's your turn.'

'No.' Trying to climb with his father watching, with the hammering of blood in his ears and the shivering of his joints, and the sipping for breath with the top inch of his lungs because to breathe more deeply might be to dislodge himself from his precarious hold – all of these were too familiar to Sam.

'Watch me, then.' Mike sighed.

His movements were so smooth as he climbed, his body seemed like water flowing over the rock. But Sam's arms wound tight around his knees as he sat watching and his breath came unevenly.

Don't fall, he prayed. Don't fall, Dad.

A moment or two later the man reached the crest

of the boulder and disappeared, then his broad grinning face looked down over the edge. 'See? Easy as pie.'

Sam felt his cheeks turning hotter, not from the sun's brightness. His father was already down-climbing, smooth and steady. And then midway he suddenly stopped.

'Now what can I do?' he demanded, flinging the words back over his shoulder into the still air. 'I'm stuck. Tell me what to do.'

The boy raked the reddish cliff with his eyes, searching the sandstone for a crack or a bulge. There were no ropes, nothing held his father safe except his own fingers or toes and now he was stuck and he would surely fall . . . he would fall and fall, and he would die.

'See anything?' Mike McGrath called more loudly. 'Any foothold?'

Sam gazed until his eyes burned.

The red rock was flat and hard, and there wasn't a dimple in it, even to save his father's life. Terror froze the sunny afternoon and silenced the birdsong, and stretched the moment into an hour.

'Wait. Maybe if you go that way . . .' He rocked up on to his knees, so that he knelt at the rock face, and took tufts of long grass in his clenched fists to hold himself tethered to the earth. There was a little nubbin below where his father's feet rested.

Too late.

'I'm falling,' the man cried suddenly. And as he did so he peeled away from the rock and his body turned once in the air, black, and as helpless as a dropped puppet.

Out of Sam's mouth a scream forced itself.

Even after Mike had executed a gymnast's neat backflip and landed upright, knees together and arms at his sides in the exact centre of the old bath towel that he left at the foot of the boulder to keep the soles of his rock shoes from contact with the ground, Sam went on screaming. The sound brought his mother running. He buried himself in her arms.

'Michael,' she remonstrated, 'what are you doing?'

She was holding the boy pressed against her as she spoke and Sam could feel her voice vibrate in the cage of her chest.

'I didn't mean to frighten him. I was just showing him it's *safe*, for Chrissakes. Sammy, I'm okay. I came off deliberately.'

'He's eight years old, Mike.'

'I want him to know what climbing means.'

Sam McGrath already knew. He knew it was what his father loved. Without knowing how to form the words he understood that Michael cared about him and his mother in his own way, but climbing was what gave everything else a meaning. Every dollar that he had to spare, every possible weekend and any vacation, were devoted to it. That was all. It was so overwhelming that in a way it was perfectly simple. And for himself, Sam also knew that it scared him speechless.

'Let him alone. He'll learn when he's ready.'

There was something here, some tension like a fine wire drawn tight between the two of them that was more uncomfortable even than his own fear, and to discharge it Sam scrambled away from his mother and stood up.

'It's okay. I'll do it now,' he said.

'That's it, fella. You see?' Michael laughed and the woman frowned.

Once Sam asked his father, 'You use ropes when I'm climbing with you. Why don't you use them when you're on your own? Wouldn't it be safer?'

He always remembered the answer.

'It's not about safety. It's about purity.'

Mike told him that a climber could make himself as safe as he chose. By knowing what he was doing and where he was going, by calculating and planning. And above all by concentrating.

'It's like a problem in math. The rock sets you a problem and you solve it. Ropes and bolts and all the other climbing aids only make muddle and add up to more danger. Real climbing is the same as making love. There's only the two of you, you and the rock, and naked is best. You're too young to know anything about that yet.'

Sam felt embarrassed and he mumbled, 'Most people except you climb with a partner.'

'I'm waiting for you to grow up. By then I'll have taught you everything I know. After you've been to college and trained to be a lawyer, you'll be rich enough to go to Alaska and the Himalaya, and climb the big hills, all the places your old daddy'll never get to see.'

Sam lifted his chin and gazed back at him, containing the defiance that he felt within himself like a stone at the bottom of a cup.

'Can I get you another?' Sam asked, nodding across

at the coffee pot. He heeled his chair back to its accustomed place and stood up. It wasn't breaking a connection between them, because there hadn't been one in the first place. Mike's attention, apparently, had barely twitched away from the television and now he held out his empty cup without comment.

Sam filled it for him, and began to make preparations for a meal. He had taken a trip into town, and bought a heap of supplies to stock the empty cupboards and the old chest freezer that wheezed in the outhouse. He didn't think Mike was taking care of himself properly and he wanted to be sure before he left that there was at least food to hand for him, even if he chose not to eat it.

'Steak and salad okay for you?'

Simple food was what Mike always liked. Sometimes he reminisced about Mary's chicken pot pie or dumpling stew, and Sam would realise how much he still missed his wife and felt guilty that he didn't live closer or make the effort to see his father more often.

'If it's what you're making.'

When the food was prepared Sam laid knives and forks on the old yellow laminate table and put the plates out. 'It's ready.'

Mike fumbled for his stick, but it still lay where Sam had pushed it aside. The old man gave a grunt of irritation and stretched awkwardly but Sam was there first. He put it into his father's hand and helped him to his feet, then guided him the few feet to the table.

'I can manage. How d'you think I get by when you aren't paying one of your visits, eh?'

'Sure you can manage. But when I'm here, I like to be able to help you.'

They ate in silence after that, the only sound the clink of their knives and forks, and the wind driving darts of ice against the windows.

'Not going to be a great night for travelling,' Mike remarked.

I could stay over, just until tomorrow, Sam thought. But he didn't want to and the realisation twisted yet another strand of guilt in him. He wanted to get out of here, back to his own place, away from the mute cohorts of their memories.

'It'll be fine. I've got to get back to work.'

That was another aspect of disappointment. He hadn't even made it to law school. Sam's business was computers, designing and managing websites, and it wasn't an outstandingly successful one.

At least the silence was broken. Mike chewed thoughtfully on his steak, then wiped his mouth. 'So you reckon that's it, is it? No chance of a rethink?'

He was talking about the running again.

Sam must have been twelve because Mary was still there, although she had begun to seem sick. Their last summer vacation, then. Sam couldn't recall exactly where the climb had been, but he remembered every crease and corner of it. There was a narrow chimney and then an awkward overhang. Mike had led the way and he negotiated the underside of the shelf as if it were a mere optical illusion.

'Climb when you're ready,' Sam heard him call from the invisible secure point above it.

The rock waited, bearing down on him. 'I don't think I can do this one.'

No answer came, and Sam sighed and began to

climb. Even as he was hanging off the first hold, beginning the calculation that would achieve the next, his mind and his will disengaged themselves. It wasn't simply that he couldn't do it. It was much more that he had no wish to. At once he down-climbed the short way he had come and called again. He told Mike that he was going down and he wouldn't be climbing any more that day. He felt a start of rebellious happiness. A moment or two later Mike reappeared on the ledge beside him. The space felt too small to contain them both.

Mike said, 'Do you want to think about that again?'

It wasn't a question, but Sam boldly treated it as if it were. 'Uh, no, thanks. I'll head back.'

'I think you should climb it.'

'I think I should go down.'

'Do what I tell you, son.'

The rock seemed to press down on their heads.

'I don't want to.'

It was self-discipline that restrained Mike. He wouldn't let anger master him out on the mountain, because anger was a loss of control and loss of control meant danger. Instead, he lowered his son safely to the ground and watched until he was unclipped from the rope. Then he turned and climbed solo up the overhang.

Sam ran the path through the woods. He made himself run faster and faster to contain his shock at what he had done. When he reached the campsite he found Mary sitting tiredly in her chair under the shade of a tree. Mary defended her son against his father. That was the year Sam took up track sports.

*

'Not for 2000, I'm afraid.'

The two of them had cleared their plates. The talk show finished and a soup commercial began.

Sam took them to the sink. 'Would you like some dessert? There's a pie. Apple.' A bought one.

'Sure, if it's there.'

He brought the helpings to the table and they ate, in silence again. That was how it was. Afterwards he washed up, and dried the cutlery and placed the dish towel – without knowing he did so – in the way that Mary always left it to dry. Mike had never bought a dishwasher.

Only then did Sam allow himself to look at his watch. 'Time for the airport.'

'You really going, in this?'

Sam tilted his head, pretending to listen to the wind. He wanted to switch off the TV in case the local weather report came on and closed off his escape route.

'Oh, it's not so bad.' He collected his zipper bag from the bedroom that still had his college sports posters on the walls and made a show of checking for his keys. 'Do you need anything else, Dad?' There was food in the cupboard, fuel in storage, current magazines on the chair. Spring would be here soon.

'Not a thing.'

'So, I'd better be going. I'll call you in the morning.' From the apartment or the office, in Seattle.

'Sure.' The old man pinched his nose and rubbed it with the back of his hand. Then he levered himself to his feet and rested his weight on his stick. From opposite directions they reached the door at the same time. Sam looked down on him.

Michael had survived a broken back, but the terrible injury and the years of fighting back from it had robbed his father of height, as well as other things. Sam thought that the way the old man lived now was truly little more than survival. Awareness of his father's loss depressed him as well as filling him with unwieldy sympathy. It also increased his own sense of being able-bodied and surrounded by opportunity, and still having locked himself into a life that didn't satisfy him, or offer any immediate chance of improvement. Mike's estimation of him as a failure only confirmed his own.

'I'm really sorry about the Trials.'

'Maybe next time, like you said,' Mike answered. They made an awkward connection, a little more than a handshake but less than a clasp. Then they stood apart. 'Thanks for buying all those supplies. I didn't need them.'

'Take care of yourself.'

'You know me.'

Well enough, Sam thought. He hoisted his bag, rested his hand for a moment on Mike's shoulder, then opened the door and closed it behind him. It was snowing hard now, and the wind rounded it into the creases of steps and walls. Sam drove through Wilding and, at last, on to the freeway. He punched the buttons on the radio, stretched in his seat and headed through the storm for the airport with unconsidered heavy metal crashing in his ears.

'I'm sorry, sir,' the American ticket desk clerk told him. 'The weather's closed right in. Maybe in an hour, if it eases.'

'I'll wait,' Sam said, as if he had a choice. From the news-stand he bought a copy of *Forbes* and from the coffee shop a latte that might take away the taste of his father's brew. Under the stalled departures board he found a seat and wedged himself between a boy with a snowboard and a woman holding a baby on her lap. He sipped his coffee and watched the refugees from the weather as they pushed in past the barrier of the glass doors. The concourse was filling up, a steady wash of people jostled in front of him and the boy with the snowboard sullenly left it jutting in their path.

Sam had been sitting with the empty styrofoam cup in his hands for perhaps fifteen minutes when he saw her.

The doors parted yet again and a flurry of windborne ice crystals spun across a triangle of the murky concourse floor. A woman blew in in their wake but she wasn't hunched over to defend herself from the weather like every one of the other arrivals. Her head was back and she was wide-eyed with exhilaration. And she appeared to be wearing nothing but a pair of slender high-heeled shoes and a faded ski parka. Her legs were very long and splashed with muddy sleet.

As well as a small overnight bag, she was negligently carrying a bridal bouquet.

Sam swore, fluently, under his breath. Some fuckwit had already married her.

He followed her with his eyes to the Air Canada desk. She went through the same exchange as he had done, then turned away. Sam was almost on his feet, on his way to intercept her, when he remembered that he didn't know her. Not yet. Instead, he watched as she bought a cup of coffee and drank it standing, her attention on the departures board. The bouquet lay at her feet, with her bag. There was no bridegroom in sight, no smirking triumphalist ready to propel her away to a honeymoon hotel. She was apparently all alone.

He stood up and placed his coat on his seat, making it the only unoccupied one in sight. He walked between the clumps of travellers until he reached her side. 'Would you like to sit down?'

Her gaze travelled over his face, level, considering, touched with amusement. 'There are three pregnant women and several geriatrics standing around here. Why me?'

Jesus, he thought. She's really something. 'Good question.'

'Thanks for the offer, anyway.' She was smiling. She wasn't beautiful, her eyes were too wide-set and her jaw too prominent for that. She was better than beautiful; she was intriguing.

'Where are you heading?'

'Home to Vancouver. And you?'

'Uh, yup. Me too.' Seattle, BC, what did it matter? Tomorrow's work waiting, Frannie – Sam folded them up and put them all on hold. It was a very long time since he had felt himself do anything so perfectly unconsidered.

'You live in Vancouver?'

'Uh, not exactly. Visiting, you know. Looks like we might have a long wait. Maybe until tomorrow.'

'I'm not giving up hope. I need to get away tonight,' she said, checking her watch. 'And I have to make some calls. Nice talking to you.' She was dismissing him.

'Sam McGrath.'

Although she hadn't invited the introduction she nodded politely enough. 'Finch Buchanan.'

He bent down and picked up the flowers, putting them into her hands. They were some kind of creamy white scented ones, spiked with glossy evergreen. Conventional, in a way that didn't quite go with her. And her fingers were ringless.

'Congratulations, by the way. Mrs Buchanan, is it?'

She laughed now, a great uninhibited snort of merriment that showed her teeth and her tongue. Jesus, he thought again.

'Actually, it was. But I only married him for his money. I shot him on the drive from the reception.'

'Wise move.'

'Thank you.'

'So now you'll be looking for a replacement?'

One try too many, he realised, as soon as he said it. Finch gave a delicate shrug. The parka crinkled around her and she pulled impatiently at the velcro fastenings to undo it. She wasn't, unfortunately, naked beneath it. She was wearing a little buttoned-up blue skirt suit that made her look disappointingly like Ally McBeal. She rolled up the parka and stuffed it into her bag.

'See you.' She smiled and strolled away towards the bank of payphones at the end of the hall.

As soon as she was busy with her call, Sam went straight to the Air Canada desk and transferred his ticket. After Finch finished her animated conversation she found a place to sit a long way off next to a group of Mexican nuns, took a book out of her bag and immersed herself in it.

Slowly, the snowstorm moved away south-westwards. The Vancouver flight was nearly three hours late departing, but on the other hand it was one of the few that left at all that night. It was full. Sam saw her as soon as he boarded, in a window seat halfway down the main cabin. He strode up the aisle to the as yet miraculously unoccupied seat beside her.

'What do you know?' He smiled and settled himself in place. She had the book open on her lap.

'I know something about the laws of probability,' she answered coolly and returned to her reading. Sam saw a guy who looked like John Belushi making his way towards them, already frowning. He leaned down and scooped Finch's flowers from where she had wedged them under the seat in front, and held them on the armrest between them. And he squirmed closer so their heads were almost touching.

'Is this . . .?' Belushi began tetchily.

Sam passed over his boarding card. 'I'm really sorry. It's your seat, I know. But look, it's our wedding night. D'you mind changing so I can sit beside my wife? She's a nervous flier.'

'Well, okay,' the man grunted and pushed onwards.

She didn't laugh now. She didn't look alarmed or disconcerted or angry – just severe. She took back the flowers and pushed them under the seat again, kicking them out of the way with the toe of her pretty shoe. 'What is all this about?'

'You think I'm a flake, don't you?'

'Yes.'

'I'm not. I just wanted to sit here.'

'Then sit,' she said crisply. He did as he was told, through the last-minute de-icing and the taxi and the take-off, and the pilot's announcement that in the wake of the storm severe turbulence was anticipated and they should keep their seat belts fastened. As the plane climbed through the cloud layers it pitched and shuddered, and the engines whined and changed key. Finch suddenly let her book drop and pushed her head back against the seat rest. Sam saw the pallor of her throat.

'As a matter of fact there was one grain of accidental truth in that load of bullshit.'

'What's that?' he asked.

'I'm a lousy flier.'

'Want to hold my hand?'

'I want a drink.'

He peered around the seat in front. As far as he could see, the crew were still strapped in. 'Not yet. Want to talk instead?'

She sighed and closed her eyes. The fuselage creaked and swayed giddily. 'If you like.'

'I had my fortune told by an old native Indian woman when I was a tiny boy. I remember to this day, her saying to me, "You are not going to die in an Air Canada 737 somewhere over the western seaboard." Do you feel sick, by the way?'

'If I vomit I can deal with it myself, thank you. I am a doctor.'

'Dr Buchanan. Specialising in put-downs of pushy men and vomit.'

The plane hit a pocket of empty space. It pitched through the vacuum for what seemed like ten seconds before hitting solid air again. A child began screaming and a moan came from an old woman across the aisle. Finch snatched at Sam's hand and dug her nails in. She had gone white to the lips.

'It's okay,' he soothed her. Her hand was clammy; he rubbed the skin on the back of it gently with his thumb. 'It's just storm turbulence. Nothing's going to happen to us. You're safe.' He reached to the seat pocket and laid the paper bag on her lap, just in case, on top of the book. He noticed now that it was *Touching the Void*, a classic account of a climbing catastrophe and its aftermath.

He nodded pleasantly at it. 'I read that. Quite a story.'

She rolled her head. 'I think I'd rather be down a crevasse than up here.'

'Thanks.'

'Look. Don't expect me to be polite and kind. Just talk to me. Tell me about yourself, if you like.'

'An invitation no male could refuse. Where should I begin?'

He told her about why he had been visiting his father and about running, and his work and its problems, trying to make it twice as interesting as it really was. He avoided mentioning Frannie, although once or twice he caught himself saying *we* and he knew she had registered it. The plane's bucking and shuddering gradually eased, and in-flight service began. By the time he was putting a large vodka and tomato juice into her hand, Finch's colour had improved. She drank half the measure down straight.

'Thanks again.'

'Steady.'

She had let go of his hand minutes ago. Now she picked up Joe Simpson's book again. 'I think I'll read some more of this.'

It wasn't until they had begun their descent into Vancouver that he broke in on her once more. 'You know all about me, I don't know anything about you. Is that a fair arrangement, do you think?'

She smiled briefly. 'I shouldn't think so. What do you want to know?'

In response to a series of direct questions he learned that she had been in Oregon for her best friend's wedding. She practised in the city with a partner, she had four brothers all older than she was, her father was an architect he had vaguely heard of and her mother was a mother. She lived alone in a city apartment. And yes, she was seeing someone at the moment. Although she flashed a warning glance at him just for asking.

They had landed and were taxiing towards the stand when he put the final, inevitable, schlocky question he couldn't think of any way around. 'Can I call you some time? Maybe we could have dinner.'

Finch sighed. She had gathered up the flowers again and they made her look as if she was headed for the altar. 'I don't think so, Sam.'

'Why not? I'm harmless, maybe even quite amusing. What have you got to lose?'

'Nothing.' They were stationary at last. Raindrops glittered on the window beyond her shoulder. 'I'm not going to be here. I'm going away for a while.'

'When?' he asked grimly. Somehow he would see her again, whatever it might take.

'In a couple of weeks. And I'm really busy before then, getting ready for it.'

'Where?'

She hesitated. Then a so-what smile crimped the corners of her mouth. 'Out to Nepal. Kathmandu. Then on to Everest. I'm joining an expedition to climb it. Medical officer.'

'You're a *climber*. You don't just read about it? That's extraordinary.' Shaking his head, he reached out mentally to all the curtains of denial with which he had shrouded his adolescence and pulled them down with one breezy sentence. 'Because I climb too. Mad about it, ever since I was a kid.'

Her eyes narrowed. 'I thought you said you were a marathon runner. A failed Olympic one.'

'That too. Where will you be staying in Kathmandu?'

'Why do you want to know?'

'I've been there. Some of the hotels are pretty dire, in my experience. Just want to be sure you've picked a decent one.'

In fact, he had never been further west than Hong Kong. He tried hard to remember anything he had ever read about the Nepali capital. Ancient. It was really ancient and seriously polluted. Would that do?

Finch sighed. 'It's the Buddha's Garden. I'm not planning to change it. And that information is of no conceivable use to you.'

The forward doors were open. The passengers ahead of them had shuffled their way out and Finch was already on her feet, bending her head under the overhead lockers.

'All information has value,' Sam said. 'Let me help

you with your bag. Or at least carry your bouquet for you.'

'I can manage.'

They were in the chilly corridors. She was slipping away from him, but it didn't matter. He could deal with that.

Immigration was about to separate them. Sam was still counting himself lucky that he had had his passport on him.

'Goodbye,' Finch said seriously. 'Someone's here to meet me, or I'd offer you a lift. Thanks for your company.'

'So long, Finch.'

Then she was gone. Sam was left alone in the arrivals hall at Vancouver airport at one in the morning, with his car and his girlfriend and his stalled life waiting for him in Seattle. From the taxi line, John Belushi was glaring reproachfully at him.

Two

It was snowing in North Wales, too. It was a different small segment of the world's weather envelope, but the local effects were the same as in Vancouver or Oregon.

Alyn Hood paid no attention either to the bitter wind or the blur of snowflakes flying into his face and weighting his eyelashes. He stood on his doorstep for a moment, gazing thoughtfully into the darkness as if it were the middle of a summer's afternoon. Then he turned and locked the door of the cottage, dropping the heavy key into his pocket. He set off down the path, bareheaded with his coat hanging loose, at a steady pace that indicated no hurry, or any awareness of the climate.

It was a long descent, down a rutted track where the potholes were already deceptively smoothed out by the settling snow. The man was a sure-footed walker. His easy pace never varied.

The track joined a lane at a gatepost where the plastic letters of an old sign, their cracked curves and serifs having acquired an eyebrow of snow, announced the name of the one-storey slate and stone cottage to be Tyn-y-Caeau. He turned left into the muffled silence of the lane and continued to descend the hill. His footprints threaded a solitary one-way trail in his wake. Half a mile further on, a tiny cluster of yellow lights showed thinly between silver-furred stone walls. There were perhaps a dozen houses here and a whitewashed pub turned grey by the insistent whiteness. There were no cars in the car-park, but a regiment of wooden bench-and-table sets in the frozen garden to the side indicated that this might be a popular place in more forgiving weather.

Alyn Hood went straight to the low door and pushed it open, familiar with its movement. A heavy draught curtain, attached to a rod on the back of the door, swung with it. There was a bar framed by glasses and bottles, a man behind its rampart polishing a tankard, and two customers. All three faces turned to the new arrival.

'Al,' the barman greeted him. The other two men nodded. One was very old, with a flat tweed cap welded to his head, the younger had a sheepdog asleep at his feet.

'Pint, Glyn,' Alyn Hood said.

'Right you are.' The barman pulled it and stood the handle glass to dribble on a bar towel.

'Bit dead tonight,' the sheepdog man said wonderingly, as if this room with its ticking clock and smoky fire usually resounded with cheering and dancing on table-tops.

'Blasted weather,' Glyn judged. 'You'd expect a sign of spring, this time of year.'

'It's only March,' Alyn Hood said mildly. He took his pint to a round table near the fire and sat down.

'When is it you're off this time, then?' Glyn pursued him.

'Couple of days.'

'Bad enough here,' said the sheepdog man.

Alyn smiled and the room fell silent again. He sat for perhaps twenty minutes, nursing his pint and looking into the red coals. A couple came in and sat in a corner murmuring together, their hands entwined.

Five minutes later the door whirled open once more, admitting a blast of cold air and a young woman who stamped her feet energetically to shed a ruff of snow. She looked around the bar and saw Al. 'Thought I might find you.'

'Molly. What are you doing here?'

'Duh. Looking for you, maybe? Went up to the house, car there but not you. Where else could you be but down the pub? Do I get a drink?'

'Coke?'

'Nn.' Molly put her head on one side. Her wiry hair was spangled with melted snow. 'I'll have a whisky and ginger ale, thanks.' She stared a challenge at her father.

'You're not old enough. You driving?'

'Get real. I'm eighteen. Near enough. And how else d'you think I got here from Betws? Mum lent me.'

Al sighed. His only child was a grown woman now, almost. Because he had missed so many of the vital, infinitesimal shifts of growth that had delivered her from sweet babyhood to this point, he knew he didn't have the right to tell her she was too young to drink whisky, or anything else for that matter.

'Very small scotch and plenty of ginger, please, Glyn. And I'll have a half.'

They took their drinks and sat opposite each other at the table. Father and daughter were noticeably alike. Their heads and hands were the same shape, and they sat in the same position with their legs pointing towards the fire and their ankles lazily crossed.

'How is your mother?'

Molly regarded him. 'The same.'

'Did she send you?'

'No. Well. In a way, I suppose. I said I was coming over and she offered me the car.'

They lifted their glasses at the same moment and thoughtfully drank.

The man with the tweed cap levered himself off his stool and headed for the door. 'Night all. See you again, I hope, Alyn. All the best.'

Molly's face drew in. The contraction of her mouth and eyes made her look angry. When the door had closed once more and the eddies of cold air were dispersed she said, 'Don't go back there. Don't. I don't want you to.'

There was a flicker in her father's eyes, a shift in his glance that acknowledged and at the same time evaded her demand. Molly saw it and Al knew that she saw it. 'I have to go, Molly. It's what I do.'

'You don't *have* to. That's a lie.'

'I don't lie to you, Moll. I try not to. Did your mother tell you to come here and say this to me?'

It was weary, over-trodden ground to Alyn. And the careful neutrality that Molly assumed in answering was a reminder that she had had to intercede for too long in the disputes between her mother and father.

'No,' she repeated. 'I came to say it myself. Dad, please don't go. I've got a bad feeling about this time.'

He smiled then, briefly, and put his hands over hers. 'You always have a bad feeling. Remember? And I always come home, don't I?'

She would not meet his eyes. He turned her hands over, looking at the smooth palms, remembering these fingers when they were baby-sized and the way they curled to grip his adult forefinger. Holding on to him hard, even then.

'Listen. I have to do this trip.' For all kinds of reasons he was drawn back to the mountain. They were not, he acknowledged to himself, reasons he would care to analyse with his daughter. 'I have to do this one and after I've done it I'll hang up my boots.'

'Do you mean that?'

From her mother, over the years, Molly had heard enough about her father's faults. She knew well enough what he was bad at and deficient in, and out of her own sense of fair play she had privately reckoned up his strengths. In order to compensate.

One of them, perhaps the foremost, was that he *was* so strong. Not just physically, although he was that too, like iron – or one of his own smooth coils of rope, that was better. Iron was too rigid, where Al was supple. It was that he never gave way or compromised or stepped down. You were always certain of what he would do and the way he would do it, and that gave him a kind of . . . serenity, if that was the word. Like a rock face, too. The weather kept on changing over and around it, but the rock stayed there, solid as.

She couldn't think of anyone else she knew who held so unwaveringly to what he believed in and wanted, the way Al did.

If you looked at it from one side it was selfishness, that's what her mother would claim. But if you took another perspective it was clarity and a sense of purpose. He held on to what he believed in and he kept on going until he was where he wanted to be. Whatever the obstacles were. That was why he was a fine mountaineer. And why she was wasting her breath now.

Love felt weighty inside her, with the nauseous edge lent by fear for his safety. It was a helpless sensation that Molly was used to. 'Do you mean that?' she repeated.

'Yes.'

It was true. He did mean to make this the last one. Or to wish it, with part of himself. And with another part he rejected the impulse entirely. It was the old, insoluble dilemma of climbing.

When you were there, doing it, you had the shot of adrenalin in your veins. This, this balance of focus and fear, was the crystallisation of reality. The brilliance of perception and nerve and concentration made you think you could pass straight into another dimension. And the mind's reaction to that very intensity, like a dull serum to counteract climbing's snakebite madness, was to make you long perversely to be comfortable and languid, and safe.

Al looked around the motionless room and listened to the clock's steady ticking. What he had seen and done made all of this peripheral. Even his daughter's drooping head. Almost as soon as you were home, safety was colourless and suffocating.

It made you turn back to the mountains. Once more and yet once more.

But he was forty-five now. Realistically, he couldn't expect to lead too many more major commercial expeditions like this one.

Alyn realised that Molly was waiting for him to say something further. 'Okay. You know I'm going to lead a group of clients up Everest for an American company called the Mountain People. These are rich men, with big ideas and they pay a lot of money for the chance to go up there. The owner of the company, George Heywood, believes that I am a good guide and he pays me well for the job. And I certainly need the money. As you also know.

'Obviously, it means I get one more chance at the summit myself. I've never climbed the big E and I want to, very much. I've done most of the other major peaks.'

'K2,' Molly said bleakly.

It was after what happened on K2, five years ago, that Jen Hood decided she had had enough. Either Alyn stopped climbing, or they stopped being married. Two and a half years later they were divorced.

Al nodded, understanding the reminder, heading off for now the memories that went with it. 'Yes.'

'Is it that important?'

After a moment Al said absently, almost as if he hadn't been listening to the question, 'Yes. It is.'

Glyn put down his polished tankard and briskly

rang a brass bell that hung behind the bar. 'Last ones, please.'

'I'll have another whisky and ginger, thanks.'

'No, you won't. You can come home and have a cup of tea with me, if you want.'

'Oh, cheers.'

But they went outside together and found that the snow had stopped falling. A glimmering blanket lay over the dry-stone walls and etched the trees, and the rock faces were black holes traced with edges of pearl.

'Pretty,' Molly commented. She unlocked the doors of her mother's rusting Metro and nodded Al inside. The interior smelled of plastic and Obsession, Jen's favoured perfume. The climb back up the hill to Tyn-y-Caeau was tricky, with the car's rear wheels skidding in the tractionless snow.

'I can *do* it,' Molly said angrily when her father tried to intervene, and she negotiated the rutted track right up to his front door.

The cottage's one main room smelled of damp and woodsmoke.

While her father went into the kitchenette to make tea, Molly dropped her coat on a chair and nosed around among his sparse possessions. There was a laptop computer on an untidy desk and a fax machine with a couple of faxes poking out of it. She read the top one; it was from the Mountain People. The message was uninteresting, to do with porters and supplies of bottled oxygen. The second one was a typed list of names with question marks and comments scribbled by hand next to them. *Hugh Rix*, she read. *British. Aged 54, experienced. Bullshitter, though. Mark Mason, British, writer, 36. Moderately experienced. Dr Finch Buchanan. Canadian, ????* The message concluded, *All will be revealed in time, mate. See you in Kathmandu. Ken.* This was only slightly less uninteresting.

The rest of Al's furniture consisted of a worn sofa and an unmatching armchair, a small shelf of books, mostly biographies and modern history, a round table and chairs, and a couple of lamps, one of them with a badly scorched shade. There was no television, no picture on the bare walls. It was the room of a man unconcerned with physical comfort and apparently indifferent to the reassurance provided by material possessions. It was cold. Molly knelt down on the stone hearth and tried to stir some life into the fire. A small flame licked up from a bed of ash.

'Thanks, Moll,' Al said when he came back with two mugs and a plate of toast and Marmite.

'Haven't you had dinner?' Molly asked when they sat together on the sofa and she watched him devouring the food.

'No. Had a couple of other things to do.'

She remonstrated, 'Dad.' As a response he took her foot that was curled underneath her and pulled it towards him. Affectionately he massaged it, kneading the arch and stretching the toes. They were both reminded of all the other separations, over the years, the times when Molly had begged him to stay with her and Al had protested, making light for her of the distance and the danger. It seemed as if there had always been another mountain, or an unclimbed line to attempt, or an expedition for him to lead. He would leave, and there would be the occasional crackling telephone call or scribbled letter, and the weeks would go by and at last he would reappear. Gaunt and weather-beaten, and apparently happy to be home. Then, almost within a week, he would be standing at the window, looking out at the sky, plotting his next departure.

Molly had loved him besottedly all through her childhood. Al was rich icing, balloons, celebrations. Jen was bread and butter, everyday, always there.

She sighed and withdrew her foot. The divorce had been grim, but she was old enough, now, to understand her mother's reasons. She resumed her contemplation of the room, looking at the titles of the books, and the Mountain People's letterhead sticking up from the fax tray and, something she hadn't noticed before, a snapshot of herself sellotaped to the wall beside the desk. She was sitting on a beach beside a lopsided sandcastle, aged maybe four or five, naked and with her hair matted in salty curls.

She didn't visit her father up here very often. Tyn-y-Caeau was twenty miles from where she lived with Jen in Betws-y-Coed and Molly had only just learned to drive a car. But she had wanted to come tonight, to see Alyn and deliver her pointless entreaty. He would come over to say goodbye to Jen and her before he left, but those visits were never comfortable. No one ever said what they thought because – they all understood this now – saying things didn't change any of them.

'I love you, Dad,' she said suddenly. Just in a straight voice, as if she were announcing what time it was, with no overlay of parodic sentimentality or swoop of melodrama to distance herself from the offering.

He looked at her and she saw two things.

One was the way he must appear to other people, women or clients or whatever, as a man. As someone you would trust with your life, because that was the responsibility he took. And the other was the way he looked at her, uniquely, because he was her father. These two were pulling in opposite directions, because the man you would trust with your life didn't go with all the dues and small sacrifices that belonged to fathers and families.

It was the first time Molly had understood this clearly enough to be able to put it into words herself.

'I love you too,' he said.

It was the truth, of course, she knew. It was both too much and not enough for her. She had to bend her head to hide the tears in her eyes. Al didn't see. He was watching the fire, seemingly.

'And I don't want you driving all the way home at this time of night. Call your mother and tell her you're staying here with me.'

After a minute, Molly took the mobile phone he held out to her and prodded out the number. Jen answered at once and gave her response. With a precise finger Molly guided the phone's little antenna back into its socket.

'She wants the car back by nine tomorrow morning.'

'Any other message?'

'No.'

She drank the last of her tea, now gone cold.

'I'll sleep on here,' Al told her, patting the sofa cushion. 'You'd better get off to bed.'

When she was lying down, he went in to see her.

She was curled on her side, with one hand flat under her cheek, just as she used to settle down when she was a little girl. He pulled the covers around her shoulders and touched her hair.

I am tucking her up, he thought. Just like . . . Only there hadn't been all that many times, in her childhood. He had always been away.

'Goodnight, Al.'

She didn't often call him by his name.

'Goodnight, baby.'

Nor did he call her that. She had never been a very babyish child.

Afterwards, he stood over the dying fire with his elbows resting on the mantelpiece and his head in his hands. My daughter is eighteen, he thought, all but. Grown up. Ready for whatever.

Silence seemed to stretch away from him, a great curve of it. It contained this house and the hillside, and the distance he had to travel, all the dimensions of it.

He thought of Spider, the memory catching him unawares as it often did and startling him with its vividness. His voice clearer than his face now, before the last trip to K2, all the years of expeditions fat with success or dim with failure, and the escapes and the drinking and the total reliance on one another that went with them. The absence of him no less punishing than it had been from the first day. And then, inevitably, came the thought of Finch Buchanan. He remembered her face.

Canadian, ???? Ken Kennedy had written. Meaning, I don't know anything about her. Meaning, we'll find out in the fullness of time and that will be soon enough. To Ken she was only a name on an expedition list, whereas to Al she was a reality, twisted up with Spider in the past and even with Jen. But no one else in the world except Finch herself knew that and Al wondered if after all this time even she remembered what had happened between them.

The snow's blanket thickened the silence, once the wind had dropped. It cost Al an effort to move, to open cupboards in search of a blanket and so to break the immense, smooth ellipse of it.

Jen's house was square, double-fronted grey stone with a purple slate roof. It stood back a little from the main road, with a short path of Victorian encaustic tiles leading to the front door. The next morning Al parked his old Audi outside the gate and followed Molly past the iron railings. The snow had melted overnight and passing traffic churned grey slush into the gutter.

Molly turned her key in the lock. 'We're back,' she called.

'Kitchen,' Jen answered. They found her at the rear of the house in the wash-house beyond the kitchen itself. She was wearing yellow rubber gloves and loading sheets from a plastic laundry basket into an industrial-capacity washing machine. After the divorce Jen had bought this too-big house with a loan from her father and had set up a bed-and-breakfast business. Plenty of climbers and walkers and fishermen came to Betws-y-Coed, even in March.

'Can I do anything?' Al asked.

Her mouth curled, briefly. 'No. I'll just get this lot in.'

'How's business?'

'Not bad for the time of year. Three last night. Full over the weekend.'

Jen was a good cook, and she also had the sense to keep the bedrooms well heated and to make sure there was plenty of hot water for her visitors. Al admired her success in this enterprise. While they had been married she had seemed smaller and less decisive. His activities had constrained her.

He reflected, not for the first time, that she was better off without him and he was touched by a finger of regret.

Molly had gone upstairs. Jen slammed the door of the washing machine, peeled off the gloves and twisted the control knob decisively. She still wore her wedding ring and the minute diamond, which was all he had been able to afford twenty years ago. 'You want some coffee?'

They went into the kitchen. The front parlour was mostly used by the guests; this was where Molly and Jen lived. There was a sofa here draped in a Welsh tapestry, and corn dollies and carved spoons and local water-colours pinned to the walls, and a big television, and a Rayburn festooned with drying socks, and a row of potted plants and on every surface, objects: shells and jugs and framed photographs and bowls of pot pourri. She was letting her natural inclinations back into the light. When they had lived together, Al had thought they shared a taste for minimal living. They had gone in for plain white walls, bare wooden floors, exposed beams.

He skirted three bowls of cat food placed on a sheet of newspaper by the back door and sat down on the sofa next to the ginger tom. Jen heated coffee and gave it to him in a mug that said 'Croeso i Cymru'. Al frowned at it. Jen had been born in Aberystwyth. Al's family came from Liverpool and even though he had fallen in love with the mountains on a school trip at the age of twelve, and had lived in North Wales for twenty-five years, he still felt like an outsider.

'Thanks for keeping her last night. I didn't want her to go, in all of that, but she would have it.'

'You don't have to thank me for looking out for her.'

'Don't I? But it's not the norm, is it?'

There it was. The old stab of resentment, still fresh as the morning's milk.

'I do love her, Jen.'

And you, although that's all dead and gone.

'*In absentia*,' Jen said coldly.

His wife: short-haired, thin-framed, boyish; mouth tucked in in anger, the same as Molly's. Now a separate person, busy with breakfasts and VAT, and – for all he knew – another man.

'Don't let's do all this again.'

'Oh, no. Don't let's. It might make you feel bad.'

Her fingers were wrapped around her coffee mug as if she needed to draw warmth from it. They listened in their separate silences to the unspoken words. He had been away too many times, for too long. He had taken too many risks.

She had never understood what drew him. To go back, to a new peak or a new line. One more time.

'So,' Jen said at last. 'When do you actually leave?'

'Tomorrow, probably. I've got a couple of things to do in London.'

'Ah.'

'Have you made up your mind about the extension?'

'I think I'm going to go ahead with it.'

They talked about Jen's plans to put two more bedrooms in the loft and about Molly's A levels, and Al asked if she needed more money.

'No. I'm doing all right, I don't need anything else.'

Even if she did, she wouldn't take it off him.

They didn't talk about Everest. He finished his coffee and leaned forward to put the empty mug on the corner of the Rayburn. The oversized cushioned sofa, the piles of women's magazines on a stool and the crowded ornaments made him think he was going to knock something over.

Jen went to the door and called out, 'Molly? Your dad's going.' He stood up at once, kicking the stool so the magazines slid to the floor.

'I've got to get to the cash and carry,' she said, unseeingly heaping them into a pile again.

Molly came down the stairs. She went straight to Al and clung on, her arms around his waist and her head against his chest.

He lifted one springy curl and let it wind around his little finger. 'Okay,' he murmured.

'I'll miss you.'

'I'll be back soon, you know that.'

He kissed the top of her head and held her close.

'Promise?'

'In June.'

Reluctantly she disengaged herself, reminding him again of her much younger self. 'Phone me.'

'Of course.'

It was Jen who walked with him to the front door. Molly had always been tactful about allowing them their private farewells. Jen turned her cheek up, allowed him to kiss it, then opened the door. Her eyes didn't quite meet his. 'Good luck,' she said. He nodded and walked swiftly away to his car.

Jen stood in the empty hallway. She walked five steps towards the kitchen and stopped, with the back of her hand pressed to her mouth. Then she swung round and ran back again, fumbling with the lock and pulling the door open so hard that it crashed on its hinges.

The step was slippery. Al had neatly closed the gate behind him. When she reached it she saw the Audi already 200 yards away. With her hands on the iron spears of the gate she called his name, but he was never going to hear. Within five seconds he was round the bend and out of sight.

Jen unclasped her hands. She wiped the wet palms on her jeans and walked slowly back into the kitchen. Molly was sitting on the sofa, her arms protectively around her knees, her eyes wide with alarm.

'It was always waiting,' Jen cried at her. 'All I ever did was wait for him.'

Alyn drove westwards, towards Tyn-y-Caeau and the few last-minute arrangements that were still to be made before he flew to Nepal. For ten miles he sat with his shoulders stiff and his arms rigid, then he saw the bald head of Glyder Fawr against the gunmetal sky. He let his arms sag and he rounded his spine against the support of the seat to relieve the ache in his back.

He knew these mountains so well. Tryfan and Crib Goch and Snowdon. The Devil's Kitchen and the Buttress, jagged black rock and scree slope. The sight and the thought of them never failed to promise liberation.

Al began to whistle. A low, tuneless note of anticipation. He was going to climb Everest. Once it was done, that would be the time to decide whether or not it had to be the last mountain. In the meantime there was a job to do, to take other people up there and bring them down safely. If Al had been given a choice, the thing he would have wished for above anything else, he would be doing it with Spider. Fast and light and free.

'Yeah, we can do it,' he heard Spider's drawl in his head. 'We can knock this one off, it's only Everest.'

But Spider wasn't here and this was now a job, the responsibility of it to be finely balanced against his own ambitions. He needed the money, just as he had told Molly. Everyone had to live and he wasn't young enough any more to scrape by from hand to mouth, like in the old days. And thinking about it, setting it against the other possibilities, whether it might be selling local maps to tourists or helping Jen in her business or sitting in an office somewhere, Al knew that it was a job he was happy to do. Even proud to be doing.

He went on whistling as he drove.

Three

The Bell A-Star helicopter rattled along the river valley between the fir trees and rocked down to the landing pad beyond the lodges, as neatly as a foot slipping into a shoe. Finch's eldest brother James stood at the window of the biggest lodge, watching the rotors darkening from a blur to whipping blades and then stopping altogether.

'They're back, Kitty,' he remarked to his wife. She put aside her book, stood up and limped to join him at the window. One of her knees was tightly bandaged. The door of the chopper opened and the pilot jumped down, still wearing his helmet.

'Ralf was flying.'

The man put out his hand and Finch took it as she emerged, shaking her head and laughing as she landed beside him. A second man wearing flying overalls scrambled out in her wake. He lifted two pairs of skis out of the basket mounted on the fuselage and handed them over in exchange for the pilot's helmet. Then he climbed back into the machine. Once the couple were out of range the blades whirled into life again and the helicopter lifted and flew away.

Finch and Ralf came towards the lodge. His free arm was round her shoulders and she looked up into his face as they walked, and laughed again.

'They look very happy,' Kitty said. She raised her eyebrows smilingly at James.

'They're in love, aren't they?' James answered.

A minute later the door swept open and Finch and Ralf came in, bringing the outdoors scent of cold air. They were bright-eyed and rosy with the exhilaration of a day's skiing, and they hopped and held on to each other as they eased off their ski boots and unzipped their outer clothes.

'Tea's here,' James called from beside the log fire.

Finch came straight to Kitty. 'How's the knee. Have you been icing it, like I said?'

Kitty had fallen the previous day and twisted a ligament. James had stayed behind to keep her company, and Finch and Ralf had had the day and the helicopter with its pilot and the blue-white slopes of the Monashee mountains all to themselves. Kitty sat down with a little wince and hauled her leg up on to the sofa cushions for Finch to manipulate the swollen knee.

'With a bag of frozen peas, just like you told me. Twenty minutes at a time. It's much better.'

'Good. Mm. I don't think you've torn anything. But it might be worth getting an MRI scan, just the same.'

Ralf Hahn stood at Finch's shoulder. The heli-ski operation was his and he had built it into a successful business catering for rich skiers from all over the world. He was Austrian, a big weather-beaten blond from Zell-am-See who had been skiing since he learned to walk. He and Finch had been lovers for nearly two years.

'You are sure you are all right, Kitty? Frozen peas is all very well. But I can fly you down to the hospital, you know, twenty minutes only . . .'

Kitty laughed, basking in their concern. 'What for? We've got the best doctor right here.'

'Where?' Finch demanded, looking around, protecting real modesty with an assumed version.

James put another log on the fire and they sat down in front of it. There was a basket of fresh-baked bread and three different kinds of cake; Ralf's chef was well qualified and the lodge food was ambitious.

Finch stretched herself with pleasure and rested her feet in ski socks on the stone hearth. 'The best moment of the day.' She sighed.

'Is that so?' Ralf teased her.

'Well, almost,' she amended after a second. Kitty looked from one face to the other.

When tea was finished Ralf said he must spend an hour in his office. Finch walked between the lodges to his cabin. The light was fading and the fir trees were black cut-outs weighted with swathes of spring snow. The last helicopter, a big twelve-seater, had just brought in a cargo of skiers and their guides. They crossed to their rooms and the main lodge, calling out to each other and to Finch. Yellow lights were showing in the windows of the pretty log buildings.

In Ralf's rooms Finch undressed and ran a bath. The place was almost as familiar as her own apartment down in Vancouver; she came up here to ski with Ralf as often as she could but this would be her last weekend of the season. In three days' time she would fly to Kathmandu.

She lay back under the skin of hot water and thought about it, with a knot of nervous anticipation beneath her diaphragm.

She had never been to the Himalaya. Friends and climbers who had seen them warned her that she might be overwhelmed by the scale and the ferocity of the mountains. They were anxious for her, but because they knew her they were hardly surprised that she had chosen to start with Everest itself. For her own part Finch worried less about the climbing and the conditions than about her job as expedition doctor. If she just kept on upwards as far as she could go, she reasoned, that would be good enough. She thought she understood the fine, fascinating balance between barefaced risk and careful calculation that was at the heart of the best mountaineering. And she would never forget the triumph of reaching the top of McKinley, or any of the other peaks she had attempted. She had been expedition doctor on McKinley too and had felt the weight of that keenly, even though the worst emergency she had had to deal with was an abscessed molar. But on Everest they would be higher and further from help, and with less back-up, and the risks were infinitely greater.

If somebody fell. If there was an avalanche. If there was a case of sudden high-altitude cerebral oedema, coma and death . . . her responsibility to deal with it, quickly and correctly. With the limited medical resources at her disposal.

Finch stared at the silver breath of condensation on

the bath taps. She knew that she was a competent doctor. She was interested in high-altitude medicine and had studied it for years. Eighteen months ago she had seen the details of the Mountain People's expensive Everest expedition and the attached advertisement for an appropriately qualified doctor to accompany them, at a significantly reduced rate. When she flew down to Seattle to be interviewed by the expedition director, who had turned out to be the avuncular, laconic George Heywood, he had asked her in conclusion, 'D'you think you can do it?'

'Yes,' she had answered, truthfully at that moment, meaning both the job and the climb.

'So do I,' he agreed.

She had got the job, and her name appeared on the expedition list and the climbing permit beneath those of the guides, Alyn Hood and Ken Kennedy.

Now she looked down at herself with critical attention. Her stomach was flat and taut with sheets of muscle, and her calves and thighs were firm from months of running and tough skiing. She worked out at a climbing gym for four hours every week so her arms and shoulders were strong too. She was fit enough, at least, for whatever lay ahead. She had made sure of that.

And this minute consideration of her body brought her obliquely to the last element of the conundrum: Alyn Hood.

Finch sat up so suddenly that a wave of water washed over the side of the bath. She climbed out quickly and attended to the mopping up, glad to have this focus for her attention. When the job was done she wrapped herself in a towel, wound another around her head, and walked through to the main room to stand by the window and look out into the dusk. She was still standing there, locked into her thoughts, when Ralf came in.

'You are in the dark,' he said, turning on a lamp and seeing her bare shoulders and the pale exposed skin of her neck.

'I was thinking.'

He came to her and untucked the towel that covered her hair. He winnowed his fingers into the wet strands and kissed the droplets of water away from her shoulders. 'About Everest?'

'Yes.'

He wouldn't say that he wished she weren't going, because Ralf was too careful and generous for that. But she heard the words, just the same. Don't go. Stay here with me and let me keep you safe. Logical and legible, secure.

Instead, he said, 'Come to bed.' He drew the curtains to shut out the dark and the trees and the glimmering snow, and unwrapped the second towel.

Lying in his arms, Finch closed her eyes and concentrated on making her body's responses tip the scale against her mind's. Ralf was a good lover and he was also a good man. She knew that he was ambitious, and hard-working and level-headed. On skis she followed his lead unhesitatingly, and elsewhere she valued his advice and opinions whenever he offered them. He spoke four languages and he made her laugh in the two she understood. In the most intimate moments, like this one, he whispered in German, tender endearments that she couldn't decipher but which made the fine hairs rise at the nape of her neck. Ralf loved her, she knew that too.

For a thin, elastic shiver of time the scales balanced exactly, thought and unthinking. And then the body's weight tipped them over. She exhaled a long breath that turned into a sigh. Ralf's mouth moved against hers, and when the moment came she opened her eyes and looked into the hazed blueness of his, and although she knew him so well it was as if she were sharing her body with a stranger.

Afterwards, she lay with her head on his shoulder and his hand splayed over her hip. 'We had a good day today, didn't we?' he murmured.

'We did.'

Finch was a good skier, but she would never be as good as Ralf. He had taken her down through a steep gully with a line of trees sheltering within it. As they carved a path between the dark boles the colours of the world changed from blinding white and silver to black and graphite and pearl. Twigs cracked and laden branches shed a patter of snow as they ducked and jump-turned between them. Then the gully opened into a wide, sunlit ledge and there was a broad bowl full of unmarked, glittering snow. Way beneath them, where the slope ran out, the helicopter was already waiting.

They paused on the lip of the slope and then there was a sweet *ssssscccchhh* as Ralf glided away. Finch watched the perfect linked Ss of his tracks. Ralf's skiing always looked as if it cost him no physical effort whatsoever. Smiling, Finch flexed her knees and reached forward to plant her pole, unweighting and letting the edge of her ski carry her into a turn. Her tracks crossed and recrossed Ralf's so the smooth arcs knitted into a chain of figure eights.

With the gathering speed whipping her cheeks she had given herself up to the rush and the rhythm. Powder crystals sprayed up and sparkled, catching the light like airborne diamonds. She was weightless, thoughtless, lost to everything but the snow and the slope. For now.

They reached the helicopter trailed by twin plumes of snow. Ralf planted his ski poles and slid forward to kiss her while they were still laughing with the exhilaration of the run.

'We are a good match,' he said now as he held on to her. She heard the vibration of his voice within the cage of his ribs and lay silent, listening. She said nothing, although he was waiting for her to agree with him.

Ralf slid away from her and walked naked into the kitchen. He came back with a bottle and two glasses, and she watched with her head back on the pillows as he twisted off the cork and poured froth and then champagne.

'This is my send-off.' She smiled. In the morning she would leave for Vancouver.

Ralf gave her a glass and lifted his to her. 'Come back safely. And when you come back, will you marry me?'

Finch understood what today had been about. He had taken her out and shown her the beauty of the back country and the perfect skiing, and the helicopter waiting like a toy in the hollow of the mountains. Now there was the well-run resort with blazing fires and log cabins and champagne, and a fine dinner waiting.

All this, he could offer her all this freedom, with marriage and loyalty and habit wrapped up in it like a leg-iron hidden under the snow.

The injustice of the response shamed her into rapid words. 'Ralf, thank you. I'm . . . only I can't say yes.'

'Does that mean you are not saying no?'

'No. Yes . . . no, it doesn't.'

'Is it because of this voyage you are making, to Everest? If it is, tell me. I know that it must be harder to decide anything at all when you are going so far away.'

In the small silence that followed they lifted their glasses and drank, their movements unconsciously mimicking each other.

Carefully Finch began, 'I have been very lucky all my life. You know that.'

He did know, of course. Ralf had met and liked all three of Finch's older brothers, and their wives and children, and he had stayed with and been impressed by the Buchanan parents and their beautiful house in Vancouver. Finch's was a remarkable, ambitious, wealthy family – held together by strong affection, as well as pride in their separate and mutual achievements. His own background could not have been more different and this solidity that Finch questioned was just one of the things he found attractive about her.

'It sounds ungrateful, spoiled, to say that there can be too much ease. But it is what I feel. I have had it easy in the world, but climbing mountains scrapes away all the layers of expectation and assumption. It's a challenge separate from the rest of my life.'

'And separate from me.'

'Yes, that's true.' She knew that she owed him the truth. At least a portion of it, the one she freely admitted to herself. 'I know that it's selfish, but it's something that I need to do. I don't find the same fixed determination or absolute satisfaction in anything else.'

Ralf inclined his head and she studied the sharp line of sun- and windburn on his cheekbones. They had discussed all this before. Finch had never been able to make him understand the force that impelled her to climb and tonight her urgency had made her speak too forcibly. She knew that she had hurt him, and she was sad and ashamed.

'I understand,' he said at length. He reached out to the champagne bottle and refilled their glasses. 'Come back safely,' he said, and he drank again.

'I will,' Finch promised, believing that she would and also understanding how much she would have to live through before that could happen. The knot of anticipation tightened again in her chest.

They finished the champagne as they dressed for dinner, then they went to the lodge dining-room and Ralf moved sociably around the tables and talked to the guests. After dinner he went to his daily meeting with the ski guides and the pilots, and Finch walked back to their cabin with James, and Kitty leaning on a stick. James was tired and went straight into the bedroom while the women wandered out on to the deck. It was a clear night, bright with stars.

With the end of her stick Kitty nudged a wooden

lid to one side and a turquoise eye opened to the sky in a column of steam. 'Hot tub?' she asked.

'Yes, definitely,' Finch agreed.

Kitty pressed the button and the water boiled with bubbles. They discarded their clothes with little exclamations at the freezing air on their skin, then slid into the pine-scented heat. They sat back, submerged to their chins and sighing with satisfaction.

After a minute Kitty asked meaningfully. 'So?'

'What do you mean?'

'You know what I mean.' Kitty was the family newsgatherer and lieutenant to Finch's mother in the battle to persuade Finch to commit herself.

'Okay. Ralf asked me to marry him. I said no.'

Kitty groaned. '*Finch*! Why not?'

'I'm not in love with him.'

'You gave a good impression of it. I thought you were nuts about him.'

'No. Not nuts enough, evidently.'

Kitty tucked a tendril of damp hair into the knot on top of her head. 'You could have all of this. All the things you like best, with a guy who adores you.'

'Perverse, aren't I?'

She wondered if James and Kitty had embarked on their partnership because they saw each other as offering all the things they liked best. There was no note of envy in Kitty's *all this*, either. James was a successful investment analyst and well able to provide for his family. They even had two-year-old twin girls, who were staying for the weekend with one of their pairs of adoring grandparents. All three of Finch's brothers were notably successful. Marcus, the eldest, was an architect like his distinguished father and

Caleb, the youngest, was a marine ecologist and film maker. His most recent film, about the pygmy sea-horse, had sold around the world. All three were married, with good-looking wives and attractive children.

Finch raised one knee out of the bubbles. The air was bitterly cold and she hastily submerged it again.

No wonder her family thought she was different, difficult. But surely it was less of a contradiction than it seemed, to reject *all the things you like best*? By which, she supposed, Kitty meant mountains and unlimited skiing, and probable financial ease, and a man who loved her and didn't threaten her.

Because by settling for them, and no more, you chose an ordinary life.

She was fearful of what might lie ahead of her out in Nepal. But she also tasted the fear with the savour of anticipation.

Kitty rolled her head against the pine walls of the tub. 'Poor Ralf. Was he devastated?'

Finch considered. On the whole Ralf didn't go in for devastation. 'No.'

'But he does love you, you know.'

'Yes.'

Finch had been in love only once in her life and it was not with Ralf.

'How does your knee feel?'

'Don't evade the issue with doctoring.'

'I wouldn't dream.'

Kitty laughed and reached out to touch Finch on the arm. 'We all want you to be happy.' All of us, the Buchanan clan.

'I am happy,' Finch said softly.

After Kitty had clambered out of the tub she sat for a few minutes alone, looking up and searching for the stars through the drifting curtain of steam.

The next afternoon Ralf flew the three of them in the helicopter down to Kamloops for their return flight to Vancouver. He walked with Finch to the departure gate, and when the flight was boarding James and Kitty tactfully went on ahead.

'You know where I am.'

Finch hesitated, ashamed to find that at this last minute she was tempted to retract everything she had said in exchange for the promise of comfort and security. Ralf was large and strong and, in retrospect, reassuring. She squeezed down hard on the impulse. 'Of course I do.'

He kissed her – not on the mouth but on the cheek, as affectionately as if he were James. 'And call me, when you can.'

'Of course I will.'

It was finished, both of them knew it.

Isn't this what you *wanted*? Finch's interior voice enquired impatiently.

He stood back to let her walk away. She turned round once to look at him, lifted her hand, then marched forward.

She took her seat in front of Kitty and James. Kitty made a small sad face, turning down the corners of her mouth, and James nodded calmly. The place next to Finch was empty and as the little plane climbed and disconcertingly rocked through the layers of cloud she thought about the man who had made himself her neighbour on the way up from

Oregon. My wife is a nervous flier, he had said presumptuously. She had forgotten his name.

Breathing as evenly as she could, Finch rested her head against the seat back. This time the day after tomorrow she would be airborne again. All her expedition kit was double-checked, packed, labelled, waiting in her tidy apartment. The medical supplies she had ordered with George Heywood's authorisation were already with the main body of expedition stores in Kathmandu. There remained only two more days and dinner with her family to negotiate.

'Everything looks fine,' Finch told her last patient of the day, as she peeled off her gloves. They chatted while the woman dressed and agreed that they would continue with the hormone replacement therapy for a further twelve months. A routine consultation, at the end of a routine afternoon surgery. At the door, the woman asked her, 'When will you be back?'

'Three months, give or take.' Finch smiled. The knot under her diaphragm was so tight now that it threatened to impede her breathing. 'Anything you need in that time, Dr Frame will be here to look after you, of course.'

'Good luck,' her patient said and Finch thanked her warmly.

She went to the bathroom and took a quick shower, then changed into a dark-blue dress with a deep V-front. She put on earrings and made up her face. It was time for her farewell dinner with the family. Marcus and Tanya would be there as well as James and Kitty, and to complete the party Caleb and Jessica were flying all the way up from San Diego where Caleb was working on a film about mother whales.

Finch locked up the surgery and drove herself to the North Vancouver shore, to the house in which Angus and Clare Buchanan had brought up their children. She parked her Honda in the driveway behind Marcus's Lexus and let herself in through the back door. There was no front door, as such. The long, low, two-storey house had been designed for his family by Angus himself. The bedrooms and bathrooms and Angus's study were on the lower level, and a dramatic open stairway led to the upper floor. Almost the whole of this space was taken up by one huge room with a wall of glass looking over a rocky inlet and southwards across a great sweep of water and sky towards Victoria. This early evening the room seemed to melt into an expanse of filmy cloud and sea spray.

Finch's parents and James and Marcus and their wives were sitting with their drinks in an encampment of modern furniture near the middle of the room. Angus and Clare collected primitive art, and their native American figure carvings and huge painted masks from Papua New Guinea seemed to diminish the living occupants of the room. When Finch was small, the mask faces regularly appeared in her dreams.

'Darling,' Clare said in delight. 'How pretty you look. Doesn't she, Angus?'

It had always been her way to insist on her daughter's prettiness. While she was still young enough to be docile, Clare had dressed her in floral blouses and tucked pinafores until Finch had clamoured for dungarees and plaid shirts like her brothers'.

'But you were my only girl, darling, after three huge boys,' Clare always protested to her recriminatory adolescent daughter. 'Can you blame me for being mad for you in pink ribbons?'

There was never any blaming Clare for anything. She had been a devoted and loyal mother, a serious cook and gardener, a recreational painter and an assiduous PR for her husband's business. She was small-boned and porcelain-skinned, and utterly intractable.

'She does,' her husband agreed. He kissed Finch on the top of her head. 'Hello, Bunny.' He always called her Bunny.

Bunny Wunnikins, Suzy would have mouthed, jabbing two fingers towards the back of her throat and rolling her eyes in disgust. Jesus, your family is just too much.

Angus was very tall and, in his early seventies, still handsome. His sons all resembled him. Finch had inherited her mother's dark colouring, but not her petite build. She moved round, now, to her brothers and their wives and kissed them all, and took the glass of Chardonnay her father poured for her.

'Good luck to you and God bless,' Angus started to toast her, but Clare cut in.

'Oh darling, wait until Caleb and Jessica get here for the speech, won't you? I so want everything to be right tonight. It's the last time we'll all be together for . . . for . . .' Her eyes went misty.

Suzy would have groaned – fucking speeches. We all love you so much. Christ! And Finch would have answered: It's okay for you. You're from a broken home.

Aloud, she said, 'I'm going to be away – doing something I *really* want – for three months, tops. There's no need to be sad about it, you know.'

Tanya pulled down the hem of her skirt to cover more of her legs. Everyone heard Caleb arriving and slamming the downstairs door.

'Here they are.'

'How wonderful it is to have all the family together.'

'Let me get the glasses.'

'So, Finch-bird. All ready for the off?'

The youngest brother and his wife appeared, straight from the airport. Their six-year-old was with Jessica's sister and Jessica carried the sleepy two-year-old in her arms. Jessica was the best-looking of the three wives. She had worked as a catwalk model in her twenties and before motherhood she had had a brief film career, now on hold, as she put it.

'Here at last.'

'Sorry we're late, guys. Stacked, would you believe? Hi, Mommy. You look great.'

'Can I make him up a little drink, Clare? If I read him a story he might just settle. He wouldn't sleep on the flight, or I'd let him stay up with his gran . . .'

'Give me a kiss. There.'

'Do you want to put him down here, with his head on this cushion, darling? Or straight into bed downstairs? Hello, sweet. Are you Granny's boy?'

They've made the effort to come tonight, to give me a send-off, Finch reflected. It's important for us, the way that birthdays and Christmases are in this family. It isn't their fault that I would rather have slipped away quietly and held the reunion after I've done something worth remarking on instead of just having talked too much about it in advance.

On the other side of the sofa arrangement Angus had launched into his speech. '. . . and so God bless you, Finch, and keep you safe,' he determinedly finished.

Everybody else made a show of raising their glasses and murmuring appropriately.

'Wish I was going.' Caleb grinned.

Caleb, the closest to her who now lived the furthest away, had always been her favourite brother. She put her arm round him and pulled gently at his hair. 'You go to enough exotic places. It's definitely my turn.'

Later, loosened up by the wine, they sat down to eat. The limed oak table made another small island in the big space. There was Scandinavian cutlery, and Italian glassware and French china, and outside the lights strung along the shoreline fractured the dark space of wind and water. As a little girl, Finch had always felt the stark contrast between the order and luxury within and the wilderness just inches beyond the glass. It had never felt like a comfortable house, for all its comforts. She was also aware that none of the others felt the same as she did. They all loved the family home. Marcus had even built himself one not dissimilar, a little further up the coast.

Over the compote of winter fruits, Marcus wondered what the next family celebration would be. 'When shall we nine all meet again?' he said jovially.

'Finch's engagement party, I hope,' Clare said.

Finch put down her spoon. It made a clatter that she hadn't intended. 'Oh, please.'

'I can wish to see my one girl safely married to a man who will make her happy, can't I?'

From a glance at their faces, Finch realised that Kitty had told Clare about her turning down Ralf. And Clare was smiling to mask her disappointment, but couldn't resist an oblique mention of it. The conversation at the opposite end of the table faded away and everyone listened uneasily.

'It isn't what I want,' Finch snapped.

In the silence that followed she could have kicked herself for her touchiness, tonight of all nights. She should just have smiled and let it pass.

Suzy would have advised: Say nothing, you dope. It's way easier. Don't you ever learn?

Caleb put his hand over his sister's. 'Hey. Lighten up.'

Finch collected herself. 'I'm sorry. Really, I'm sorry. I know what you want for me and why you want it. I'm so pleased that we're all together tonight. And seeing you all . . . maybe it makes me feel I *should* be settling down.'

There was a little chorus of disbelief. After she qualified Finch had worked for a year in Asia and had travelled like a nomad. And once she had come back to live in Vancouver there had been the regular mountaineering expeditions. Except for Clare, they accepted that that was the way Finch lived.

Angus said, 'We all liked Ralf, you know. We'd have been glad if you had chosen him, but as you didn't – well, that's fine too.'

From down the table Kitty silently signalled her

apology to Finch for unleashing all this.

'You've got plenty of time, darling,' Clare said. 'You go and climb Everest . . .'

'I'm not going all the way. I'm only supporting the serious mountaineers.'

'Do you think we believe that?' Caleb laughed.

'. . . and then come home. And after that, maybe you'll be ready.'

Suzy: For the serious business of life.

And Finch thought she heard her friend saying that straight.

Maybe, she silently rejoined. Maybe I can only find that out by going.

There was, after all, some buried instinct stirring in her, making her dream at the deepest level of something that the rest of her life appeared to deny. If there had not been, then she would not have chosen to join this expedition, this particular one of so many.

'Who *is* taking you to the airport tomorrow?' Angus was asking. 'Your mother and I would like to, you know that.'

'Dennis is,' Finch said firmly. 'We will have some last-minute things to settle. Patients, management, bits of business.'

Dennis Frame was Finch's medical partner. She had known him since high school and after Suzy he was her closest friend.

'I was, in fact, the very last child in the world to be named Dennis,' he said, but he refused to answer to Den or Denny. He was tolerant, slightly introspective, and gay. Finch greatly admired him. With the help of two other physicians, he would look after Finch's patients in her absence.

The evening was coming to an end. Caleb's and Jessy's son had slept through the dinner but now he had woken up and was starting to cry. Tanya said she had an early start in the morning and James was flying to Toronto. They moved from their seats and crossed the spaces of the room to embrace and exchange the shorthand assurances of families. Write. Phone. All the news. Mail me.

This was Finch's matrix. She felt restricted by it when it was tight around her, like tonight, but she knew when she stood back she would see the firm knitted strands of it and value it in theory.

All eight of them came out to the driveway to wave her off. The air smelled of rain and salt.

'I shouldn't have said anything. Will you forgive me?' Kitty whispered.

'I'm pleased you did. It saved me having to bring it up.'

Each of the boys hugged her and warned her to be careful. Their concern made her feel like the little girl again, trying to demonstrate that she could run as far and jump as high as they could.

Tanya and Jessica kissed her, wishing her luck in clear incomprehension of why she would want to go at all.

Clare and Angus took her hands and wrapped her in their arms, and tried not to repeat all the things they had said already.

At last, Finch climbed into her car. Her family stood solid against the yellow lights of the house, waving her off. She drove back to the city, to the apartment that already seemed unaired and deserted. There were a few books, some cushions and candles that had mostly been given to her as presents, but otherwise the rooms were almost featureless, as if she were just staying a night or two on her way to somewhere else. Finch didn't want to copy the grand architectural effects of her parents' home, and if she had given her own taste free rein she would probably have cosied her rooms with knitted afghans and pot plants and patchwork quilts. She left them altogether unadorned for simplicity's sake.

It was after midnight. She stepped past the neat pyramid of her expedition baggage and stopped with her back to the hallway. Her shoulders drooped and she pushed out her clenched fists in a long cat-stretch of relief and abandonment. The boats were burned, completely incinerated, and she was actually going.

She had a job to do, a team to fit in with and the biggest challenge of her life waiting to be met. Now that it was happening she felt relieved and ready for it. What would come, would come. She clicked off the lights and went into her bedroom.

Sam sat at his computer in his apartment in Seattle. It was late, gone midnight, and the enclosing pool of light from his desk lamp and the broad darkness beyond it heightened his sense of isolation. From beyond the window he could just hear the city night sounds – a distant police or ambulance siren and the steady beat of rain. A humdrum March evening, seeming to contain his whole life in its lustreless boundaries.

He tapped the keys and gave a sniff of satisfaction

as the links led him to the site he was searching for. He tapped again and leaned back to wait for the information to download. The teeming other-world of netborne data no longer fascinated him as it had once done. And as he stared at the screen he asked himself bleakly, what does interest you, truly and deeply? Name one thing. Was it this he was searching the Net for?

An hour ago Frannie had come to look in on him, standing in the doorway in her kimono with her fingers knitted around a cup of herbal tea. 'Are you coming to bed?'

He had glanced at her over the monitor. 'Not yet.'

She had shrugged and drifted away.

The website home page was titled 'The Mountain People', the logo outlined against a snow peak and a blazing blue sky. Quite well designed, he noted automatically, and clicked on one of the options, 'Everest and Himalaya'. And there, within a minute, it was. Details of the imminent Everest expedition. Sam scrolled more impatiently now. There were pictures of previous years' teams, smiling faces and Sherpas in padded jackets. Then individual mug-shots of the expedition director and his Base Camp manager, and two tough-looking men posing on mountains with racks of climbing hardware cinched round their waists and ice axes in their hands. This year's guides, he noted, accompanied by impressive accounts of their previous experience that he didn't bother to read.

Here. Here was what he was searching for.

Dr Finch Buchanan, medical officer and climber.

Her picture had been taken against a plain blue

background, not some conquered peak. She was wearing a white shirt that showed a V of suntanned throat and she was looking slightly aside from the camera, straight-faced and pensive. She was thirty-two, an expert skier and regular mountaineer. She had trained at UBC, worked in Baluchistan for UNESCO, now lived in Vancouver where she was a general medical practitioner. Previous experience included ascents of Aconcagua in Argentina and McKinley, where she had also been medical officer. In the course of her climbing career she had developed a strong interest in high-altitude medicine.

That was all. Sam read and reread the brief details, as if the extra attention might extract some more subtle and satisfying information. He even touched the tip of his finger to the screen, to the strands of dark hair, but encountered only the glass, faintly gritty with dust. The dates of the trip blinked at him, with the invitation to follow the progress of the climb over the following weeks via daily reports and regular updates from Base Camp. She must already be on her way to Nepal, Sam calculated.

There had been a total of perhaps five hours from the moment she had blown with the storm into one airport, then disappeared into the press of another. He had been thinking about her for another fifty. Sam swivelled in his chair, eyeing the over-familiar clutter on his desk and trying to reason why. Not just because of the way she looked, or her cool manner, or the glimpse of her vulnerability in her fear of flying, although all of these had played their part. It was more that there had been a sense of purpose about her. He saw it and envied it. She looked through him to a bigger view and the vista put light in her face and tightened the strings that held her body together. The effect wasn't just to do with sex, although it was also the sexiest encounter he had ever had with a total stranger.

Sam sighed. Everything about Finch Buchanan was the opposite of the way he felt about himself. His life seemed to have narrowed and lost its force, and finally dried out like a stream in a drought. Work yawned around him with its diminishing satisfactions. His father was disappointed in him and vice versa. The energy and effort he had put into competitive running now seemed futile. And the woman he shared his life with was asleep in another room, separate from him, and he couldn't even make himself care properly about that.

I wish I were going to Everest too, he thought.

The wildness of the idea even made him smile.

And then it was so unthinkable that he let himself think about it.

The climbing he had done as a child with Michael had frightened him. He knew his father had pushed him too hard; the terror still sometimes surfaced in his dreams. And yet this woman did it and it – or something related to it – gave her a force field that sucked him towards her. He was drawn closer and now the fear had transferred from himself to Finch. Even before she vanished at Vancouver airport, even as he sat down beside her on the plane, he had known he would find her again. He had imagined that he would wait until she came back, then track her down in Vancouver. But the aridity of his life made a sudden desert flower of an idea swell and burst into iridescent colour in his mind. He didn't have to wait for her to come back. He had been prescient enough to ask where she was staying.

He could go out there.

Maybe just by being close enough inside her orbit he could make sure that she was safe.

Ever the optimist, McGrath, he thought. The woman's a serious mountaineer and you flunked out of it at the age of fourteen. And you still imagine you can look after her? She'll just think you're some weird stalker.

He'd have to deal with that. Optimism was good; it was too long since he had felt it about anything. Seize the moment.

Sam sat for a few more minutes in front of his screen, reading the rest of the Mountain People's seductive sell.

When he slipped into their bedroom he found to his surprise that Frannie was still awake, propped up on her side of the bed reading a gardening book. The angle of a fire escape outside a city apartment wasn't enough growing space for her. She wanted a house and a garden for her plants, and Sam couldn't blame her for that. He sat down beside her on the edge of the bed and she lowered the book to look at him.

'Working?'

'Yeah.' He undid the laces of his sneakers and eased them off his feet, then unbuttoned the cuffs of his shirt. Frannie lay back, watching him, waiting for him to climb in beside her. They had lived together for three years, and the sediment of their joint existence was spread around them on the shelves and in the drawers. A blanket from Mexico, their last holiday together, covered the bed. There were invitations in their joint names on the dresser. Even in the fluff of pocket linings and trouser turn-ups there would be the forensic evidence of their inter-related lives: sand from walks on the beach; dust from cinemas; carpet fibres from the homes of their shared friends. The extent of their separation within this unit was too apparent to Sam.

'Switch the light off,' Frannie murmured as he lay down. She turned on her side to face him and her breath warmed his face as she slid closer. 'Mm?'

Sam lay still, contemplating the redoubt of betrayal.

'What's wrong?' she whispered.

He lifted his weighty hand and rested it on the naked curve of her hip where the T-shirt she wore in bed had ridden up.

'I don't know,' he lied. Could you say, I feel trapped by this life, I don't want to stay here, you deserve a man who will treat you better than I do? How did you do that, instead of making love like he proceeded to do now, with a flare of guilty optimism battened down inside you?

Afterwards Frannie fell asleep with her back curved against his belly and Sam lay awake, thinking out how he would make the next moves and trying to plan the gentlest words he could use to tell her.

Frannie was a teacher and always woke up early to prepare properly for the day at school. When her alarm went off at 6.50 a.m. she got out of bed at once, and padded around between bed and bathroom while Sam lay with the covers hiding his head. He heard her taking a shower, rummaging for clothes, peering in the mirror while she applied a slick of mascara. When she went into the kitchen to make coffee he sat up abruptly and followed her.

'Toast?' she asked, with a knife slicing the air. They didn't usually have breakfast together. Evenings were their time, when they drank wine and talked and collaborated over the cooking. Or used to.

'Just coffee.'

He sat at the table, looking into the cup. 'Fran. I want to go away for a bit.'

As soon as the words were out he knew she had been anticipating, probably fearing them. The tension of it had been in the air between them. Her face creased now and her mouth drew in sharply. 'Where to?'

'I want to go . . . to Nepal. Maybe to see Everest.'

She gazed at him. 'Oh, of course. When?'

'Now. I suppose.'

Fran shook her head. There were red marks like thumbprints on each cheekbone. 'Why?'

Because I need to get away from here? Because my work isn't satisfying and because I can't run as fast as I want to, and because you and I don't make each other happy? Because I've just been to see my father and we can't talk to each other, and I know I have disappointed him? Or just because I saw a woman at an airport and thought, *I want her*?

Sam mumbled, 'I can't tell you why. I want to go because I had the idea.' This was cowardly. But would the truth be kinder?

There were tears in Frannie's eyes but she stood up and turned away. She rinsed her breakfast plate, an angry plume of water splashing up from the sink. 'You always do what you want.'

He was surprised at that. Sam generally felt that he spent his life approximately conforming to what other people wanted – clients, friends, Frannie. Maybe as an ineffectual compensation for not doing it for Michael. He had been feeling ineffectual for too long. 'Do I?'

'Yes.' She began to shout at him. 'You keep it quiet, but you do. And you evade everything you don't want to do. You're never full on. It's like you're always looking out of the window at some view the rest of us can't see. I hate it.'

'I'm sorry, Fran.' His inability to please her was just part of the scratchy disorder that his life had become. He was profoundly tired of it, he knew that much. His resolve hardened.

She flung some cutlery into the sink. 'What happens if I'm not here when you come back?'

Their eyes met.

'I will have to deal with that when it happens.'

There was a silence. Through the wall hummed their neighbour's choice of morning radio programme.

Fran jerked away from the sink. 'I've got to get to school. We'll have to talk later.'

'It isn't a whim,' he said quietly.

'I don't care what it is,' Frannie shouted.

After she had gone Sam walked to his desk. His jacket was creased on the back of his chair, where he had shrugged it off last night. He picked it up and absently smoothed the lapels. He had to get to work too, to a meeting with a travel agent who wanted a website to sell last-minute budget ski packages.

Go, Sam advised himself. Maybe the reasons for it were shaky, but he couldn't come up with a single one against going.

Four

'You coming?' Adam Vries asked Finch.

A group of seven men were standing outside the dining-room of the Buddha's Garden Hotel. In their plaid shirts, combat pants and cheery slogan T-shirts they might have been any group of tourists, although a closer inspection would have revealed that they seemed noticeably fitter than the average. They had just eaten an excellent dinner and they had the rosy, expansive look of people intent on enjoying themselves for much of the rest of the night.

'Yeah, come on. We're going to Rumdoodle.'

'What the hell's that?' Finch grinned.

'She's a newcomer, isn't she?' a big, grizzled man teased in a broad Yorkshire accent. His name was Hugh Rix; the front of his T-shirt proclaimed 'Rix Trucking. Here Today, There Tomorrow'.

'Bar,' Ken Kennedy said briefly. He was in his early forties, short but broad-built. His colourless hair was shaved close to his scalp and his rolled shirtsleeve showed a scorpion tattoo on his left bicep.

'Uh, I don't think so,' Finch demurred. 'I'm going to sleep. In a bed. While I still have the chance.'

'Coward.'

'Leave her be, Rix. She'll be seeing more than enough of you before the trip ends,' Ken said.

'Night,' they all said to her and in a solid phalanx moved towards the door. Of the ten-strong Western contingent that made up the Mountain People expedition, George Heywood had eaten a quick dinner and gone off to a meeting with the climbing Sherpas and Alyn Hood had not yet arrived. The word was that he had taken a two-day stopover in Karachi.

Finch went upstairs to her small single room and switched on her PowerBook to send an e-mail to Suzy.

Hey, married woman.

Good honeymoon?

Here I am. Flights not too bad, hotel plain but reasonably clean (as my mother would say). Dinner tonight with the rest of the group except lead guide who isn't here yet. They're okay!!! George Heywood I already met, Adam Vries is communications manager, pretty face (but your type, not mine), poses a bit. Ken Kennedy's the second guide, acts tough, sports a tattoo, probably has a heart of gold. Clients are Hugh Rix and Mark Mason, both Brits, know each other from back home. Rix (as he calls himself) is the self-made-man type, probably won't stand any nonsense unless he's generating it. Mark is quieter and more sensitive, although not by a long way. There's a longhair Aussie rock jock named Sandy Jackson and two determined Americans, Vern Ecker and Ted Koplicki, who were here last year and turned back from Camp Four. Now they've all gone out for a beer.

For me, bed. If I can sleep, with excitement.

I wouldn't be anywhere else in the world, or be doing anything different. You know that. Give Big J a kiss from me xxx

Before she climbed into bed, Finch stood at her window. She opened the shutter and looked out over the trees of the garden and a carved statue of the Buddha to a corner of the busy street just visible beyond the gate. The traffic rolled and hooted through the haze of pollution. Kathmandu lay in a hollow ringed by high hills, and the smoke and exhaust fumes hung in the air like a grey veil. As she stood absently watching, a man walked in the darkness across the grass and through the gate into the roadway. He lifted his hand to a bicycle rickshaw man hopefully lingering near the hotel entrance and hopped into the hooded seat. The old man stood up on the pedals, his lean legs tensing with the effort, and the rickshaw trundled away. Finch stood for a moment longer, resting her shoulder against the window frame and breathing in the scent of woodsmoke and joss and curry that drifted up to her. Then she pulled the shutter to and finished her preparations for bed.

It was surprisingly snug in the rickshaw seat, with the hood framing the view of haphazard streets and ancient wooden houses leaning out over the cobbles. Piles of rotting debris carelessly swept into the angles of walls gave out a pungent vegetable smell. Sam leaned forward to the driver. 'Very far?'

A triangle of brown face briefly presented itself over the hunched shoulder. 'No, sir. Near enough.'

Sam had landed at Kathmandu six hours earlier. He had found himself an acceptable hotel close to the Buddha's Garden, changed his clothes, eaten a meal that he didn't taste and couldn't remember, and shaved and showered with close attention. The unfamiliar feeling in his gut was nothing to do with the soupy dal bhaat he had eaten – it was anticipation. It was a very long time since anything in his life had given him the same sensation. Even running didn't do it for him any more. He had tried to summon it up before he competed at Pittsburgh and had failed. There was a part of himself that warned the rest that it had been a long way to travel from Seattle to catch up with a woman he had spent barely five hours with. But Sam told himself that in any case it wasn't just to do with Finch. He was in Kathmandu, he was doing something other than withering away at home.

When he finally reached Finch's hotel the obliging receptionist told him that yes, Miss Buchanan was resident there. But he believed that all the climbers had gone out – just gone, sir, five minutes only – to a bar in the Thamel district.

Armed with the name and directions, Sam set out again. The quickest way through the steaming traffic looked as though it might be this bicycle-propelled pram. He sat even further forward on the sagging seat, as if he could urge the driver to pedal faster. His eyes were gritty with travel and he blinked at the waves of people and cars with a yawn trapped in the back of his throat. Maybe he should have gone to bed and waited until tomorrow to find her. But the thought of being so close, and the fear that she would somehow disappear into the mountains before he could reach her, was too much for him.

At last the old man sank back on his saddle and the rickshaw wavered to a halt. They had come to a doorway wedged in a row of open-fronted shops, where multicoloured T-shirts and cotton trousers hung like flags overhead, and a press of wandering shoppers threaded through narrow alleyways. There was a thick smell of spicy food, and patchouli and marijuana. Two dogs lay asleep on a littered doorstep.

The bar was up a flight of wooden stairs. Sam found a big room, noisy with muzzily amplified music and loud talk. Most of the customers were very young Westerners with the suntans, bleached hair and ripped shorts of backpackers, although there were a few Thais and Japanese among them. He edged his way through the babble of American, British and indeterminate accents to the bar, and positioned himself in front of it. He searched the crowd with his eyes, looking for her.

Finch wasn't there. Within a minute he knew it for certain but he still examined each of the groups more carefully and drank some weak beer while he waited in case she had gone outside for five minutes. It took him much less than five minutes to identify the group of Everest mountaineers. They were older than most of the other drinkers and were gathered in a tight group around two rickety little tables. One of them had a goatee and wore his long hair tied back in a lank ponytail, another had an effete blond fringe, the rest had brutally short crops. They all had worked-out, hard-looking rather than muscular physiques. The look was familiar enough to Sam: for years he had seen men with similar bodies high on the pillars in Yosemite, or drinking beers with his father and exchanging the arcane details of routes and lines and remote peaks.

There was an empty chair at the far side of their group, next to the blond man. Sam strolled casually across the room and hesitated beside it. 'Mind if I take this?'

'Sure. Help yourself.'

He sat down, carefully placing his drink on the table. He relaxed for a minute, gazing into the room with unfocused eyes and letting their conversation drift around him.

'The man's an asshole. Forget the hills. I wouldn't go as far as the Bronx with him leading . . .'

'. . . into a heap of shit. So I say to the guy, this place is a *latrine* . . .'

'A brand new camera, a Nikon AX.'

'I'm ready for it. But if I don't make it this year I'll be back. And I'll keep *on* coming back until I do make it.'

'You'll do it, man. George Heywood's put thirty-five clients up there already. Why not you? And Al Hood's a fine leader.'

'He's never climbed it.'

'He's climbed every other fucker in the known world.'

Meditatively, Sam drained his glass. These men were going to be Finch's companions for two months. 'You heading up for some climbing?' he asked the blond in a friendly voice.

'Yeah, man.'

'What're you planning?'

'The big one. Everest.'

Sam gave a soundless, admiring whistle. 'Is that right? I envy you. You all going?'

'It's a commercial expedition. Six clients, or five if you don't count the chick medic. Two guides, Ken here and another guy. The boss is out here this trip as Base Camp manager. He's climbed the hill twice himself. I work for the company, supplies and communications manager, but I'm kind of hoping to get a shot at the summit. Have to see how things pan out, though.'

'Ahuh. Sounds good.'

'You climbing? My name's Adam Vries, by the way.'

'Sam McGrath. Not this time,' Sam said cautiously. He didn't want to exclude himself from the company that included Finch.

'Pity. Want some of this?' He held up a jug of beer and Sam nudged his glass across. Adam filled it up for him.

'Thanks. So, where're you from?'

Adam named a little town in Connecticut but said that he spent most of his teenage years in Geneva. Under the careful pressure of Sam's questions he hitched his boot on the rung of a chair, locked his hands behind his head and talked about climbing in the Alps. His fine, slightly girlish features lit up with passion as he reminisced about the big faces of the Eiger and Mont Blanc, and Sam found his initial antipathy melting away. Even though he had dismissed Finch as the *chick medic*, this was a nice guy.

For a climber, he was an exceptionally nice guy.

In turn, Adam extracted from Sam the details of his own mountain history. He shook his head disparagingly. 'Man, that's tough. But you can still climb, can't you? Without your old man, I mean.'

'I suppose I could.'

He had merged into the group now. The two British expedition members had introduced themselves as Mark Mason and Hugh Rix – 'Just call me Rix,' the blunt-faced man insisted – and Ken Kennedy stretched out a hand and shook Sam's. His grip was like a juice presser.

The jug of beer was filled and refilled, and the level of noise and laughter rose.

'What are you doing in Kathmandu?' Rix demanded in his loud voice.

'Just travelling. Taking a break from the world.'

'Sounds like a waste of good climbing time to me.'

Sam laughed. 'Could be. Do you reckon you're going to get to the top?' With Finch to treat your frostnip and your constipation, and monitor you for oedema on the way, you bullet-headed bastard?

Rix leaned forward. He was red-faced with beer and the drink made his Yorkshire accent even more pronounced. He put his big, meaty hands flat on the table. 'Listen up. I know what people say. The old brigade of professional climbers who had bugger all in their back pockets and that mountain in their dreams, who clawed their way to the summit or died in the doing. I know they say the South Col route is a yak track and that any fat fucker with fifty grand to spare can get himself hauled up there if he can be bothered to go to the gym twice a week for a couple of months beforehand. They claim that Everest's been turned into an adventure playground for software salesmen by the commercial companies dragging along anyone who can pay the money.

'And that may well be true, mate. All I know is that I've dreamed of standing on that peak since I was a snotty kid at home in Halifax. I've climbed Makalu and Cho Oyu and Aconcagua, and enough peaks in the Alps, and I'm still as hungry for Everest as I was when I was a lad. I was out here this time last year and I got turned back by the weather at 25,000 feet. But I've made my money and this is the way I choose to spend it, and no bugger's going to stop me. I'll climb the hill. It's not a question for me.'

'No,' Sam said thoughtfully.

Adam was three-quarters drunk now. He propped his blond head against the wall. 'Rix's right. I know it. I know that feeling. Ever since I started, from the first climb, it's what I've existed to do. It's been the focus of my life. Every time I reach the summit of a new mountain I know no one can take that away from me. It's concrete. Like, there it is. Mine. And you know' – he waved his hand along the group around the two tables – 'there's this family. If you're some Yank kid lost in a Swiss school where you can't even talk to the class losers let alone the cool kids, and your old man's always travelling and your mom goes shopping, you can go climbing and you find people who'll be with you. You're in the mountains and you're not lonely any more. It's . . .' His head rolled and his eyes drifted shut. 'Hey, I am *wasted* . . . it's everything you need in the world.'

There was a small silence, then Adam's eyes

snapped open again. 'You know what I'm saying, man. You climb yourself.'

Seven pairs of eyes looked at the newcomer.

'Yes,' Sam said.

Much later, by the time the bar was closing, everyone except Ken Kennedy was drunk. 'Come on, the lot of you. Get to your beds,' he ordered.

Adam and Sam made their way unsteadily down the stairs together, Adam's arm looped over Sam's shoulder.

When the thick-scented air hit them they staggered a little and Adam coughed with laughter. 'Need a scotch to settle my gut after all that beer. You coming back to the hotel for one more?'

Even with his head spinning, and his ears and tongue clogged with the dull wadding of jet lag, Sam was just able to work out that it wouldn't be clever to present himself at the Buddha's Garden in this condition and risk bumping into Finch.

'Nope. But I'll come by tomorrow and see you.'

'Don't make it too early,' Adam groaned.

It was past noon when he strolled back through the leafy garden. The strong sunlight laid wedges of indigo-blue shadow under the trees. Sam had slept for ten hours, then dressed in a clean white shirt and pressed chinos. He was not going anywhere or doing anything else until he had tracked down Finch Buchanan and made her promise to have dinner with him.

In the lobby Ken Kennedy was sitting under a ceiling fan with a balding man Sam didn't recognise. They were frowning over a sheaf of papers and Sam passed by without interrupting them. The desk clerk gave Sam Adam's room number and pointed to the stairs. Sam ran up two shallow flights and found the number he was looking for. He knocked on the door and was greeted by a wordless mumble that he took as an invitation to come in.

Adam was lying on a disordered bed, naked except for a pair of shorts. One limp arm hung over the mattress edge, the other shaded his eyes from the dim light filtering through the closed shutters. 'Uh, it's you.'

'What's up?'

'God knows. I've never puked or shat so much in my life. Can't just be the beer.'

'That's rough. Can I get you anything?'

'How about a gun to put to my head? *Jesus*.'

Adam hauled himself half upright and vomited a couple of greenish mouthfuls into an enamel basin. Sam grimaced and tried to look in the other direction while Adam spat and then sank back on the pillow. 'You could go down to the bar and get me a couple of bottles of water. Room service doesn't do much in this place.'

'Sure,' Sam said.

It took ten minutes to locate a barman, pay for the mineral water and make his way back to Adam's room. This time he opened the door without bothering to knock.

Finch was standing with her back to him, staring at her watch and holding Adam's wrist loosely in her hand. After another five seconds she finished counting and turned her head to see the intruder. She was wearing a sleeveless khaki bodywarmer with pockets and a white T-shirt with the Mountain People's logo on the front. She looked less tense and therefore younger than she had done on the Vancouver flight.

'I brought him some mineral water.' Sam smiled. 'It's nothing serious, I hope?'

'This is the doc,' Adam said.

She was looking at Sam, the total surprise in her face distinctly shaded with irritation.

'What are you doing here?' Finch asked coldly.

'I told you. Bringing the sick man some water.'

'Do you mind leaving us alone while I examine my patient?'

'It's okay. He doesn't have to go on my account. Do you two know each other?'

'Yes.'

'No. Now then, how long ago did the vomiting start?'

'Twelve hours.'

'Right.' Finch took a phial out of her medical bag and shook out a large capsule. 'I'm going to give you something that should stop it.'

Adam held out his hand and gestured for the bottle of water.

'Not orally, you'll vomit it straight up again. It's a suppository. To be inserted in your rectum. I can do it for you, or you can deal with it yourself, whichever you prefer?'

'I'll manage.'

'Good. Try to drink some water over the next few hours, don't eat anything.'

Even the mention of eating started up another bout of retching. There were dark sweat streaks in Adam's blond hair. Finch watched him with her fingers resting lightly on his shoulder, then she took the bowl from him and rinsed it in the bathroom.

She's an angel, Sam thought. If I were ill, would she look after me like this? Put her hand on my shoulder?

'Okay, Adam. It's food poisoning. You should start feeling better soon. Try and rest, and I'll be back to see you at about six. Your friend will stay and keep you company I expect.' Finch smiled sweetly.

'Actually, I was hoping . . .' Sam tried.

She snapped her bag shut. 'See you later, Adam. Good-bye . . . um . . .'

'Come on, you know my name.'

Finch was already halfway out of the door.

'Wait a minute. Look, I'll be back,' he called over his shoulder to the wan figure in the bed.

Adam had covered his eyes again with one arm. 'Don't mind me,' he muttered.

Sam ran down the corridor after Finch. Realising that she wasn't going to shake him off so easily she turned with a flicker of anger and confronted him. 'Right. So here you are in Kathmandu. What do you want, exactly? I'm busy, I've got a job to do.'

'I want to take you out to dinner. Is that too much to ask?'

'Did you *follow* me all the way out here?'

'Yes. I got here twenty-four hours ago.'

'Why?'

'That was how the plane times worked out.'

'Don't try to be more of an asshole than you are already. Why did you follow me?'

Sam hesitated. 'Look, I know it seems flaky. I met you, we talked, I wanted to see you again. But it isn't as weird as that makes it sound. You talked about Everest and I loved the way it lit you up. My life is at a kind of static point right now, so taking off out of it for a while seemed a good idea and I thought, why not here? I've never seen Kathmandu before.'

'That's not what you told me.' She did look faintly mollified now.

'Why would you have told me where you were staying, if I hadn't claimed some familiarity with the place?' Candour, he thought, was probably the best defence.

They were standing in an angle of the main stairway. Rix, Mark Mason and Sandy Jackson came up the stairs from the lobby, and each of them gave Sam a friendly greeting as they passed.

'Hey doc, how's the patient?' Sandy enquired over his shoulder.

'He'll live.' She returned her full attention to Sam. 'You know everyone.'

He shrugged. 'Well, sort of. How about tonight?'

Finch sighed. Her hair was tied with what looked like a bootlace and he wanted to slide his finger underneath and hook it off.

'Listen . . .'

'Sam.'

'Yes. I do remember. Listen carefully, Sam, and save yourself from any more impulses to do with me. One, I am responsible for the health care of a total of twenty people on this expedition. Two, I am here to climb as high as I can go on Everest. I don't expect to make the summit, necessarily, but I want to do myself justice. I can't afford it, but I have saved up the money to pay for this. I've made a lot of physical and mental preparations. I don't have room for anything else in my life right now. *Nothing*.'

She's saying the same things as those guys last night, Sam thought. Climbers. Peak pervs. Monofocal mountain morons. But even so his longing to untie Finch's bootlace, to put his fingertip to the corner of her mouth, to hear her voice in his ear, never even wavered. Her steeliness only impressed him and made him want to be with her even more than before. He held up his hands and smiled. 'It's only dinner. Two glasses of wine and a curry, dessert optional. It's not an addition to your workload or an emotional commitment.'

She studied him briefly, working out whether he was threatening or harmless, then put her hand briefly on his arm. 'No. No thanks, Sam.'

She smiled in a finite way and removed her hand again. Sam was not especially pleased with his way with women, but it did strike him that even in circumstances as unusual as these he had never been turned down with quite such cool certainty. There was more here, he thought, than immediately met the eye.

'Wait. Do you want to do something genuinely helpful?' she added.

'Yes.'

'Then sit down for a while with Adam Vries. I have to check over my supplies because they've just come in from the airport.'

'I'll make sure he's okay.'

'Thank you.' She inclined her head and walked away down the stairs. Sam followed her with his eyes, remembering her long legs under the ski parka.

Adam had shifted his position. 'Huh. I shoved the thing up my butthole. How does she know I'm not going to shit before I puke?'

'Brilliant medical judgement.'

'Mh. I wasn't going to have her sticking her index finger up there.'

'No. Although, I don't know . . .'

Adam managed the ghost of a smile. 'You too? Forget it. Used to know a brutal med student like that at college. The Fridge, we used to call her.'

'Is that so?'

Sam settled himself in a chair and rested his feet on another. He could see through a chink between the shutters to the top of a tree and the side walls of some houses. On a balcony level with his sightline an old woman was peeling vegetables over a plastic bowl. A plump baby played at her feet until a young woman, hardly more than a girl, came out and swept him up in her arms. The baby's thumb plugged into his mouth at once and his head settled on her shoulder. The mother cupped the back of it with her hand, stroking his hair. Sam watched until she had carried the infant inside, then sat for a while with unfocused eyes, wondering what Finch would look like with a baby.

Whatever Adam might think she wasn't a fridge. Something in her eyes, the turn of her head and hips, made him certain of that.

When he looked again he saw that Adam had drifted into a doze. He would have liked to slip away and maybe go out for a beer with Rix and the others, but he was afraid that if he moved he would wake him up. He leaned his head against the chair back and let his own eyes fall shut.

Last night had made him think of his father.

Michael would talk about mountains in the same way, using the very same words. He remembered conversations overheard. Michael and Mary outside the tent on summer nights when he was supposed to be asleep, and the timbre of his father's voice in response to Mary's questions *why*, and *what for* – and the always unspoken but equally ever-present words within his own head, *danger* and *falling* and *dead* –

'I need that reality. If I don't climb, my grip on reality fades and I feel like nothing exists.'

'Not me? Or your boy?'

'Of course. But not in the same way, Mary. Nothing's the same as the way you feel up there with the rock and space. I'm no good with words, you know that. I can't explain the need for it, the being more alive than alive. But it's always there, once you've tasted it.'

'So am I always here, so is Sammy. We don't want anything to happen to you.'

Sam remembered that he would squirm in his sleeping bag, trying to bury his head, to bring his shoulders up around his ears so that he couldn't hear any more. But the voices came anyway, as much from within his head as outside it.

Michael would give his warm, reassuring laugh. 'Nothing will happen. It's concentration. If you keep your mind on it you don't make mistakes.'

Sam thought of Michael as he was now, moving painfully around the old house, all alone, with only the television freak shows for company. When I get back, he promised the dim room, I'll see more of him.

Maybe it's time to move the business a bit closer to home. If there still is a business when I'm through with this caper.

An hour later Adam woke up again. 'I've got a thirst like the desert,' he whispered.

Sam passed him the water, but held it so that he could only take a sip or two at a time. 'Otherwise you'll spew it straight up again.'

'Thanks, nurse.' He rubbed his cracked mouth with the back of his hand.

Sam went into the bathroom and found his face-cloth, rinsed it in cool water and handed it to him.

'Nice. But I'd still rather have the doc to hold my hand.'

'Fuck you.'

'Is that what all this is about? You should see me when I'm really looking my best.'

'She told me to keep an eye on you.'

'Ah. I see.' Adam lay back again. 'I appreciate it. I think I may go back to sleep. Don't need you to watch me any more. Honestly.'

Sam stood up. 'I'll catch you later.'

'Ahuh.'

There was no one to be seen downstairs. Sam hung around for a minute or two, hoping that Finch might appear again, but in the end he gave up. He found a bar a hundred yards from the hotel gates and sat at a rickety iron table under a bamboo awning, keeping watch.

He didn't have much of an idea about what he was going to do next.

*

Al was in a taxi on his way in from the airport. He had been to Kathmandu a dozen times before, so did not have much attention to spare for the congested road and the scrubby concrete housing that lined it. He sat motionless in the back of the worn-out Mercedes, his eyes apparently fixed on the grime-marked collar of the driver's blue shirt.

Karachi had been a last-minute diversion, a visit to an old climbing friend. They had sat for a long time over too many glasses of whisky, not talking very much, merely pursuing their memories in one another's company. When it was time for Al to leave again Stuart had come to see him off.

'Drop in and see me on the way back, when you've got the big hill in your pocket.'

'I might just do that.'

Stuart stood watching Al's back as he moved in the line of veiled women and men in loose shalwar kameez towards the barrier. He stood a full head taller than anyone else, and he looked fit and relaxed. Just before he disappeared Al glanced round and nodded a last goodbye. Stuart lifted his hand and held it up long after Al had gone. They had known each other for many years and had said casual goodbyes before a score of expeditions. That was what happened and this was no different. History made no difference. It was the present and the future tenses that counted for climbers.

As his taxi approached the Buddha's Garden Al was acknowledging to himself that the stopoff to see Stuart Frost had been a delaying tactic. He hadn't wanted to get to Kathmandu, to join this group, until the last moment. But now that he was here he focused his mind on what was to be done. It was a job, like any other, as well as a climb.

As he was checking in, with his weather-beaten packs piled beside him, George Heywood came out of the bar. He shook Al's hand, enclosing it warmly in both of his. George was bald, with a seamed face and sharp grey eyes.

'Good to see you, Al. Thought you might be going AWOL at the last minute.'

'Why?'

George laughed. 'Now I see you I realise I was worrying about nothing. You look good.'

'Everyone here?'

'Yup. You're the last.'

'Good.'

'Ken's in the bar, with Pemba and Mingma. You want to go and change or something, or will you come and join us?'

'I'll come,' Al said.

The three men stood up when they saw Al's tall frame following George to the table. Pemba Chhotta and Mingma Nawang were the climbing sirdars – experienced Sherpa mountaineers who would be sharing the guiding duties with Al and Ken. They had worked with Al in the past and they showed their liking for him in broad smiles of greeting.

'*Namaste*, Alyn,' Pemba said formally.

Ken was more laconic. He clasped Al's hand very briefly. 'Yeah, mate. Here we are.'

'Ken. I saw Stu in Karachi. Sends you his best.'

Their eyes met briefly. Everyone sat down and George ordered more drinks. There was the business of supplies and logistics and porters and yaks to be discussed, then George briefly described their six clients, mostly for the benefit of the two Sherpas who would act as second guides to Ken and Al. The two Britons had been on Everest the year before, but with a different company who they believed had let them down. Now they had come to George and his US-based Mountain People to make one more attempt. The two Americans were experienced mountaineers too; the Australian was a less well-known quantity but he had been recommended by previous clients.

The Canadian doctor, George explained, had climbed McKinley in a group led by Ed Vansittart. Everyone at the table nodded. Ed had written to him to say that Dr Buchanan was an excellent medic, who really understood the demands of high-altitude climbing. She was in a unique position in the group because she had a staff role, but she was also a client who hoped to reach the summit with the rest of them. Although not highly experienced herself, she was physically strong and as tough-minded as any mountaineer he had ever met. She was also good company, he had added.

'I think we're lucky to have her with us,' George concluded. 'Al agreed with me.'

'Seems A-okay to me,' Ken said.

Al listened impassively to all of this, with the edge of his thumbnail minutely chafing the corner of his mouth.

George was folding up his lists. 'And Adam Vries is sick.'

Ken clicked his tongue.

'What's the problem?' asked Al.

'Just a gut thing. A day or two, the doc says. We

leave the day after tomorrow, as planned.'

Once the last pieces of equipment and batches of food supplies had been assembled, there was nothing more for the expedition members to do in Kathmandu but enjoy what would almost certainly be their last hot baths and clean sheets for two months.

'Another beer?' George asked them all, by way of a conclusion.

Ken had glanced up. 'Speak of the devil,' he said in a warmer voice than he had used before. The rest of them looked in the same direction.

Finch was hesitating in the doorway. Filling most of the wall behind the little group of climbers was a huge colour photograph. Against a hyper-real blue sky stood the huge bracket ridge and summit of Nuptse. Everest stood to the left, farther back and seeming smaller than its neighbour, and in the foreground was the monstrous spillage of the icefall and the dirty grey rubble of the Khumbu glacier.

George beckoned cheerfully, his head bobbing up to obliterate the South Col. 'Here's our doc. Come and join us, Finch.'

She stood at the edge of the group. Ken levered himself out of his wicker chair and offered it, but she only smiled at him. 'I've just been to see Adam again.'

'And?'

'It's a bad bout. But he should be okay to leave as planned.'

'Finch, this is Pemba, and Mingma.' She shook hands with each of them. 'And Alyn Hood.'

Al had risen to his feet. He was much taller than Finch but when their eyes met they seemed on a level.

'Hello,' Finch said quietly.

Al said nothing at all. He held on to her hand for one second, then carefully released it. In the confusion of introductions no one else noticed the way that their eyes briefly locked and the flash of acknowledgement that passed between them. No one could have guessed that they knew each other already, or deduced a single episode of their history from the way they moved quietly apart again.

Five

The helicopter ride was nothing like flying the trim A-Star with Ralf across the serene silvery expanses of the Canadian mountains. The Asian Airlines flight from Kathmandu to Lukla was a pensioned-off ex-Russian machine that lifted off the runway abruptly, without pre-take-off formalities, and juddered over the grey haze of the valley towards the mountains.

Finch sat in her metal seat and tightened the webbing strap across her lap, trying not to think about crashing into the fields beneath them. Her knees were wedged against a mountain of expedition baggage secured under netting that filled the centre of the cabin. She had checked them on board already, but she searched out the barrels in which her medical supplies were packed and kept her eye on them as if they might jump up and roll away. Anything was better than looking out of the porthole behind her head, either at the view down to steep ridges striped with different coloured crops or upwards to the blanket of mist that blotted out the peaks. Bundled up beside her with his chin on his chest was Adam Vries. The noise of the engines made conversation difficult, but she nudged him and raised her eyebrows, *you okay*?

He nodded wearily. Two days of sickness had left him grey and listless.

The helicopter tilted sharply and changed direction, climbing steadily. Finch closed her eyes and swallowed hard to equalise the pressure in her ears. When she looked up she saw that Sam McGrath was grinning at her from his seat on the other side of the netting. She gave him what she intended as a glare in return. He had seen her abject fear on the bad flight up to Vancouver and she wasn't pleased to have him watching this fresh ordeal.

She wasn't quite sure yet how he had insinuated himself, but he was here for the ride and maybe a couple of days' trekking with the expedition on the walk-in towards Base Camp at the foot of the Everest icefall. She hadn't seen him for the whole of the last day in Kathmandu and had concluded that after all he had been easy enough to shake off. Her relief at this had, she was certain, been entirely untinged by regret. And then, in this morning's bleary dawn at the airport, there he was again. Standing joking with Rix and Mark Mason at the check-in for Lukla, towering over the packs of Japanese tourists who were waiting to see if the weather would lift and allow them to embark on sightseeing flights around the Everest massif.

'What's he doing here?' she had murmured to George.

'They went out on the beer again and Rix and Sandy just asked me if he could come along for part of the walk. All the guys seem to have really taken to him.' George shrugged. 'Makes no difference to me, so long as he pays his way. Might even be helpful. He looks in good shape. You know him anyway, don't you?'

'No. I just met him once, on a flight into Vancouver.'

'Coincidence.'

Finch noticed that Sam fitted easily into the group. He wore well-trodden hiking boots and similar clothes to the other men, and he looked just as fit and testosteronically confident. But of course, she remembered, he was an almost-Olympic marathon runner. He was probably stronger than any of them.

'Good morning,' he said cheerfully to her. And then, 'You're not happy about this, are you?'

'Is my happiness or otherwise particularly relevant?'

'Of course it is.' He had mobile eyebrows and they flattened now in a straight, sincere line. There was a puppyishness about him that irritated her.

She made an effort to sound neutral. 'It doesn't make any difference to me if you walk in with the expedition. It's just a few days' hiking.'

He smiled at her. 'I'm looking forward to it. Magnificent scenery, I believe.'

Thin veils of mist blurred the blue view through the portholes and the helicopter rocked through the bumpy air. The mist thinned into streaks, and above and beyond puffed great towers of cumulonimbus. Warm, moist air was sucked up from the valleys to funnel upwards. The weather up here was usually changeable, often threatening, always unpredictable.

She looked along the line of faces. Mingma and Pemba were flanked by two other Sherpas and beyond them was Al. He sat with his head tipped back and his eyes closed, apparently asleep, oblivious to the white-knuckle flight. Two deep lines hooked the corners of his mouth. She glanced away again, afraid that he might suddenly open his eyes and catch her looking at him. At the communal dinner table last night it was he who had been watching her. Under his gaze she felt herself grow self-conscious, thick-fingered with her cutlery. Across Vern Ecker's shoulder he had asked how she was and if she felt ready for the climb. Yes, she had assured him. She was glad to be here and she was ready for the challenge. The buzz of other people's conversation swelled between them.

'Hey Al. Tell Ted about the time you were with Vansittart on Lhotse.'

He had turned away and Finch found herself staring down at her plate, at a mess of congealing food.

The airstrip at the mountain village of Lukla was very short, sloping uphill and terminating abruptly beneath a rocky cliff. As the helicopter descended Finch was pleased at least not to be in a fixed-wing plane. The fringes of the tiny airfield were packed with people and the rough brown backs of yaks.

As they gratefully disembarked Sam said to her, 'Better than the last flight we were on.'

Al heard him and looked sharply from Sam to Finch. He frowned slightly, apparently noticing Sam for the first time.

The expedition baggage was manhandled into the open air. Another shipment had been flown up the day before and it was waiting, tagged with Mountain People labels, to be loaded on to the waiting yaks. The porters who had come down to meet the flight surged around the barrels and packs, with George and Pemba directing their removal. There was a hubbub of shouting and counter-commands, and a press of people. White-faced, Adam tried to pitch in and establish order. Seeing that she would only compound the confusion, Finch walked slowly away. She sat on a low stone wall and looked up the valley. The slopes of the steep hills were clothed with trees and the heights beyond were shrouded in cloud. The cold air was scented with smoke and yak dung. Lukla was a peppering of whitewashed stone houses skirted by muddy lanes.

Two small children sidled along the wall and stopped in front of her. The older one, a girl, wore a long skirt of printed cotton and dirty pink socks inside very large boots. The headscarf she had tied over her jet-black hair made her look like a miniature old lady. She held very firmly with one hand to the wrist of her much smaller brother. His face was a dirty, beaming mess of dried mucus.

'*Namaste*,' Finch said quietly.

They returned the greeting even more quietly, their mouths just framing the word as they stared at her.

It took almost two hours for the train of porters and yaks to be loaded and ready to leave. The climbers set out at an easy pace, in twos and threes, following a track that slowly unwound away from Lukla. They were already at a significant altitude, almost 3000 metres, and there were good reasons for not moving too fast. Finch stretched her legs to find her stride and flexed her shoulders under the weight of her pack. A pinch of nervous tension tightened in her stomach and eased again as her muscles warmed to their work. The grey-white waters of a glacier-fed river ran in a chasm in the rock and from time to time the path was carried across it on high, swaying bridges made of rope and planks. The loaded yaks plodded over, one or two of them balking until the porters whacked their hindquarters with sticks.

It was pleasant walking on the firm, well-trodden ground. The trees were budding and under their knobby branches lay the thick layers of many seasons' dead leaves. The air was moist and pleasantly cool. Ahead of her Finch could see Rix's big grey head and Mark Mason's close-shaved skull bobbing together. Occasionally Rix gave a noisy hoot of laughter but the note was dampened and swallowed by the crash of water. Finch gazed upwards to see how the rest of the expedition was faring. Ted and Vern, the two efficient Americans, moved quickly and comfortably.

She had been half dreading that Sam McGrath might clamp himself to her side all the way, but after asking politely as they were setting out if she needed any help he had fallen in beside Sandy Jackson. Sandy's ponytail extended over the top of his pack like a small dead animal. Ken Kennedy was a little way ahead of them with Pemba and George. Al walked alone, seemingly without expending any effort, but still at a loping pace that carried him a steadily increasing distance ahead of the group.

After a while Finch looked round and saw that

Adam was way back at the rear of the column, behind Mingma who had been given the job of backmarker. Adam was walking very slowly, with his head down. She sat on a rock at the side of the path, pretending to rest, and waited until he caught up.

'How are you doing?'

'So-so,' he muttered.

She offered her water bottle to him but he shook his head. 'Had plenty. Anyway you don't want me spitting germs into it.'

'Still feeling rough?'

'Just a bit.'

Finch lifted her pack again and walked on beside him. They passed through two or three settlements, little groups of low stone or whitewashed houses with slate or corrugated roofs. Children ran out to watch them go by and the women nodded their greetings, *Namaste, namaste*.

In the middle of the second day's walking they crossed a plank-and-rope bridge suspended hundreds of feet above the gorge. Immediately they left the valley and the river in its cleft of rock, and began to climb in earnest. Looking up, Finch could distinguish the zigzag of a path marking the face of a steep wooded cliff. This was the way to Namche Bazaar, the ancient capital of the Sherpa people. The route was busy with files of trekkers and yak trains, and groups of villagers with heavy baskets supported by bands around their foreheads, heading to the Saturday market in Namche.

It was a long ascent. Finch laboured in the wake of the expedition's heavily laden yaks, stopping often to rest and to let her breathing steady itself. This was the first serious test of altitude acclimatisation and she felt a warning thumbprint of pain at the front of her skull. The river dwindled in the valley bottom and the path still climbed. It was shady under the overhanging trees, with their moss-festooned branches, and very quiet, and she concentrated on the physical effort and let her mind wander. The pressure in her head gradually eased. Flowering rhododendrons made lakes of pink and yellow in craters of sunlight.

When she looked back she saw Adam turning a bend further down the mountain with Mingma beside him. He was walking more steadily now. No one else had reported any ailments.

Mark Mason had a cough, she had heard it when she woke last night, but when she asked him about it in the morning he had shrugged off her question. 'Just the filthy air in Kat. I'll be fine, all the way up here.'

Rix's exuberance and aggression made his companion seem relatively quiet by comparison, but Finch still saw that there was determination in every line of Mark's tense posture and in his flat, unemphatic voice.

It was late in the afternoon when the column of climbers and porters wound into the town of Namche, set in a horseshoe on a ledge like an amphitheatre above the steep gorge. The houses and lodges were square, flat-faced with small-paned windows framed in bright-blue and with shallow blue or green roofs. The steep streets were muddy, lined on either side with haphazard shops selling hippy clothing, food and second-hand climbing gear. The altitude was just over 3000 metres and as soon as the sun went down the air grew cold. Finch took off her pack and pulled out a fleece jacket and a hat with ear flaps as she plodded up the steps to the expedition's guest house. The first arrivals from the expedition were already sprawled on a balcony overlooking the street.

'Wanna beer?' Sandy Jackson called down to her in greeting.

'Tea,' she shouted back.

Vern Ecker and Sandy made room at the wooden table and a young Sherpani put a glass of black tea in front of her. Finch drank thirstily. From here upwards, they would all aim to drink four litres of liquid a day, to counteract the dehydrating effects of altitude. Mark was coughing again.

'Everyone okay?' she asked the group. Al Hood was sitting a little to one side. He had taken off his boots and his feet in thick socks were resting on another chair.

'Yeah, pretty good. Is Adam here?' Vern asked. His face was already stubbled with a growth of pepper-and-salt beard.

'He and Mingma were just behind,' Finch answered. 'Should be here any minute.'

Sam came across to the table. He had zipped up a red parka around his chin and he looked eager and bright-eyed. Finch sighed inwardly.

'Can I join you?'

The other climbers shuffled their seats but on the crowded balcony the only spare chair was under Al's feet. He shifted them slowly, unwillingly.

'We haven't been introduced,' Sam said, sitting

down and smiling at him. 'I'm Sam McGrath.'

'Who are you?' Al asked.

'Sam McGrath.'

'I heard your name, Sam. I was asking who you are.'

'That's a big question. Who is any man?'

There was a small beat of silence.

Sandy wound his forefinger in his ponytail, fondling it as if it were a pet as he listened to the little exchange with a pucker of a smile.

Al's expression didn't change. He waited until Sam had to step down and offer him a different answer.

'I met these guys in a bar back in Kat and we kind of got along. I'm travelling alone and they invited me to come out for a walk with them. I've never been up this way before.'

'Are you a climber?'

There were heavy boots scraping up a wooden staircase somewhere close at hand, the clink of beer glasses on a tray and a snap, followed by the roll and click of balls as someone broke on the pool table inside the bar.

Finch had asked him the same thing, back on the flight into Vancouver. He was aware of her sitting to one side, half hidden by Ted Koplicki, and of Alyn Hood's stare that challenged him – defied him – to prove himself. And he thought suddenly of his father at home in Wilding, watching the daytime chat shows and waiting for nothing.

'Yes.' The answer sounded a note of certainty that surprised him.

'Ahuh.'

Al had already shifted his attention. George

Heywood was standing at the balcony doorway, the young Sherpani was taking orders for more beer. Cloud had risen to obliterate the mountains and the end of the street was blotted with a thin, chill mist. Ted got up and strolled into the bar, leaving an empty seat between Sam and Finch. To his surprise she smiled at him, a flicker of friendly sympathy.

'Here we are,' he said and inwardly cursed his own banality.

'Look at all of this.' Her gesture took in the street, with its traffic of Sherpas and Tibetan street traders with trays of turquoise and coral and silver metal jewellery, and the smell of apple and cinnamon from the bakery below, all of it slung on an apron of mountainside with – somewhere above and behind them – the invisible dreamed-of Himalayas close enough to beckon and to remind them of their presumption. They were both thinking of the mundane press of the airport where they had first met and the shuttle up the coast to Vancouver, and the corridors of familiarity and routine that they had left behind. The memory and unspoken acknowledgement of it was the first common chord that had been struck between them.

Sam saw the way her skin stretched over the cheekbones in the cold air and her eyes dazzled with eagerness for the place and the adventure. 'What are you doing tonight?' he asked.

'The same as everyone else. Eating and then sleeping. I hope.'

'Have dinner with me.'

Finch began to laugh. 'In Namche? Shall we go Cal-Ital or French, or maybe you'd prefer sushi?'

'There's a curry house, I passed it on the way up.'

He saw her hesitate.

She was going to give way. She was going to spend an hour or so sitting over a bowl of yak korma in his company, instead of with Rix and Sandy and the rest of them.

He felt like beating a tattoo of triumph on the table-top. Seattle or even Vancouver would have been much easier, but Namche Bazaar gave this first taste of victory an extra savour. Mingma edged his way around the backs of the chairs. He had taken off his coat to reveal a pink Lacoste polo shirt. Most of the Sherpas proudly wore clothes inherited from Western climbers and trekkers.

'Madam, doctor? You come to see Mr Adam. He sick.'

Finch stood up at once. 'Where is he?'

'Inside.'

'I'm sorry, Sam.'

He watched her retreating, then sat and stared down into the muddy chasm of the street.

Adam was lying on the lower bunk nearest the door of a room containing three two-tier beds. He was grey and exhausted, and he shielded his eyes with one hand. Finch took one look at him and snapped open the catches of her medical kit.

The sixth sleeping place in the room was Sam's, and when he edged into the confined space after half an hour waiting alone on the chilly balcony he found George and Al as well as Finch standing in a quiet group around the patient. Adam's eyes were open and his knees were drawn up under a hummock of sleeping bag. Plainly a serious discussion was underway.

'Hi, fella,' Sam said quietly to him.

'They're trying to send me back down,' Adam said at once. 'I don't want to go. I told her to wait till tomorrow and then check me out again.'

Finch motioned to him to lie back. 'You need to lose some height,' she said gently. 'Rest a few days, down at Phakding. Then you can come back up and try reacclimatising.'

'No need for that,' Adam insisted. 'I've never had an altitude problem before. I'll be fine tomorrow.'

'I'm going to send Mingma and one of the porters down to Phakding with you tonight,' George said. 'They're getting ready.'

'No.' It was a flat refusal now.

George raised one eyebrow at Finch, who shook her head.

Sam read the desperation and defiance in Adam's drawn face, and the expression was deeply familiar although it was stored in the recesses of his memory attached to a different set of features. He understood how much the other man wanted this opportunity to climb the mountain. It was cruel to have it denied before the peak was even in sight. 'Give him a chance,' he interceded.

Al's head turned and he fixed his eyes coldly on Sam as if seeing him for the first time. 'I have watched a man die from cerebral oedema. It wasn't a party game.'

Finch glanced quickly at him, then when Al's attention remained fixed on Sam she twisted her stethoscope into a loop and pushed it back into her medical bag. 'I'm not saying that he has oedema. Headache, fatigue, nausea and dizziness all point to acute mountain sickness and we are at the altitude where that is what I would expect to be the problem. But the point where AMS develops into cerebral or pulmonary oedema is often difficult to distinguish and if there's any doubt, descent is the best medicine.'

Sam said, 'Can't he decide for himself whether to go or stay?'

'Not while I'm employed to lead this expedition, he can't. He does as I say, acting on the doctor's advice,' Al said.

Adam still protested, but more feebly. 'Look, I've got a job to do up here. I'm sorry, George.'

George's rim of grey hair stood out like a frowsy halo around the egg of his head. He was unshaven and his pleasant face was creased with concern. His plaid flannel overshirt was thrown on anyhow, with the hem caught up on one side under his arm. 'I agree with Al and the doc. Don't worry. We'll get by until you reacclimatise. You can catch us up further up the track.'

Mingma appeared in the doorway with a porter at his shoulder. The porter was as gnarled and ribby as a tree trunk and somewhat stronger. He spent his life carrying loads up and down the tracks to Everest for a few rupees a day. One more climber to be hauled down to the safety of thicker air was all in his day's work.

'Ready to go,' Mingma said. He had put his coat on again over the pink polo shirt. There was silence while Finch and Sam helped Adam to his feet and fastened his down parka around him.

The small convoy shuffled out to the main street. Mingma led the way with a pack on his back and

Adam was supported by the porter, who reached up to his shoulder. 'Christ, my head,' Adam muttered as he began walking. All three men wore head torches, although the two Sherpas knew the road blindfold.

'I'm coming back. Don't think I won't be,' Adam managed to say over his shoulder. His disappointment and the threat of individual failure hung round all of them, clammy as the mountain mist. Each of them, except for Sam, had come out here with the intention of going as far and as high as they could. That one of their number should have to pull out at this early stage was an unwelcome reminder of their fallibility.

'Sure you will. See you in a couple of days.' It was Sam who said it.

The torch beams swung across the house fronts.

The other members of the expedition stood in a huddle, watching the retreat.

When they were gone Al turned and said to Sam, 'You. Don't intrude in the business of this expedition. Right?'

Sam was ten years old again, dressed down by his father in public. He fought with a queasy mix of childish indignation, humiliation and adult anger. 'Screw you,' he snapped.

Al simply walked away, back to the guest house. The other climbers only lingered long enough to be sure there wasn't anything as interesting as a fight in the offing. In the end only Sam and Finch were left standing there.

'Al's not the way he seems,' Finch said.

'How do you know? Why do you apologise for him?'

'It doesn't matter. I liked the way you stood up for Adam.'

'But you made him go back anyway.'

'I'm here to do a job as well, Sam. It doesn't mean I don't feel sorry for Adam, or understand his disappointment, because I want to climb the mountain as much as he does. But medically it was the right decision, and that's what George expects from me and what Al relies on. Okay, he might have been all right in the morning. Or he might have been seriously ill. Up on the mountain it's not so easy, but why take the risk down here when you can be sure?'

Sam considered this, and the delicate balance that Finch had to maintain between being a staff member and a client at the same time. He realised belatedly that his interference hadn't helped her. 'It's just that his expression reminded me of someone.'

'Who? Am I allowed to ask that?'

She was standing close to him and he could see the cloud her breath made in the damp, cold air. The alignment between them had changed. It had taken on a dimension of friendliness. 'My father,' Sam said.

'Go on.'

'Over dinner.'

'Sam, not tonight.'

'What do I have to *do*?'

She smiled suddenly, a small glint of white in the dim light. A burst of music escaped from a bar behind them. She pulled the zipper of her fleece jacket beneath her chin with a metallic snap and a new cloud of condensation followed her exhalation. 'Let's think. Um. Climb Everest?'

'Is that all?'

Amusement crackled between them, brittle as spun sugar.

'Absolutely all. Do it and I'm yours.'

'Consider it done.'

They strolled back towards the guest house.

'And you'll tell me about your father?'

'Not tonight. See, I can play hard to get as well as you.'

Finch laughed. 'I'll get it out of you.'

Rix and Vern Ecker were playing pool, watched by a gaggle of Australian trekkers. Their wager money, a pile of crumpled rupee notes, sat on a nearby table weighted with an empty glass. 'Sam, are you getting the beers in?'

Finch had one of the lower bunks in the other dormitory. She laid her sleeping bag on the grimy mattress and stuffed her down jacket inside a cotton bag to make a pillow, the familiar expedition routine, then climbed into bed in her thermal underclothes.

'How do you manage about washing and stuff, on these trips?' Suzy had asked her once. Finch smiled, now, at the thought of Suzy's recently elaborated beauty routines and her bathroom shelf crowded with Clarins and Clinique. Somewhere in the course of their long friendship they had exchanged roles, Finch metamorphosing from Vancouver princess into mountain boho as she moved further out of her mother's orbit, and Suzy taking on the well-groomed assurance of fashionable pediatrician, fiancée and now Mrs Jeffery Sutton.

'It's cold, okay? You don't sweat so much. Or get so dirty.'

'So basically you don't wash?'

'Basically.' It was at these lower, warmer altitudes that it was tricky. Finch's smile widened at the idea of Suzy even glimpsing the horror of the bathroom down the hall from here. But it was okay, she reasoned, if everyone was in the same boat. Everyone just smelled the same.

Mark was already asleep in the bed opposite her so Finch didn't turn on her head torch to try to read. She lay in the darkness, listening to the noise. A trio of dogs barked incessantly in the yard beneath the window. Boots tramped over the wooden floors overhead and music filtered tinnily up from the bar. Doors banged, and the wooden beams and supports of the bunks creaked as the guest house began to settle for the night. Namche was not a restful place. It would be quieter further up, on the glacier, under the ring of high peaks.

Al sat alone on the balcony overlooking the street. It was cold in the misty darkness. Everyone else was inside in the pungent warmth of the bar, but he preferred the solitude out here.

His irritation with the interfering boy, whoever he was, had rapidly dispersed. He didn't think about the episode at all now. Instead, he was mentally reviewing the personalities and probable abilities of his six clients as he understood them so far, and their chances of reaching the summit in the light of that. He judged that the two Americans, Vern and Ted, were fit and strong, and should make it if the weather permitted. Rix was a bullshitter who talked too much, but he had a high degree of determination too. Mark Mason seemed always in his shadow and Al feared that if Rix dropped out for any reason Mark might not have the individual stamina to go on alone. But I could be wrong, he thought. He had seen quiet, self-effacing people turn out to be the embodiment of will-power. Sandy Jackson was more worrying. He was neurotic, Al reckoned, and took pleasure in stirring up discord. He wouldn't be a team player and that might cause trouble. Al had taken a dislike to him, but he would do his best not to give any sign of that. Spider always used to say that energy, ability and tolerance were the three essentials for serious mountaineering, and that tolerance was the hardest to maintain in some crappy high camp with a storm blowing.

'Especially for you, boy.' Spider would laugh.

As a professional guide it was now part of Al's job to be even-handed and to attend to the morale of his group. It was a shame about Adam Vries. He was likeable and his good humour might have raised everyone else's spirits at all the low points that would no doubt come. Maybe a couple of days' rest down at a lower altitude would solve his problem.

And there was Finch Buchanan. Whatever she did, she would do well, with the edge of seriousness that characterised her. Al let himself think about her for a few moments. Tomorrow. Maybe tomorrow he would even find an opportunity to talk to her, away from the eyes and ears of the rest of the group.

He stood up abruptly, directing his considerations back to the expedition for now. It wasn't a bad group; he had had more unpromising aspirants to lead up high mountains.

Automatically, Al glanced up at the black sky.

Everything that he could do to minimise the risks for them would be done. But he knew that danger wasn't always foreseeable and when it came in the mountains it came quickly. They were at the mercy of the weather, the ice and the wind, and their own small aspirations in the face of much greater forces.

None of these speculations was new to him. Shrugging his jacket around him, Al went inside out of the dark.

One by one the other men came to bed. As soon as the door opened Finch knew when it was Al, from the way he moved, from the shape of his shadow. She lay motionless as he peeled off his top clothes and dropped them on the floor, then realised that she had forgotten to breathe. Air sucked into her lungs in a gasp that sounded deafening. His bunk was in a line with hers. He lay down with his head at the opposite end. There was a brief twisting of his sleeping bag as he settled himself, then silence. The only light in the room was a greyish streak at the side of the window. Mark Mason was snoring. Finch's feet were almost touching Al's. The contact was the closest they had made since the expedition set out. It was comical, this lying toe to toe in a narrow bunk room that smelled of male feet, dust and spilled clothes, but the effect of it made her lie rigid in her down cocoon, her eyes stretched so wide open that they smarted.

It was a long time before she drifted into a sleep overcrowded with dreams.

The next day was spent in Namche, for acclimatisation purposes. Some of the climbers rested, either in their bunks or loafing in the bars and cafés. Finch chose to take a walk, to gain some height before descending again. She knew from experience that sleeping at an altitude lower than the day's maximum made for a better night's rest, and she felt weary and dazed after the uncomfortable night that had just passed.

A track led steeply out of the village, between low stone walls. She climbed doggedly, hands in the pockets of her jacket. Up here, somewhere, there was the promised first view of Everest itself. But today there was little chance of even a glimpse of it. Thick clouds swirled up from the gorge below Namche and all the prospects above were blanketed.

After half an hour of steady ascent she stopped and rested on an outcrop of rock. The short grass at the foot of it was blue with the petal cups of gentians. She saw that someone else was following the same path behind her, climbing quickly.

It was Al. Without moving Finch watched him come closer.

She was trying out sentences in her head, the nervy fire of questions and explanations, but as soon as he stopped in front of her she understood the irrelevance of words. Instead, she stood up silently, sharply aware of the slippery turf under her boots and the insulation of the swelling mist.

He put his hands on her arms and they looked at each other. A minute went by and then another while they explored the lines and shadows of each other's faces. Still without speaking he tightened his grip and drew her closer. Their mouths touched, cold in the cold air. They kissed for a long time and it was not an exploration but an admission.

When they moved apart he still held her, as if to prevent her escape. There was too much to say now. The words swelled up, pushing between them.

'Five years,' Finch said wonderingly.

'There hasn't been a day . . .' he began and she smiled at the sound of his voice and at the protestation. He read her amusement and he kissed her again.

'Eighteen months ago I saw your name in a fax and it was like seeing the translation of something that had always been in a foreign language. Once I understood it I knew that what would happen was this. I only had to wait.'

'A fax?'

'From George. He said you wanted to join as expedition medic. Listed your experience and qualifications. Asked if I knew you or had heard of you.'

'Ah. So what did you say?'

'I said . . . I knew you by reputation. And that I was sure you would be ideal for the job.'

'Thank you. So he took me on. You knew I was coming, then?'

'Of course, Finch.'

Of course. Nothing was ever out of Al's control. She stared straight back into his eyes. 'I thought you might have forgotten what happened. Forgotten me altogether.'

He didn't flinch. 'No, I hadn't forgotten. It wasn't bullshit, I meant it. There hasn't been a day when I haven't thought of you.'

'How is your family?'

'They're well, thank you. Molly's almost grown up.'

It seemed suddenly absurd to Finch that they were having this polite conversation about the man's family and at the same time standing in each other's arms, after five years, hungry to pull off the layers of padding that kept them apart. At least, she thought, I'm hungry. I don't know about him. I never really knew.

She stepped back, her face tightening, but he held her closer. He was rough, on the edge of hurting her.

'Jen and I separated. A year after I got back. We've been divorced for more than two years.'

The tightness in Finch's face broke up in ripples of bewilderment. 'Why didn't you . . .'

'Tell you? Come to look for you?'

'Yes.'

'You are a strong woman, Finch. Not a child or a dependant or half of someone else. Who was I to presume to walk back into your life again, any more than you did into mine?'

'So you waited for a fax.'

He thought about that for a moment. 'I knew we would meet again. I didn't know where it would be, or how long it would take, but I was certain it would happen. And I was also afraid of what it would mean, for all the reasons you know and understand about me.'

Yes, Finch thought. Reasons of commitment and loss of freedom, all the things that climbers were always afraid of.

'Then I saw your name. Like a translation.'

He was honest. Back then, he had been honest too.

He was looking around, checking the pearly sky and the upwards turn of the path. There was a low stone building a few yards away facing down towards the gorge, and he took her hand and led her to the back of it. He unbuckled his pack and dropped it, and eased Finch's off her shoulders.

'Let's sit down.'

They sat, leaning back against the crumbly stone. The sun's warmth was beginning to burn off the mist. Overhead the sky carried the palest suggestion of blue. Al took a chocolate bar out of a pocket and unwrapped it, then opened a red metal water bottle and held it out to her. She drank warm black tea, and he broke off squares of chocolate and put them into her cupped hand, licking his fingertip to pick up the crumbs from her palm before eating them himself. The intimacy of this small gesture touched her more directly than any sexual overture. She closed her eyes with the urgency of wanting him and let her head fall back against the wall, feeling the sun's heat on her forehead. The residue of chocolate tasted voluptuously rich in her mouth.

'And you?' Al asked.

There wasn't all that much to summarise, when it came to it.

Work, interesting and valuable, and well enough paid and always enlivened by Dennis's company. Suzy and her other friends, mostly married and settled now. Her family and the ring fence of security. And Ralf, until a couple of weeks ago. Then for the last year or more there had been this expedition and the preparations for it – occupying more of a space than there should have been to spare in her life; Finch understood that well enough. She told Al this, briefly, not considering any of it worth further elaboration.

When the chocolate was all gone they sat quietly, listening to the low jingle of yak bells.

'Why are you here?' Al asked at length. Their shoulders and hips were just touching, they had settled in the same attitude with their knees loosely drawn up.

'I want to climb.' It was true, although in Finch's case the need wasn't to do with fear, exactly, although the thought of it certainly made her fearful. Finch knew that she was rich and lucky, and there was a chip of ambition in her that dismissed her achievements in the privileged world and made her look elsewhere for a colder, more absolute challenge. 'And because I saw your name on an expedition list that was short of a doctor. I thought that if you weren't going to come for me, I would have to do it, even if it involved taking on Everest as well.'

Honesty deserved honesty in response, she thought. Al seemed to be studying his folded hands. Finch waited, looking at the spring flowers in the grass without seeing the colours.

'Thank you,' he said at length. And then, 'Look.'

She lifted her head. The sun had burned off the last shreds of mist. Above them a great silver-rimmed blue rent had appeared in the clouds and riding through the space like the sails of huge galleons were the distant peaks. Their disembodiment made them look more threatening and magnificent. Finch recognised the ridge and peak of Nuptse and behind it, with a diaphanous scarf of spindrift torn from the summit, was Everest.

In the village, from a table on the blue-painted balcony, Ken and George were watching the main street. It was packed with Sherpa families and trekkers making their way to and from the Saturday market. Two women were swaying downhill, each with a tower of aluminium pots and pans balanced on her head, and another carried a basket of plump red and green chillis.

'Where's Al?' George asked.

Ken yawned and shrugged. 'Saw him at breakfast time. Gone for a hike, I guess. Always the same Al, never says two words where none will do. Any news about Adam?'

'Finch and I called him up first thing. He's better than he was last night. But still not good. The rest of them are okay, are they?'

Ken nodded. 'Oh, yeah, no worries yet. Mason's got a chest problem, Rix's mouth is too large, otherwise fine.'

'Just the question of Adam's job, then. If he doesn't get back on his feet in time. We might need some extra porterage. The supplies I can handle on my own, communications I'm not so sure.'

'How difficult can a couple of radios, a satphone and some e-mail bulletins be, George? Al and you and me can sort it between us once we get Base established.'

'Sure we can.'

Sam McGrath came up the street and climbed the steps to the balcony. He had a bag of tiny, misshapen apples from the market in one hand and his down parka swinging in the other. The midday sun was hot.

'Sam, you want a drink?' Ken asked.

'Trade you one for an apple.'

Ken caught the fruit in one hand and flicked it straight on to George. Sam sat down astride the nearest chair. For a minute or two he busied himself with taking out a penknife and paring a perfect spiral of peel. He bit into the yellow flesh and chewed thoughtfully.

'Mind if I talk to you guys for a minute?'

George nodded an invitation.

'I want to ask if I can fill in for Adam Vries.'

Ken laughed with what sounded like real amusement. George was turning the gnarled apple over in his fingers.

'I appreciate the offer, Sam. You're a fit-looking man, but it's a serious hill and this is a commercial expedition. My duty is to my clients – to give them the best chance of success and to do that partly by offering the best support climbing team possible.'

'Minus Adam, now,' Sam said pleasantly.

'Adam's been climbing big mountains since he was a boy. He's just been unlucky this time. It can happen to anyone. But he had all the right qualifications for the job.'

'He was supposed to look after supplies and communications, right? And the bulk of the supplies work is done, isn't it? Getting the gear and provisions this far?'

'More or less.'

'Okay. Now, I majored in communications technology. Design, theory, practice. Right now I work as an information architect. Bringing all the separate elements together to design a website. I know the difference between a GIF and a JPEG. I can code the HTML, JavaScript or CGI . . .'

George held up his hands. 'Whoa.'

'So rigging a generator and a transmitter or a satphone or even a PC with e-mail isn't going to present *too* much of a problem. I also have an MBA. If you brief me, I guess I can handle whatever planning and overseeing Adam was supposed to do with the stores.'

Ken laughed again, his windburned face creasing into puckers. 'You're a trier, boy, I'll give you that much.'

Sam didn't even look at him. His attention was all on George.

George said, not unkindly, 'Listen, kid. You could be the world's greatest information architect, maybe you already are for all I know. But that isn't going to get you any distance up this hill. Adam wasn't brought along just to make lists of tinned food and twiddle a few knobs. He was here to provide back-up to Al and Ken and the climbing Sherpas. I'm an old wuss now. I'm going no higher than Base Camp.'

Sam sat easily, with his forearms resting on the chair back. He let a minute or two of thoughtful silence tick by. Then he said, 'My father's Mike McGrath.'

George put the apple down. 'Mike? You're Mike's kid? I thought he was . . .'

'No. He lives in Oregon, still. He doesn't climb any more. But when I was a kid he took me everywhere with him. He always said I'd climb the Cap before I was twenty, like he did. I'm sorry now that I didn't. I don't know if you've got kids of your own, George?'

'Three. One boy. Works in the film business in LA.'

'. . . but part of the deal seems to be turning your

back on whatever your old man wants for you.'

'Yes. That seems to be the deal,' George said quietly. 'I don't know that that's such a bad thing either, when your old man's married to the mountains. Like your dad was, and like Ken and Al and I have been.'

'Maybe. I took up running instead, long-distance. Marathons mostly. My best time over the distance is two hours twenty. I didn't qualify for Sydney, unfortunately, but the Trials were only six weeks ago and I've been training regularly since then. I'm still race fit.'

'I'm sure you are, son.'

'I can climb, George. And I can carry the same loads as Adam would have done, and if getting the clients to the top is the deal I'm up for that as much as you, or Ken.'

The two men were looking at him.

'Give me the job,' Sam begged.

'It's hard work, poorly paid, low on glamour. If anyone's getting to the summit it's the paying customers, first, second and third. Why do you want it so badly?'

Sam met his eyes. 'It would please my old man.'

George nodded.

Bull's-eye. And what's more it was true, Sam thought. It would please Mike, as far as anything his son did was capable of pleasing him. It was also true that he was an information architect and he did have an MBA, although the bare facts didn't give a properly accurate account of what a crock of shit his life had become lately. He wanted to stay with the expedition because he didn't have very much else to do with his time right now. And because he wanted to go on being close to Finch, even if it was a romantic illusion. Everyone needs something in life to hold on to, Sam told himself. If Finch Buchanan is what I want, and it *is*, I've got more than I had a month ago.

'Okay,' George said. 'Ken?'

The other man shrugged. 'Yeah. What have we got to lose?'

'I'll make a call, see if there's a chance of getting your name on the permit in place of Adam's. But if Adam comes back, you're off the team again. And Al's the expedition leader. He has the final say.'

'I understand,' Sam said calmly.

Al and Finch sat looking at the mountains until the clouds came and hid them again. She shivered a little because it was cold sitting still once the sun was obscured, so Al took her hands and lifted her to her feet. He kept them folded between his as Finch studied his face. In the past when she had thought about him she was afraid she had forgotten what he looked like. The separate features, eyes and mouth and hair, she could have described, but the set of them together and the play of expression eluded her. Now, she was surprised at how entirely familiar he seemed. They had spent such a short time together, and yet he had stayed with her, inside her head. That seemed unspeakably precious and important.

'What happens now?' she asked.

He tilted his head upwards, towards the mountain. 'We are going up there.'

'And then?'

'And then we will have done it.'

This tight focus was so entirely characteristic of him that Finch started to laugh, and there was an answering flicker in Al's dark face that loosened the lines around his eyes and mouth until he began to laugh with her. They held on to each other, shaking with it, when he cupped her face suddenly in his hands and kissed her again. The laughter faded away as they tasted each other and wanted more.

'I don't know anything else. But I'm so pleased you're here,' he said, moving his mouth against hers. 'Jesus. How tepid does that sound? It's beyond pleasure, beyond anything I had hoped, just to see you and touch you. I don't deserve it, but thank you.'

'You do. And I don't deserve thanks for doing what I want to do.'

Happiness seemed brighter than the vanished sunshine. It coloured the grass and the gentians, making them seem other-worldly in their brilliance. The blue and green roofs of the village houses laid out in a horseshoe beneath them were pin-sharp in the still air. They looked at the view for a minute longer, standing in each other's arms.

'I have to get back down there,' Al said regretfully.

'Let's go, then.'

He took her hand and they made their way back down the track.

Ken was leaning over the balcony, watching a pair of well-built Australian girls in board shorts making their way up the street. 'Look at those two, will you? Uh, here's Al coming now, with the doc.'

A moment later Finch came up the steps with Al behind her. Ken was already talking about something else and didn't see their faces. But George did and he sat back heavily in his chair as a thought struck him.

Sam looked too and he read the happiness there as plainly as if it were written on a Times Square billboard. He had never seen Finch look that way before: as if she had been soothed and gentled. He heard a booming in his head and ears, as loud and terrible as an avalanche breaking away.

'Al, have you got a minute?' George asked drily.

'Sure.'

'Sam, here, has suggested himself as a replacement for Adam. He seems to have pretty good credentials. I said we might give him a try, if we can fix the permit. How does it sound to you?'

Al seemed hardly to hear. 'Well, fine, why not?' He held out his hand to Sam. 'Welcome to the team.'

Finch tried shaking her head, tried signalling her disagreement from one to the other, but none of them would see it.

Six

The lama sat cross-legged on a plush-cushioned stool. Behind him under an ornate canopy was a great gold statue of the Buddha swathed in muslin drapes. The monks sat on padded stools at right angles, muffled in their dark-red robes against the cold, continuing a low chanting that was hardly more than a spoken murmur. The climbers silently shuffled into the dim temple, past the carved and painted pillars, and little leaded windows looking out on the cloudscapes and toothed mountains, and made a bulky, over-tall and padded line in front of the lama.

When Finch's turn came she presented him with the gift that Pemba and George had instructed her to offer, a white fringed scarf called a *kata*, and when she knelt the old man blessed her in return, fastening a red silk cord around her throat. His fingers were dry and surprisingly warm as they fumbled with the knot. Her head felt so muzzy with the chanting and the clouds of incense that when she stood up she almost overbalanced. She caught at Mark's arm and awkwardly shuffled away, soft-footed in her socks, emerging into the searing daylight in the temple courtyard. The climbers' boots were arranged in a pungent circle beside the door. She sat down on the steps to put hers back on and saw Al leaning against a pillar.

'Didn't you go in?' she asked, reaching up to touch the red thread. It chafed against her skin under her collar and she twisted it between her fingers to make it sit more comfortably.

'I've been blessed before,' he told her. 'I feel blessed now.'

There were strips of cloth tacked over the windows and the breeze caught them now so that they rippled like surf breaking. Al and Finch were still looking at each other as Sam and the other climbers came crowding out and jostled to retrieve their boots.

The monastery at Thyangboche stood on a ridge dominating the Everest track. The rest of the day's route took them winding uphill away from it. Once or twice Finch looked back and saw the gilded pinnacle that surmounted the roof piercing the sky like a dart.

The walk from Namche to Base Camp took an easy four days. They stayed in tea houses at night, smoky little stone buildings that were crowded with trekking parties and climbing expeditions all heading up to the Khumbu. The men ate big meals and sprawled around the stove afterwards, playing cards or chess, conserving their strength. Finch read, or wrote in her diary, or chatted to whoever happened to sit next to her. There was no privacy. Sam beat everyone at chess and made no special attempt to single her out. He was polite to Al and obliging to the rest of the group. Mingma and Pemba liked him especially because he taught them to play frisbee with a silver plastic disc that he produced from his pack. They hooted with laughter when he tried flashy catches and theatrically missed them, panting with exertion in the thin air. A beaming column of the Sherpas and porters lined up to take a turn and demonstrate how much better they could do. One afternoon Sam and Sandy organised two teams and played a soccer match.

Climb Everest. After a couple of days, Finch convinced herself that Sam couldn't have taken her flippant challenge seriously. He had his own reasons for talking himself on to this expedition.

Leaving Al to his discussions with George or Ken, Finch either walked alone or with one or another of the five clients. She learned more about Rix's absolute determination to summit out, this time, 'Whatever. Believe me, doc, *whatever*.' Mark Mason told her that he was more of a weekend climber than the fanatical Rix. He walked uphill doggedly, generally with his eyes fixed on the ground ahead rather than on the peaks above them. He was a travel writer who was sending back reports of the expedition and his own summit bid to a British newspaper, as a way of partially financing the climb.

Vern and Ted, Finch discovered, were both very rich men who regarded the conquest of Everest as a natural follow-on to their business successes. Ted owned a series of real estate development and sales companies across the Southern States and Vern a company that designed and manufactured the latest hospital equipment. In the course of their talk she had heard much more than she could hope to absorb about the ground-breaking design features of the latest high-dependency crib for special-care baby units.

Sandy Jackson was more difficult to place. He talked about the recent ending of his relationship with someone he described as 'my woman'. He divided his time between Perth and Sydney, and was apparently involved in the sportswear industry. Finch wondered if he might be a drugs czar, but decided he wasn't smart enough for that. Probably he just had a rich father, she concluded.

What the men all had in common was a level of commitment to the expedition's goal that was frightening in its intensity. They wanted the summit. Although they fenced with each other through jokes there was no comedy in them. They made her feel dilettante and tentative and female. She had used all her savings and taken out a loan to pay even the reduced expedition fee to George Heywood, but the summit's image had not been burned in her brain tissue the way it had in theirs. Maybe that was how they had made themselves rich, by thinking of every obstacle as a peak to be conquered. Or as a barrier in the path of their egos, to be flattened and ridden over.

She had come because of Al Hood. She wanted to climb too, the mountains dragged her gaze upwards, but it was the pursuit of their unfinished connection that brought her here now.

Whenever she thought of this Finch was ready to laugh at herself, but still she always looked to see where he was, walking in the midday warmth with his shirtsleeves rolled and his heavy pack seeming weightless on his back. And the sight of him always made her lose her rhythm, so that her breath came irregularly and she had to stop and rest to even it out again. They barely spoke to one another but she knew he waited and looked for her just as she did for him.

They had time ahead of them now, everything else would happen eventually.

The expedition reached the terminal moraine of the Khumbu glacier at 16,000 feet. The wilderness of rock and grit and ice was crusty with winter snow-pack – there would be no glimpses of softening greenery from here on. It was a bitterly hard, monochrome world. On a bleak plateau beside the glacier there were dozens of simple stone cairns. Each one of them was a memorial to a climber who had died on Everest.

The highest settlement along the track was Pemba's and Mingma's home village. Just outside it there was a stupa, a little shrine built of rock beside the path, and Finch changed her direction to pass to the left of it according to custom. A row of prayer wheels mounted in a recess in the wall were still lazily turning and she had set the first one spinning faster before she saw Sam sitting just beyond the shrine. Deliberately she spun the other wheels and moved on. He fell into step beside her and they walked in silence for a way, looking up to the ring of peaks.

'I couldn't think of a prayer that wasn't to do with not dying up there,' he said at last. She glanced sharply at him. It was impossible to imagine Ted or Rix or one of the others saying any such thing.

'I know. I felt the same with the lama.'

'You're scared as well?'

'Yes. Looking up there, how could anyone not be?' She had been afraid ever since she had seen the mountain riding in its sea of cloud. The scale of it was so fearsome. 'Why are you doing this, Sam?'

'Because you won't have dinner with me otherwise.'

'What's the real reason?'

'Do you think that isn't real?'

When she didn't answer he laughed. 'And because I want to see what I can do. I'm surprised by the urge, but there it is.'

'It's the same for me.'

'But that isn't quite all of it.'

He didn't frame the words as a question. After a moment Finch said quietly, 'No.'

The village was just a huddle of grim stone houses on steep ground above a polluted trickle of a stream.

The expedition cook's boy was waiting for them at a turn of the path with a big enamel kettle between his knees. He jumped up as soon as he saw them and filled two enamel mugs. 'Tea, sir. Tea, madam.'

'It's Sam,' Sam said to him, taking the cup and handing it to Finch.

'Yes, sir.'

They drank the hot tea. There were Khumbu women along the path, greeting their men as they came home. It would be a busy evening in the village *chang* house, over the local sweet rice beer.

'How long have you and Al known each other?' Sam asked, staring straight ahead. 'Don't . . . at least don't pretend that you don't know what I'm talking about.'

There was the low jingle of yak bells and the train

of porters and animals came slowly by heaped with Mountain People baggage. Finch watched them pass.

'Five years,' she answered. 'We met in the Karakoram, near K2. It was only a few days and we haven't seen one another since then.' She didn't enlarge. It wasn't for her to explain that Al had been married then.

Sam was standing motionless. The fires of burning yak dung made the air rank and the rocks were turning a forbidding grey as the light faded. 'It won't change anything if I go up there, will it?' he said. Disappointment burned in him, a slow fire that would go on smouldering whatever he might do.

'You knew that anyway. Unless it changes something within yourself.'

'Unless,' he agreed heavily. 'So I'm here for the ride. We can talk, maybe get to be friends, can't we?'

She liked his directness when he stopped flirting and angling with her. An instinct for warmth made her want to put her arm through his, but she resisted the impulse. 'Yes. You were going to tell me about your father, remember?'

'That's a *long* story. You'll have to trade one for it.'

'Okay. There's always my mother to talk about.'

He laughed again. 'It's a deal.'

They began walking uphill, towards the lighted windows of the tea house.

The next day the expedition reached Base Camp at the foot of Everest itself.

This was another village now, temporarily bedded in the snow and rocky rubble of the glacier. It was a complete canvas settlement, brave with colour but dwarfed by the chaotic walls of rock and ice that soared around it, and weighted by the cold sky.

The Mountain People established their base tents in an orderly huddle at the western side of the encampment, ten separate dome shelters for the climbers and leaders, two big green structures for the mess tent and kitchen, another for the medical and communications centre, and a fourth for the Sherpas to sleep in. The line of yaks and porters had wound their way up here and offloaded the mountains of supplies, then plodded unweighted back down the long track again.

George Heywood stood in the last of the evening's light surveying the arrangements made by the other expeditions who also had climbing permits. The nearest were a small group of Swedes who evidently believed in travelling light and crammed themselves into a pair of tiny tents, a stripped-down French outfit aiming for a speed ascent, a large and outwardly chaotic party of South Americans and a honed Indian Army team aiming for the summit of Lhotse.

In all, there were more than a hundred tents. People stepped between the various outposts, busy with establishing their dominions. It was the beginning of the season. This village would represent home and security for most of them for the next six weeks. There was an atmosphere of highly charged optimism and expectation.

The Mountain People's equipment and accommodation looked more opulent than most of their neighbours'. Clients who paid big money, as Rix and Ecker and the rest had done, expected to have their chances of summit success backed up by the best possible material resources. In George's long experience it was worth providing, and charging for, the best: the latest weather-resistant tents, the most meticulous planning, the most dedicated guides.

A heavy arm sleeved in a down jacket clamped around George's shoulder.

'Busy as Broadway up here,' Ted Koplicki said.

George nodded. 'They'll spread out up the hill in the next few days. And we'll help each other out.'

'Sure.' Ted patted him on the back. 'Looks good to me.'

'I think so. If we get the weather.'

'Sure we'll get the weather.' Ted laughed. He didn't believe in taking a pessimistic view.

George looked upwards. His skull tilted on the pivot of his spine, back and back, until the vertebrae in his neck cracked in protest. As the earth turned and the sun sank behind Pumori, the conical peak to the west, a line of darkness consumed the rock and ice faces above him. It extinguished the silver and steel, and left instead formless caverns of ink-blue and black that were less threatening, in their invisibility, than the gaunt reality. Above the shimmering snow reaches that were still washed with light, the sky itself had a dark-blue depth like outer space. Atmosphere's envelope was thin up there. Suspended above the icefall and the western cwm, over the Lhotse face and the South Col, floated the summit of Everest. It was a quiet evening down on the floor of the glacier but up there in the jet stream the winds were tearing snow and ice off the rocks. Standing in camp, with the night's cold beginning to clamp itself around him, George could hear in his head the shriek and batter of that wind. He had been up there and he shivered at the remembered sound.

'Coming to eat?' Ted asked.

'Be right with you.'

George was also listening to the faint clink of Sam McGrath trying to repair a damaged antenna on the radio transceiver. He was hunched in the mouth of the medical tent and in the quick darkness he had turned on his head torch. He was humming quietly as he worked. The boy was adaptable and seemed capable enough, George thought. But he would count no chickens until Sam managed to get the generator going tomorrow and until he had seen if he could climb with a loaded pack on his back.

Sam glanced up and saw that he was being watched, then gave a quick smile. 'Shouldn't be too much trouble. Do you need it tonight?'

'No. The weather report can wait until tomorrow morning. Come and get some food.'

There was a sudden roar of laughter from the South American tents. Outside here in the yawning space it sounded puny and defiant, quickly damped by the vast area.

Sam put the radio carefully aside and glanced over his shoulder into the tent's lamplit interior. Then he followed the other man across to the mess tent. Their boots crunched on the gritty rock.

Finch was in the medical half of the tent. A canvas screen was pegged across the divide to offer her patients some privacy. She was unpacking her barrels and checking the supplies of dexamethasone, acetazolamide, nifedipine and the rest against the inventory. Everything was intact. This establishment of order restored some of her confidence. The walk-in had not been too demanding. And now that the first major mountaineering obstacle, the icefall, reared directly above her she felt less intimidated. It was a terrible jumble of crevasses and precarious seracs and treacherous creaking ice, but now she had seen it she could envisage how they would fix the ropes and lightweight ladders, and begin transporting supplies upwards to the next camp. The summit was 3500 metres above her head.

From somewhere beyond the canvas wall she heard Mark coughing and struggling for breath before the next bout. Finch took a phial of capsules out of a watertight case and slipped them into her pocket. He should take an antibiotic, although at this altitude there was no guarantee that it would work.

The guides and all the other climbers were already sitting at the table in the big mess tent. Just for tonight it was lit with kerosene lanterns, but from tomorrow there would be electric lights powered by solar panels and with the generator providing sturdy back-up. There was a library of paperbacks, a CD system and a selection of music. Once the solar panels were rigged it would even be possible to heat meltwater and deliver it, via a barrel and a system of tubes, as a hot shower. All of this Finch had known in theory but to see it materialising, up in this bleak canyon at the toe of the highest mountain in the world, made her look with renewed admiration at George Heywood. In nine years of commercial operation he had put thirty-five clients on the summit.

Anticipation quickened her heartbeat and chased away the apprehension.

Why not, why not me too? Finch thought. Ambition suddenly shivered through her like a sexual charge.

'Come and sit down.' George waved to her. 'We'll eat first, then there will be a briefing.'

She took the last chair. Ken and Al sat on either side of George, with Pemba and Mingma next to them. The other eight Sherpas – four climbing porters, two base Sherpas, Dorje the cook and the cook's boy – ate in the kitchen tent. Looking at the circle of faces Finch saw that everyone was smiling. Sam forked fried potatoes into his mouth and cheerfully avoided taking issue with something Rix was saying about how kids were all work-shy nowadays. Al sat with one arm hooked over the canvas backrest of his chair, watching his charges. He was satisfied that they had all made it comfortably this far, with Adam Vries the only minor casualty. They were a strong bunch. Now the work could begin.

He allowed himself a brief glance at the woman with the glowing face at the other end of the table. At once their eyes connected. The look in hers made him think of choices. There were possibilities in the future that were not tied to cold and danger, or bending the will as well as the body to fight a way up another mountain. There might be a gilded, luxurious space somewhere that contained happiness because, amazingly, it contained Finch Buchanan.

He had to turn away, bending his height to match Mingma's and catch something the second sirdar was saying, in case his expression might give away the sudden and disconcerting joy.

Finch read his face too, as if she had known him all her life. She made herself look at the other climbers instead, watching to see how they ate. The food was hot and palatable enough. Altitude depresses the appetite but everyone managed to eat a decent meal tonight.

George clinked his fork on a tin cup and they all turned to look at him.

'Welcome to Base Camp.' He smiled. 'Now. Let me outline the plan of attack.'

Attack was the right word. The planning and organisation of this expedition was on a military scale.

George's recipe for successful summit bids was based on slow and thorough acclimatisation to altitude. Rix and Mark, as well as Vern and Ted, had all been on Everest before, but they listened as intently as the three newcomers. The first objective was to establish a camp 2000 feet above where they were now sitting, on the lip of the icefall in the western cwm. They would each travel up and down again, probably twice, and on the second visit to Camp One they would stay overnight. At the same time the Sherpas would porter cumbersome loads of food, oxygen, cooking equipment and tents onwards to a second camp, Camp Two, at the head of the cwm.

'Al and I won't expect you to carry any loads, but if you feel like lending a hand with some of the gear the offer won't be refused. You may also find it develops your stamina and assists your acclimatisation.'

Rix smilingly tilted in his chair with his arms folded. 'What are we paying good money for, George?'

'To have your gear carried for you, as I have just said, if that's your preference,' George answered pleasantly.

In turn, two more high camps would be established, on the Lhotse face and in the South Col, and acclimatisation time would be spent in each, with descents back to Base for rest and recuperation.

'We'll make for the summit from the col but we also hope to place oxygen, food and a tent high up on the south-east ridge, for use in an emergency. Al and I'll talk to the other leaders so we don't end up with a traffic jam of climbers making for the top on the same day. But weather permitting I estimate we'll make our summit push in the second week of May.'

It was now the end of the first week of April. All around the table, heads nodded eagerly.

Al took his turn to speak. 'We'll be working in two teams. Mingma and me with Rix, Mark and Sandy. Ken and Pemba take Vern, Ted and Finch. This is intended to be flexible and may well change when we get up high. But that is the arrangement for now, at least as far as Camp Two.'

Finch studied her hands. He's right, she told herself. It's better this way. Don't complicate what is already demanding enough with what your heart demands. Not until this is done.

'I'd like to help with some loads up there. Which team shall I work with?' The question was Sam's.

Al raised an eyebrow at George who shrugged as if to say, give him a try. 'You can come with me,' Al said shortly.

'Thanks.'

There was a beat of silence. Mark Mason raised one eyebrow and Rix grinned insinuatingly. The common goal seemed suddenly only the most fragile envelope to contain this combustible mix of separate ambitions and egos. Finch waited. Amity might suddenly get blown away like a tent in a storm.

'Tomorrow,' George continued smoothly, 'You will please assemble your equipment so that Al and Ken can check it over. Make sure that you've got everything you need, in good order. Sam and I will continue with setting up the support systems here. The day after, all being well and the route up the fall being ready, we'll start the climb. Everyone happy with that?'

There was a murmur of assent.

'Also tomorrow we make *puja*,' Mingma added. He was a slightly built man with a patient face and a tranquil manner, older than the more ebullient Pemba.

'Tomorrow. And now I don't know about the rest of you guys, but I'm going to get myself a long night's sleep,' George said.

Al and Mark and Vern followed him, and when they had gone Rix brought out a bottle of Johnnie Walker. 'A small tot. Drink to success, eh?' He poured generously into tin mugs.

Sam clinked his against Finch's. 'Good luck.'

With the others, she echoed the words. She drank too deeply and choked on the first drink she had tasted since Kathmandu.

'Easy, doc,' Ted remonstrated.

Sam shook out a clean bandanna from his pocket and gave it to her to mop her eyes.

By the middle of the next day the Mountain People's camp area looked like a garage sale. Kitbags had been unpacked and gear was spread everywhere. Finch laid out her plastic mountaineering boots and crampons, her climbing harness, safety tether, jumar clamp and ice axe, and put her glacier goggles and head torch beside the heap of fleece and pile and down clothing. Spare gloves and goggles, and her water bottle and some energy food, were stowed in her pack. A few yards away Sam and George were tinkering with the solar panels. Al was sitting in the doorway of the mess tent reading a sheaf of computer printouts and marking up loads for the porters. In the sunshine the mountains looked benign, even the great silvery scarf of snow that flew from the summit of Everest.

Ken crunched through the rind of ice to Finch's tent and bent down to inspect her equipment. He held up her boots approvingly. 'Well broken in, I see. I've had guys turn up here with brand-new ones. Chopped their feet into raw mince in two days. Let's have a look at your crampons.'

He ran his thumb over the cage of spikes that would attach to the soles of her boots and give purchase on slippery snow and ice. 'Sharp as a knife and clean as a whistle. Just like you, doc.'

Finch laughed. She liked Ken. 'I'll take that as a compliment.'

Ken stood upright again, ready to move on. 'You know each other, don't you? You and Al?'

'Is it so obvious?'

'He never said anything. He's silent as a granite wall, at least about anything that matters to him. Just me putting two and two together, like.'

Finch nodded.

'Well. It'd be a relief to see him acting like a man

instead of a robot once in a while.' Ken spoke brusquely but there was affection in his face. 'I wish you well.'

'Thank you,' she said.

Three of the porters passed by carrying big stones. Under Mingma's direction they were building a *puja* altar to the side of the camp.

By the end of the afternoon it was ready. A neat cube of rocks was surmounted with a tall wooden pole from which four bright strings of prayer flags were tethered to the ground beyond the corners of the altar. An aged lama made his stately way up from Mingma's village to conduct the blessing ceremony that would bring good fortune and the mountain's benevolence to the expedition.

Finch pulled on her down jacket and left the tents to watch. The Mountain People's Sherpas clustered attentively around the altar and the climbers stood in a row behind them, huffing in the chilly air.

The rocks were still festooned with mountaineering gear and in the communications tent Sam had already rigged the satellite phone and fax. At the same time the lama made his way clockwise around the stones, chanting and throwing out a small handful of rice and flour at each corner, north, south, east and west. Mingma lit a few juniper branches on top of the altar and the pungent smoke drifted and mixed with cooking smells. Dorje and the Base Sherpas would keep the fire alight until the last of their climbers was down again.

The scarlet and saffron and emerald of the prayer flags and the dark-red of the monk's robes seemed to bleed into the colourless air, as if this hostile place were greedy for their warmth. Finch shivered in spite of her padded clothes. The contrast between the respectful grace of this ritual and their own brash assault preparations was uncomfortably sharp.

The little ceremony was soon over.

'Amen,' Rix said.

The lama shuffled casually away again and the Sherpas went back to work, except for Mingma who stirred at the smouldering twigs and placed fresh ones nearby.

George patted Finch's shoulder as he passed. 'We don't ever climb without making *puja*.'

Everyone was ready now. Even the competitive talk faded. The climbers slipped away early to their tents and the whisky bottle failed to make a second appearance.

When Finch reached her own shelter, Al was hunched beside it in the darkness. He glanced at the silent tents. 'Good luck,' he said quietly.

'And to you.'

They both knew how big a part luck always played. He kissed her on the corner of her mouth and touched his hand to her cheek. Then they moved apart, to their separate canvas domes.

Sam slept fitfully. Altitude made him restless and the thought of the next day dried his mouth and throat. At 4 a.m. he was up, checking his equipment yet again and listening to the breakfast preparations and the sounds of the other climbers getting ready. He had bought a pair of second-hand mountaineering boots and crampons in Namche. Most of the rest of his gear belonged to Adam. A label reading 'Adam

Vries' was stitched to the breast of his red down suit. He sat at the door of his tent to lace his boots, zipped the flap behind him and clambered over the moraine to the mess tent.

'Here we go, fellas.' Ted was rubbing his hands. He had already eaten his rice porridge.

'Yeah, man,' Sandy echoed. 'Let's kick it.'

Finch was quietly drinking tea in a corner.

Al came in, looking at his watch. 'Ready to go by half past, please.'

They would hope to reach Camp One at the top of the icefall, turn around and get back to Base again before the sun's melting heat made the glacier ice even more unstable.

Pemba was hovering near Al and Mingma was just a black hump in the pre-dawn outside the door.

'Mingma's unhappy,' the sirdar muttered to Al.

Al drew him inside, where he could see his face. But Mingma wouldn't look at him. The Sherpa's face was ashen. 'What's wrong, Mingma?'

Vern and Sam, who were nearest, turned to listen.

'I have bad dream. See dead men sitting beside this fire, in our camp, here.'

Al nodded. 'We all have bad dreams. Too often, in the mountains.'

'Not good for climb.'

'I understand. But do you want to stay behind?'

The grave little man hesitated, then pulled himself upright. 'I come.'

'Okay. That's good. Thank you, Mingma.'

The climbers and guides and the two sirdars assembled in the pre-dawn light. There was a thin moon in a clear sky and the light reflected off snow buttresses made head torches almost unnecessary. The four climbing Sherpas were already on their way, with huge loads on their backs.

George Heywood shook everyone's mittened hands as they filed past. 'Good luck. Weather report is clear today and most of tomorrow. Changeable after that.' Global meteorological updates were faxed or phoned to Base Camp from Seattle and were supplemented by local reports from George's agents in Kathmandu.

'Hey, man, you wish you were coming with us?' Sandy shouted.

'Yeah. I do,' George answered. 'See you at lunch, guys. Watch your step.'

Al indicated the load that was waiting for Sam. He picked it up obediently and hoisted it on to his back, then slipped his arms through the straps. About forty pounds, much less than the porters carried. Even so it felt like a crippling load. The two guides were just as heavily laden; for today the clients carried only their own lightweight packs.

It was 5 a.m. The eastern sky was grey. Eleven people plodded away across the moraine to the spilling ice.

Sam tightened the straps of his crampons and neatly fastened the tongue through the buckle. When he stood the blood pounded in his cranium. Looking up, all he could see was a solid torrent of grey and pearl ice, ribbed and fluted, jagged with menace.

The glacier spilled over the lip of the canyon above them and moved down to the valley at the rate of three or four feet every day. It was always shifting, cracking open new fissures and crumpling yesterday's together like wads of tissue paper. It threw up towers of ice and sent others toppling without a second's warning. The sound of its perpetual motion was a low creaking and grinding, a murmur of threat that was all the more fearful for being everywhere, all around, and never specific. Sam had read about the icefall in Mike's books and magazines. He knew it was the most dangerous section of the mountain. More people had died here than anywhere else on the great expanse of it. Most of them were porters ferrying loads up to the western cwm and beyond.

He kicked forward experimentally in his crampons. The weight of his pack momentarily unbalanced him and he stumbled, then toppled sideways because Adam's climbing helmet cut off his peripheral vision. As he hoisted himself upright again he saw Al Hood coldly watching him from the back of the line.

Rix was already ascending in front. Mingma was leading the way, with Sandy eagerly streaking up right on his heels.

'You right, mate?' Rix called down.

'Yeah,' Sam answered, inwardly cursing. He swung his foot forward and the forward-pointing spikes of his crampon bit into the ice. With his right hand he chopped with his ice axe to make a secure purchase.

It was a long time since he had done any climbing, longer still since Michael had dragged him into the Oregon ice and snow.

He heard his father's voice, over the glacier's threatening mumble: 'Always aim for three secure points of contact.'

He stepped up firmly on his two hollow hooves of

spikes, grasped the shaft of his axe and slid his safety tether up the fixed line. None of this was like anything he remembered. In those days he would have been securely roped in Michael's wake.

Joined to his father by the braided perlon umbilical cord that he had fought to sever all through his adolescence. And now he was hovering at the icy hem of goddamn Everest. The irony of it made him let out an involuntary gulp of laughter.

'What are you waiting for, Sammy?' Mason wanted to know from beneath him.

Today they were all climbing separately, linked for safety to the fixed rope that snaked up into the heights, instead of to each other. The whole distance of the icefall was roped and breached with aluminium ladders. George's expedition, and most of the others now climbing, had paid thousands of dollars to the route pioneers for the use of the ropes and ladders they fixed at the start of the season. Sam's waist line was fixed to the rope by a metal clip called a carabiner. If he fell, he would do no worse than slither down to the next screw or picket that anchored the rope, then dangle there like a fish on a hook. Unless the fixings themselves worked loose, through the glacier's restless shifting or the ice melting in the sun.

Don't think about that now, Sam advised himself. Just fucking climb.

He struggled upwards, toehold after toehold. Slide and step. Slide and step. Chop with the axe pick and haul himself up when the angle was too steep just for stepping. The heavy pack threatened to pull him backwards. Every breath was a struggle to suck some nourishment out of the etiolated air.

For the first thirty minutes Sam thought he had no chance of making it to Camp One. It was unthinkable how many hours of today's hideous battle still lay ahead, let alone how many more times he would have to follow this same route up and down in order to acclimatise enough to reach the summit.

Rix was a long way above him and the grit and chunks of ice that his progress dislodged rained down around Sam's head and pinged off his helmet. Mark Mason was far below, and Sam could hear the rattle and gasp of his cough. When Sam stopped to rest and drink some water, he saw Al moving easily up the rope in his wake. Finch's and Ken's group were further behind. The route was too tortuous and meandering for him to hope to see what they were doing.

But then, an hour into the climb, he realised that what had seemed impossible only a few minutes earlier now felt no worse than extremely uncomfortable. The crampons began to seem like useful extensions to his feet instead of stumbling blocks, and the rhythm of his stepping and chopping grew smoother. The sun was rising invisibly over Tibet and daylight flooded over the ice wilderness. Sam even found the strength to look around him.

The landscape had a bizarre beauty. It was a haphazard jungle of iridescent ice towers, leaning over chasms of silver and blue and iron-grey, all fantastically jagged and toothed, and feathered with rime. Patches of ice that the sun had melted yesterday were refrozen and sinisterly gleaming like newly exposed bone, and the steel pickets and screws that anchored the rope bit into them like a surgeon's brutal implements. The Minotaur's route now led under an ice pinnacle that leaned over at a crazy angle and skirted a deep crack. Sam edged sideways along the foot-wide ledge, gripping the rope and pressing his shoulders and groin against the hip of the pinnacle as if he wanted to mate with it. The alternative was to hang out over the lip of the crevasse.

When he rounded the next corner he found Rix crouching beside the crack that now widened to about twelve feet. The sides of it were smooth and colourless near the rim, but deepening to voracious deep-blue below. Sam didn't want to peer any further than he could already see.

'Serac looks a bit dodgy,' Rix superfluously remarked. If the massive pinnacle toppled – and it was a statistical certainty that sooner or later it would – and if anyone happened to be passing beneath it at the time, there would be no chance of surviving the impact of thousands of tons of ice.

Sam didn't want to think about the precarious serac; it was behind him now, for the time being. Ahead was the crevasse. In two or three places along the route so far, aluminium ladders had been fixed in place on the steepest ice walls. He had clambered upwards, glad to use the short cut instead of having to kick his own way with front points and axe pick. But now the ladders had developed a hideous new application. Two of them were lashed together end to end, and were fixed horizontally to make a narrow bridge. Ice screws spiked through the metal eyes at either end, pinning them to the grinning lip of the crevasse. The safety rope languidly trailed across beside the bridge. On the other side, Sandy was sucking at his water bottle, looking exhausted. Mingma waited impassively with his mittened fists thrust in the armpits of his jacket.

'Onwards and upwards,' Rix muttered. He shuffled to the ladder edge and checked that his tether was clipped safely to the rope. He stood upright and stepped out on to the ladder. One foot in front of the other, stopping while the aluminium struts creaked and bounced under his weight, then moving forwards again, he inched his way across.

Sam watched, his stomach twisting with horror.

No way, his reasoning self insisted. No fucking *way*.

Rix reached the far side and punched the air with his fist. How has he got the energy left for that? Sam wondered. He could already hear Mark treading warily around the serac. There were only two options: either to turn round and ignominiously slither past Al Hood on the way down, or to do the balancing act over the ice chasm.

He shuffled to the edge and checked his tether, as Rix had done.

Then he put one boot on the first metal rung. Look ahead, balance. Take another step. The pack was heavy, trying to pull him over backwards. His crampons clinked on the ladder and the whole structure swayed precariously.

When he reached the middle point, where his weight made the bridge sag and creak, he glanced downwards. Between his straddled legs he saw the blue shaft plunging into the bowels of the glacier. If he fell, he would dangle from the safety rope while the ice gullet sucked at him.

His movements immediately froze and he clenched his buttocks, to counteract the involuntary loosening of his gut.

If the fixing screws came adrift. If the lashed joint between the two ladders parted. If the crevasse itself suddenly shifted and the jaws widened . . .

'Come on, man.'

Rix was standing five feet away as if he were on a golf course waiting for his partner to catch him up on the green. Sam groaned and somehow shuffled another step. Another, and Rix reached out an arm. Sam grasped it and almost fell the last two steps off the ladder and on to the near-safety of the crevasse lip. Mingma was laughing, a little *tee-hee* sound. Sympathetic amusement creased his broad face. He seemed to have recovered his spirits since the early morning.

'God in heaven,' Sam muttered. When a trickle of moisture ran down his forehead he realised that he was sweating. He batted it away with the back of his mitten.

'Easier next time,' Rix told him. Mark was already making his apparently unconcerned way across to them. Mingma set off again, following the rope through the vicious maze.

For the next four hours they climbed, up and over the irregular ice, crossing crevasses and detouring around seracs. It was hard going, but not impossible. So long as Sam kept his mind closed to all the what-if speculations and focused it firmly on the next step.

Sandy had started very strongly, pushing right behind Mingma, but he began to fade after two hours. He stopped more often, grey in the face and gasping for breath, and moved ever more slowly. Eventually he dropped behind Sam and the others, and fell so far back that he and Al were no longer in sight. The two Britons moved steadily and confidently. Sam was impressed by their stamina.

The sun grew strong and it became uncomfortably warm.

'Time going very fast,' Mingma said, peering upwards into the unruffled blue sky.

By 11 a.m. the four men were heaving themselves up the last hundred feet of the climb. The western cwm was revealed as a vast, gently sloping canyon that ran upwards to the sheer Lhotse face of Everest. The sun bored down into it like a power drill. As he stumbled towards the Mountain People's Camp One, Sam shielded his eyes with his forearm as if even his glacier goggles were not enough to protect his eyeballs from the punishing glare.

There were four small tents set in a ring. Two of the four climbing Sherpas were waiting for them, with tea in a billycan. Sam tottered the last dozen steps and sank in a heap on the snow.

'You make good climb,' Mingma assured him with a sly smile. 'Maybe a little bit scared to die on ladder.'

'Give me tea,' Sam croaked. The warm sweet liquid tasted like nectar. He drank it and stared up the slope to a pair of toiling black dots. It was the other two Sherpas making for Camp Two with tents and the first cache of oxygen and food.

Twenty minutes passed before Pemba arrived, with Ted and Vern and Finch just in front of Ken, then Al and Sandy.

Sandy was hardly moving. He sank down at the

edge of the group. 'Man, I'm wiped,' he whispered.

Finch went straight to Mark. 'How does your chest feel?'

Sam gazed at her. She looked tired, but far less exhausted than he felt. She must have crossed that terrible ladder bridge and performed all the other feats of the morning that he had barely managed himself, and she was still doctoring. She was the most amazing woman he had ever met and he had fallen for her without knowing anything about her just because she had appeared to be naked underneath a ski parka in a stormbound airport.

She had never encouraged him, never attempted to paint matters any differently from the way they really were. Obdurately following her all the way out here, trussing himself up in another man's climbing gear and hauling himself up that gaping hell's kitchen of ice now looked to be the most jejune, embarrassing and fruitless effort any man had ever made for the sake of a woman.

Al radioed down to George at Base to report that they had all made Camp One safely. He nodded at the two Sherpas, who piled the stove inside one of the tents and zipped everything securely, then scurried for the top of the icefall again. They would check all the fixed ropes on the way down. This safety attention was part of the dues that George paid for the use of the route.

Sam gazed upwards, up the blinding slope of the cwm. He was surprised to realise that he didn't regret what he had done.

Six members of the South American team came over the top of the climb and struck out in a line towards their tents. They nodded some weary greetings as they filed past.

'When you're ready,' Al said to his group. The down climb waited for them.

'Give me five more minutes,' Sandy begged.

Al looked hard at him. 'Okay. You're with Ken. Finch, you join us.'

She shouldered her pack and picked up her ice axe at once.

When she stepped into line Sam grinned at her. 'So how was it for you?'

'Tell you at the bottom.'

They threaded their way downwards through the maze. Sunshine turned the ice slopes to sweating slabs of unhealthy grey and the shadows lightened to ethereal pale-blue. Sam was thinking longingly of his tent and the opportunity to rest his aching limbs and head when out of the air came a sharp crack, followed by a noise like a huge roll of thunder. The rumble of the avalanche breaking away and gathering speed seemed so close that he dropped into a crouch and wrapped his arms round his face to protect himself. After a jagged pause, when no wall of snow descended on him, he looked up again. The other climbers were similarly frozen.

'Below us,' Al said tersely. They resumed their dogged descent.

A few metres further down Mingma suddenly sprang forward. Looking past him Sam saw a man splayed in the snow at the top of a jumble of moraine. It was Namje, one of the two Sherpas who had gone ahead. He looked up at them, imploring.

Because they were checking the fixed ropes the two

men had been independently roped together for safety. The avalanche had swept them both away and taken the rope route out at the same time. Somehow, by a superhuman effort, Namje had dug in with his axe and then his feet, and arrested their downhill plunge. Now Ang, his partner, was somewhere below him, either buried or hanging at the end of the rope.

By the time Sam had this worked out, Al was already below the Sherpa and following the straining rope out of sight.

'He's here,' Al's level voice came up to them. 'Crevasse. Rix and Mark, you body belay. Mingma and Finch rope up and come down to me. We'll have to lift him out.'

Immediately the two Britons began chopping at the precarious snow slope with their ice axes. They cut two saddle-shaped seats with hollows for their legs and left a solid tongue of icy snow between them to provide resistance against which to brace their bodies. They sat down in their saddles and passed the ropes around their waists to anchor Finch and the Sherpa if they should fall. In this quiet rush of intense activity Sam waited helplessly.

Once the two clients had made themselves as secure as they could, Mingma and Finch tied the ropes into their harnesses and clambered down to Al's vantage point. From here they could see that Ang was unconscious, left dangling after the avalanche's rush had tipped into the chasm. Somehow, the fall had pulled him halfway out of his harness and now he hung precariously in the void.

Sam gnawed at the back of his mitten as he watched the careful manoeuvres.

Very slowly, roped to Mingma, Al lowered himself over the edge. Finch leaned back with her crampons and axe dug firmly into the snow, and an extra loop of Mingma's rope around her waist. Above her Rix and Mark sat motionless in their snow belays, braced for the sudden rush and jerk of another falling body. There was a long minute that stretched into several more while Al was out of sight. Finch waited with her head bent, apparently studying the avalanche debris.

'Take him up,' Al's voice came at last.

Mingma took the strain on the rope and began hauling. Ang's inert body appeared at the surface and with a concerted heave the rescuers pulled him out. Al scrambled out beside him. Finch was already busy, freeing the injured man from the rope cradle and pulling open his clothes to check his breathing and pulse. Al ran his hands over the splayed limbs. Detachedly now, as if it were a scene in a film, Sam watched how instinctively they worked together.

Namje sat with his head in his hands. He was shivering. Rix put one arm around his shoulders.

There was a huge gash across Ang's forehead, running up to the top of his head. The black hair was sticky with blood.

Pemba and the other half of the expedition came up behind them. The two guides conferred and Ken took out the radio to talk to George.

Al said, 'We'll have to lower him down to Base.'

Finch put a dressing over the wound. The man's head lolled as he was lifted and roped under the arms, and through his harness, and she struggled to support it.

'All of you will go down with Pemba and Mingma,'

Al told his climbers. 'Ken and I will bring him down, with Finch.'

'Let me help,' Sam said.

Al didn't even look up. 'Do as I say.'

In silence, the column moved obediently away. Below the site of the little avalanche the fixed ropes remained in place.

Twenty minutes later they reached the glacier floor. George and the Base Sherpas were waiting there. It was another half an hour before the rest of the convoy came in sight. Ken and Al carried Ang between them; on the steepest sections they lowered him in his harness. Finch moved carefully alongside, monitoring the casualty. As soon as they had him down the Sherpas lifted Ang gently between them and began the rapid clamber to the Mountain People's camp. Ang was ferried straight into the medical tent with Finch and the two guides.

Dorje the cook brought Sam a mug of tea.

'Very bad,' Dorje said. 'First day.'

Sam nodded. He sat down with his back against the stones of the *puja* altar. It was warm in the sun. Mingma silently came and stirred up the juniper fire.

Seven

That night Sam had his recurrent dream. He was in the old ridge tent, in his sleeping bag, curled up in the dim green light. From outside there was the clink of pans as his mother tidied up after the evening meal and the low mumble of his father's voice. Everything was safe and familiar, and he was holding his dream self very still, afraid of the safety melting away. And then, as always happened, he was elsewhere. A place he didn't know. A needle against the sky, rock, a sharp tooth biting the blue, with birds rising around the summit. There was a spider on the needle, climbing like a man, reduced by the dizzy height to a black scratch almost too tiny to see and too far to save, and Sam knew that he needed to be saved because it wasn't a spider at all, it was his father.

Help me, his father's voice called. Tell me what to do.

Sam's mouth moved, no words came.

I'm falling.

The spider shrivelled as if touched by flame and spun through the air, endlessly somersaulting, and then it had hands and feet, legs and arms, and it fell still shouting I'm falling, and then it touched the ground. Sam screamed and the vibration of it was still in his throat as he clawed himself awake in his sleeping bag at Base Camp. He rolled on to his back and pulled the hood away from his face. The terror of the dream slowly released its hold and ebbed away. Sam lay with his eyes wide open and tried to steady his breathing. He knew from experience that he wouldn't sleep again after the dream.

He heard someone making a scrambling rush out of one of the other tents and then the sound of retching.

At breakfast Vern was missing but then later in the day Sam discovered him resting in a canvas chair at the side of the mess tent. 'You okay?'

The big American looked pale and uneasy, but he managed a smile. 'Sure. I had a real bad headache after yesterday morning. Couldn't move with it for a couple of hours and couldn't keep the painkillers down. Like the worst migraine. So I had kind of an uncomfortable night, but the doc fixed me up with something to stop the vomiting and then the dope kicked in, so now I'm fine. Just acclimatising. It's happened before.'

'That's tough luck.'

'Ah, nothing to worry about. Good that we've got a rest day today. How d'you feel?'

'Fair.' In fact, Sam hadn't slept after the dream, as he had known that he would not. In its wake he felt sick and languid, and the prospect of climbing the icefall even one more time, let alone several, was completely unendurable. But still he knew that he would do it because the alternative was to back down and walk away. A wedge of comprehension was driving under the piled-up judgements of his father and tipping all his perspectives sideways.

Vern nodded sympathetically. 'You did pretty good yesterday.'

'Thank you. I'm not sure Al would agree with that.'

'Bit of a bastard, isn't he?'

Sam shrugged. He didn't want to enter into a discussion of the expedition leader. He wandered around to find Dorje instead and drank a cup of tea while he gazed down the valley. Cloud had flooded upwards to blot out nearly all of the view.

The camp was quiet. Most of the climbers were resting in their tents or reading in the mess. The sound of water splashing behind a canvas screen next to the kitchen indicated that someone was taking a shower.

Yesterday afternoon, after Finch had stabilised Ang as far as possible, Al and two of the Sherpas had carried him to Pheriche, back down the valley, where there was a Western-run medical clinic. Al had called George in the evening to report that the injured Sherpa was conscious again and had had his head wound stitched up. He had a dislocated shoulder, crushed ribs and lacerations, but there was no doubt that he would mend. Al would spend the rest day walking back up to Base Camp.

George was sending faxes in the communications tent. He greeted Sam with a tilt of his head.

'Any chance I could make a call, when you're finished?' Sam asked.

'Sure. You rigged it. Six dollars a minute, to the US.'

'Thanks.'

Five minutes later, Mike answered the phone in Wilding, Oregon.

'Hi, Dad. Do you want to guess where I am?'

George Heywood darted a glance, then tactfully wandered out of the tent.

Listening to the faint, satellite-borne echo of his own voice Sam thought of all the times he had heard his father fantasising about Everest. *You'll climb the Cap before you're twenty, kid. And then you'll go and do all the big routes in the Alps and the Himalaya, places your old daddy'll never get to see.*

'I thought you were in Kathmandu.'

'Close. But much better.'

'I don't know, son.' The old man sounded tired.

'Everest Base Camp.'

There was a moment of crystalline silence, then a laugh, disbelieving and yet longing to believe.

'Honestly. Yesterday I went up the icefall as far as the cwm and down again.'

'How come?'

'A lucky break. I got a job on an expedition. Mentioned your name, as a matter of fact.'

'Sam. This wouldn't be one of your jokes, would it?'

Did I ever make a joke like that? Was I so cruel?

He gripped the slippery handset and thought, I'm going to *cry*, goddamn it. After all this time I'm going to weep. 'No. It's the truth. I told a man called George Heywood that I'm your son and he took me on as a substitute for a guy who got sick. I'm here to support the clients trying for the summit, but you never know. I might get to go a bit higher yet.'

'I think I remember George, from the old days up in Yosemite. He was just a kid, then. Listen. Take a look outside. Tell me what you can see, will you? Tell me everything.'

Sam stepped forward so that he could peer out of the tent flap. He described the view and added a few embellishments because the cloud was thickening.

'You can see the summit?'

'Yeah, I can see it.'

Mike breathed out a long sigh. 'That's something,' he said. 'That's really something, isn't it?'

Sam stared very hard at the convolutions of rock and ice. 'I wish you could see it too.'

'This is nearly as good. Listen, son. You're going climbing, like I knew you would. I can hear the sound of it in your voice, so don't tell me it's just a job. But I want you to be careful. Remember how I used to tell you about concentration?'

'I remember.'

'And when you get on top, just say my name, and your mother's.'

'Dad, I'm not . . .'

'Just *say it*.'

'Okay, I will. But it's a huge if, not when. I'm only hanging on the hem of this expedition. If the guy who's sick recovers and makes it up here, I'm off the trip.'

All the way from Wilding, he heard a strange sound that could have been his father chuckling. 'Sure you are. But you'll remember, won't you?'

'Say your names.'

'I meant be careful.'

'Yeah.'

'Remember all those times when I took you out when you were a kid?'

'I was crap.'

'You learned plenty.'

Sam became aware that there was a shadow beyond the tent flap. 'I'm on the expedition satphone, Dad, at six bucks a minute. I'd better go.'

'Sure. I'm real proud of you, Sammy. Have a good time.'

When he stumbled out of the tent Sam found Finch turning away from the doorway. He collected himself with an effort. 'Sorry. You wanted to get to the med room?'

'I was going to try a call too. Is anything wrong?'

Sam shook his head and Finch edged past him into the tent.

She wanted to talk to Suzy. Her laptop e-mail didn't work up here; incoming e-mails were received at the office in Kathmandu and hard copy was carried up by mail runners from the Lukla airstrip. She had sent faxes announcing their safe arrival at Base Camp but now a conversation, a proper talk regardless of distance, was what she needed.

The icefall itself had been fearful enough. She had known in theory about the effort it would cost her, and about the shifting menace of it and the extremes of heat and cold, but the reality had been much more disturbing. Yesterday her own physical cowardice had appeared ahead of her, moving as solidly as another climber, or loitering malevolently on the lip of the crevasse and under the precarious seracs. She had thought she was courageous enough but the apparition rose up and blocked her way. Sometimes the effort of will needed to take one more step alongside it had seemed beyond her. And then almost at the end of the struggle there was the avalanche and Mingma's imploring face looking up at them, and the moment when Al lowered himself out of sight into the chasm. She had wanted to scream like a child and run forward to claw on the rope and pull him back again.

All the time she had been helping with the rescue and doing what little she could for the injured man she had been watching herself detachedly, thinking, you are a fraud and a liability here. You haven't got what it takes. You will let Al down.

After the men had carried Ang away down to Pheriche her sense of helplessness increased. She hadn't done enough for him. There was no treatment room here, no battery of equipment nor any of the medical resources she and Dennis took for granted back in Vancouver. Her duty to all these people in this hostile environment made her wonder how she could have taken on the responsibility so blithely. It had been a long, uncomfortable night.

Jeff answered the phone but a minute later Suzy was on the line. The warm familiarity of her voice briefly eased Finch's isolation.

'Yeah, I'm fine. Rest day today. Bit of an epic yesterday.'

She described the avalanche and the tense minutes of the rescue, and gave an account of Ang's injuries.

'Oh, God. It could have been you,' Suzy exclaimed. 'Did you know it was going to be like that? You can't have realised it was going to be so dangerous and still wanted to go?'

Blithe was the word, Finch thought. For taking on the medical responsibility and for thinking she had the courage for the climb. 'I don't know, Suze. Maybe

I wouldn't have come if I had known and I'm still glad that I'm here.'

'Finch, all of this is crazy. I'm scared for you.'

'Don't be.' I'm scared enough for myself. Any more fear would be entirely superfluous. 'How are you, anyway?'

Suzy paused, then laughed, 'Pregnant.'

'*What*?'

'First shot, too. Not bad, eh?'

'That's good news. That's so good, Suzy.' They were both laughing now. They talked for a minute about dates and trimesters, suddenly not medical but motherly, and Finch forgot where she was and the days that were waiting for her.

'You sound fine,' Suzy said at the end of it.

'I am.' Maybe she was, after all. She was with Al. This was her own choice, whatever was coming.

'I'm thinking about you every day, up there.'

'And me about you. Even more, now. I've got to go, George wants to get the weather report.'

'Climb it and get back here, will you?'

'Watch out, primagravida.'

Outside, there were thick towers of cloud colliding and obliterating the sky and the peaks. A thin wind pulled at the nylon flaps of tents and dragged the prayer flags horizontal, and a few specks of snow whirled out of the grey air. Sam had taken a walk around the perimeter of the camp, restless, wanting to shake off a sense of confinement. He saw Finch as she emerged.

'Who's in the mess tent?' she asked him.

'Everyone, pretty much.' There was a card school and Sandy was playing a CD of Van Morrison's greatest hits. Sam added carefully, 'Except Al. He's not back from Pheriche.'

'Ah.'

'You could come back to my apartment if you don't fancy the mess tent.'

Her smile, when it came, was a reward in itself. 'Thank you. That sounds nice.'

The Mountain People's tents were big enough for two. Sam's was tidy, with his sleeping bag neatly folded and his clothes and books in small piles at the inner end. Finch settled herself to one side with a kitbag for a backrest and Sam reclined on his sleeping bag. The wind was getting stronger, slapping and straining at the little dome so they had to raise their voices.

'I just heard my best friend's having a baby.'

'Is this a cause for celebration?'

'Definitely. She's just married, it was her wedding I'd been to when we met at the airport.'

Sam liked this acknowledgement of their history, for all its smallness.

'Let's break out the chocolate, then.'

He found a bar, undid the foil wrapping and broke off a piece for each of them. Finch gnawed at hers, hungry and nauseous at the same time. Altitude, she thought absently, not pregnancy. Eat what you can manage and drink as much as you can.

'Were you calling home? Your girlfriend?'

'My girlfriend and I reached a point of . . . realising there wasn't any point, just before I came out here.'

Finch examined her chunk of chocolate, choosing not to pursue this.

'I was talking to my father.'

She did settle back now, squirming her shoulders into the improvised cushion and quietly waiting for what he would tell her. The tent's confined space, the dim greenish light and the synthetic, gluey smells reminded Sam of the expeditions with his parents, and the dream. It was disturbing to be with Finch in this intimate enclosure. Yesterday's danger and the avalanche's aftermath had stripped a layer of reserve. They looked at each other candidly now. He wanted to put out a hand to rest on the smooth swell of her calf muscle. Instead he began to talk.

He told Finch about his childhood and the house-high, alarming boulders Michael had wanted him to climb. He tried to convey the angry childish incomprehension he had felt, for his father's obsession and the obscure equation of risk and achievement.

'I never understood. Never even began to understand it, until yesterday. And then suddenly I was unhanded with terror, practically incontinent with it, but I still wanted to go on. I have to go back up there.'

Finch said, 'I know the feeling. Every one of us here knows it.'

'I called my father to tell him where I am and what we did yesterday. He had no idea. He didn't even know about me hitching a ride on the tour.'

'And what did he say?'

'He told me, when I get to the top, just to say his name and my mother's.'

She smiled again.

'And he said he was proud of me. He must have told me that before, I guess, but I don't have any memory of it. Or of when it might have been.'

'Go on,' Finch said after a moment.

Sam raised his eyebrows.

'There's something else, isn't there?'

'He fell,' Sam said.

It was nearly ten years, now. Sam had not been there when it happened, of course. He had long before made it clear that he didn't want to climb, with his father or with anyone else. No one at all had been there. It was always Mike's preference to climb free and solo.

It's not about safety. It's about purity.

He had been working his way unroped up a pillar, following a route he had devised himself and named Jam Today. It was a tiny crack, just offering enough purchase for fingertips, running vertically upwards to an overhang eighty feet from the ground. It was the equivalent of a gentle afternoon stroll for Michael McGrath, who loved the dizzy cliffs of Yosemite and relished a delicate ascent up thousands of brittle feet of frozen Alaskan waterfall.

He had been making the dynamic move that transferred his fingers from the vertical crack to a tiny hold out of sight on the overhang above his head. There was no way to do it successfully except by springing upwards and locking into the invisible crevice.

When there is no way to move upwards except by relinquishing the safety of the existing holds, climbers talk about committing. *Commit yourself, son,* Sam remembered his father calling up or down to him as he fought to find the will for a similar manoeuvre. *You have to commit.*

This mild Saturday afternoon, on the crux of a climb he had done a dozen times before, Michael committed himself too late or too hesitantly and his fingers missed the hold.

He fell eighty feet to the ground and lay there.

It was the black, tumbling figure that Sam had seen in his premonitory dreams and had unwillingly revisited in his imagination too many times since then. No one witnessed the real fall but it was vivid, stamped and imprinted and ineradicable, in Sam's head.

Michael broke his lower back and suffered other injuries. He lay conscious and in agony for an hour until two hikers passed by and found him. It was an unfrequented piece of country and he was lucky that it wasn't much longer.

Sam was in his freshman year at college. He was out running and his room-mate was away for the weekend. The first news he had of the accident was a telephone message taken by a stranger living down the hall and left pinned to the door of his room. Call this hospital, this number. Speak to Dr Shapiro.

'I didn't concentrate,' Mike said bitterly, when Sam arrived at his bedside. 'Just once, I took what I could do for granted.'

Michael came home to the old house in Wilding in a wheelchair. At first Sam had to look after him, lifting him into bed and on to the lavatory. He gave up college and, with a grudgingness that he was ashamed to remember, prepared to devote himself to caring for an angry, crippled man. He took a job as a computer salesman at a discount warehouse on the other side of Wilding.

But he reckoned without his father's iron will.

Michael learned to walk again, one precarious step

from his chair to the kitchen table and then two, then with the swing of his powerful arms and shoulders and the slither of his legs that took him from his bed to the chair. He kept on even when he was in severe pain, lurching from the chair to the table in the uncared-for kitchen.

But the atmosphere in the house threatened to poison them both. Sam suffered from claustrophobia and from his father's tongue. Michael knew that he would never climb again; the doctors were pessimistic even about the chances of his walking unaided, and the frustration and rage found a vent in his dissatisfaction with his son.

Sam escaped by running. He ran hundreds of miles, pushing himself to cover greater distances in ever shorter times, keeping the focus of his concentration tight. When he came back, to find his father brooding in his chair or making the painful two-step shuffle, his impulse was to go straight out again and run further and harder.

Gradually, Michael regained some control of his lower body. He learned to walk around the house with the aid of crutches, then with two sticks, then with just one. He began driving his car again, as far as the grocery store, or into town. One day he said abruptly, 'Go on.'

'Go on where?'

'Back to college. I don't need you here.'

A year after the accident, Sam resumed his studies. His sports scholarship had been held open, and he repaid the faith by winning the Oregon State championship and a series of national events. It wasn't easy to share any of these triumphs with

Michael, who held the bitterness of his own physical captivity like a tumour in his gut.

The wind across the glacier was getting stronger. Sam had to raise his voice again over the drumming of the nylon capsule.

'That's about where we stayed. I wouldn't climb for him and he didn't care about anything else,' Sam concluded.

Finch had listened intently to all of this, watching his face as he talked. 'I think he sounds remarkable. Medically, that is.'

'Maybe all this is because of him. I have had a buried, subliminal, unacknowledged but burning urge all along to climb Everest and win my father's withheld approval at long last.'

Finch considered. 'I very much hope so. Because it means none of that bullshit about me and dinner has any truth in it.'

They both hesitated.

Then Sam took her hand and held it, and she let it lie there. He was separately and vividly conscious of her warm fingers, and the oval nails and the relaxed crook of her thumb. 'There isn't anything for me to hope for, is there?'

'No,' she said gently.

'I want to kill him.'

'No, you don't.'

'Okay. If you say so.'

He gave her hand back and she nodded.

'I've got some things to do, Sam. Mark Mason's still coughing and I ought to go and check up on Vern. Thank you for – telling me all that.'

'Sure.'

They were crawling out of the confined tent and into the full force of the wind. There would be plenty more time for talk, they were suddenly aware. The sprawl of camp looked small and vulnerable on its glacier bed, and they were trapped in it by the capricious weather. There was nothing any of them could do but crouch and wait until it changed again.

Finch pulled her insulating wind jacket around her. Snow scoured the triangle of her face that was left exposed. She saw Al standing talking to George but looking directly at her, only a few feet away, with snow on the hood and shoulders of his parka, and frosting his new growth of black beard. He was back from Pheriche at last. George clapped a hand against his shoulder, sending snow spinning, and they ducked into the mess tent together. A shaft of light shone briefly on the snowy, hummocked jumble of glacier rock.

Finch followed them into the tent. All the climbers except Sam and Vern were gathered around the big table, waiting for it to be dinner time. Two or three of them were reading, Ken and the others were playing cards. Al had slumped in a chair at the near end of the table.

Finch went straight to him and put her hand on his shoulder.

She was aware at once of the suddenly stilled activity and the eyes on them, and then the whisper of conclusions being drawn.

That was right. She wanted them to know. And then she forgot that there was anyone there but Al.

Al acknowledged her claim by grasping her wrist

and looking straight up into her face as he spoke. 'He will be all right.'

'That's good.'

'Thank you for what you did.'

'It felt like too little. What about you?'

'A long walk, that's all.'

They moved apart. Finch became aware of everyone hurriedly resuming their activities, so as to seem not to have noticed anything. Sandy Jackson was smirking over his hand of cards. She took a spare chair at the table and desultory conversation continued around her. Sam and Vern came in together. Within a few minutes the cook's boy arrived with fistfuls of forks and knives, followed by Dorje with the food.

Vern ate almost nothing. 'I'll be right tomorrow,' he insisted to Finch.

Everyone else picked at their platefuls.

At the after-dinner briefing George held up the weather report. 'We're looking at two or three bad days. It's a matter of sitting it out, as you all know. It's lucky we're not higher up the mountain. Take the opportunity to rest and conserve your strength.'

There were plenty of climbers from other groups in camps up as far as the South Col. The wind and the chill at that height would be fearsome. Sporadic news was radioed down to the various bases and circulated around the camp. They would try to sit tight, confined in their tents, until the storms blew themselves out.

'Al?'

Al leaned forward in his place. Sam had been watching him, unwillingly, but unable to stop his gaze being drawn back every time he looked away.

There was an inner stillness in the man that was reflected in his wintry face. He wasn't impassive, his expression was subtly responsive to the demands of the conversations around him, but he was self-contained. He had considerable presence without giving away anything of himself.

Finch had been right, Sam didn't hate him at all. He wanted to, but what he felt was closer to respect.

'As you all know, Ang was seriously but not critically injured yesterday. He is now at Pheriche, receiving medical attention. Thank you all for your assistance on the mountain. You have heard the weather report.' He broke off, tilting his head to the sound of the wind. 'As soon as it eases again, we'll go back up to Camp One and spend a night there. The same groups as last time.'

Sam opened his mouth to ask the same question as before, but Al's glance silenced him.

'Anyone got anything relevant to add?'

No one else spoke.

'Okay. Stay focused.' He nodded to dismiss them. People began to ease back their chairs and drift away from the table.

'Have you got a minute?' Al spoke directly to Sam.

'Sure. Of course.'

Al nodded to the tent flap. Sam stood up and followed him outside. It was too windy to talk comfortably and Al indicated the communications tent. Once inside it, he said without preamble, 'Have you ever had a pair of crampons on your feet before?'

'Yes. But not recently.'

'It didn't look like it.'

'I'm sorry about that. I thought by the end I was doing pretty good.'

'I don't need anyone to fuck up out there.'

'No.' Sam kept his voice level, hanging on to his composure.

'You claimed to be a mountaineer.'

'Actually, I think I just claimed to be strong and willing.'

Al studied him. 'Why are you here?'

'I don't think that's any of your damned business.'

'I'm leading this expedition, kid. Everything that happens here is my business.'

It was the *kid* that did it. Added to the knowledge that Finch loved him and he could understand why she did so.

Anger and humiliation flooded through Sam. He clenched his fist, swung his arm and punched Al in the face, not very effectively. Al hit him right back again, much more capably, and Sam staggered sideways into the table with the satphone and radio on it. Everything skidded and shook, and Al calmly reached to steady the table. Blinking and gasping, Sam fingered his cheek and jaw, wondering how many molars he had lost. His face felt as if it had split open. He sat down in a heap in George's chair.

When he had made sure that there was no harm done to the communications equipment Al put his hand on the crown of Sam's head and turned it to look at the damage. 'Bruise. You'll live. Won't even spoil your pretty looks.'

'Did you do that . . . because of her?' Sam muttered, using the tip of his tongue to investigate the pulpy mess inside his mouth.

Al put his hands in the pockets of his fleece, giving the question proper consideration. 'Did I? No. Tell me, are you here because of her? You might as well be honest. It doesn't make any difference to me.'

It wasn't even arrogance, Sam thought. It was simply the truth. He was an irrelevance, as far as Finch and Al Hood were concerned. He rested his elbow on the table and cupped his undamaged cheek in one hand. 'That was how it started, yes.'

'But something has changed, since yesterday?'

Sam thought of the climb and then his talk to Michael. 'Yes.'

'I thought so. I was watching you up there.'

'Great. Sneering at my technique.'

'Snotty little arsehole, aren't you? As a matter of fact I noticed that you're fit and strong, and pretty determined. Much better than some of my clients, I might say. And the reason I asked you in here for this little talk was to say that I'm now short of a highly experienced climbing Sherpa. I can replace Ang with equivalent manpower, but not the niche he filled in the team. New faces can cause problems. So if you want to help out with some portering, and by doing exactly as you're told, there's a job for you on the expedition even after Adam gets back.'

'I was scared shitless up there.'

To Sam's surprise Al laughed. 'We're all scared shitless, man. Every time we step up. But we keep doing it. And if you're not afraid, you're probably not paying enough attention. Do you want the job? I don't pay, but you get to climb alongside the rest of the group.'

'Yes,' Sam said, without hesitation.

'Fine. And about the other business. Finch Buchanan knows her own mind.'

'Yes,' Sam acknowledged. 'She does that.'

'So it might seem like a load of bollocks for you and me to be sitting here discussing who is going to possess her.'

'And punching the lights out of each other.'

'Call that a punch?' Al laughed again, apparently in real amusement. 'Now, I have to make some calls. I'm glad to have you working with us. Maybe you want to ask the doctor to look at your face, make sure there's no real damage?'

'No, I don't think I'll bother.'

'Goodnight, then,' Al said coolly.

Sam went back to his tent. He lay in his sleeping bag listening to the tumult of the wind. He remembered that in tenth grade both he and Ricky Arnaz had been in love with a girl called Linda Camino – long legs and a pixie face – and although he had hated Ricky intensely and creatively he still felt a bond with him.

It was a dismal two days.

The storm blew relentlessly and the expeditions who had climbers stranded higher up the mountain battled to keep in radio communication with them. An atmosphere of anxious apathy settled over the whole Base Camp community as the groups waited and watched the weather reports, and tried to keep busy, and stay relaxed and not get on one another's nerves. Every communal tent shrank to a squalid tangle of food debris, cluttered possessions and inert bodies, and the individual tents became claustrophobic repositories for stinking clothes and the nervous dreams of inactive sleep. The ice and rocks between and around the tents were furled with fresh snow that was then scoured by the wind into an iron crust with the sheen of beaten egg white.

George Heywood's clients had formed a congenial group in Kathmandu and on the walk in from Lukla. Now it suddenly seemed that they had learned enough about each other's histories, and individual idiosyncrasies became annoying rather than amusing.

Rix's loud voice was grating and constantly audible. He had few reserves of patience or self-containment. The other clients eased themselves away from him in the mess tent and Mark Mason, his partner, spent most of his time with his head down writing reports to fax back to his newspaper in England.

'What is there to bloody say?' Rix demanded irritably of him. 'There's fuck all happening.'

'So what I'm writing about is that fuck all's happening,' Mark answered and eased away to the fax machine.

'I wouldn't pay to read that,' Rix shouted after him and Ted Koplicki frowned over the pages of his Carl Hiaasen.

Al and Ken went to a meeting with the leaders of the South American team to discuss sharing some resources in the high camps and in his absence Sandy Jackson asked Finch, 'Where's your boyfriend gone?'

Sam glared down at the letter he was writing, wanting to rip the man's ponytail out at the roots and force him to eat it.

'He isn't my boyfriend.'

Sandy grinned insinuatingly. 'So what is he, then?'

Finch considered. 'He is my friend, I hope. He's also the leader of the expedition you and I are both a part of, and that's the most significant relationship for now. If you need him urgently I'm sure he won't be far away.'

Her coolness made Sam want to kiss her. Sandy's smirk faded slightly.

Finch found the inactivity, the confined spaces and the apprehensive waiting very hard to deal with. She tried to concentrate on the needs of her group. Sam had a large contusion on his right cheekbone. She looked hard at it, then at him and he stared straight back, challenging her to comment on his injury. She held her tongue.

Vern's headache cleared completely and his cheerful good humour came back. She liked both of the Americans; they were optimistic about their chances and confident of their abilities without being pushy or dogmatic. Mark Mason's cough improved a little, mostly with rest, she thought, not because the antibiotic treatment was particularly effective. One of the porters cut his finger slicing vegetables and she put two stitches in the wound. Another came to her and shyly revealed that his neck, elbows and the backs of his knees were a mass of scaly, weeping eczema sores. She sent him away to wash, then applied hydrocortisone cream and told him that he must come back to see her every day to get more medicine.

'Yes, madam,' he whispered, smiling and showing several gold teeth.

Ken Kennedy had diarrhoea. He joked about it and complained in graphic detail, but it was bad luck. He needed all his strength for the job and a persistent bad stomach would sap it very quickly.

'You know the deal, Ken. Step up the fluids. Don't take anything for a day or so; let it work itself out of your system.'

He nodded stoically and tramped away again to the latrine tent.

Outside her clinic hours, Finch spent her time reading, thinking and sleeping, like everyone else. The noise of the wind was exhausting and inescapable. The cold battered her whenever she ventured between the tents, but claustrophobia forced her outside. She went to drink coffee with three Frenchmen in their compact mess tent. Two of their party were dug in on the South Col, waiting for the break in the weather that would allow them to make the dash for the summit. If it didn't come soon they would run out of food and have to retreat.

'*On espère*.' The handsome base manager shrugged with admirably assumed casualness. '*On verra*.'

For an hour on the second afternoon, when by some freak chance they had the communications and medical tent to themselves, Sam and Finch drank black tea and ate more chocolate and talked again.

'I wish I hadn't let everyone see what they saw the other night,' Finch confided. 'I just thought, it isn't a *secret* that I care about him. Why should it be? But it only makes it more difficult. Goddamn Sandy Jackson and his dirty laugh.'

'What does Al think?'

Finch turned her hands outwards, a little gesture

of gentle frustration and affection. 'What chance have we had to talk about it? But I don't think Al cares.'

Careless bastard, Sam thought.

'He just wants to do the job,' Finch added softly. She looked past Sam to the door of the tent and beyond it. Her face was warm and she was contemplating a place that he couldn't reach or even imagine and sadness arrowed into him. 'He wants to get everyone to the top and safely down again. And then.'

There was no confining the anticipation of *and then* into dry words, but Sam's imagination was vivid enough.

'Tell me how you met each other,' he asked instead. But Finch only shook her head. She told him about her family, as she had promised she would. At the end of it he understood a little better why she should wish to be here instead of sitting comfortably in Vancouver with the spring sunshine reflecting off the straits.

The more he knew about her, the more he wanted to know.

That evening, the wind died. From a whirling black space the sky slowly unshrouded itself and became a silent dome of stars. There were more of them and they shone with more cold brilliance than Sam had ever seen before.

At the after-dinner briefing that night George held up the weather report. It confirmed what they could already see, that storms were giving way to a ridge of high pressure moving from the south-west. So much fresh snow made the going much harder and greatly increased the risk of avalanche, but it was what all the groups cooped up in their tents were waiting to hear. There was the possibility of movement again.

Word came from the French base that their two climbers on the South Col were ready to make for the summit. They would start at 1 a.m. Ripples of anticipation discharged the sluggish atmosphere of the last two days.

'What's the plan, boss?' Rix said. He sat back in his chair, hands expansively clasped behind his head.

Al said, 'We wait another day down here.'

There was a collective mumble of dismay and disappointment.

'Every other fucker'll be up the hill.'

'So I think we should allow them some space.'

Rix and the Americans protested, but Al was adamant. The routes would be reopened by other people's efforts and the avalanche slopes would be tested. The Mountain People would bide their time.

'Waste of a day,' Rix muttered sourly, but Al ignored him. The climbers dispersed one by one to the unwelcome confines of their tents.

Finch lay in the stuffy down cocoon of her sleeping bag, reading by the light of her head torch. When she moved, the beam made a little greenish flicker on the nylon close to her face. She heard someone picking his way over the snowy rubble close at hand, so when a voice murmured at her she didn't jump.

'You're awake?'

It was Al.

'Can I come in for a minute?'

'Of course.'

He unzipped the flaps and crawled in, a big dark bulk in the dimpled concentric circles of torchlight.

Finch moved aside on her sleeping mat and he lay down beside her. For a minute each listened to the sound of the other's breathing. Then Al took her in his arms and pulled off the torch, brushing back her hair so that he could kiss her forehead. His skin and the bristles of his beard felt cold from the outside air.

Finch pressed her mouth against his cheek, breathless with his closeness. 'Why are you here?' she whispered.

She could feel all the little complex muscles in his face doing their work to make his smile.

'Don't you want me to be?'

'You know better than that.'

He did. Her question was to do with all the eyes and ears surrounding them. The Sherpas were superstitious about behaviour that might offend the mountain; the Westerners could question Al's authority if he appeared to have time and attention to spare for anything except guiding them to the summit.

He breathed warmth into her ear. 'I just want five minutes with you. Only this. You smell so good.'

His smell was woodsmoke and sweat, overlaying the intimate clean scent of his skin that she had never forgotten even through the five years of separation. She wanted to lick him. Her body tingled inside the trap of the sleeping bag. She didn't think she had ever wanted anything so much as she wanted Al now.

'And so do you.'

The torch was buried under a fold of nylon. They were in darkness, motionless, hidden and yet exposed to the ears of the night and the savage cold stars.

His mouth found hers.

After the kiss he said, 'We both have a job to do. There won't be much time for two weeks, maybe three.'

'I know that.'

'But maybe I can call a break just before the summit bid. Maybe we can go back down for a night or two.'

She put her mouth against his again to stop the words. 'It doesn't matter. There will be plenty of time, afterwards.'

Al didn't answer. Fear came out of nowhere and stroked a cold finger over her heated face.

'Al?'

'Yes. I'm here. Let me touch you.'

He ran his hands over her body, blurred as it was by the swathes of padding. Finch's head fell back and she gave a long, sweet sigh.

Al's hand rested heavy for a moment. Then he shifted himself away and propped himself up. 'If I don't go now, I'll never be able to make myself. I'll be here all night, and what would Rix and your American boy make of that?'

She accepted the space that he put between them, as he had done before, just when it seemed that nothing could ever separate them. 'Did you hit him?'

'Who, Rix? I wish I had.'

'Not Rix.'

'Ah. Yes, but as a matter of fact he hit me first.'

'Why?'

'I was uncomplimentary about his crampon work.'

Finch coughed with unwilling laughter.

'Goodnight,' Al said. He kissed her again, quickly,

and sat back on his heels. 'Listen, I came in here to tell you something. I'm happy you came on this trip. That sounds so lukewarm, but it's the truth and I can't think of any other words for it. I want you to be happy too, as well as all the other things I know you're feeling.'

'I am happy,' Finch said simply.

'I love you,' he told her, for the first time. Then he ducked backwards out of the tent. He zipped the flaps carefully behind him, consigning her to solitude once again.

The morning was clear and still. When the sun rose, the two French climbers were visible, two specks seemingly immobile on the blinding crest of snow above the western face. Most of the other teams had headed for the icefall long before dawn, but the diminished population of Base Camp watched and waited.

At 1.10 p.m. there was a yell from the French tents and the handsome base manager ran out into the sunlight. The two climbers had just radioed down to him. They were on the summit. It was the first successful climb of the season. Finch and Sam danced up and down on the rocks before slapping each other's hands. Dorje produced chips and meat curry for a celebration lunch and Rix sat smiling next to Al when Mark Mason brought out his camera for a group photograph.

The next morning, at 4 a.m., the two groups were climbing again. They reached Camp One at the top of the icefall by midday. They made an afternoon climb part of the way up the cwm, over the wide slope of the glacier, then came back and settled themselves for a long evening in the cramped tents. They spent the night restlessly turning, listening to the sighs and murmurs of their companions, and wishing for sleep.

Eight

The sun was overhead, a solid white eye in a harsh sky. As midday approached Finch could stand the glare and the heat no longer and she stopped near a jumble of rocks that offered a narrow margin of shade. She held up her hand to Saddiq, her Hushe guide, and when he halted the two porters who followed in their tracks obediently shuffled to a stop as well. The older one immediately rolled the pack off his back and rummaged in the pouch around his waist for tobacco to fill his thin clay pipe.

'I'd like to rest now, Saddiq. Maybe drink and eat something?' Finch said.

The guide nodded. He had led the young American lady for two weeks, up the Hushe valley in the Karakoram and over the Gondogoro La pass towards Concordia. Now they were in the mountain amphitheatre itself, under the high peaks on the border between China and Pakistan. The solitary white massif of K2 stood out hard and brilliant against the sky, directly behind them.

The doctor lady had barely faltered in twelve days of walking. It was hardly suitable that a young, unmarried Western woman should be making her way alone in such places, Saddiq thought, even under the impeccable guidance and protection of a man such as himself, but he could find no fault with her strength or stamina. She had been as tough as any man and she had won his respect. If the lady wanted to call a rest stop now, high up on the Baltoro glacier and barely a morning's walk down from K2 Base Camp, then she had earned the right to do so.

Finch took off her own pack and sat down in the band of shade offered by the rocks. The glacier was a jumble of bare rocks, dirty ice, grit and wind-flayed snow. She stretched out her legs and rested her head against the stone, sighing as luxuriously as if it were a feather pillow.

Her eyes fixed on the high peak. K2. Only the second highest, but a far tougher and more brutal climb than the ordinary routes on Everest. She had been as close to it, now, as she would ever get but it still drew her eyes and her imagination.

She didn't hear the porters murmuring together as they lit the stove to boil a pan of water. She was daydreaming as Saddiq supervised the brewing of tea in a billycan and the pouring into her tin mug.

But she heard the man's voice so clearly that it cut into her head and settled into the chambers of her skull. Afterwards, long after he had finished, not only the words but the pure sound, the separate notes, vibrated minutely in her inner ear.

He asked the abrupt question as if these were the first words he had uttered for long days. 'Can I have some of that?'

It was a British voice, with a faint unplaceable secondary accent.

In the following instant she looked to see where the voice came from and saw him with his back to the ring of mountains, and with the sun hard over his head. Her first impression was of a black beard masking a gaunt face with skin flayed raw by the weather. Saddiq straightened up and moved protectively in front of her. The porters stepped closer to the discarded packs.

He saw their suspicious reaction. 'I only want a drink. I'm thirsty.'

'Here.'

Finch scrambled to her feet. She held out her untasted tea.

He took the tin mug in both hands, apparently warming them in spite of the sun's heat. Then he drank, finishing the tea in a single long swallow. The tendons in his neck strained. Finch saw that he was very thin, almost emaciated.

The man handed back the empty mug. 'Thank you.'

'Would you like some more? Something to eat?'

Saddiq's mouth pinched in a thin line.

'What have you got to spare?'

'Dried fruit. Crackers. Canned and packet stuff. Not a big choice. We're on our way out.'

The man passed one hand over his face. He was exhausted, she realised. She motioned to Saddiq to refill the mug.

'Thank you,' the man said again. His mouth was painfully cracked.

'We can share,' Finch said. Showing their disapproval with every movement, her companions went back to preparing food. The kerosene burner hissed at their feet.

The man was carrying a huge pack on his back. Finch pointed to it. 'Take it off. Sit down and rest.'

He did as he was told, absently, as if his whole attention was elsewhere. He sat down at a little distance, his back against a rock and his face turned to the mountains. He didn't gaze at the high peak in the way that Finch had done, with awe and fascination. He stared at it blankly, as if he would look anywhere else if he could, knowing that his eyes would be dragged back to it whenever he tried to turn away.

'Are you a climber?' Finch attempted.

'I was,' the man said curtly. Nothing in him invited conversation and she made no more attempts. He took the plate of tinned tuna and reconstituted mashed potato that Saddiq passed to him via Finch and ate. He cleaned the dish mechanically, without visible relish, eating because he knew that he must rather than with the pleasure of appetite.

'Thank you,' he said for the last time when he had finished everything. He drank another mug of black tea and accepted the fistful of dried apricots that Finch gave him. He tucked the fruit into a side pocket of his pack, then lifted the load once again.

'Can we help you with anything else?' she asked.

'No. I have to get out, that's all. I'm just getting out of here.'

He turned away, the pack tipping briefly sideways on his back before he wearily shrugged it upright and secured the straps. Finch watched him go. For a man who was clearly close to his physical limits he moved very fast. Before Saddiq and his porters had cleared the remnants of the meal and dismantled the tiny stove, the man was no more than a speck on the blinding expanse of the glacier.

'Dangerous fellow,' Saddiq muttered.

'No, I don't think so. Desperate maybe, but not dangerous.'

Two days later, Finch and her companions reached the trail-head village of Skardu. It was the end of their expedition together. The porters were paid off and headed away immediately to their villages back in the Hushe valley. Finch was expecting a hired jeep to ferry her back down the Karakoram Highway to Islamabad, where she would pick up a flight home. Only there was, it transpired, a small problem with the jeep. Maybe it had broken down en route, or maybe another traveller had commandeered it for a better price. Saddiq was not sure, or was not prepared to give the full story. Finch's options were to wait, to hitch a ride in another vehicle, or to trust herself to the local bus. Having checked out the alternatives, to wait was not a difficult decision. The thicker air at this lower altitude made her feel strong. She could easily put her life on hold for a few more days.

Saddiq assured her that he would stay too, to see her safely into the keeping of the jeep driver. 'Skardu dangerous place,' he said darkly. But he anxiously chafed his moustache as he spoke and his eyes shifted sideways. Finch guessed that he must have another trekking party lined up and was worried about losing their business.

He had found her a place to stay. It was a two-storey mud-and-stone building with a corrugated-iron roof.

It was hot under the roof in the daytime and chilly at night, but Finch had an upstairs alcove to herself and a wooden bed with a cat's-cradle of string lashed between the supports to make a mattress. After the nights of camping high on the glacier, this was almost luxurious. The guest house appeared to be owned by several generations of women. The oldest sat all day in the shade of the doorway with her black garments tightly drawn around her, the intermediate generations swept, scrubbed and prepared food to her exacting standards, and those who were too small to contribute played in the dirt of the yard among the scrawny chickens. Some of the places in town looked as if they might not be reliable refuges, but Finch felt comfortable in this one.

'I want you to go, Saddiq. I know you have business. I am *strong woman*, remember?'

He had told her as much, with a touch of archness, at the conclusion of their journey.

'Not possible, madam,' he began. 'More than my reputation is worth.'

But it was only a form of bargaining. Saddiq was open to persuasion. After an hour of negotiating he was ready to go, handsomely paid and maintaining the impression of unwillingness until the very end. He didn't shake her hand as he left, bowing formally instead. 'I wish you safe return in America.'

'Canada,' she corrected gently, not for the first time.

Saddiq's smile was wide and tender, and infinitely uncomprehending. She was sorry to see him go. He had been friend and family all the time they had been walking, and he had looked after her well.

Finch walked away from the guest house down the chaotic main street towards the river. Animals, people and vehicles spilled around her, and the yammer of incomprehensible language. She felt her loneliness in this isolated place.

She came to a little open space nearby, not quite a public square but a dry expanse of scraped earth underneath some stunted apricot trees, where two or three old men sat with their pipes. Another figure sat to one side, motionless, looking nowhere. It was the glacier man.

Finch stopped a yard in front of him. 'Are you all right?' she asked.

His face was all hollows and shadow. The look in it shocked her. She moved forward without thinking and stooped in front of him, bringing her eyes level with his. 'You can talk to me.'

Something shivered inside the mask of beard and windburned skin. There was a long moment of silence. 'He died,' the man said.

'Who died?'

'I couldn't save him.'

A trio of boys in ragged colourless clothes ran past. A dusty ball wheezed between them and a starveling dog skidded in their wake.

'Who died?' she persisted.

He passed a hand across his face, the same weary gesture she had seen up on the glacier. 'A friend of mine. Oldest friend. We were climbing and then he died.'

The ball bounced in the dirt, close at hand, and the children ran after it and then stopped short and eyed the Westerners. Finch trapped the ball beneath the toe of her boot and nudged it towards them.

The man stood up abruptly. 'Come for a walk with me.'

'If it will help.'

They walked in silence down a muddy defile towards the river and then began to pace along the bank. The water was milky white and it funnelled noisily through a rocky gorge. There was a stretch of turbulence and a pool where women were soaping clothes on stones at the water's edge. Finch became aware that the man was staring at her, as if he was noticing her for the first time.

'What are you doing here?'

She answered slowly, in a calm voice barely loud enough to be heard over the swirl of water. He just wanted to hear someone talking; it didn't matter what she said. She told him about her walk from Gondogoro to K2 and Concordia. She explained that she had worked for a year for UNESCO in a vaccination and medical education programme in rural Baluchistan. This walk was her private adventure before she finally went home to Vancouver, to join her old med school friend Dennis Frame in medical practice. She didn't mention that for the past eight months she had been living with an agronomist called Michael Dickinson, because that was now over. She finished by telling the man her name.

He listened to all of this. Then, when she stopped talking, he seemed to collect himself by an act of will. 'I was lucky you were up there on the glacier, Finch Buchanan. I was out of food and close to my limit.'

'What happened?'

He looked down into her face. 'You said I could talk to you.'

'I meant it.'

They were beyond the outskirts of Skardu now. The path was overhung by mossy trees and the air was sharp with the scent of juniper. The man whose name she didn't know walked with restless speed, driven by images she couldn't see. She wanted to stop him, hold his face between her hands, force him to look into her eyes. She felt no need to question any of these impulses. They seemed natural. From the moment when he had made his demand on the rubbled ice of the Baltoro his voice had been sounding in her head.

'I've known Spider since we were kids. We were in primary school together. His mam and dad lived two streets away from us.'

The faint accent that had troubled her because she couldn't place it grew momentarily stronger and she thought of John Lennon. Sitting at a piano crooning 'Imagine' into a mike. That was it. Liverpool.

'We learned to climb together. Bunking off school to hitch to Llanberis. Summers in Chamonix, living on porridge and café leavings, and whatever we could thieve. Telling each other we'd climb K2. Oh, shit. Fucking *shit*. The bastard died.'

The last words came at a shout. The man stumbled and he pressed the heels of his hands into his eye sockets. He was weeping.

Finch took his arm and guided him to a rock so that he could sit down. She folded her arms around his head and held it against her, and the impact of his sobs thudded against her ribcage. Resting her cheek against his stiff hair, she breathed in dirt and sweat, and the underlying smell of himself, and his grief and anger stirred a response in her that was just as strong. 'Cry,' she told him and her body loosened with desire for him.

The storm was brief. A moment later he lifted his head and drew away from her. He swept his face with his hands and when he began talking again his voice was level. 'I can't believe he's gone. We were high up, but descending. We'd made the summit, by the south face, like we always planned. Climbing by fair means.'

Finch knew what that implied. It was a phrase coined by Reinhold Messner, the great climber. Meaning no bottled oxygen, no teams of porters, no fixed ropes or pre-established camps or mounds of supplies. Just two men on a rope, like the early alpinists, climbing and belaying and depending on one another for their lives, in perfect symbiosis. She also knew that the south face was three and a half thousand metres of almost vertical rock and ice, riven by gullies that threatened avalanches and overhung by splintered swords of precarious glacier. It was an undertaking of immense bravery, as well as of self-confidence. To succeed would have been an achievement almost beyond her comprehension. But they must have believed that they could do it, because they were there.

'We were coming down again by the Abruzzi Ridge. Late, and the weather deteriorating. Spider was moving slower and slower. He said that he couldn't see properly. I thought it was just disorientation brought on by exhaustion. I wasn't thinking that clearly myself, no doubt. The wind was fierce and new snow had wiped our footprints. We were wandering by that time; I knew we would run into serious trouble if we kept on. We had a lightweight tent and I decided to bivouac. We were past doing anything else, really. I got the tent up and we crawled inside. Spider was shaking his head from side to side and muttering about not being able to see a thing.

'The storm came. The wind blew all night and through the next day, and then slackened off as it grew dark. We had almost no food left and very little fuel, so we couldn't melt snow to drink. Spider had been lying quietly in his sleeping bag all this time. I decided we should try to descend in the darkness to a camp belonging to some Spanish climbers and ask them for help, and I told him to get ready to go.

'He couldn't put his crampons on. He was holding them in cupped hands as if they were some kind of . . . rare fruit. Staring like he'd never seen anything like it before.

'I told him we had to get moving, started trying to fit them on his boots for him.

'Then he said, "Mikey, there's a pain in my head." Mikey's his big brother.'

Up until now the man had told the story quietly, unemphatically. Now he hunched his shoulders and crossed his arms across his chest, unable to speak through the throb of pain.

'Ataxia, confusion, hallucination,' Finch repeated mechanically. 'Cerebral oedema.'

Meaning excess fluid on the brain, increased blood flow, cerebral thrombosis and petechial haemorrhage. At that altitude, without support or anything more than basic medical supplies, and at the mercy of a storm, it meant coma almost certainly followed by death. Every mountaineer knew the danger of it, prayed that it wouldn't happen to him or her and went on climbing. The dead man would have felt the warning headache, the onset of disorientation and loss of physical co-ordination. To attempt K2 alpine style was in itself a brave gamble, but to ignore the onset of high-altitude symptoms was pure recklessness. Presumably, in his mentally impaired state the dead man had judged the risk worth taking and had gone on, and his body had finally proved him wrong.

The glacier man abruptly resumed his narrative.

'I couldn't get him down the mountain, I couldn't do anything for him up there. We lay down again and I held on to him. He said, "I'm sorry, mate." But mostly he was away on his own. By the time the morning came he was in a coma. I waited the rest of the day with him. I'd worked out that by the evening I'd have to leave him there anyway, dead or alive. I couldn't melt any more snow and I'd have no chance myself unless I got going. But he died quite quickly. I wrapped him in the tent, covering his face and head. And left him up there on the south shoulder. I climbed on down and by a fluke I found the Spanish camp where they'd been waiting out the storm. They gave me some hot soup and I lay down in one of their tents for a few hours. I won't tell you what my dreams were like.'

Finch was still standing in front of him with her hand resting on his shoulder. She looked upriver at the torrent of glacial meltwater and the roar of it churning through the rocks seemed to swell in her ears.

'At first light I made my way down to Base Camp and straight on down the glacier to where I met you. I had to get there and telephone Spider's wife to tell her he was dead. After that I had to call my own wife and tell her too. She met Spider on the same day she met me.'

Of course he had a wife. He was somewhere in his forties. A husband and family man, as well as a mountaineer. She kept her eyes firmly fixed on the milky water.

The man tilted his head forward again very slowly so that his forehead just rested against Finch's ribs. She unclenched the fingers of her right hand and slotted them very gently through the stiff spikes of his hair, rounding his skull beneath her palm.

'It was my fault.'

She considered the facts. 'Only in that you both went up there in the first place, in the way you did, and your friend made that choice of his own free will.'

She felt under her hand a slow nod of the head. 'Don't go away. Don't leave me,' the man said quietly. 'Just for today.'

'I won't go,' Finch promised.

His hand found her left one and held it tight. 'My name is Al Hood,' he said.

They sat on the river bank for a long time, until dusk came and then the envelope of darkness. It was a clear, cold night and the sky was a metallic sweep of stars. When they walked back into town Al kept hold of her hand. She showed him her guest house but he led her past it to a roadside mechanic's workshop with a rough pyramid of worn-out truck tyres stacked to the side of it and an open space behind where an old truck was parked under the spreading branches of an ancient pine tree. The truck had a high cab and a rear superstructure of canvas stretched over metal hoops. Al Hood undid the secure lacing of the back opening and helped Finch up over the tailgate. She ducked under the canvas and blinked when he lit a kerosene lantern and hung it from one of the hoops. There were rolled-up mattresses at the cab end and metal benches bolted to either side with locked chests underneath. Al groped for some keys and unlocked the nearest chest. It contained a neat stack of canned food and a camping stove. The next one along was full of beer.

'This is base. We borrowed the truck from an old mate of ours who lives in Karachi and drove it up here. Meant we could travel cheaply, and walk in and climb really light.'

He took out a beer, ripped off the ring pull and handed it to her. Finch sipped at the silvery froth.

'Do you want to eat?'

'Yes. If you're going to.'

So they ate beans and frankfurters from tin plates, sitting opposite each other on the floor of the truck.

When they were drinking more beer afterwards Al took from the pocket of his fleece jacket a penknife and a watch, and wrapped them in a handkerchief before stowing them in the most secure box. He told her that they were Spider's and that he would take them home to his family. 'One boy,' he said, in answer to her unspoken question. 'Fourteen, now.'

'And you?'

'I have a daughter a year younger than Spider's son. Molly. Are you married?' He looked at her fingers, curled around the beer can.

'No.'

It felt odd to be exchanging this basic information after what had already passed between them.

Out of the same pocket as the watch and penknife Al took an old carabiner, worn smooth and silvery. He twisted the screw between his thumb and forefinger. 'This was his too. He's had it for twenty-five years, carried it everywhere with him, for luck. I think he would want me to have it.'

They sat in silence for a moment, realising that it was already late. The town had settled into quiet except for the dogs barking at the sky.

'Will you stay?' he asked.

Finch thought, and didn't think. 'Yes. If you want me to.'

He unrolled the two inflatable mattresses and laid them in the well between the seats. The space was so narrow that they overlapped almost completely. There were two ordinary sleeping bags. Finch guessed that the two men would have taken light-weight survival bags with them up the mountain. Spider would still be wrapped in his. Al blew out the lantern.

They lay down with one of the sleeping bags spread over them. Their faces touched and Finch felt that he was shivering. She put her arms round him and held him until the trembling stopped. His breathing slowed and steadied, and almost immediately he fell into the deep sleep of physical and mental exhaustion.

Finch slept too. She had no idea how much later it was when she woke again but she knew that Al was also awake. Their mouths met.

He imagined a reluctance in her that she didn't feel.

'Spider's dead,' he said, his voice the same as the first time she heard it. 'We are still alive.'

To answer him she took his hand and found the buckle of her belt with it, and they undid it together. Greed for each other enveloped them. The struts of the seats penned them on either side and Finch hit her head when she lifted up her hips to him. The smell of engine oil and musty sleeping bag was thick in the back of her nose and the darkness was full of sharp edges and booming metal, but she wanted him to go on fucking her for ever.

Afterwards, in a twist of damp nylon and skewed mattress, they fell asleep.

In the morning Finch opened her eyes and stared up at the khaki canvas tunnel overhead, and the blur of sunlight warming it. There was no one lying beside her.

She scrambled to all fours and winced, putting her fingers to the lump on the back of her skull. The memory of how it had come there remained in her joints and viscerae, physical satisfaction as a languid weightiness that denied rationalisation or regret. For now. She crawled to the canvas opening and peered into the morning's brilliance. Al was sitting on the ground with a tin bowl of water and a mirror propped on a stone in front of him. He had shaved off a neat half of his beard.

Finch laughed at the sight and he looked up at

once to see her and a smile split his face too, intensifying the bizarre contrast between pale skin and bushy blackness so that she laughed harder.

He stood up and turned his profile from side to side for her consideration. 'What do you think?'

'Hm. I rather like the beard. I think you should keep it.'

'Bugger.'

They ate beans and franks again for breakfast, replacing beer with tea.

'What now?' Finch asked.

'I have to go to Islamabad to make formal statements about Spider's death. Then drive the truck back down to Stu in Karachi. Come with me?'

'Yes.'

Finch had a few days to spare before she was finally due back home. They drove south, away from the mountains, perched on the torn plastic seats in the oily capsule of the truck cab. They were three days on the road. They talked as they drove, raising their voices over the drumming of the engine and the whine of the transmission, filling in some of their histories for one another. There was never any talk of the future. Finch wished for it, but Al never gave her any margin for hope. She learned that his marriage was a difficult one, and that climbing cut a rift between him and his wife that could only slice deeper now that Spider was dead. But that was all. A statement of sad fact. No *if only*, no *maybe some day* . . .

In a way she was relieved. It made the sudden suffocating intensity of her longing for him easier to handle, knowing that it was contained and cut off by this journey through the dust and heat of Pakistan.

Al didn't talk much more about the death of his friend, either. After the manifestation of grief beside the river up in Skardu, he took it inside himself and lived with it there. Finch knew that was what he was doing because she lay beside him at night, and heard the terror and the restlessness of his dreams. His refusal to include her or to acknowledge the procedures of mourning was the most telling sign of Al's fixed will and his solitariness.

Just once, she tried to challenge him. 'Why don't you talk to me about it? Are you ashamed, or something, of the way you let me see what you were suffering, back there?'

He looked her straight in the eyes. 'You said, "You can talk to me." Do you remember?'

'Yes, I remember.'

'I knew I could as soon as I saw you and if you hadn't appeared there, in front of me, I don't know what I would have done. And I did talk to you. I'm grateful. You came with me and stayed, and I'll never forget that. But you can't go on and on. I'm not ashamed of anything, except that I couldn't save my friend's life. Nobody could have done. Some mountaineers do die and others survive, and other people go on living. You have to keep on moving.'

Finch wanted to answer, no, it's not so simple or so cold. Human loves and griefs are messy and unquantifiable and surprising, and you can't codify them according to your own wishes. But she said nothing, only looked out of the windscreen at the dun-coloured landscape, a camel staring at the roadside and a group of women walking with sinuous curved pots balanced on their heads.

They passed through Multan and Sukkor and Hyderabad. At night they lay down between the bench seats, and retreated through sex and the intimacy beyond passion into the wordless oblivion of sleep. The last night of their five they spent in the disorientating luxury of a white wedding-cake hotel in Karachi.

They lay in a deep, hot bath in a white marble bathroom of blinding order and cleanliness.

'This is our honeymoon,' Al said. He soaped her skin and rinsed the grime from her wrists and knees.

'And our swansong.'

He lifted her out of the water and carried her into the bedroom. The large bed seemed too big and too soft, after the trough between the seats in the truck. When they had made love Al held her and looked at her for a long time. They fell asleep and when she woke in the middle of the night Finch was disorientated and couldn't find him when she reached out. In the truck, in the intervals of their disturbed sleep, he had always been there, close up against her. She groped a little further and her hands connected with the curve of his shoulder. He was asleep with his back to her and in all the sudden space he had moved away to the edge of the bed.

Early in the morning they took the truck back to Al's friend Stuart Frost. He lived alone in a villa screened from a busy road by a fringe of eucalyptus trees. The sparse rooms smelled of disuse and solitude. Stuart was short and pale-coloured, with thick arms and hands. He couldn't have looked less like Al physically, but still she was struck by their resemblance. It was in their eyes and in the way they admitted nothing. They were two men with their ghosts.

Stuart said, 'I'm sorry, mate.'

Finch went out and sat on the veranda, watching the glitter of traffic beyond the trees. Ten minutes later they came out to find her and Stuart poured tea into glasses. Later he drove them to the airport.

Finch's flight left first. Al walked with her to the gate and held her in his arms for a moment before she walked through. 'Thank you,' he said, exactly as he had done up on the Baltoro when she gave him her mug of tea. She had told herself that when the time came, she would let him go and she would never look back. But it was the hardest thing she had ever done, to turn away and walk down the tunnel to the aircraft.

That was all, just five days and nights, then back to their ordinary lives and five years of separation.

There was not one day in all that time when Finch did not remember Alyn Hood.

Nine

In their Camp Two near the head of the western cwm the Mountain People lay in the two-man tents, recuperating from the third ascent of the icefall and the long slog up the cwm. With the enforced rest and acclimatisation periods down at Base Camp added in, they had been climbing for three and a half weeks.

Their new objective, Al and George had announced, was to climb via Camp Three on the Lhotse face that now reared black as pitch above them and to reach Camp Four at the South Col. They would stay at altitude for a night or two. Then, acclimatisation complete, they would descend again to Base Camp or even lower to rest, eat and sleep, marshal their physical resources and wait for their turn with the other expeditions and the right spell of weather for the summit push.

'When will the attempt be?' asked Vern.

'I don't like to talk about summit *attempts*,' George had joked. 'With the right degree of determination and a measure of luck with the conditions, every one of you can get up there. You are a strong group.'

Team spirits were high.

'This is it, this time,' Rix said, pounding his fist into

his palm. 'No question. I feel better than I've ever done.'

Mason lay beside him with his head pillowed on one crooked arm. He had been murmuring into the tiny dictaphone he kept in his inner pocket, but even this had, for once, failed to irritate his climbing partner. He rotated the rim of his head torch to extinguish the beam and pulled the hood of his sleeping bag around his ears. The tent became a rustling cell of stuffy darkness anchored to the glimmering grey immensity of the cwm.

'I feel like shit, as it happens.' His cough had never abated and now it felt as if his ribs were splitting every time a spasm overtook him. 'But I still think it's going to come good this time.'

Rix chuckled fruitily. 'Sure it is. You got the piss bottle on your side there?'

Mark wearily unrolled himself, groped for the bottle and handed it over.

There was an upheaval of grunting and sighing as Rix relieved himself and finally settled. 'What would I give for a decent crap. My bowels feel like I ate concrete,' he remarked. Mark closed his eyes and tried to focus on sleep. Just an hour or two would be something, before the crawl upwards began all over again.

In their tent a metre and a half away, Ted and Vern were already asleep. Beyond them, Finch and Sandy Jackson also lay side by side. Sandy had recovered his confidence after finding the first forays up the mountain so difficult. Today he had been on Pemba's heels all the way up, and as a result had been noisily self-congratulatory in the interval between arrival in camp and settling to sleep. He and Finch had eaten their meal, noodles and sachets of meat sauce followed by chocolate and a muesli bar, squatting next to the door of the tent to minimise the risk of spilling food into their sleeping bags. Mingma had brought them a pan of frozen snow and they had melted it on a propane gas burner to make a mug of tea each. Sandy had talked all the time, about places he had been and other adventures he had starred in. Finch concentrated on taking steady mouthfuls of food she felt almost too nauseous to ingest. The hot tea was a welcome aid to digestion.

Now they were settling to sleep. At least Sandy had had the tact to turn his back while she peed effortfully into an empty chocolate tin she kept for the purpose. The male anatomy was much better adapted to mountain conditions, she thought, not for the first time.

Sandy gave a long sigh and audibly suppressed a belch.

If you are going to vomit, Finch silently warned, just keep yourself and the contents of your alimentary tract well away from me.

Her tent partner had cannily taken the lower side of the sloping floor. She had to brace herself awkwardly to avoid the unthinkable prospect of rolling into him.

His sigh turned out to be one of satisfaction rather than internal discomfort. 'This is better than I could have hoped. Want to come a bit closer?'

'No. I don't,' she said coldly. 'And how come you've got the energy even to think about it?'

Sandy chuckled. 'Energy's not my problem.

Expedition leader gets first pick, does he? How long have you and Al been an item?'

'I don't think that's any of your business and in any case we aren't an item.'

'No?'

When she wouldn't answer Sandy chuckled again. 'Goodnight, doc.'

In the silence that followed Finch could hear small rummaging and licking sounds. She imagined that he was picking his nose.

To shut him out she thought of the Karakoram and the long drive southwards to Karachi. Every moment of that time, the smallest details of it, had grown shiny with constant revisiting. It gave her a beat of amazing happiness now to think of the reversal, that there was after all a sequel to that brief story. The future seemed to broaden ahead of her like a wide river delta in the sun. And the present, even the cramped tent and the gnawing of constant fear and the consuming physical effort, was better than anything that had happened to her before. In this benevolent light even Sandy Jackson became lovable. Finch drifted into an uncomfortable doze.

Al and Sam were in the next tent. Al hadn't even considered doubling himself up with Finch. His plan was to make a very early start for Camp Three, and to move fast in the immediate wake of two Sherpas portering a load of food and oxygen cylinders. He and Sam would also carry some supplies, and they would check out the route as they went up and concentrate on the proper establishment of the third camp as soon as they reached it. Ken, Mingma and Pemba could bring up the clients at a more leisurely pace. Ken wasn't yet at full strength after his gut complaint.

He noticed that Sam had made good progress up the icefall and over the crevasse territory of the cwm. He might even turn out to be an asset, Al thought, if he stayed strong and well. The boy's attention to Finch hardly crossed his mind. Even Finch herself was only in the back of his mind, although he looked automatically and as often as he could to check that her harness was properly secured and her crampons strapped correctly, and that her safety line kept her clipped to the fixed ropes. But he did the same for each one of the clients. Finch got no special treatment.

'Will you be ready to start early and carry a load up to Three with me?' Al asked curtly as he and Sam wiped out their tin dishes after the meal.

Sam looked quickly at him, trying to judge whether he was being tested or punished, or maybe even subtly rewarded. He felt tired, but not annihilated. His head ached, but not unbearably. 'What time?'

'I'll wake you about three.'

Michael had looked at him with the same expectation long ago. The same delicately insinuating challenge. To respond to Al's request was to go back in time, to turn himself into a kid again, to make a different choice. Sam stowed his plate and lay back on his sleeping bag. The down filling exuded little puffs of air around him. 'Sure,' he said.

By 3.30 the next morning they were climbing away from camp with weighty packs on their backs.

It was an hour's walk up the slope of the glacier to the beginning of the cwm. Sam kept his head down and his eyes on Al's tracks in front of him. The entire glacier was riven with crevasses and buckled into towers and cornices of ice. The gradient wasn't steep, but the obstacles meant that every step required concentration. Even though mighty jet-stream winds hammered the summit a mile or so overhead, there was barely a breeze in this sheltered canyon, and Sam listened to the rhythmic crunch of his boots in the ice and the clink of carabiners slung from his harness.

He was thinking about Michael again. It was tempting to attribute all of this to his father's influence, to a belated need to make reparation, but this morning he felt that wasn't the truth. In the biting cold air, with the steel glimmer of the ice all around him, he recognised that he was doing this for no one but himself. The demands of it, the way it took every particle of his strength and concentration, diminished the confusion of the rest of his life. Running, failing business, Frannie, even Michael, all seemed manageable in comparison with the scale of this mountain.

He tilted his head upwards, just briefly. The two porters were already on the face, two little blots of light shivering up on the vertiginous wall. Above them the heights of the South Col, the south-east ridge, the summit. Sam's imagination greedily soared upwards. Not even because of Finch any more. The man climbing steadily ahead of him was his rival, but now Sam felt only a kind of kinship with him. The curve of rope umbilically connecting them seemed the symbol of it.

One step followed another, a hypnotic rhythm of upwards movement. Towards the top. *I'm going to do it. We're going to make it.*

After an hour they reached the bergschrund. The huge convoluted chasm that separated the head of the Khumbu glacier from the mountain wall gaped like a mouth full of ice teeth. Between the fangs was a system of fixed ropes and ladders across which Al launched himself without hesitation. From the upper lip he called tersely to Sam, 'Climb now.'

Sam did as he was told. The weight of the pack as he balanced on the ladder threatened to drag him off backwards and he rotated his shoulder in an effort to regain equilibrium. The windproof fabric of his suit scraped the ice and a shower of tiny crystals stung his face. As he clattered upwards with the ladder bouncing gently under his weight he realised that the roaring in his ears was his own breathing. He fixed his mind on the next move and the one after that, and the rest of the universe dwindled to a dot in the distance. The steel spikes fixing this goddamn ladder better hold, he thought. Otherwise he'd be dangling in hoary space at the end of a rope, like a chunk of pork fat hung out for the birds.

And that was the best-case scenario.

'Okay,' Al said as he reached the opposite side. 'Let's get up there.'

They glanced up at the shiny, dirty jumble of rock and ice. A thin scarlet thread of nine-millimetre perlon rope dangled uninvitingly from the heights. Al undid the rope that had connected them for the glacier crossing and neatly coiled it. He stowed it in an ice hollow to one side of the fixed rope ready for the return traverse, clipped his safety tether on to the red line and began smoothly climbing. From now on they would all climb individually, relying on the fixed ropes, instead of in the interdependent pairs that were the routine on the glacier.

As Al moved upwards Sam clipped his own tether to the line. He took his jumar clamp off the loop on his harness and fastened it on to the rope. The jumar slid smoothly up the rope when he moved it forwards, but in the reverse direction a camming device bit into the perlon and acted as a brake. Sam found a purchase for his crampons and stepped up, slid the jumar up the rope and stepped up again, gaining a meagre few feet every time. If he wanted further purchase he swung his ice axe so the pick bit into brittle ice. If he needed to rest he let the jumar grip so he dangled from the rope in his safety harness.

Dawn was just breaking.

After an hour of this procedure Sam's glacier optimism was entirely gone. His arm and shoulder muscles screamed. Every step upwards was a fight against breathlessness and the dead weight of his load. As they gained height the temperature dropped and a tricksy wind sucked fine snow off the cliff and sprayed it into his face so that he shivered inside his down suit. His throat ached from sucking icy air into his squeezing lungs and his fingertips grew worryingly numb. Just once he looked down, to the tiny coloured blobs of Camp Two, and then to the specks that were Finch and Ken and the others at the bottom of the face. He tried to send a telepathic message to her, a jumble of warnings and wishes that flashed wordlessly through his mind before vanishing into the snow spray, then bent his body back to the task. He made it his goal and only thought to keep the red rear of Al's Mountain People staff uniform windsuit always the same distance ahead of him. If it seemed to recede he pushed himself to increase the step rate until his head pounded and the breath seared in his chest.

How much further?

They climbed for four hours and at the end of it, with Sam feeling closer to expiring than he had ever done at the finish of a marathon race, they reached Camp Three.

Four tents sat on a series of tiny ridges that the Sherpas had chipped out of the ice and snow at an altitude of 24,000 feet. The two porters were perched on a shelf to the right, their faces turned to the new arrivals with expressions of pleased amusement. Sam sank on to all fours in front of the nearest tent and sucked thin air into his lungs like a drowning dog.

'Very good, Sam,' one of the Sherpas teased. 'High climb for you next.' The other one giggled with delight.

'Home sweet home,' Al murmured, dropping his pack between the tents.

When Sam could speak again he whispered, 'I didn't think I was going to make it, back there.'

'Oh, you had no real worries. It must be in the genes. And it will be much easier the next time you come up here.'

'Pray God you're right.'

Al helped him off with his load and handed him a bottle of warm lemon drink the porters had prepared. Sam tipped it to his mouth and drank and drank. After he had emptied two litres of liquid into his parched system he was able to sit back and look at the world. 'Jesus,' he whispered.

For the first time he was looking down at the view instead of gazing upwards. The wind had died away and sun was pouring into the canyon now. A great silver balloon of space shimmered in front of him, trapped by the flanks of Lhotse. At the bottom of it lay the minuscule tents and the floor of the cwm. From up here the glacier looked almost smooth and almost innocent. Far beyond and below that was the grey curve of it as it flowed away from Everest, and the icefall and Base Camp, down the valley towards the yak pastures of Lobuje and Pheriche. Sam's vantage point now allowed him to look down on the summits of lesser peaks that until now had towered against the sky. Little swirls of cloud floated around their slopes like veils of gauze.

'Jesus, that is something,' he murmured. He had forgotten, just for the moment, his raw throat, numb fingers and craven body.

Al was dividing and reapportioning the loads of supplies. Over the next week or two, while the clients were making their own nervously intent preparations for the summit, the Sherpas would make a series of relays up and down the mountain to establish the highest camps. It was with these logistics, in the form of lists and menus and computer printouts detailing every last tin of sardines and gas canister and sachet of lemon drink, that George Heywood busied himself down at Base. Nothing was left to chance. Sam was fully able to comprehend why commercial big-peak expeditions charged their customers so many thousands of dollars. And he had recovered enough from the morning's exertions to remember the extraordinary lucky break that had delivered him to the middle of the Lhotse face, almost for nothing.

If this *is* luck, he thought. He only realised that he was sitting there grinning when Al looked up and raised his black eyebrows sarcastically. 'Thanks for your company,' he said. 'But if you would like to make a start on melting snow so our clients can have drinks when they get in, that would be a double bonus.'

Sam took up his ice axe at once and began chipping snow and packing it into a pan. It was a fiddly job to get the flame burning, but he managed it in the end. When he had time to examine the tips of his fingers he saw that there was no trace of frostnip. That was good. Nothing must go wrong now. Summit fever flared up in him again.

Climb Everest. Then I'll have dinner with you.

He glanced at Al. He didn't feel the jealous fury any more. Only a desire to do what was expected of him as well as he could, because the man commanded his respect.

'Thanks,' Al said quietly, approving his work with the stoves.

The Sherpas were already inching their way up the 2000 feet that separated them from their next destination on the South Col. The forty-pound loads on their backs looked bigger than they did.

Al's walkie-talkie whined and crackled, and he took it out of the recesses of his suit. It was George, down at Base.

'Yeah, George, it's good. Three is in. Sam and I are here, the rest are on their way.' He leaned forward and peered down the precipice. 'Slow, but not bad.

Another hour for the front ones, maybe. Perhaps an hour more for the tail-enders. Looks like Jackson and Buchanan, from here.'

Further instructions and information were exchanged, then Al said, 'Yeah. Here he is.'

To Sam's surprise, he handed him the radio. George's voice sounded clearly from 8000 feet below. 'Sam? Someone here to speak to you.'

Another voice drawled, 'Hey man, you're wearing my gear.'

Automatically Sam looked down. The name tag on the front of his Mountain People windproof read 'Adam Vries'.

'Adam! How're you doing?'

'Jeez, have I been ill. But I crept up here real slow and I feel okay now.'

Sam looked around him, at the tiny tents on their precarious lip of snow, and the wedge of Pumori and the other peaks floating below him. Adam was left behind in the communications tent down at the deserted Base. 'I'm sorry I took your place.'

'Yeah, me too. Get your ass back down here in one piece and we'll talk about it.'

'I'll try to do that.'

He gave the radio back to Al who was busy with foil sachets of food. 'I feel bad about Adam,' he said.

Al shrugged. 'Don't waste your energy. These things happen. Get on with the job.'

An hour later, Pemba arrived at camp. 'They all okay, Al, I think.'

Ted and Vern came up one after the other. They were gasping for breath and they flopped on to the ledge in front of the tents just as Sam had done, but they clapped their hands on Al's shoulder as he greeted them and took the drinks that Sam handed over.

'More room than last time.' Vern approved of the camp after he had drained the liquid. 'You can stretch your legs without them hanging over the edge.'

Ken was next to appear. He set down a load of supplies. 'Mason's struggling today.'

Rix unclipped himself from the rope. He laid down his ice axe on the steep incline instead of burying the pick end in the snow. It was skidding into space in the direction of Mason's head way down on the rope as Pemba caught it. Rix shook his head slowly. 'Sorry. Not thinking. It's a bugger today. A right bugger.'

Al was looking downwards for the last three climbers and Mingma, but he turned briefly to Rix. 'You'll be okay. A night's rest and you'll be up there.'

Rix rubbed his beard with a gloved fist. Ice crystals rasped and glittered. 'I just hope so, mate.'

Mark Mason was making one upwards step and then resting for what seemed like a full minute. Every two or three steps he hung inertly in his harness as a coughing fit tore through him. Just once he glanced upwards, searching for a glimpse of the camp. His face looked utterly blank behind the shield of his glacier goggles.

Al called, 'Another twenty feet, that's all. You've made it.'

Al and Pemba pulled him up the last metre. He was coughing as if he were going to die.

It was thirty minutes more before the last trio came within earshot. Finch was leading the way, very slowly, but reasonably steadily. Sandy came behind her, head down, apparently lost to everything but the effort each step cost him. Mingma climbed patiently in their wake with another load of supplies towering on his back.

Sam crouched at the lip of the ridge, watching the red curve of Finch's hood. Al and Ken were helping Mason away into his tent. At last she was within reach. When she gained the ledge he unclipped the carabiner that secured her to the line and steered her to the front of the nearest tent. Her eyes were invisible behind goggles, but she pulled a silk mask away from her mouth and sucked air greedily into her lungs. Her legs were barely supporting her. She looked completely spent.

'Well done,' Sam said gently.

She was too exhausted even to acknowledge him. He put a flask of warm lemon into her hands and watched her drink. Sandy stumbled into the camp. The climbers, except for Mason, rested shoulder to shoulder in a row along the tiny jut of their refuge. They looked like a line of seabirds battered by a storm. Pemba and Mingma murmured together. There was no space in Camp Three to accommodate their tent. They would have to climb to another ledge a hundred feet above and shelter there.

'Finch?'

It was Al, from Mason's tent. Sam saw her shake off the fog of exhaustion and lack of oxygen, and sharpen herself into the doctor again. She edged past Ted and Vern, and crawled in beside Al.

Mark was lying on his side in the yellow nylon capsule. She frowned at what she saw. Another bout of coughing shook him as she knelt over him. Al was preparing an oxygen cylinder with its regulator and face mask. When the spasm subsided Mark lay back with a weary shrug and gasped, 'Same cough. Less air.'

Finch listened to his chest and felt his forehead. There was some tachycardia but she couldn't detect the crackly, bubbling sound of fluid on the lungs. However, its absence didn't necessarily mean that he didn't have pulmonary oedema. There was no fever.

'Headache?'

'No,' Mark muttered. 'Or no more than usual.'

The guides and Finch all carried emergency first-aid kits in their packs. She opened her box now and took out a nifedipine capsule. Mark swallowed it without comment. He was an experienced enough mountaineer to know what the altitude-related drugs were and why they were used.

'Another one in six hours. In the meantime, oxygen and rest, and we'll see how you respond to that.'

'I've had it for this year, haven't I?'

He took the mask and gratefully pressed the black rubber to his face, drawing greedy breaths. Al adjusted the flow via the regulator.

'I think you probably have,' Finch said levelly.

'You don't have to decide now,' Al countered.

Finch's eyes met his. This was an area of contention between them. They had never discussed it, never even referred to it, but they both knew that it was there.

Mark was breathing more easily. Finch replaced the phial of capsules, then crawled backwards out of the tent.

The guides and climbers were arranging themselves for a long night fastened on the ledge. The exertions of the climb, the new height they had gained and their isolation in this precarious position drew them into a tighter team than they had been before. There were other expeditions camped on the face, but they were distant now instead of pushed together in the claustrophobic huddles of the lower camps. The Mountain People passed around their squares of chocolate, throat lozenges and tubes of lipsalve with rekindled generosity. Pans of snow were melted on the butane stoves and foil-wrapped ready meals heated up. In the tedious waiting times they forgot their irritations and praised one another for the day's achievements, and speculated about the test to come.

Once he had rested, Sandy Jackson grew lively again. He and Finch crouched in their tent and doggedly spooned warm beans and rice into themselves. With her cracked lips, burning throat and persistent nausea Finch found it a struggle to swallow more than a mouthful. Sandy used his pocket knife to saw chunks off a piece of salami. He offered her one speared on the point of his knife and she gagged at the sight of the pink meat and glistening fat globules.

'Sorry,' he said, with genuine sympathy and put the meat where she couldn't see it. 'Want some cheese instead?'

'Thanks. I'll just have the rice.'

'How do you feel?'

She considered. She was sharply homesick for Vancouver, and Dennis, and Suzy. She was beginning to feel the strain of being the only woman on the expedition. The men largely contained their fears and projected their self-confidence but if there had been just one other woman, Finch thought, she might have been able to share her misgivings about her abilities and exchange reassurances. She made no criticism, in her mind, of Al. It was his job as head guide to keep up group morale. It was also his responsibility to look after all of them and understandably that took all his attention. It was true that Sam had demonstrated his difference from the others, in the few opportunities that they had had to talk privately. But what she felt tonight in the cramped tent with Sandy Jackson wedged alongside her was still an almost suffocating loneliness. And she was tired beyond anything she had ever experienced or imagined.

She answered, 'Not bad. All things considered. Thanks. And you?'

'Oh, shit. Keyed up, like my mind's fighting my legs. This little expedition's taken every dollar I've got and even more that I've borrowed. I've got to climb this sucker. There's no way I can go home without the photo of me on the summit. Business reasons, personal reasons, everything.'

For Sandy, this speech amounted to a major emotional revelation. Finch nodded in sympathy. 'But you can only go as far as your body allows.'

Sandy gave a bark of laughter. 'Fuck, no. You can go a way further than that, if you've a mind to.' He lay back on his sleeping bag in a mess of food wrappers and salami skins, and damp, stinking clothes, and knitted his fingers contemplatively across his chest. His half-full pee bottle sloshed against the tent wall.

'Just you wait and see.'

Finch looked at her watch. The little thermometer clipped to her outer jacket indicated that it was –5 degrees inside the tent. She was fastening her outer boots and strapping on her crampons. To venture outside without them was to risk a slip off the ledge and a 2000-foot plunge to the floor of the cwm.

'Okay, whatever you say. I'd better go back and take a look at Mark.'

Sandy chuckled, for no evident reason. 'Ever the good doc. You mind your step out there.'

Outside the tent the cold and the sting of wind-blown snow made Finch pull the edges of her hood tight around her face. She masked her mouth with one mittened hand and crept the tiny distance to Mason's tent. The responsibility of providing medical care in these conditions weighed more heavily on her than anything she had ever undertaken in her life.

Mark was dozing, with Rix bundled in a heap of outer clothes beside him.

'Is it me, or is it a bit cold in here?' Rix remarked facetiously.

Finch listened to Mason's chest again, checked his pulse and shone her torch into his eyes. There was no deterioration and his breathing was much easier.

Mason looked particularly English, Finch thought, with his wide, ruddy face and a thatch of stiff, colourless hair. The weight he had lost in the course of the expedition made his heavy bones look close beneath the windburned skin.

She took his hand and held it between hers. 'With that cough you really ought to go down. Tomorrow morning.'

'I've been coughing all the way from Namche.'

'I know. I'm sorry. It isn't going to get better up here and you could deteriorate very quickly.'

'I want to try for the South Col,' he said.

'I think that would be inadvisable.'

'It's his decision in the end, isn't it?' Rix demanded.

'Only if his decision does not affect other climbers who might have to rescue or help him. Maybe we should talk to Al about it.'

'Al already agreed he could go on tomorrow if he felt like it.'

'Let him speak for himself, can't you? Is that right, Mark?'

Mason nodded. 'I'm not a quitter. Al knows that.'

Finch hesitated. Again the unspoken rub between them. Of course Al wanted to get as many clients to the summit as possible. The reputation of George Heywood's company as well as his own worth as a guide depended on it.

'Nobody's suggesting you're a quitter,' she said quietly. 'But do you want to risk your life on it?'

All of these people, she thought, all of them with their different motives and yet pushed together on this fearful rock face by their common ambition. Herself included. Listening to the wind and watching Mark Mason's grim face, the value of that ambition seemed utterly paltry.

'I'll decide after I've had some sleep,' Mason said with finality.

There was nothing more for Finch to do but crawl out into the dark again. Al had eaten his meal in the tent Sam was now sharing with Ken and he emerged at the same moment. He put his hand out to steady

Finch as she was assaulted by the force of the wind tearing down from the ridge above. It made a noise like an express train in a tunnel. She began to shout something at him about Mason's condition, but realised the absurdity of trying to have any spoken exchange out on this ice strip, with the black abyss barely a metre from her boots. She simply pointed at Mark's tent and made a rocking gesture with her palm to the ledge. Al nodded. He knew what the situation was. The beam of his head torch slid over her face as he moved closer, just touching one mitten to her cheekbone. Warmth spread from beneath her ribcage and seemed to flood into her limbs.

He withdrew his hand and pointed upwards. The four tents and eight people in the group occupied all the available area. Al would have to climb another hundred feet to the next ledge and share a snow bivouac with Pemba and Mingma. He kicked his way to the fixed rope now, clipped his safety line and began to climb. His torch made a tiny yellow blur through the snow blowing down from the heights above. Finch watched the man she knew she loved, with every fibre of her body and all the facets of her consciousness, as he hauled himself up the ice-bound rock with the wind trying to peel him off and hurl him into space. Fear and cold threatened the warmth Al had given her. After a last squint at his retreating torch she unzipped her tent flap and crawled inside. She removed her boots, crampons and down suit, and pulled her sleeping bag over everything else.

The nylon skin over her head slapped and vibrated in the wind. She had thought that Sandy was asleep, but after a moment he put his hand on her shoulder and briefly squeezed. It was a gesture of companionable warmth and she was grateful for it.

Finch managed to doze for a few hours, broken by intervals of queasy restlessness. In the last waking stretch she realised that the wind had eased. What seemed like a moment later Ken was at the tent flap.

'We're going on up. George has been on the radio. Forecast's okay, sky's clear. You've got forty-five minutes to make a drink and eat something.'

'And Mason?'

'Yeah, him too. He says he feels okay. Al's given him the go-ahead, if you agree.'

She sat up, every muscle protesting, then held her head. Sandy stirred and groaned too. The night's volume of their exhaled breath had frozen to the tent inner. It made it look like the grotto of a malevolent ice fairy.

They lit the stove and laboriously melted some snow for tea, and ate a muesli bar apiece and a handful of dried fruit. Then Finch crawled across to Mason's tent.

He was pale, but breathing easily and the cough had subsided. 'I want to do it,' he insisted. Against her better judgement, she signalled her consent.

The group moved out of Camp Three at 4 a.m., with Ken in the lead and Sam at the rear. Pemba and Mingma were already climbing, and Al attached himself to the column as it clambered by.

The South Col with the various camps dotted on it was the most forbidding place Sam had ever seen. The area was wide, as big as two or three playing fields with the drop down the Kangshung face into

Tibet as the northern boundary and the Lhasa face as the southern. The south-east ridge rose forbiddingly in one direction, the route to their distant goal, and in the other was the summit of Lhotse.

The Mountain People straggled exhaustedly into their Camp Four through the middle hours of the afternoon. Their tents were waiting on an expanse of ice that had been burnished by the wind to an ugly grey sheen. Outcrops of rock and hummocks of snow pocked the surface of it, together with discarded oxygen cylinders and rusting tin cans, and refuse blew into every faintly sheltered corner before whirling away into infinity. In places the snow and ice were stained yellow with urine, and dotted with the frozen coils of faeces. The camps of three other expeditions occupied the other reaches of the Col and their occupants moved slowly and lethargically between the tents. Even though it was a fine day and the sun shone from a clear sky, the wind was like a living thing, battering and assaulting the creeping climbers. From the summit ridge a huge, silky-looking banner of snow blew out over Tibet.

'Welcome to the South Col,' Al shouted as Sam tottered the last twenty metres to the camp.

'Jesus Christ,' Sam mouthed in response. However hard he gulped there seemed to be no oxygen, no nourishment in the air at all. They were at 26,000 feet.

Ted and Vern had already reached their tent. Rix crept towards the refuge of his, bent almost double in the wind. Sandy was next in line behind him.

Al was chipping snow for melting when Sam came and crouched beside him. 'Where's Finch and the others?' he yelled. It was as if the climb had brain-washed him. For the last hour he had been unable to think or recollect, to do anything except realise the pain of lifting one foot and then the other. Now, having reached the goal, he remembered that Finch was still somewhere out there.

Al nudged him into the tent and gave him a drink.

'Okay, I'm okay,' Sam insisted. 'I want to know where she is.'

Al studied him. 'Sure you do.'

He took the radio out of his inner pocket. 'Ken? This is Camp Four. Ken, can you give me an update please?'

He pressed the button and there was a buzz of static. Sam imagined Ken hanging from the fixed line in his safety harness as he reached for his handset. There were other far worse things that he could have imagined but he deliberately blocked them out.

After a long interval Ken's voice came back. 'Camp Four, Camp Four. We're still climbing. Mason's bad but he's moving. Pemba just reached us. Over.'

'I sent Pemba back down to see if he could help,' Al told Sam.

'Where's *Finch*?' Sam repeated.

'Ken, hello, Ken. Got you. What about Buchanan?'

'Keeping steady. She wants to stay with Mason.'

Sam closed his eyes. She had the strength to do that climb and to look out for some other guy at the same time. She amazed him, at every turn and in every way. If he couldn't have this woman, he thought, he couldn't imagine how he would ever settle for another. And it was certain that he couldn't have her, because she was in love with Al Hood.

'Okay, Ken, good. We've got a brew on here for you.'

'Great stuff. Out.'

Al slotted the radio back into place. He busied himself for a moment with firing up the stove and balancing a pan of snow on the flame. Then he looked straight at Sam. 'Don't have too much on your mind. This is mountaineering. It takes concentration.'

'I always knew I fucking hated it.'

Al laughed. When the frown lines eased he looked young. 'I think you're in denial. You love it, really.'

'Maybe. Look, Al, I'm sorry. I can't help it, the way I am, about her. I know it won't lead to anything. I know how things are with you and her. She told me. I think you're . . .' He tried for the right word to describe all the things he thought Al was, but his tired brain denied it. 'Lucky,' he finished flatly.

The stove was tipping on the uneven floor of the tent. Al steadied it and held the pan in place. It took a long time to melt enough snow to make a drink. He didn't look at Sam this time. 'Do you think I don't know that?'

'No.'

Al nodded. 'I'm not surprised you love her. I would be more surprised if you didn't. It's strange, how these things work out. Did she tell you how we met?'

Sam shook his head. He wanted to lie down, pull his sleeping bag around him and sleep for a year. He wanted to go outside and watch for Finch's approach over the glazed ice. He didn't want to hear how she and some other man had fallen in love, even though the other man was Al.

He liked Al quite a lot, he realised, as well as admiring him. He had even made him think differently about his father. And about mountains and the sharp, siren challenge of them.

'Some time, I will,' Al said. 'When we're some place with a beer in our hands and not freezing our arses on the South Col with Rix and Jackson for company. Go and check on our clients for me, will you? And see that Mingma and the guys have got enough brew water on for everyone.'

Sam obediently hauled himself out of the tent. He was here to do what Al told him to do. *Climb Everest* . . . the frivolity of it, Finch and he knowing nothing, would have made him laugh now, if he had had a particle of energy left.

An hour later, Finch and the others were crossing the last few metres to the camp. Mason was shuffling, supported on either side by Ken and Pemba. His head hung forward on his chest as if he could no longer find the strength to hold it up. Finch plodded in their wake. With every step her crampons felt as though they had welded themselves to the ice.

Al and Sam came to meet them. Sam's arms came around her as Al went to Mark Mason. 'You're here. You're okay. You made it.'

The sun was sliding behind Pumori. Finch pushed the goggles off her eyes and fought for breath. She was afraid of suffocation. The wetness of exhaled breath through her face mask had frozen into a secondary mask of ice.

'Tent, here. Hot tea,' Sam said.

She couldn't speak. She tugged at the mask until Sam pulled it away from her mouth for her. The pain of the skin ripping with it made her cry aloud. He put the bottle of tea into her hands and helped her to hold it steady while she drank.

Finch tasted warmth and sugar, and she sucked greedily. Only the most basic awarenesses remained – pain, cold, thirst and hunger. She let Sam lead her to the tent and he made her sit down while he removed her gaiters, crampons and plastic boots. He pulled off the inner boots and felt her socks. They were wet and icy, but not frozen. He opened his down suit and nested one of her feet in each armpit. She lay back against someone's pack and drank. It was twelve hours since she had eaten anything and lemon juice from the water bottle in her pack was all she had had to drink. The climb had been endless and awful.

Al's face appeared in the tent mouth. She tried to smile at him but her lips cracked so painfully that the smile turned into a wince.

'How is she?' he asked Sam.

'Pathetic,' Finch said.

'Amazing,' Sam said simultaneously.

'Come and check out Mason, when you're ready.'

Her fifth awareness returned, a shrivelled and reluctant version of it but still imperative. Responsibility. 'I'll be right there.' She removed her feet from the warmth of Sam's armpits and squatted to retrieve her boots.

Mark was prone on his sleeping bag again. Finch had climbed all day within shouting distance of him, but she was still alarmed at the sight of his sunken face and glazed eyes. Al had put him on oxygen. He finished a bout of coughing into the face mask. 'Can't breathe. Like drowning . . .' he gasped.

Silently Al handed her the medical pack. Finch prepared a shot of dexamethasone and another of nifedipine, and administered them. She had no stethoscope up here. She put her ear to Mason's chest instead, listening for a long moment.

Finch smiled a reassurance she didn't feel. 'I'm going to put you in the bag for a couple of hours. Do you feel okay with that?'

His eyes flooded with fear but he managed a nod. Al backed out of the tent while Finch settled Mason as comfortably as she could. A moment later Al came back from the main supplies deposit with an orange canvas zipper bag. He opened it up and smoothed out what looked like a deflated air bed. Between them Finch and Al helped Mark into the bag.

'I'll be right here,' Finch reassured him. 'Here's the window. We can watch each other the whole time you're in there.' She closed the airtight zip on him.

Al connected a foot pump and began working it. Someone would have to keep pumping all the time to prevent the build-up of carbon dioxide. Within ten minutes the chamber was fully inflated. Mark lay prone inside, staring up through the porthole, his eyes dilated with terror. He looked as though he was in his coffin. Finch knew he must be feeling the similarity to the point of panic. The increase in atmospheric pressure inside the bag was equivalent to an altitude drop of 1500 feet, but claustrophobia for the patient was inevitable. She leaned close to the window and said reassuringly, 'You will start to feel better very soon. Al and I will sit here with you.'

They were both intent on Mark. They waited in silence, keeping their opposite opinions to themselves for now. Al radioed down to George, warning that a helicopter evacuation might be necessary from Base Camp. Even at that altitude the chopper would be operating at its highest limit.

Ken came in. 'How is he?'

Finch said, 'We have to get him down.'

The guides looked at each other. 'Ken, you take Pemba and Mingma and start with him as soon as it's light. Don't risk it before then. I'll lead the rest of the group with Sam.'

'Right.'

The other clients were all comfortable considering the altitude, eating and resting, Ken reported. 'South Col bloody Hilton,' he said. Ken's personal mountaineering preference was for fast and free, the opposite of George's heavyweight excursions.

After another hour Finch judged that Mark should be released. Al turned a tap to deflate the chamber and the patient was peeled out of his meta-coffin. He lay still while Finch listened to his chest once more. His breathing had eased again. She put him back on the oxygen mask.

'You get to sleep with me tonight, Mark,' she told him. 'Rix can go in with Sandy.'

He coughed weakly. 'What a waste.'

Al laughed. 'Just wait. When you get back down to Base it'll be like you're nineteen again. Always happens to me.'

Finch was moving the compression chamber aside. She kept her eyes down but she couldn't stop herself blushing. The incongruity of it, the place and the time and the circumstances. But still, that was the way he made her feel.

They sat with Mark for another hour, monitoring his breathing. Al was silent, and Finch knew that he was remembering another tent and another critically sick climber. He hadn't had the pressure chamber then, or a doctor and a team of Sherpas to help him. Either climbing K2 alpine style was the farthest reach of bravery, as she had once believed, or it was the definition of insanity. Finch thought now that it was closer to the second. She looked across at Al's grim face. For the first time his tenacity made her angry with him, as well as turning her inside out with love. 'Go and get a couple of hours' sleep,' she told him. 'Then come back and help me put him in the bag again.'

Al did as she suggested. Sleep was a safety factor for tomorrow.

Finch lay beside Mark and dozed, and woke again every few minutes to listen to his breathing. When Al returned they gave him another two hours of compression, and more nifedipine and dexamethasone. It was a long night, and the cold and the unending howl of the wind lengthened it until it seemed eternal.

In the morning Mark was feeble, but lucid and composed. He knew as well as any of them that his only chance of survival was to get down the mountain. Finch and Rix helped him into his boots and windproofs. He ate nothing, but managed to drink a litre of warm lemon. Ken and the sirdars were at the tent.

'Let's go, mate,' Ken said.

Mark got to his feet. The Sherpas each took one side of him and Ken led the way. Al clipped on to the rope at the top of the Lhotse face and prepared to guide the rest of them down the mountain. At the same time the other three Mountain People climbing Sherpas were heading the other way, to establish an emergency camp with oxygen and food in a snow cave high on the summit ridge.

The healthy climbers reached Camp One on the lip of the icefall in the middle of the afternoon. Al and Finch waited there for Mason and his supporters; the rest of them went on down. Ken reported by radio that their progress had slowed because Mark was barely able to walk. They were more or less carrying him between them.

Al was watching them through binoculars as they crept down the cwm. 'Come on, come on, you can do it,' he muttered. The rescue helicopter was on standby on the airstrip at Namche.

Mark was more dead than alive by the time they got him to the icefall. Finch gave him two more shots of drugs, and they began the fearful descent through the seracs and crevasses. Mark could hardly keep his footing. It took the efforts of all five of them to steady him and to lower him on the ropes.

Al called George again. 'Get the chopper in. We'll be down in an hour.'

That was optimistic beyond reason, Finch thought. But as they descended through the last twisted gorge of ice she heard the faint gnat's buzz of the helicopter.

Fifteen minutes later Mark was being lifted into it. 'Thanks,' he murmured exhaustedly to Finch. There was more gratitude in the one word than she had heard in plenty of ten-minute speeches.

'You made it to the South Col.' She smiled at him. Privately she thought that he should never have tried to do it, nor should Al have allowed him to.

'Just about,' he conceded.

Five minutes after that the little machine was a dot against the sky.

The sun was down as the group trailed back to camp from the helicopter landing. George and Dorje came to meet them, walking with a third man. Adam had stitched a home-made label to the front of his sweater that read 'Sam McGrath'.

Sam looked him up and down. 'Shit, I've piled the weight on. I'm a real porker. And check out my hair.'

'You are a bastard,' Adam retorted. 'An opportunist, sneaking, conniving bastard. When you've got your breath back, I'm going to hit you.'

'Been done,' Sam said drily.

Mingma went straight to the fire on the *puja* altar and stirred the ashes with a fresh juniper branch.

Later, after they had eaten in the mess tent, and drunk Mark's health and their own, and to the future success of the summit push in black tea faintly laced with whisky, Finch was sitting in the medical tent. She had written a report of Mason's condition and his evacuation in the expedition log. Her anxiety for him had diminished, but her mind was full of the Col and the threat of it. There were faxes and e-mails for her, but she couldn't detach herself enough yet to read them.

Al found her sitting with the sheaf of papers on her lap. He took them out of her hands and touched his forefinger to the raw mess around her mouth left by the ripping face mask. 'I can't even kiss you without hurting you,' he murmured, with his face against her hair. She turned her head away and moved a little distance from him.

'Finch, what's wrong?'

'Mark Mason should never have gone up to the Col. You shouldn't have said he could go on, I shouldn't have agreed to it. We sent Adam down just from Namche after you told him that you'd seen a man die from oedema and it wasn't a party.'

Al rubbed his forehead with the back of his hand. 'Yes. I know. I know what you think, as well. I saw it in your face up there. But Mark's a client. He paid to take his chance. And he did make it to the Col because he really wanted to, and all the way down again, and he will be all right now.'

'Is that what matters? That he paid his money and reached some arbitrary point on the mountain because you and I let him risk his life in the process?' She was suddenly shouting at him.

Al sighed. 'Look. We're not on opposite sides here. I'm only a guide, you're a doctor, but we're trying to achieve the same thing. Which is to allow the people who want to do it to climb as high as they can, using our expertise to limit the risks for them as far as possible. That's what I'm paid for. But we can't eliminate the fucking risk altogether. Mason was set on doing what he did, he *chose* it, and I'm pleased he reached the Col and even more pleased we got him down again. You and I did a good job. Why moan about it now? What's more, if he'd died up there, I'd still think the same thing.'

'Is that what you think about Spider?'

Their eyes met.

Quietly Al said, 'Yes. But more so. He did what he wanted, just like Mason. And it was pure for Spider and me, pure ambition. Simple. Not complicated by money or business or amateurs who want a picture of themselves on top of Everest. I'm proud of what we did on K2. If I wasn't, I don't think I could live with myself or the loss of him. And there still isn't a day when I don't hear his voice.'

Finch bent her head. She understood what he was saying, even though she couldn't comprehend the will behind it. Then she looked up and smiled at him, full of love. 'I'm sorry. We are on the same side. I'm only an amateur, though.'

He put his arms round her again and held her. 'Yeah. But a very professional one. Listen, will you run away with me?'

'Yes.'

'Tomorrow?'

'Yes. Where shall we go?'

'What about down to Pheriche, to see how Ang is?'

'Damn. I thought you were going to say Venice, or the Caribbean.'

'Venice? That'll have to be next year,' he said, smiling back at her.

Ten

'It's paradise,' Finch said. 'Compared with the truck.'

There were trees here, their branches spun with moss that hung down like locks of hair. The paths were slippery with mud and the air was so thick with sap and dew that it seemed to leave a lush coat of moisture on their skin and tongues.

Finch and Al had left camp and walked back down the valley. In the medical clinic at Pheriche they enquired after Ang and were directed to his cousin's house.

They found the Sherpa sitting motionless by a dung fire in a smoky hut. But he gave a wide smile at the sight of them, then hunched the once dislocated shoulder until it almost touched his ear. 'See? All mended.' He laughed.

There was a pucker of fresh pink scar slanting from the bridge of his nose up into his hairline. Finch turned his head to the light so she could examine it. 'So you are,' she agreed. 'And here?' She indicated his ribs.

'No good for laughing yet.'

'Difficult, then.'

Ang laughed all the time.

'Back to work very, very soon. Drink *chang*, gamble money, must earn rupees.'

Ang was the most abstemious of men. The joke masked real need, Finch knew quite well. While they were drinking tea together and when Al was looking the other way, she slipped a little roll of money into his hand. When it was time for them to leave, Ang came out into the sunshine to say goodbye and shaded his eyes with his hand to watch them as they descended the path.

'He was lucky,' Al said.

'This time.'

Later in the day they had walked into the village of Deboche with its mossy trees and stone walls. There was a tea house here, sheltered under a steep curve of the hillside.

The Sherpani owner was evidently an admirer of Al's. She adjusted the beads and braids in her hair and removed the sacking apron she wore over her red skirt before taking his hand between both of hers. '*Namaste*, sir.' She smiled coquettishly. 'You come back at last.'

'I always come back, *didi*.'

The woman gave them a knowing smile. 'And today you bring your wife.'

Al inclined his head.

'I give you a special place. Come with me.'

They followed her out across the dirt patch where the family yak grazed on refuse. They climbed some stone steps to the upper floor of a barn and the wooden door creaked open on a small bunk room. The window was a hole in the wall looking back up towards the mountains. The wood floor was rotten in places and a strong smell of yak percolated from below. There were two bunks and a table and chairs, and a stone hearth with a neat stack of wood beside it.

'Thank you,' Al said gravely and their hostess withdrew.

They stood in the middle of the floor and looked around. The light shining through the window illuminated a narrow shaft of dust particles and left the rest of the room in shadow. Now that they were here, they were momentarily uncertain of each other.

'We could go on down to Namche . . .' Al began.

Finch shook her head. Namche was full of climbers, people who knew Al or knew of him. She couldn't share him.

'Good.' He smiled.

He knelt down in front of the hearth and lit twigs and kindling, stirring them together to make a hot orange blaze before steepling the branches around it. Damp wood sent billows of smoke to mingle with the dust, so that Finch rubbed her smarting eyes. Her skin looked grey with dirt, where it wasn't crimson sun- and windburned, and her hair was stiff and matted. She couldn't remember when she had last looked in a mirror or worn a full set of clean clothes, and none of this mattered because what she brought to Al was herself. With the calm of absolute certainty she watched him cosseting the fire. There was nowhere else she wanted to be, nothing else she needed to struggle for, because this man was here.

Her eyes widened at the realisation and stung even more painfully in the smoke.

After all the incredulity she had directed at her friends for expressing the same feeling, after the wishful attempts at it with Michael Dickinson and Ralf, and half a dozen others, it had come to her so simply and completely. She reached out her hand and touched the curve of his spine as he bent towards the hearth. He was solid, like a boulder or a heavy wood carving.

There was a dull red core to the fire now. Al turned his back on it and they knelt, facing each other in the dust. He took her face between his hands and held it.

'I love you,' he said. He touched the corner of her mouth with his thumb and triggered a smile.

'And?' he prompted her, teasing.

'And you know that I love you. Shamelessly. From the moment you appeared on the Baltoro, looking like a man possessed. Thirsty and starving and desperate.'

The memory of that day shivered between them.

The spectre of the dead man and a legion of others suddenly crowded into the firelit room and stood in the shadows, faceless, voiceless.

'Don't,' Finch suddenly whispered. 'Don't climb any more. I don't want it to happen to you.'

She might almost, Al thought, have been speaking with Jen's voice.

He understood that this was the crux, like the point of greatest difficulty on a climb, that he would have to negotiate before moving upwards. It was a physical and a mental problem combined: whether to commit and make the leap and so risk the fall, or whether to cling on, fingers hooked in the existing hold, and try to make an easier move.

He had never made the leap for Jen.

He had never committed himself to a life that

didn't contain climbing and so he had lost her. The evasion, deferring the promised from one expedition to the next, through year upon year, had seemed the easier route but in the end it had caused the catastrophe. Jen's love had worn thin and frayed, and then it had snapped altogether, like an old rope finally bearing too much weight.

'It won't,' Al said, as he had said to his wife a thousand times.

'That's not enough,' Finch said. 'You can't make that assertion, because it isn't based on certainty.'

The crux.

Give up a life, the construct of risk that he understood and had existed with on and off for so long that he could remember nothing else. Or lose her, as he surely would because Finch was not Jen and would not allow even the lease that his wife had given him.

'This trip,' he said, looking down at their knees, almost touching, and upwards to the fuzzed surface of Finch's fleece jacket and the zipper at her throat with its little tongue of braid. 'Just Everest for both of us and no more once it's done. Although I don't know what we'll live on.'

Or *by*, he could have added, if it wasn't mountains. He had lived in the way of them, and among the people who talked their terse and unadjectival language, for the whole of his thinking life.

'We'll find something.' She smiled, her face bright with conviction. She was so sure, he thought. So unshaken by the world and so confident of her place. The thought of anything happening to her that might shake this confidence was like a cruel thumb pressing on a bruise. He tilted her face again and kissed her, gently, mindful of her scabbed mouth, and the fragility of her neck and the small, arched bones of her shoulders.

'Here.' He spread their windproofs on the floor-boards and lay back with his knees drawn up. She curled herself like a cat and rested her head on his belly, and they watched the fire together. Outside, close at hand, in fact, but seeming a long way off, were the sounds of children's voices and dogs barking.

'I'd like to hear, if you wouldn't mind telling me, that is, if it isn't intrusive or too painful, about why your marriage ended.'

It seemed to Finch that there were a hundred loose ends snaking out of the tangle of history. There was time, plenty of time to unravel everything, but she caught hold of this end and pulled on it anyway.

'Jen got tired of waiting for me to be there. She had had enough of explaining my absence to Molly and being father as well as mother to her. But it was the uncertainty that undermined our marriage. She hated it when I was away. She said she never knew, when she thought about me at a particular moment, whether I was even still alive. We got older and she could never understand why I didn't open a mountain equipment shop or get a job in the building trade.'

Finch thought of the wind and the South Col, and Mark Mason's fear of death from drowning in the effluents of his own lungs. 'I don't think I understand either.'

'But you are *here*.'

'All the more reason, because I have seen it.' Her

face was dark, and Al's fingers slid among the strands of her hair and then tightened.

'When I came home after Spider died Jen was implacable. He was her friend too, they were always close. I was jealous of him, sometimes.

'She said to me, *this is enough*. Meaning, enough deaths. Falls, avalanches, oedema, disappearance. But I went on another expedition and then another after that, because it was what I did. It was how I identified myself.'

Finch stirred and twisted her head so that she could make his eyes meet hers.

'No, all right. I went because I didn't want to stop going quite badly enough to make it happen. And there wasn't the same desire to be at home anyway, because I had met you.'

'I didn't want it to be anything to do with me,' she said sadly.

'Of course you didn't. But it was.'

She took that into herself, turning her eyes back to the fire.

'Jen left me. Took Molly and went to her father's, and then bought herself a business. She's good at it. Two years after that we were divorced.'

'Does she have someone else?'

Under her ear, infinitesimally crimping the skin of her cheek and jaw, she felt his muscles tighten.

'I don't know. Maybe.'

'And did you, in the time since we met?'

'Yes. Just as you had men. It doesn't matter.'

This had turned playful now. They were minutely taunting each other, testing the sexual ground. His hand moved from her hair to her shoulder and down to her breast. She held herself still for a moment, then stretched out on her back, arching herself beneath his hand.

A moment later they rolled in each other's arms.

'I'm so dirty,' Finch said with her open mouth against his. 'And I don't care.'

He unzipped her jacket. 'Scent, soap, manicure, make-up. All artifice. I don't want them. I only want you.'

'Soap isn't. Soap's good.'

'Take off your clothes.'

The room was dark except for the fireglow. It was cold, too, with the unglazed window that was now a square of chilly blue and the draughts through the broken boards. Finch stood to shed her clothes and scattered them around her. Cold was nothing any more, she had lived with it for weeks and it was her constant shadow. She was aware of the pallor of her skin and the sharp bones beneath it. Living at altitude and expending so much energy and eating too little, her body had started to consume muscle because there was no fat residue left.

Al was naked too. He was all black and white, black hair and beard, and skin that matched hers. Touched hers, now.

'I would say, come to bed. If there was one.'

The bunks were just wooden boards.

'What do you mean? We have a choice of two. It's luxury.'

He laughed and the deep, warm vibration of it filled her mouth and her throat.

'Compared with the truck.'

*

There were years of time to make up. Finch and Al stayed for three nights in the Deboche barn and talked and slept, and went walking on the hills in the intervals of sunshine. Finch learned more about Al's childhood in Liverpool. He told her about his sister Cath, fifteen years older than he was.

'Cath looked out for me, always. I loved her.'

'Are you close to her now?'

Al looked away. 'Not so much. I should be, I wish I was. Climbing got in the way. And the men she went for.'

He changed the subject, to the first time he and Spider went to North Wales and saw the rocks. The years after that were an unbroken line of increasingly severe climbs. It was only in his thirties that Al bothered to win the formal guiding qualifications that enabled him to take clients and lead commercial groups. Until then he had climbed first and lived on whatever came to hand afterwards.

'Jen usually had a job. If it came to the worst,' he said. 'And she climbed herself, until Molly came along.'

'And then?'

'You don't need a lot, living the way we did.'

'Were you happy?'

They were sitting at the table in the barn. They had eaten fried potatoes and mystery meat curry in the tea house, and afterwards Al had brought back cans of beer and lit candles to stand in the corners. Everything they needed, a complete universe, was contained in this shadowed space.

'Sometimes. With Molly, when she was tiny. I remember a day when I took her to the beach, just the two of us. And in the hills, much more often. Even on K2. Otherwise, there was a lot of restless space. I'd come home and I'd look at the time to be filled, and I would start wanting to go again. Just to feel the burn that it gave me. I was always looking for an experience that would be more real than reality.'

Finch looked steadily at him until he laughed.

'You think I sound ridiculous. Or like a junkie muttering about the next fix.'

'No. I don't.'

She had told him more about Vancouver and med school, and her work abroad, and then going home again. He had listened to her and seen in his mind's eye the grand house overlooking the Sound, and her patrician father and elegant mother, and the large, confident, assertive brothers. He understood entirely why she needed to climb McKinley and come out to Everest. To get out from under all that weight of patriarchal privilege and fraternal regard. To fashion herself for herself.

She even showed him the e-mail that had come from Suzy while they were up on the South Col. 'It's weird, I've been looking after babies for all these years and now I am going to have one myself and until now I never understood what it feels like. Finch, you have to come home safe. This is bigger than a mountain. I want you to know what it's like. Making a whole new life.'

'I think maybe she's got a point,' Finch mused.

Her expression turned hazy and inward, even though she was still looking at him. The idea of a new permanence and all the attendant potential of their future induced a shiver of vertigo that he never suffered on the most exposed and precarious ridge. He waited coldly until the sickness subsided, as it must do, then reached out his hand and covered hers with it. 'Did you tell her about me?'

'No. I never told anyone about you, even Suzy. I kept you for myself.'

'Were *you* happy?'

'Not unhappy. But I don't think I ever understood what it meant, until now. And once you do know happiness you never can forget what it is. Even though it might not always be there.'

In her way she was as wary as he was. He was so disarmed that he stood up abruptly and knocked over his chair. The crash reverberated and started the dog barking in the space beneath the floor. He came and put his arms around her shoulders and held her against him. 'I love you. One of the reasons why I love you is because you can say what you feel. There isn't some stone in your mouth that stops you uttering it.'

'Stone?' she repeated vaguely. She stood up to meet him and put her mouth to his. With her hands on his hips she pulled him closer. It was dark again outside. She felt untied, disconnected, adrift with happiness. Only one more night and then they would have to go back to camp, and after that they would be free to begin everything else together.

The next day they walked down to Namche and Al telephoned George. They had a long conversation, with Al leaning on the door jamb of the rough cubicle and abstractedly toeing the scraps of litter at his feet. Finch sat out of earshot, looking down to the river gorge where the afternoon's cargo of fat clouds puffed up from the warm depths.

'It's okay up there,' Al reported when he emerged again. They began walking back up the main street, ducking under the clothes and second-hand climbing kit hung out for sale from the low eaves of the shops. 'Mason's recovered and he's flying out to London tomorrow.'

'Good,' Finch said composedly. She still thought he had been remarkably lucky.

'Your young men, Sam and Adam, are fooling around like a couple of kids.'

She could easily imagine it and the thought made her smile. Although Sam McGrath had hardly entered her mind for two days. 'Mine?'

'Don't dismiss him,' Al warned her.

The admonition stopped her short. 'I didn't mean to.'

'He talked to me about it. About you, rather. He said that he knows how things are with you and me, and he was sorry about the way he felt, but he couldn't help it. It was when we were up on the Col and you hadn't appeared, and he was quite obviously shitting himself with worry about you.'

'I didn't know that.' There had been too much else happening and no space left to give consideration to Sam. She had kept the idea of his devotion in a box in her mind labelled *adolescent fixation*. But Sam wasn't an adolescent, he was a grown man. 'I didn't ask him to follow me, or to latch on to the group.'

'I know. If it makes it any easier, he may have come out here mainly because of you but he stayed for other reasons. The old peak hunger started gnawing in his gut. He claims it's for his dad he's doing it, but I know he's climbing for himself. You can only climb for yourself. There's no other imperative.'

'You like him, don't you?'

With a part of his mind Al had been thinking about Molly. It came to him how much he loved her, and regretted all the absences and broken promises.

Don't go, she had begged him this time. *I have to*, he had repeated, as he always did.

How would that change, now? Maybe the only difference would be that he was breaking the same promises to a different woman. Wife, daughter, lover.

'Yes, I like him,' he said.

Perhaps Molly would find herself someone like Sam. He liked the thought of her with a partner, a man who would take care of her.

'What are the others doing?' Finch asked.

They were negotiating the steep slope that led the same way that he had followed Finch on the rest day in Namche, near where she had caught her first sight of Everest. There was no view today, the peaks were swathed in cloud. The weather had temporarily deteriorated, and he had learned from George that two or three of the other expeditions had brought their climbers down from the Col and beyond. Bad weather and enforced waiting increased the pressure on the summit when conditions did improve enough to allow further attempts. Too many people were climbing under too many restrictions.

'Rix and Sandy are bullshitting each other and complaining to everyone else about too much waiting and time-wasting.'

'Sandy's okay,' Finch said, remembering the way he had squeezed her shoulder in the tent.

'Vern and Ted have been climbing Kalapathar and exercising, and probably sharpening their crampons.'

'They're keen. It means a lot to them.'

'You are all keen. You wouldn't have come this far, otherwise.'

She walked with her hands in her pockets, watching the rising ground in front of her. They came to a *mani* wall and passed to the side of it with their heads bowed. The tracks were much busier than they had been when they had passed this way a month ago. Yak trains and trekkers pushed upwards towards the high valley.

'What's up?' Al asked, after a long interval of silence.

It was the same question that had troubled her the night Mark Mason had been flown out.

'Where do you set the line between their eagerness and your own professional ambition for them, and the bounds of unacceptable risk?'

She knew when his answer came quickly that it was because he had thought about it for a long time.

'Risk has two aspects. There's the objective one – weather, altitude, avalanche, exposure. We all *know* it's dangerous up there, we all accept it and try to minimise the danger by being careful. That's good mountaineering. The second aspect is personal, buried deep in each one of us and different in every individual who goes up into the mountains. You, me, Rix, Sandy Jackson, whoever. It's what risk means to us alone and how close we're prepared to let death come to achieve whatever the goal is. For Spider and me it was K2 alpine style. You know what that cost. For Mason it was the South Col and he made it. The risk was huge, but it was his alone. His gamble with himself made everything more difficult for me, and you and Pemba and the others, but we accepted that probability when we took the job. And before you bring it up all over again, I sent Adam down from Namche because I wanted him fit again to do his.'

'The risk was Mark's alone,' Finch repeated softly. 'And Spider's, and yours alone too. What about Spider's wife? And Jen and Molly?' And me, she might have added.

He flicked her a glance, hearing the two words even though she hadn't uttered them. 'I'm a mountaineer,' he said. Simply, flatly, and – Finch understood – without compromise. He might believe he could give it up for her, might even intend to do so, but she knew that he never would. Not while he could still pull on his boots and put one in front of the other. To accept him in spite of that was her own risk. Then Al laughed. 'And you are a doctor. You save lives. It's hardly surprising that we think differently.'

'I'm sorry,' Finch said, with a prickle of anger.

'Don't be. You have the right to your opinions. We're doing different jobs here, that's all. And I am in your admiring debt for the way you looked after Mason.'

'You're not in debt to me for anything . . .' she began incredulously, but he stopped her.

'Let me be proud of you. And let me ask you

something. Why do you talk about the clients as *them*? Don't you include yourself in this group any longer? Because if anyone is capable of getting to the top of the hill it's you, Finch. You and Sam McGrath. I don't say that because I'm in love with you and because I think Sam's a decent guy I wouldn't mind seeing my daughter with, but because it's my professional opinion.'

He was right about risk, Finch decided.

It was the essence of the experience and the clients knew that. It was partly what drew them and their excess of dollars here in the first place. The difference in her own case now was that she had the pressure of happiness within her. It changed the colours of her internal scenery and it affected her emotional appetite as radically as Suzy's pregnancy affected her physical one. Risk seemed suddenly superfluous.

None of this was Al's responsibility, except that he existed in the first place, and had come to her and had changed everything for her.

She stopped walking and turned to face him. 'Al, I'm not criticising anything you do. I'm awed and humbled by it. I think you're brave beyond reason and I've thought it ever since you told me what happened to you and Spider. I don't wish for anything to be different. Least of all you.'

He took hold of her. The feel of him burned her and she looked at the rocks and grass, and the crows circling in the sky, wishing for the haven of their barn and for more time, and for the end of the expedition to come and release them.

'Come back with me now,' he whispered, after their

mouths had briefly met and they had drawn apart again. They began walking once more, up the stony path to Deboche.

Later, they lay in each other's arms in the darkness.

The window hole was a just-discernible rectangle of thinner dark, more clearly delineated by the cold draught that sliced straight through it. Finch shivered and he tightened his arms.

'Cold?'

The truth of it was closer to fear. He scented it on her skin, and kissed her cheeks and tight shoulders to soothe her. 'Go to sleep. You're safe now.'

'It's not just for me . . .'

It is for us. For the smooth, perfect egg of this happiness, that I can never forget now I have held it in my hand.

'Go to sleep,' he whispered again.

Seek oblivion.

Two days later they were walking back into Base Camp, through the settlements of the other expeditions, exchanging greetings and hearing the latest news. The South Americans had put two climbers on the summit, despite the weather. The Indian Army was high on Lhotse. Another porter had been injured in the icefall. There were disputes about the maintenance of the fixed ropes.

'So what's bloody new?' Al muttered.

The Mountain People were disposed around their tent circle. They had the look of climbers who had spent more than enough enforced leisure time camped on a slag heap of gritty rock and ice. The return of the leader and his doctor provided a major focus of interest.

Sandy smirked and Rix made a lewd gesture covertly intended for Al but intercepted by Finch as well. She gave him an unblinking stare. The two Americans welcomed them back and George poured mugs of coffee from the vacuum jug that sat in the mess tent.

Sam and Adam had been playing three-card brag with Pemba and Dorje. There had been shouts and Adam crying *Hey maaaan*, but they stopped as soon as they caught sight of the new arrivals.

Sam's eyes went straight to Finch, then slid away again. Her features looked soft and blurry, almost unformed.

A small silence bled inwards, until Adam folded his cards and pitched them on the table. 'I guess that's that,' he said.

George came in with the faxed weather report and the rest of the clients crowded in. Now that Al was back it was as if something was guaranteed to happen. Finch moved away and took a seat at the rear of the group while Al and George conferred. She could see the back of Sam's head and the exposed nape of his neck where his collar had fallen away. There was a line where sunburn abruptly faded into pallor, and the sight of it made her suddenly aware of him as a man, a separate individual only half known to her with his cargo of hopes and dreams.

She transferred her gaze quickly to George. They were all waiting expectantly.

'Okay. Today is May the second. I have here the medium-term forecast and there is a spell of clear weather moving in advance of the monsoon. You are all fit, rested and acclimatised. We will wait at Base for another two days . . .'

'Why wait if we're ready to go?'

The rumble of protest was led by Sandy, but George silenced it with a glance. '. . . to allow two other expeditions room to make their attempts and on May the fifth you will leave for the summit. This isn't a race, and all the camps are stocked with food and oxygen in sufficient quantities to allow leeway for weather and personal variations. However, I hope to have you all on the top of the hill on May the eighth.'

There was a rush of collective indrawn breath and then a little chorus of cheers.

'Whooee, it's real at last,' Sandy said. 'Let's do it, guys.'

Finch slipped away from the team spirit in the mess tent. She hunched inside her own and took out a sheet of paper to write a fax to Suzy. It was late in the day to be telling her any of this, but she wanted her friend to know about Al. 'Dearest Suze,' she wrote. 'This will surprise you, and you may be hurt or angry because I haven't told you about this man before. If you are, then I'm sorry, but just know that I want to tell you everything now. In two days we're leaving to do the climb. In a week, I believe . . . *hope* . . . we'll be back down here again.'

She told the story of herself and Al, then signed the note: 'Thinking of you with love, F.' She folded it without reading it through and put it aside to send in the morning.

*

At 3.30 a.m. on 5 May the line of climbers were ready to leave Base Camp for the last time. George and Dorje and the Base Sherpas shook their hands in turn as they filed away.

Adam stood with his hand raised in salute, his face clouded with disappointment. He had never acclimatised fully and even now he was troubled by headaches and breathlessness. 'Good luck,' he said to each of them. 'Even you,' he added to Sam.

Finch had had a call from Suzy. 'I'm happy that you are so happy,' Suzy had said. 'Now I just want to hear that you're back down again. God bless you.'

Al walked at the head of the line as they made for the icefall, Ken at the rear. It was a crystalline night, with a cold crust of stars paling the sky.

Eleven

The wind screamed across the South Col, driving fresh snow off the rocks in a solid white wall. To walk six steps against such a wind at sea level would have taken strength and determination; at 26,000 feet the effort required every human ounce of combined muscle and will. Digging in with his ice axe to anchor himself, Al Hood crawled on hands and knees from tent to tent. The tiny domes caved and juddered, and bent under the gale's assault.

It was 4 p.m. on 7 May. Summit day was just eight hours off. Weather permitting.

In the first tent Vern Ecker was hunched over a cooking stove, trying to melt snow. Ted Koplicki was setting out equipment next to his empty pack. He kept lifting up the jumar clamp and putting it back next to his water bottle, and moving the energy bars from one end of the line to the other. He was frowning and muttering to himself. Al unzipped the flap and crawled in, disturbing the precision of his arrangements.

'I've forgotten something.' Ted shook his head. 'I'll get out there and I won't have it, and I'll be fucked. Mittens, goggles, food, jumar. Food, goggles, mittens . . .'

Al said, 'Just try to get some sleep, on oxygen. Flow rate point five, okay? You've got your bottles for tomorrow?'

Ted picked up a face mask with trailing tubes from his equipment parade and looked distractedly around him. 'Uh, yeah, here we go.'

Four three-kilogram bottles were lying in the corner of the tent. Each client would carry two and a further one apiece had been cached at the emergency high camp near the south summit.

'Ready to leave at midnight, please. Sweet dreams and good luck.' Al shook each of them by the hand and backed out of the tent. The two Americans would do fine, he thought. He wasn't worried about them.

Rix and Sam McGrath were lying in their sleeping bags. They had already eaten what they could manage to force down and their oxygen masks were strapped to their faces. Rix chafed his hands and stared up at the straining tent roof. The whole structure rocked as if the slightest increase in wind speed would tear it from its anchorings and whirl it into Tibet. Al arrived with a flurry of driven snow and the two men propped themselves up to listen to him. He had to shout over the shriek of the gale.

'This wind should drop before the morning. There's a mass of fresh snow but the forecast's good enough, so we leave at midnight. Please be completely ready.'

'I'm ready right now.' Rix's eyes glittered and he repeatedly pumped his fist against his palm.

Al looked appraisingly at him and then turned to Sam. 'Feeling fit?'

'All things considered.' The long climb back up to

the South Col had been no picnic, but it had been easier than the first time. If he was going to get any higher, it would have to be done soon and done quickly. At this altitude and above, the human body was existing beyond its survival zone. From the heaviness of his limbs and the slow, confused working of his mind Sam had no doubt of that.

Al nodded. 'Get some rest, both of you. And good luck.'

'Wait,' Sam said. A glance assured him that Rix had retreated into his tranced contemplation of victory. 'I guess it's because you went along with it that I've got this far. I wanted to thank you for giving me the chance of tomorrow.'

Al looked straight back at him. 'You did a job. Upwards from here no one really knows what may happen. If things go awry tomorrow, for any reason, I'll be looking to you to pull your weight with me and Ken.'

Sam smiled. 'That's a compliment. A big one.'

He put out his hand and Al shook it. Instead of releasing his hold the guide tightened his grip. 'If anyone in the group needs extra help and I'm not right there to give it . . .'

He didn't say her name, because there was no need to do so.

'I will be there.'

'Thank you. I hope you manage some sleep,' Al said.

Finch and Sandy had made a brew of powdered soup and now they were drinking it, hunched side by side in the confined space. Finch laced her fingers around her mug and gazed at the little heap of her belongings. Her boot inners were frozen solid. The plastic outers must have started to leak somewhere on the second ascent of the Lhotse face. Probably because she had been too tired, or made careless by lack of oxygen, when she put them on she had either laced them wrongly or secured her gaiters awry, and snow and ice had penetrated inside the shell. She was thinking that if she nursed the inners in her sleeping bag for a few hours they might thaw out enough to be bearable tomorrow.

If her mind had been working better she would have accorded the frozen boots the status of a serious catastrophe. Ordinarily she knew how important it was at least to set out each morning with feet that were approximately warm and dry. But now she was exhausted and confused, and she wearily accepted her boots as just one more source of discomfort as she pushed the inners down into her sleeping bag.

The climb back up to the Col was already nothing more than a hideous blur of cold and breathlessness. She felt much more fatigued than she had done the first time up here and she was aware that she was now probably the weakest of the group. What if Mason were here this time? she wondered. What if someone else gets sick? Her brain came up with no answer.

A blundering at the tent flap revealed itself as Al. He hauled his bulk inside and squatted in the cramped space to give them the weather news and their instructions for the start.

'All ready? Everything okay?' he asked them both.

The list of things that were not okay seemed to Finch too lengthy to enumerate. She nodded listlessly instead and he came closer, shuffling on his knees through the sordid chaos of spilled food and icy outer garments.

'Sure?' His beard glittered with points of ice and she met his eyes for a minute. He was looking at her not as he did in the valley, but in the narrow way a guide assesses a client and a mountaineer. For tonight she was another summit seeker to be encouraged to the top and shepherded down again. But this was the last time. He *had* promised her, surely, down in the firelit barn?

'Sure.'

'Sandy?'

'Yes.'

He patted Sandy's shoulder, then his mittened hand briefly cupped Finch's cheek. 'You can do it,' he said.

'Is it worth it?' she mumbled.

He did look at her then, a flash of the man suddenly visible through the mask of his professional concern. 'You are the only person who can answer that.'

She grappled with the thought for a second and then abandoned it. Just to get down, merely to be warm and not to have to haul her craven body any higher, that was all she wanted.

'Good luck, both of you.' Al pulled the hood of his down suit closer around his face, ready to head out into the wind again.

'And to you,' Finch called after him, too late, when the swirling snow had swallowed him up again.

Sandy was too weary to snigger or insinuate. Looking at him, Finch saw his oozy, red-rimmed eyes and cracked, flaking lips, and the way his skin appeared to have tightened over his sharpened bones. She knew that she looked just as bad, or even worse.

There was just tomorrow to endure and after that they could head out of here.

Ken was stowing gear into the deep recesses of his guide's pack.

'Everyone okay?'

Al eased himself across the heap of kit to his own side of the tent. He rubbed his beard with the flat of his hand, feeling the scrape of ice. 'Yeah. You?'

Ken hadn't really recovered his full strength after the gut infection. Nothing was going to get any better at this stage. 'So-so. I talked to Pemba and Mingma, like you said. They'll leave at eleven and break trail. Namje and Dos Santos's guys will be working on the ropes.'

An Argentinian expedition was sharing the summit day with the Mountain People. Their lead guide had detailed two of his Sherpas to work with Al's to repair wind and storm damage to the fixed ropes.

'Okay. Do you want a brew?' Ken shook his head. 'Then get some kip, mate.'

The other man settled his balaclava over his bristly skull and rolled himself up in his sleeping bag. Al pulled his pack towards him and took out a little waterproof pouch. Inside it was a photograph, Molly aged five, sitting on a beach with sand silvering her plump limbs and her corkscrew curls caught by the breeze. There was also Spider's old carabiner, worn shiny with long use, that he had shown to Finch in the truck. When he took the watch and the penknife home to Spider's wife, she had told him to keep it. In any case, the carabiner's history predated her by several years. It was Al who had been there when Spider, aged seventeen, deftly nicked it right off the belt of a loud-mouthed once-a-year climber in a pub in Capel Curig.

'To those who have shall be given,' Spider had murmured as he slipped it into his pocket. 'And then we shall take from them.'

Al smoothed the photograph and zipped it into the inner pocket of his down suit. He screwed the carabiner shut and open again with a practised twist of finger and thumb, then clipped it on to his harness. It was too old to use, but it was his talisman. 'I miss you every bloody day, Spider,' he said aloud.

Ken didn't stir. The boom of the wind drowned everything.

Finch lay huddled in her bag. The boot inners were a melting ice block close to the pit of her stomach. Rigid cold inhabited the core of her body like a steel rod. The oxygen mask clamped over her mouth and nose made her feel that she was suffocating, but she had just enough reasoning power to know that if she pulled it off her face the surrounding air would be so much thinner that she would be left gasping like a landed fish. She closed her eyes and forced herself to breathe slowly and evenly. At her back the tent fabric strained and slapped, and the wind seemed to grow ever fiercer.

There were maybe five hours left before it would be time to get up and make ready. Finch did not expect to sleep but she unlocked her limbs from their tense angles and tried at least to rest.

*

With the arrival of darkness the wind gradually slackened.

At 11 p.m. the climbing Sherpas plodded away from camp, followed by the rope-fixing party. The climbers lurched unwillingly from their sleeping bags and gnawed at scraps of food, dry-mouthed and nauseous. They heated the water that they had laboriously melted in the afternoon, drank and filled their thermos bottles. Finch tucked hers inside the bib of her down pants where it radiated a tiny glow of warmth through her chilled bones. She put on a dry pair of socks and pulled the part-thawed inner boots and plastic shells over the top, praying that by some miracle they would not freeze solid again.

Sam was dressed and ready to go. He checked his watch and craned for a look at Rix's altimeter. Bubbles of anticipation and apprehension rose in his stomach. He was thinking that now the time had finally come, now the highest place in the world was within reach, there was nowhere on earth he would rather be. If he couldn't have Finch Buchanan, then to claim this vicious and beautiful mountain with her was a partial compensation.

Rix squatted heavily next to his pack, his fists clenched on the shaft of his ice axe. His eyes seemed glazed and he kept muttering, 'Come on. Come on.' At 11.50 p.m. they crawled out of the tent and secured it to await their return.

The wind was still brutal enough, although it had lost most of its earlier force. Swirls of spindrift raced across the rock and ice, and blurred the beams of their head torches. The temperature was –32°C. Vern and Ted joked a little mechanically with Ken, while Al crouched over his radio handset for a final conference with George down at Base.

'So you've got a good day for it,' George's voice crackled. 'There may be some snow later. Go on up there and good luck.'

'We're on our way. Out.'

The group assembled. They looked like a line of spacemen in their fat padded suits and their face masks, and they moved as clumsily.

Al said, 'Last check. Do you all have everything you need?'

The huge heads robotically nodded. He moved from one to the other, checking the assembly of their oxygen bottles and regulators, making sure that the supply was switched on and the flow rate properly adjusted.

'For Chrissakes. Are you going to try and carry us up there?' Rix demanded, his voice raw with nerves. 'Let's just get started.'

'Take it easy,' Al said.

He moved a step backwards so they could all see him. 'Can you hear me?'

The heads slowly bobbed again. 'We are going to move as a group as far as possible. I will be leading, Ken'll take the rear. The order is Ted, Vern, Finch, Sam, Rix, Sandy. That may change according to how fast you each move and how often you need to rest.'

Sam swung his head to look at Finch. Al was giving her into his care. He would follow her all the way, step for step.

She didn't see that he was looking at her. She stood with her head bent, apparently studying the dirty ice in front of her feet.

'Pemba, Mingma and Namje will be waiting for us at the south summit. Further oxygen and emergency bivouac supplies are stashed at Camp Five just below it and you will see that as we pass.

'There is one more thing. The most important. At two o'clock we turn around. After that time, no one will be going a step higher. Wherever you are on the hill, when two o'clock comes you start moving down. Understood? Ted, Vern?'

They mumbled their assent. Sandy, Finch and Sam nodded yet again.

Rix was kicking his feet in the ice.

'Rix?'

'Let's get going, for fuck's sake. I'm getting frostbite here.'

'Steady, tiger,' Vern warned.

Al looked at the great dark bulge of the ridge rising from the flat table of the Col. He eased his shoulders under the straps of his pack and took a step away from the group. 'Enjoy yourselves,' he called back to them.

They trailed away in a line across the Col, stepping through the little circles of light thrown by their head torches. The Argentinian group was ahead, glimmering yellow points revealing their whereabouts.

The flat ice became a slope of snow and crumbling rock. Finch's crampons skidded on a smooth rock slab and she thrust down with the shaft of her ice axe to steady herself. The small effort made her catch her breath and gasp into her face mask. It was an agonising minute before she got herself under control again. The gap between her and Vern was already too wide and she sensed Sam treading right on her heels. She bent her head and grimly hauled one foot after the other. In her lethargic state the effort was immense. One step, then one more. One step, endlessly. The slope grew steadily steeper. Patches of rock alternated with deep, unstable snow. At least away from the exposed Col the wind was less fearsome.

Somehow an hour passed. Finch kept thinking, this is only the easy part. The slope would become much steeper. She peered upwards through her goggles, the beam of her torch making a feeble yellow swathe against the black sky. The ridge beetled above her, reducing their figures to tiny, crawling specks. After two hours they had climbed three hundred metres. There was nothing in the world but the dead weight of her limbs, the brutal incline ahead of her and the abyss of space on either side. Her feet had gone numb.

When she first glimpsed the hunched grey shape in the snow ahead and to the left of the line of steps made by the climbers, Finch thought it was a rock. Her torch beam crept towards it and lit up a boot. Yellow plastic and the tattered remnants of a neoprene gaiter.

The dead man was lying on his side and either the wind or his death throes had torn parts of his clothing from his upper body. His back and shoulder were naked, grey, frozen as solid as his terrible surroundings. His head was hidden by a hood, tied in place with rope.

There were other corpses exposed on the mountain, left where they had fallen for the last time, as well as those which were buried under the great pinnacles of ice and snow. Finch knew they were there, had even smiled at mountaineers' macabre jokes about dead meat. But this was the first one they had passed close at hand. The pathos of the sight halted her struggling steps and she was unable even to turn her head away and leave him to the dignity of darkness. She just stood there, watching at the wind tearing at his shreds of clothing, seeing his frozen face in her mind's eye.

Suddenly she knew it must be Spider. Exhaustion and lack of oxygen confused her but lent the confusion a brilliant, hyper-real clarity. This was Al's friend, lying where Al had left him. She couldn't pass by. She had to go and touch him on the shoulder, make certain that he was dead. If he was still alive she must help him. And if he was really dead then she would tell him he wasn't alone, because they were all up here with him.

She moved out of the tracks and immediately stepped into deep snow. She stumbled two more paces, her eyes fixed on Spider. There was someone shouting her name and she turned, intending to wave them away. This was private, her first meeting with Al's friend.

Two people were coming after her, one from above and one from below. A third was waving his arm, pointing her the way back to their tracks. Rix, that was who it was. The two men reached her. In their masks they looked identical but they were Sam and Ken. Somewhere in the back of her mind she knew that much.

Sam took her arm. She pointed backwards,

unintelligibly blurting through her mask, 'He's got no clothes. He needs help.'

The men looked at each other. Ken went round behind her and turned the regulator on her oxygen cylinder to increase the flow. He removed his own mouthpiece. 'He's a German guy, died last year on the way down. Come on. Keep going. You're doing well.'

She let them steer her back on course. One step, another and another. Gradually the extra oxygen seeped through her, pushing back the strange crystal confusion. She was hypoxic. Of course the man lying there wasn't Spider. He was on K2. This wasn't even the same mountain.

Vern was way ahead of her and Al so far above she couldn't even see him. The mountain was so vast. Their presence was utterly meaningless in these desolate wastes. She feared Everest now and she hated it with the last reserves of her energy.

Sam watched her moving up ahead of him. She was slow, but steady enough. The sight of the dead man had plainly disturbed her but she must have been able to put it out of her mind.

Behind Rix, Sandy Jackson was climbing much more erratically. He would put on a surge of speed so that he almost bumped into Rix's backside, then he would stop altogether and lean over his axe as if too spent to take another step. Ken had to keep steadying and encouraging him, and Sandy would shake off his attentions with a gesture of weary impatience. He looked round constantly, straining upwards to see where they had to go and backwards to assess the distance they had covered.

Rix was different again. Ever since they set out he had been moving with robotic determination. He kept his gaze intently fixed on his goal.

Sam was relieved that so far he was experiencing no major difficulties. The bonus of oxygen made him feel a little stronger than he had done below the Col. The slope was relatively gentle as yet, and there was even a certain pleasure in the contemplation of where he was and what he was attempting.

Nepal to the left, Tibet to the right. Above, the south summit and the peak itself. Maybe another eight hours and it would be theirs. *Mine, and Finch's.*

He found himself in a rambling dialogue with his father: *I'm sorry I never did what you wanted. El Capitan and those other big climbs you used to scare me with when I was a kid. I wish I had done. But this beats it all, doesn't it?*

Close to his shoulder Mike gave his ruminative chuckle. *It does. It sure does. You wait till the sun comes up, boy, and you see all those peaks below you painted gold.*

You've never been up here, Dad. How do you know what the dawn will look like?

I know because I've dreamed it. I can't climb but I can still dream.

What else do you dream?

That your boy will do it better than I ever did. They say talent skips a generation, don't they?

Or it could be my daughter, of course.

There was Finch ahead after all, the exemplar, the strongest woman he had ever known.

The chuckle came again. Michael was unreconstructed. Women stayed down in camp, if they came climbing at all.

Sam was jolted out of his reverie by Rix. The man

pushed up alongside him, almost knocking him aside. He jabbed his axe angrily towards Finch.

'What's the matter with her?' he bellowed through his face mask. 'Why's she going so slowly? Do you know the time? I want to get past her.'

'Al gave us the order. She's doing all right.'

'What the fuck do you know?'

Rix was enraged. Nothing was going to impede his path to the top. Ken came up and Sam turned away, leaving the guide to remonstrate with him. The sky was turning grey and the stars were fading.

Finch's feet were completely numb. A textbook picture of the black swellings of frostbite kept coming into her mind and getting mixed up with the image of the dead climber's ice-coloured flesh. There seemed to be no air coming through her mask and the fight for breath became so desperate that she reached up a mittened paw and clawed it away from her face. At once she was gasping, gripped by the fear of suffocation. Somehow she pressed the thing back over her chin and sucked inwards again. She stopped in her tracks and Sam was beside her. Rix came past, not even glancing at them, thrusting his axe shaft into the snow holes and hauling himself upwards.

'Al?' Finch heard herself say.

'He'll be at the south summit. Waiting for you. Come on, Finch.'

The slow torture began once more.

Al was resting with Ted and Vern in the little hollow of snow near where the Sherpas had left the stash of emergency supplies and oxygen. Beside him Pemba and the others were passing a water bottle between them and licking tsampa porridge. It was daylight. The vista of a dozen snow peaks rearing beneath him was gilded by the oblique rays of the rising sun, and the Kangshung glacier far below in Tibet still lay in shadow like a vast brown tapestry. This was the highest point he had ever reached on Everest. Anticipation fluttered inside him and he deflected it, turning his attention to the clients.

It was 6.30 a.m. The two Americans had been climbing pretty strongly, as expected. The rest of the clients were coming up; close at hand he could see Rix, hunched over his axe, iron will in every line of his body. Below him was Finch, a tiny figure in red windproofs. His heart contracted at the sight of her. The kid was right on her heels, and Sandy Jackson and Ken were not far behind that. This was a strong group. Time was going too quickly, but they should still all make it, barring accidents.

Al looked upwards across the vast white sprawl of the Kangshung face, to the jagged line of the north-east ridge. Rix heaved himself the last two or three metres and sank in the snow beside him.

'Time?' he gasped, when he had recovered himself.

'Still okay,' Al reassured him. He didn't like this desperation. He gestured to indicate that Rix should change his oxygen bottle. The empty ones would be left here and collected by himself and the Sherpas on the way down. Mingma and Pemba were already moving upwards, leaving Namje behind with the group, and heading for the upper ridge and the fixed ropes on the Hillary Step. The Step was the last major obstacle before the summit itself. The Sherpas had no sooner started moving than Rix began to stumble after them.

'Wait here,' Al ordered sharply.

Finch blundered a crooked path towards them. A little way from Al she dropped to her knees in the snow, then sank forwards on her hands. He slithered down to her and checked the regulator on her tank. It was knobbed with a lump of frozen dribble. He took off his own mask and removed hers, pressing the good one to her face. She gasped and stared at him with wide, terrified eyes.

'Your O was iced up. You'll be okay now.'

Sam crouched beside them. 'I should have seen that. I should have checked it for her.' He tried to support her with his arms but she wearily pushed him away.

'Let her rest.'

'Drink,' she managed to say. Al unzipped her suit for her, found the flask stowed inside her clothes. She gulped at the warm tea. Sam cleared her regulator and fixed it to a fresh bottle.

Sandy and Ken reached the hollow and squatted to rest, Sandy's head hanging while he panted for air. The guides conferred as the sun forced the lines of shadow back down the distant rocks.

'Let's move,' Al said.

'Yeah, boss,' Ted answered. The rest of them reluctantly stood up and shuffled into line.

No further, Finch thought. Please, no further. But still her limbs obeyed some subconscious imperative buried deep within her cerebral cortex. She took a series of steps that cost her almost all her tiny remaining reserve of strength and clambered up on to the south summit. There was a narrow spine rising away from her, the overhanging cornice of snow so undercut that it looked like a huge wave about to break and send a flurry of spume up into the skies. At the top, in the distance, was a cliff. The Hillary Step. The miniature figures of the South American climbers toiled towards it.

She moved like a robot, with pain in her head and chest. Her numb feet felt as if she were dragging blocks of stone. After a few agonising moments she slowed and then stopped altogether. It would be such a comfort to lie down and rest. Just lie and let everything cease. Someone was leaning over her: mask, goggle eyes. Pulling her cruelly to her feet again.

Looking back, Al saw what was happening. He nodded Namje onwards with the two Americans and turned back. He had to make a detour off the ridge steps because Rix didn't even look at him, let alone make room for him to pass.

'Finch, can you hear me?' She nodded and he tried to see into her eyes. 'You can do this. I know you can. You must just keep going.' Now her padded head moved in the other direction, signifying *no*. 'Yes, you must.'

The kid, Sam, was on the other side of her. 'She's exhausted. Her oxygen's on four litres a minute, it won't last her.'

'There's more.'

Sam breathed hard. 'Fuck you. Listen to her. She doesn't want to.'

'Finch?'

Slowly she raised her head and looked at Al. He cupped her face in his gloved hands. There were dark feathers of hair sticking to her cheeks and he tried to stroke them away. He forgot Sam, and Ken and Jackson leaning over their ice axes.

'I love you,' he said. 'Come with me.'

He couldn't see it, but he was sure that a smile softened her face. She put out her arms and he hoisted her to her feet again.

'Just follow in my steps.'

Sam snatched at his arm, shouting over the wind, 'Don't take her up there.'

They both ignored him. Finch was already following Al's lead. Sam swung round to Ken for support, but the other guide only shrugged. There was no contradicting Al.

'You are a fucking liability, not a guide,' Sam yelled at him. 'Can't you see she's had enough?'

Al hardly turned. 'Get in line.'

The ascent was much steeper and the ridge only a few steps wide. The sun threw their monstrous shadows hundreds of feet out over the abyss. Close at Finch's back, Sam watched her every move instead of glancing to either side of them. Vertigo hadn't troubled him yet but he felt the open mouth of it begin to nibble at him now.

Finch's mind was a jumble of disconnected threads, memories and questions and faces, all distorted by hypoxia. The thinking part of herself, what was left of it, was detached from the protesting body. She was climbing beside someone else, another woman who was partly Suzy with her gappy smile and partly herself, but ancient and wizened, and hunched over with pain.

The minutes passed and the hours. They came to a series of almost vertical rock steps with fixed ropes snaking up the faces. The climbers wearily clipped on and began the slide and hitch of jumaring upwards. Rix's progress was noticeably slowing. Al asked him a question and by way of answer Rix just pointed on upwards. Finch hadn't lifted her head from the rock and ice in front of her. She seemed to move by the effort of will alone. When Sam put his arm to her shoulder she started in fright.

'Finch? Talk to me. Do you want to go back down?'

The sound that came from her mask was a sigh.

It was nearly 11 a.m. when they reached the towering rock Step. On Al's instructions, Vern and Ted were waiting at the foot of it with the two Sherpas. They had been there some time and were chafing with impatience. The Argentinian party had already clawed their way up the fixed lines.

'That's good, really good. We won't have to hang about,' Al said. He kept his fears about their slow progress to himself.

Pemba led the climb, followed by Ted and Vern.

When Rix's turn came he forgot his safety tether. Al had to pull him forcibly back down again and clip him safely. 'Watch yourself,' he warned.

Rix's progress up the fifty-foot cliff was agonisingly slow. He would make one upward shift, then hang inert in his harness for half a minute. Pemba watched anxiously from the ledge at the top.

Finch huddled in a heap at the bottom. For a moment, everyone's attention was on Rix. Like a drowsy eye opening, a window of reason cleared in her mind. She was confused from lack of oxygen, that was all. No head or chest pain, or none significant. Nothing more serious internally. But she knew for certain she could go no further, she could not climb the Step.

Her mittened fist thumped her boot. The full dimension of the catastrophe belatedly dawned on her. There was no sensation, nothing, it was frozen. She must be in the early stages of frostbite, at the very best. The worst was unthinkable up here. If she tried to go any further she would die.

Shock briefly galvanised her. She took off her oxygen mask.

'I can't,' she said aloud. '*I can't*.'

It was the first time she had said it. Was this the first time in her *life* she had said it? At once she felt weak and relieved, and touched with elation. I can't, I can't. I can't. Nothing happened. The skies did not crack open. She heard herself beginning to laugh. At once people leaned over her. There was Mingma's mouth close to her face, asking a question. Sam took her foot and rested it on his lap, examining the gaiter fastening. Al held her by the shoulders.

'I can't,' she repeated to him and now she was crying instead of laughing.

They were looking at her foot.

'Why didn't you tell me?' Al shouted, unbuckling her crampon and gaiter. 'Your boot is frozen. It must have got wet.'

'Yesterday,' she admitted.

They were kneeling on either side of her, Al and Sam. Their faces swam, changing shape. They became Caleb and Marcus, playing some game that involved teasing her, hiding something that belonged to her.

'Give me the mouse,' she begged. Why were they staring at her like this?

There was a secret, they were looking at each other now, signalling.

Then Al became Al again when he held her face between his hands. 'Finch, listen to me. You have to go straight down. Mingma will take you back to the Col. I will see you there.'

He was unstrapping his pack, taking out a plastic toothbrush container with a syringe inside it. They made her turn over in the snow and she lay unprotesting, feeling warmer now, even sleepy. They pulled at her clothes and she felt the tiny stab of the needle in her hip.

'It's dex, Finch.'

Dexamethasone, for oedema. Foot frozen, brain fluid. Ha. Doctor, doctor.

Al's mind raced. Jesus, Christ Jesus, how could he have let this happen? She had frostbite, she was confused. An hour ago she had seemed so strong. Had she? Or had he just wanted her to be? He had wanted to give her the summit. To share it with her because he loved her and it was the best he could give her, and instead he had dragged her into grave danger.

Was it going to be the same all over again? The weight of a body in his arms. Don't die, don't die, when he knew it was already too late. Spider.

No time for thinking that now. Let it not be too late this time. Undo the mistake, get her on her feet and lose some height.

'Stand up. Mingma, get her on the rope.'

Between them they hauled her to her feet and roped her to the Sherpa.

'I'm going with her,' Sam said. He took one look at the scar of rock towering over them and turned his back on it.

'No need, I will look after,' Mingma said. 'You climb.'

He had worked on Everest for years but he had never been all the way to the summit. An ascent would add to his reputation and increase the wages he could command in the future, but he was making no complaint about being sent down with a client.

'No,' Sam insisted.

Finch seemed to collect herself. 'I don't want you to. Go on up.'

'I'm coming with you.'

Al hesitated, trying to make a rapid decision. He was angry with himself, poundingly enraged and horrified that he had let Finch – *Finch*, of all the clients – get this far, this high, with frozen feet. But with the self-control of long practice he coldly blotted out his anger and love in order to think more clearly.

He wanted more than anything to go down with Finch himself, it was no wonder Sam did too. There was no question of Al abandoning the rest of the group, but reason and experience told him there was no need for Sam to go either. The boy loved Finch and would sacrifice anything for her, even his chance of the summit. That was good, Al was glad of it. But he knew better than Sam did himself how important it was for him to climb this mountain.

He could do it, easily. It would be a matter of just a few more hours. Mingma was the best there was and

Finch would be down at Four when the boy and all the rest of them got back from the top. However bad Finch's feet were, whatever his own responsibility was for that, to let Sam give up his chance of the summit would make no effective difference to her chances.

Putting all the authority he could muster into his voice Al said, 'You'll stay with the group. You've got a job to do.'

Rix had reached the top of the cliff at last. Pemba hauled him off the rope and gestured down for the next climber to clip on and start the ascent. Sandy and Ken sat to one side, drinking from their flasks and waiting for the problem to be resolved. The morning sun was strong, warming all their heads in spite of the wind.

'Get going,' Al snapped at Sam. They stared at each other for a long moment. The promises Sam had made were now at odds. To do what he was told for the good of the expedition, to look after Finch whatever came.

'Don't make me have to insist,' Al said. He had made the decision, now, and the quieter he became, the more he insisted. But there was another lengthy pause before Sam capitulated.

At last he put one clumsy hand on Finch's shoulder. 'Take care.' In this place the warning was pathetic but she nodded her head obediently. Then he wrenched himself away and tramped to the dangling end of the line. He kicked in the front points of his crampons and began to climb.

'Go on,' Al said quietly to Mingma and Finch. And he added to Finch alone, 'Mingma will take care of you until I get back to the Col. I will be back soon.

And then . . .' Her wide, frightened eyes locked on his, as if she wanted to suck the confidence and reassurance out of him. And then, he thought. But he didn't finish the sentence. The promise slid away from him, like a fish into deep water.

The argument had tired them all. Mingma and Finch obediently began to shuffle away from him, linked by the blood-red rope. Al stood completely still and watched but Finch suddenly stopped and turned round. The rope went tight, restraining her like a dog on a leash so she stretched one imploring hand back up to him. He stumbled down to her and held her fingers and tried to kiss her but her face was insulated by the oxygen mask.

'You must go down, look after your feet. I have to take the others to the top. Wait just a few more hours for me. Then we'll never have to be apart again. I promise you.'

There, there was the promise. Surfacing again like a fish rising. He couldn't even see whether she was crying or smiling. Her eyes were opaque now, unreadable behind her goggles and she was slipping away from him, and he longed to go with her instead of taking these other people higher and further up the implacable mountain.

Mingma gently pulled on the rope. Finch visibly wavered and at last she just touched her mittened hand to Al's face. She took one slow step away from him, then another. He stood watching until her head descended out of his sight below a convex curve of the ridge.

Al climbed back up to the remainder of the group. No one had even looked back down to the little scene with Finch. None of them had attention to spare for anyone but themselves. Up here, it was everyone for himself. Survive or die.

Sam was nearing the top of the Step. 'You next,' Al said curtly to Sandy.

'He's pretty knackered as well,' Ken muttered, once the Australian had awkwardly manoeuvred himself on to the line. 'Like me. We are getting too old for this game, mate.'

Al looked up to check on Sandy's progress and back to the point where he had lost sight of Finch. 'This'll be the last one for me. I told Molly it would be.'

He reached into the warm inside of his windproof for the walkie-talkie to call George and report that Finch had turned round.

At the top of the Hillary Step there was no sign of the rest of the group. It was past midday and Pemba had led the Americans and Rix on towards the summit.

'Let's get going,' Al said. 'Jackson, come in behind me.'

Sam began counting. Ten steps, tottering with exhaustion, and then a rest. Ten more steps and a series of gasping breaths.

The ridge was like the rough spine of some huge white creature, rising out of the depths of a limitless sea. It curved upwards, away from him, into blue infinity. Looking down, Sam saw a few white puffs of cloud rising from the Khumbu. Down there, tiny shavings of colour dotted on the glacier, were the tents of Base Camp. Perhaps George was out watching their progress through binoculars, as he and the others had watched climbers from earlier expeditions.

The last ridge had seemed so high, so far off, and now he was climbing it. A worm of excitement twisted inside Sam. He hadn't gone down with Finch, it was too late to regret that now and he was left with a strange debt to Al for insisting that he continue.

Ten steps, kicking with his crampons and hauling on the shaft of his ice axe. Rest and then ten more.

Rix was ahead of them. He had stopped moving. His companions, Ted and Vern with Pemba, were still going steadily for the summit.

'Tired,' he muttered when the others reached him. 'Rest a bit.'

'Come on,' Sandy said. He was moving on auto-pilot, his eyes fixed ahead.

'You go on with Ken and Namje,' Al ordered him.

Al checked and found that Rix's second bottle of oxygen was already finished because the man had turned the flow up to maximum. His own second was in his pack untouched, so he changed them over and left the empty one standing in the snow. He would have to summit and get back down to the cache at Camp Five on what was left in his first.

'It's one thirty,' he warned Rix. He was moving so slowly that he stood no chance of reaching the top before turn-around time.

'Fuck the time,' Rix snarled. 'I'm this far and I'm going on.'

'You have another thirty minutes,' Al said and led on. There were climbers descending towards them, the successful Argentinian group. There was a brief exchange of congratulations and encouragement as they passed by.

At 1.50 p.m. Pemba and the two Americans stepped up on to the summit. They looked at the spread-out jagged silver and blue and sepia infinity and then at each other, touched by awe.

'We did it!' Ted shouted. They clapped hands and reached for their cameras.

Pemba crouched down and reverently touched the tips of his fingers to the crown of the world. He closed his eyes in a prayer.

Ten minutes later they were on their way down again. There was a thicker mat of cloud in the Khumbu valley now. At 2.20 they met Ken and Sandy. Sandy Jackson was on a rope and it looked as if Ken was towing him upwards.

'Time late, Ken,' Pemba warned.

'Al's still climbing too.' Ken shrugged.

'We gotta make it,' Sandy mumbled. He was shaking his head from side to side. 'Can't get this close and give up.'

Further down the ridge Namje and Sam waited, while Al and Rix disputed. The wind was rising and they had to shout to make themselves heard.

'It's one hundred fucking metres. That's all. You piss off. I'll go alone.' Rix was raving, taking great gasps between breaths. He pulled himself away from the guide and began stumbling up the slope, weaving too close to the edge of the cornice. One more careless step and the crust would break and send him pitching thousands of feet down the Kangshung face.

'Get back,' Al howled as he plunged after him.

They swayed in a clumsy embrace, inches from oblivion.

'Bad place,' Namje murmured, grey in the face. 'Very bad.'

Sam was rooted in helpless terror. They watched as the two men retraced three and then five steps, back into the line of bootprints. Rix had hauled himself free and was climbing again, face turned blindly up towards his goal.

Al had his hand up to his mask. When Sam reached him he gestured tiredly. 'He's right out of it. I can't stop him so I'll have to follow.'

'I'm coming too,' Sam said. There was no time or space for contradictions now.

'Namje?'

Like Mingma, the young man had been subdued ever since the icefall avalanche had almost claimed Ang.

'I wait here.' He hunkered down in the lee of a rock.

They began the last ascent without him, Sam kept close behind Al, moving in the same rhythm, as if they were part of the same organism. Al was on Rix's heels and each step was slower than the last. Pemba and his group came down to them. The Americans were flushed with triumph and their elation only emphasised the grimness of the climbers still trailing upwards.

'I know, I know.' Al brushed aside Pemba's remonstrances.

Ken and Sandy Jackson reached the top at 2.45. Sandy was so exhausted that he seemed hardly to know where he was. Ken extricated his camera from the inner pocket of his suit for him and took the victory picture. By this time it was 3 p.m. Ken could see Al and the others toiling towards them. At worst, they were twenty minutes off.

In the event, it was 3.30 and Rix was more dead than alive when they finally made it. Ken and Sandy had already abandoned the summit and begun the climb down.

'Two minutes on the top and then we're out of here too,' Al promised the other guide as they passed by.

The sun was drifting downwards through a green veil on the western horizon and the east face of Pumori was slate-grey. Overhead the sky was still blue, deep-tinged with purple, and the rising wind whipped up a spray of spindrift that glittered with points of iridescent light. In every direction a thousand peaks lay below them, tongued with the tiny streams of huge glaciers. The Tibetan plateau stretched away, a brown desert, to the lavender-grey horizon.

The three men stood and gazed in silence. The summit itself was big enough for the three of them to stand, close together. A tattered little string of prayer flags that someone had anchored there snapped in the wind.

'Oh, God, thank you,' Rix whispered. All the big man's grit and rage had melted away and he was openly weeping. The wind blew tiny sparkling droplets of tears and mucus away into space.

The summit of the world. Sam turned and Al put his arm around him. They stood for a moment half supporting one another. Their exchange was mutual and fluent. It rubbed out the disparate years and experiences, and acknowledged the bond that transcended them. It required no words. In that moment of epiphany, all the pain and effort the climb had cost them were forgotten. They had done this thing together. It would always connect them.

The sky's blue was fading fast into eerie green. It was late.

Two hours ago he might have allowed them all to linger, even indulge his own triumph, but now Al collected himself and gestured to his companions to take out their cameras quickly. He had meant to extract the picture of Molly from his inner pocket and show the summit to her, but there was no time left for that. He photographed the other two, posing as conquerors, and submitted in his turn. The rising wind was troubling him. Time, time to start the descent. At last they were ready. Al stabbed his finger towards the snake of the ridge. Down, down. A warning blur began to smudge the sharp edges of his awareness. The oxygen in his cylinder was running out. Five. Down to Camp Five.

Sam still lingered. He turned in a circle, taking in the panorama and storing it in his mind. The light had turned luminous. It seemed to shimmer with electricity.

'Michael and Mary McGrath,' he said softly but the wind and the spindrift tore the words from his mouth and obliterated them. He repeated their names, yelling them this time into the booming air. Triumph edged exhaustion out of his consciousness. He felt free of earthly bonds.

Al was twenty steps down the ridge, beckoning sharply. Sam stayed for five seconds more, then reluctantly kicked his way forward and began the descent.

Finch crossed the icy waste of the Col in Mingma's wake. The climb down had almost finished her. She was clumsy on her numb feet but the Sherpa had guided her every step as she blundered her slow way down the ridge and slid down the fixed ropes. Without his help she would have fallen a dozen times. Now the tents were only a few yards away, visible through the whirl of spindrift. The wind was rising ominously, and cloud funnelled upwards and spilled over the lip of the Col.

Ten more steps and she was at the tent, with Mingma kneeling to open the entrance. She fell to all fours and crawled inside, collapsing at once on her sleeping bag. Knowing that she was alone and that Al and Sam and the others still had to make the fearful descent, she offered up a wordless prayer, to God or to the cruel mountain itself, *please*, before drifting into a stupor of exhaustion.

She did not know how much later it was that Mingma came back with hot tea and made her sit up to drink it. The wind had gathered the same shrieking force as the night before and although they were close at hand, she could only just hear the clamour of shouts from the South American tents. They sounded more warning than celebration.

'Are they back?'

The descent down to the Col, the rest and the fluid had cleared her mind. Her confusion was replaced by sharp fear, darkening the simple relief at her own survival this far. Al. Where was Al?

'Not yet,' Mingma said without emphasis. 'Wind strong again. We take a look at your feet now.'

It was a tricky job to pull away the outer and inner boots and to tease the icy socks away from the skin. The left foot was revealed as yellowish and leathery, only superficially frostbitten. But the right one was as hard and solid as a piece of white meat just removed from the freezer.

'Bad.' Mingma whistled.

Finch was recovering enough of her faculties to attempt a medical assessment of her injuries. She made herself calculate the extent of the damage with careful detachment. She thought that the left foot would recover, slowly, once thawed but only time would tell about the other. In any case she knew that there was nothing to be done up here. Even if they had been able to produce enough hot water to immerse the feet, it was impossible to walk at all on tender, swollen, unfrozen tissue. She would have to descend to Base, somehow, as quickly as possible and treat the condition there. She wrapped the grotesque extremities in her sleeping bag to hide them. There were more urgent questions.

'What can we do to help Al?'

Mingma lowered his eyes. His broad face was expressionless. 'Only wait.'

Al and Sam descended with Rix close between them. After the climb and the summit all the will-power had oozed out of him. He seemed smaller, flabbier. They passed the spot where they had left Namje waiting, but he was gone. Al's oxygen was finished. He could only make himself concentrate by a major effort of will. Namje would have joined Pemba, or Ken and Sandy Jackson. There was a line of prints leading down the ridge but the wind was so strong now and the coils of spindrift so dense that they were becoming difficult to follow. The smallest detour would be fatal. Watch, watch for the cornice overhang.

He began to think of the two women. Finch and Molly. Jen and Finch. Voices. *Don't go. Come back.*

But he had done it, he was on the way down. The last time, the biggest one. He was happy to give up now. Why had he ever thought that he couldn't give up, exchange this pain and struggle for ease and warm places?

A window seemed to be closing in his mind. He looked back at Rix and Sam, then blinked and shook his head. His vision still refused to clear. Oxygen. His system cried out for it. Get to the south summit, to the high camp. Shelter there.

Wait, something in the snow here. Orange, an O bottle. A gift, a miracle. Let me breathe.

He was on his knees, wresting off his old cylinder, when he remembered. This was Rix's empty one they had left on the way up. He took it up and stuck it in a loop on his harness.

The other two were at his back. 'Bushed,' Rix muttered. Sam looked dazed too. They were all exhausted. Bad, this was going bad and he must look out for all of them.

They came to the Hillary Step. Al squeezed a knot of concentration in the forefront of his mind and watched them in turn as they clipped in and slid down. Now his turn. Spider's old carabiner clinking on his harness.

They grouped at the bottom of the rock face. Rix was stumbling and gasping.

'Keep going, stay tight,' Al ordered. 'Sam?'

'Okay,' he mumbled.

More steps, down and down, following the blurring line of prints. Fresh snow in the spindrift now.

Finch heard them arriving, voices and metallic clattering in a second's lull in the wind. With her heart thudding she shuffled on her knees to the tent flap. It was Pemba with Ted and Vern. The Americans were half out of their heads with elation and relief.

'Hey, we made it. Just about. Wow. It sure was something up there.'

'Jesus. Tough, tough luck, Finch.'

She looked straight into Pemba's eyes. They were wide and black, and full of foreboding.

'We pass them, yes. Still climbing. Maybe half past two, three o'clock.'

Still climbing, so late. With this renewed storm coming up on them.

Please.

They seemed to have been stooping and threading their precarious way for endless hours. The light was almost gone and the wind drove the snow horizontally into their frozen faces.

Reach the south summit and the hollow below it. Oxygen and food, even emergency shelter.

The next time Al looked round, Rix had stopped yet again. He was sitting down in the snow, beyond even speaking. Sam rested a foot away, silently shrinking from the wind. Al uncoiled the rope from around his shoulders and tied the end into Rix's harness. He hauled him to his feet and began to tow him onwards like a dog on a lead.

It was *impossible*, surely, even in his hypoxic state, that they hadn't reached the south summit yet?

Wait. There was the sound of whistle blasts. And someone looming out of the grey wall. A Mountain People uniform parka. It was Namje, but the whistling was coming from somewhere else.

'Boss. Sandy,' Namje managed to say.

'Where is he?'

'Lost. He just lost. One minute, in front. Then, gone.'

The whistling was Ken. A minute later the guide stumbled back along the line of steps.

'Al. Thank God, mate. Jackson's disappeared. The vis. went right down, I turned round to go back for him and there was no one but Namje. I've done a right-angle search of the tracks, there's nothing. He can't have overtaken me.'

Rix collapsed again, almost pulling Al over at the end of the rope. Al untied the inert bundle while his mind tried to work out what to do.

'Ken, you take Rix down on the short rope. Sam, go with Namje.'

'No.'

There was nothing left in any of them now. Al shrugged. He took Spider's carabiner off his harness and began to bang the empty bottle with it. Sam held out his hand to Ken who put the whistle into it. He lifted it to his lips, pushing aside the mask, and blew a thin blast.

'Help Ken,' Al said to Namje. Ken and Namje shuffled on down with Rix between them and left Sam and Al together, banging and whistling their signals into the exploding air.

They continued the search for Sandy Jackson, although feebly. Lack of oxygen, exhaustion and dehydration robbed them of reason and urgency. Their steps tended downwards, although they were not aware of it. At last they saw something.

Ahead of them was a faint line of prints, blurred by fresh snow, wavering leftwards and down. They followed them, until Al suddenly flung himself backwards. Just visible a metre from his boots was a jagged hole and the line of the cornice smooth on either side of it. The prints led straight to the hole and through it they could see nothing but space.

Sandy had wandered away from the tracks, fallen through the cornice and plunged straight down the Kangshung face.

He was certainly dead.

Sam grabbed Al's shoulder and hauled him away from the overhang. When they had crawled and clawed their way from the immediate danger they knelt in the snow together, gasping and retching with shock and exertion. At last, Al raised his head. He knelt upright and looked down at his empty hands. He had lost Spider's carabiner and Sandy Jackson was gone.

What now? What could he do now, except try to keep the flicker of will to survive himself?

But there was someone else with him. That's right, Sam was here.

They were alone on the mountain. That was right,

too, in some way he couldn't piece together. They belonged together. They were halves of a whole. It was getting dark. He was dully aware that he didn't know where they were.

How far down had they come? How much further, to reach the Col and Finch?

There were more voices and the sound of more people coming into camp. Finch heard them through her stupor of exhaustion and crawled to the tent door again, crippled by her frozen feet. She saw Rix, being half dragged through the snow by Ken and Namje. Pemba and Mingma had run out to meet them. She called weakly to Mingma once Rix had been hauled into his tent and the Sherpa came back and knelt beside her. 'I don't know, madam. I will send Ken.'

At last Ken came. He kept his head bent so she couldn't see his eyes. 'How's the feet, doc?'

She pushed his arm aside, knowing that he was stalling her. Pulses of fear throbbed in her head. 'Where is he?'

'They made the summit, but very late. After Jackson and me.' Of course, the thought just slid through her head. Sam was out too. 'They had Rix with them and he wasn't up to it but he insisted on going on. Then they caught up with us on the way down.'

Finch waited, her eyes on what she could see of the guide's face. If they had caught up, where were they now?

'It was Jackson. I turned round to check on him and he'd gone.'

She listened as he explained. The wind was louder

and louder but every word was too clear. Al and Sam were still up there, searching for Sandy. And here was Sandy's sleeping bag in a heap next to her, his bundle of spare clothing, damp socks. At last, Ken did meet her eyes. For a brief second. 'No worries. Al will get them all down.'

Finch nodded. 'Yes.'

'They just have to get back up a few metres to Camp Five. They weren't so far below it. They can shelter there, if they have to.'

She lay down again, suspended between the day that had passed and whatever would come. Fragments of fear and hope filled her mind, tiny random magnetic impulses that clung together and then spun apart again. She was too exhausted for proper thought.

Al and Sam crept on through the wind. The light had almost gone, both of them were out of oxygen.

This is the worst, Al's reasoning mind told him. The wind and snow had obliterated all the old tracks. We're lost. Weather deteriorating. Dark coming. Find Camp Five, and the oxygen and food and bivouac. At the same time another fraying strand of awareness warned him, too far. You've come down too far and the high camp's above you.

He halted his stumbling steps and Sam bumped against him. Stay together. Nothing to be done for Jackson now, all they could hope for was to stay alive themselves. They stood head to head, hunched against the wind, disorientation lapping them. A couple of feet away, protruding from a mantle of snow and ice, was a big rock like a pair of shoulders.

Al remembered it now. It was way below the emergency cache at Camp Five, too far to think of climbing up again even if they could find their way.

'Have to dig in here for a few hours,' he told Sam. And Sam nodded, a single lethargic dip of his head. They knelt together, as if in prayer, and began to scoop snow from the lee of the rock. It took a huge effort to create a tiny hollow. Al fought to open his pack and dragged out a folded nylon fabric emergency shelter. He tried to spread it so they could crawl inside but the gale made a snatch at it. It was torn from his grasp and they had a brief glimpse of an ungainly blue wing, flapping away into nowhere.

In the end they lay down in the sketchy shelter of the snow hollow. They pressed their bodies close together and the wind filled their heads, while the cold locked their limbs into a stiff embrace. It was completely dark now.

'Stay awake,' Al commanded. 'Talk.' Their faces, mouths, were almost touching. Close to a kiss.

In a slurred voice, Sam did as he was told. Michael, Yosemite, Wilding. Running, Mary, Fran, Seattle. Dreams, disappointment. A tired, disconnected litany.

'Now you,' Sam prompted sleepily.

'It's over,' Al said.

Sam smelled the faint warmth of his breath. He waited, but there did not seem to be any more.

'No. We'll get down. Just have to stay here, stay awake.'

There was the sigh of his exhalation again. 'You will.'

'You have Finch,' Sam said urgently. 'You can marry her. Have children together.' Instead of the snow and the blackness that whirled into his eyes he could see it all. A vivid picture. Three little children, Finch's feathers of dark hair. A yard and a sugar maple tree in spring leaf. He could smell the rich scents of earth, grass, blossom.

The world was all there, waiting. He could get it back again. Walk down out of the ice and wind. Back into his life. It was precious, whatever he was going to find.

'Finch,' Al said, so quietly that Sam thought it was just another breath.

They clung together for an hour, then another hour. The wind was like a third person, their companion.

Al thought of the mistakes he had made. The other kid dead, Sandy. Finch with frostbitten feet, urged on too high. The others on the mountain, too late. Then he let it go, all of it, and let fall the ends of his life that he had never been able to knit together. The broken circles, staying broken now. It was Molly he saw behind his frozen eyelids. The girl she had been when he left, a young woman, curled up in his bed the last night at Tyn-y-Caeau. Black hair spread on the white pillow, warm skin.

He felt warmer himself.

It wasn't good to feel warm, not here. Not sleepy like this, great feathery billows of sleep rolling over him.

No matter. But Sam, he mattered. Finch and Sam. Of course.

Al pushed back the tide of sleep and made an

effort to shift his heavy body. He rolled himself on top of Sam and curved his back and arms around him.

At Base Camp, George Heywood sat at the mess table with his head in his hands, waiting. Ken had radioed the news down to him from the Col. Sandy Jackson missing, Al and Sam McGrath out on the mountain. No radio contact made or received.

They would have to wait for first light. Try to reach them then.

In the darkness Finch woke from a dream and sat bolt upright in her sleeping bag.

The tent was empty, there were only Sandy Jackson's belongings heaped beside her. The camp was silent. The others were all lying in their tents, beaten by exhaustion and the storm. Beaten by the mountain itself, which they had tried to subdue.

She felt with absolute certainty that Al was dead.

The sky was white, the colour of ice, the colour of cold itself. Sam's eyelashes were heavy, crusted with rime, but he had forced his eyes to open and he knew it was the real sky above him. There was a weight on top of him, pinning him down. He turned his head and heard the rustle of ice-stiffened windproofs. There were arms across his shoulders, the weight was a man's body. Al's face was close. His beard was frozen, his cheeks and eyes and hair were all frozen and there was a blanket of snow like a bedsheet or a winding sheet folded over his shoulders.

Slowly, effortfully, Sam's oxygen-depleted mind

tried to marshal the realities out of the snippets of dream and delirium.

Dawn had come. They had lain out in the snow all night. The man protecting him was dead.

Move. A stab of urgency needled his dull brain. Move, while you are able.

Al's body was stiff. He was heavy, hard, like a log of wood. Sam slid and crawled from underneath him. The wind had eased again. The ridge curved away and down, cruel with ice, but visible. Get down. Nobody else here. He would have to summon everything he had and get himself down to the Col, because there was no other way to survive.

A terrible, hard determination to live took hold of Sam.

He knelt over the other man and pulled his neck zipper open. His fingers were too numb, he leaned down instead and searched with his mouth for the carotid pulse. Nothing. The skin was frozen. It was as if the warmth had flowed out of Al and into him.

Don't think. Unzip further. Find the radio. Call up and ask them to come to meet him. Warm drink, oxygen.

The radio was in the inner pocket of the down jacket. Sam extracted it, then realised his hands were too frozen to operate the buttons. He dropped it and it slithered away from him, gathering speed on the ice. Why did they not use it last night? They had been too tired and confused. And who could have come to their rescue, up here in the storm?

Something else here. A shiny fragment. He was

turning away when he saw that it was a photograph. He balled it up in one frozen hand, creasing it, and stuffed it into his pocket.

Now move. He staggered to his feet and without a backward glance began a lumbering walk. Down, down, away from here.

From Base Camp George spoke urgently to Ken. 'Can you go back up? Take Pemba, tea and some food. They'll be up at Five, waiting it out.'

Ken lifted his head. He didn't believe he had the strength to make the climb again. The three Sherpas sat in a line, waiting and watching him. The clients were still in their tents. Finch Buchanan was the biggest worry. She would have to be got down somehow and flown out to hospital.

'I can't raise them and neither can you, George. What do you think?'

The answer crackled out of the handset: 'I think we've got to do every last thing.'

'Yeah.'

'Ask Dos Santos if he's got anyone.'

'Yeah.'

The Argentinians had already been across to offer assistance. They could help Finch and Rix in their descent.

'Pémba and I'll be on our way in a few minutes.'

'Good luck. Ken?'

'Yeah.'

'Thanks. Out.'

The guide and the Sherpa loaded their packs with food and warm drinks, and the last two cylinders of oxygen, and made the slow traverse of the Col to the rising ridge. Finch rested on her knees in the isolation of her tent.

'He's dead,' she said aloud, to nobody.

Michael McGrath was sitting in his armchair in the kitchen of the house in Wilding. A pot of coffee had gone cold on the table and the remains of an almost untouched meal congealed on a plate. The light outside was softening towards twilight and Michael had been watching it without seeing anything since before noon. There was a heavy silence in the house. He had not switched on the television, or the radio tuned to the country music station.

When it was almost dark outside, with the sun down behind the big trees that backed the house, he shuffled to his feet. Leaning heavily on his stick he made his way to the telephone. There was a notepad beside it with some pencilled numbers. Sam had read them off to him and he had absently written them down, knowing that he would never dial some number in Nepal, to speak to people in camp at the foot of Everest.

But all day, foreboding had been gathering in the pit of his stomach like nausea. The old instincts, the climber's superstitions and sixth senses, had woken up in him again and now they crawled through the labyrinths of his imagination. He had to talk to Sam, now. To give him advice. To encourage him and warn him to watch his step.

The satellite phone buzzed in the communications tent and George Heywood picked it up with a heavy hand.

Michael stood looking out of the window in the

dusty hallway. The lights of a car came down the road from town, soft yellow in the thickening dusk, and slowly swept past the house.

'Your son reached the summit late yesterday afternoon,' the man said.

George Heywood, his name was – Michael dimly remembered him from years back. Surely he had been an earnest and careful young man, eager but not intuitive on the rock?

How the memories burrowed away and then wormed their way to the surface again.

'I'm afraid he hasn't returned to the Col yet. We have every hope that he has spent the night at a high camp, with the lead guide. As soon as we hear any more news from the group up there I'll call you, Mike.'

Michael slowly replaced the receiver. His fingers closed over the head of his stick, but he stood still.

Come down, son. It's important. Don't go now, not yet, before I have had a chance to tell you what you mean to me.

He has climbed Everest. Sam went out there and climbed the fucker. He must not die in the doing.

'I'm not going,' Finch cried.

The big Argentinian shrugged his shoulders in frustration. He had come to help down the American doctor with frostbite and now she wouldn't move. 'You must. You risk your feet. Maybe yourself altogether.' He made a chopping motion horizontally across his windpipe.

Tears ran unimpeded down her face, salt stinging

the cracks in her cheeks and mouth. 'I can't go without him. Not until I know where he is.'

Mingma and the climber glanced at each other, furtive, acknowledging the woman's raw grief but lacking the courage to confront it.

'We leave now,' the man said. He was uncomfortable, but his own needs were at the front of his mind.

Finch put her hands on his arms, then feebly shoved him away. 'Go. I won't change my mind.'

He nodded his head and backed off. Mingma resumed his crouched position beside her. Ted, Vern and Rix had shrugged their belongings together. They were waiting in a silent huddle, speechless, all the noise and bravado leaked out of them. It was time to start descending. They were all too exhausted to spend any more hours in this punitive place.

With his head hanging, Sam plunged and stumbled like a drunkard. Sometimes he gave up and slithered on his back down the icy slope, skidding until some instinct made him stab with the pick of his ice axe to arrest the slide.

He didn't think or remember. All that remained of his conscious self was a node of determination. Get down, keep moving. Save yourself. Stay alive.

He passed the corpse. The other dead man.

Not me. I am not going to die.

The light was getting stronger.

In the far distance, way below on the ridge, he saw two tiny figures. He couldn't tell if they were moving, they were just dots in the cruel landscape. He thought they were himself and Al.

They can't be. Al's dead. Save yourself. Move, fuck you. *Move*.

The figures grew bigger.

'Look,' Ken said, pointing upwards. A climber was coming down the slope.

'He is ours, I think,' Pemba said.

'Only one.'

They tried to move faster towards him.

Sam came close enough to recognise the Mountain People uniform parkas. His legs were failing him. He tripped and fell forwards, snow filling his mouth and eyes. It was the hardest thing he had ever done to lift his head once more instead of lying where he fell.

An arm came under his shoulder and supported him. Another lifted his body, pulling back his hood. His face was covered in snow, his beard iced and goggles obscured his eyes.

'It's Sam,' a voice said.

Mingma knelt, unscrewed a flask and put the hot drink into Sam's hand but he was too numb to hold it. Liquid cascaded over his legs. Mingma caught the flask again and held it this time for him to drink. Warmth filled his mouth and he swallowed a luxurious gulp.

'Sam, can you hear me?' Ken Kennedy, his pale face grey as the ice. A nod, to signify yes.

'Where are Al and Sandy?'

Try to find a voice. No more than a croak, but he said it. 'Dead.'

In the silence he drank another mouthful of tea.

They prepared a fresh oxygen cylinder for him

and helped him to put it on. He breathed deeply and the life-giving gas flowed into his system.

'Are you ready to go on down?'

Another nod and he was on his feet, moving painfully between them.

Finch watched them approach across the Col. Sam's slow steps tended straight towards her and he sank down at the open flap of her tent. 'He's dead.'

Her eyes were dry and hard now. 'I know.'

There were helpful hands trying to move them both, but they ignored them.

Sam's mouth worked, an awkward shape forming around a dam of frozen words. 'He saved me.'

Finch looked into his eyes and measured what she saw there. Then she inclined her head so that her forehead briefly rested on his shoulder.

Ken radioed the news down to George Heywood. The imperative was to get the survivors down as quickly as possible. The weighing up would come later, with the insights that their situation was too precarious to permit now. They spoke briefly and then he came back to the stricken group to give directions.

'We make our way down to the cwm immediately. Andrea Dos Santos's people will wait at Camp Three to assist. We'll stop briefly at Camp One and make our way down the icefall at first light in the morning. George will have the chopper up to Base to evacuate Finch and Sam as soon as they are down.'

He looked at the blank faces. 'We need to help each other.'

Rix was the one who answered. 'We can do it. Al showed us that much and we have to do it once more now.'

They formed themselves into a silent line. With Pemba in the lead and Mingma and Namje supporting Sam and Finch they began to move. Rix, Ted and Vern plodded with them, and Ken brought up the rear of what was left of the Mountain People's expedition.

The telephone rang again in Wilding, Oregon. Michael took long minutes to reach it, but the caller let it ring.

'He's alive and up at the Col, Mike. They are bringing him down now.'

'And?'

'He was out all night. Hypothermia, frostbite. I don't know yet how bad. But he made most of the descent unaided. He is very strong. Two other people didn't make it.'

'I'm sorry,' Michael said.

After he had rung off he stood still, looking expressionlessly at the rough grass where Mary's garden had once been and the empty road. An old man with a tough face and a crippled body, shifting around inside himself the unwieldy awareness of how much he loved his only child and wondering why he had never had the ability to tell him so.

Angus Buchanan sat in his black leather chair in his office in a bronze glass tower in Vancouver. He took the urgent call that his secretary put through to him and listened to the news.

'As soon as we can get her down here to Base Camp, there'll be a helicopter waiting to fly her on to hospital in Kathmandu,' George concluded.

'No.'

Angus thought quickly. He was a man used to making executive decisions, surrounded by expanses of ash-blond wood, inlay and veneer and polish. Finch might not know it, but she was his favourite child, his adored and admired only daughter, and if necessary he would move the entire world to get her home a single minute sooner. 'I want her flown out of there at once. Hong Kong and on to Vancouver. It will add another twenty hours, maximum. I will arrange it with the airlines.'

'Of course,' George said.

At first light the next morning, after a black respite at Camp One, they left the huddle of tents and began the last descent of the icefall. Finch had to be lowered most of the way. The tissues of her feet were beginning to thaw and the pain made her clench her teeth against the need to scream. With the loss of height and the intake of food and fluids, Sam was stronger. He made his own way, locked into silence. As they reached the flat of the glacier they heard the faint buzz of the helicopter labouring its way up the Khumbu.

Finch was helped to the medical tent. They passed by Al's closed-up tent and she turned her head, just briefly. Adam Vries was standing to one side of it, his sunny face dark with shock. On the stone *puja* altar the twigs of the juniper were still smouldering.

In the tent she gave herself a shot of diamorphine

and another of antibiotic, and prepared two more for the journey. She took off her boots and peeled the socks from the tissue. The skin was blackened and swelling. With the help of George and Dorje she dried it and wrapped her feet in clean bandages.

'Where's Sam? Let me look at his feet and hands before I go. He'll need a shot too.'

'Sam will be okay. He's tough.'

He saved me. That's what Al did. She knew it from Sam's eyes. The look in them was new, with a fathom of sadness and awe where before there had been only the easy glitter of laughter.

The helicopter landed and the rotors stirred a flurry of snow that mimicked in miniature the conditions higher up. They all turned their faces away from it.

At this altitude the machine could only carry a single passenger. Finch would have to go first. With her arms over the shoulders of George and Adam as they lifted her towards it she looked up, just once more, towards the summit of the mountain. Then she turned to see Sam. He lifted his hand and attempted a smile. A shiver of recognition passed through her and flowed between them.

They were connected by what they had seen and lived through, and the connection was forged through Al. They could not break it, even if they wished to.

George helped her into the seat and buckled her in. The pilot nodded and spoke into his headset.

'I'm sorry,' Finch said.

The whine of the engines drowned her words. The

helicopter lifted and rocked precariously, then carried her away down the valley.

Sam sank down on a rock, his hands hanging loose between his knees. His fingers and toes were frost-bitten, and Dorje was heating pans of water to begin thawing them. After the noise of the helicopter died away the desolation of the place amplified their individual silences and despair.

George Heywood asked him, 'Tell me exactly what happened.'

Sam described it all and the finality of Al's body weight resting on him.

At the end George said, 'I have to go and tell Al's ex-wife.' He walked away, his boots crunching on the grit and ice.

Adam came and sat beside him. Neither man spoke. Absently, Sam reached into the pocket of his windproof, still labelled with Adam's name, and hooked out the crumpled piece of shiny paper. He nodded to Adam to take it from his numb grasp. The other man smoothed it and they looked at it together. It was a picture of a little girl on a beach, windblown and laughing up at the camera.

'His daughter,' Adam said.

'Put it back in my inside pocket,' Sam said. 'I'll take it to England and give it to her.'

Dorje came with the pans of warm water and Adam helped his friend to lower his feet into them.

After an hour, the buzzing of the helicopter became audible again. A few minutes later the black dot materialised against the blue sky.

Adam helped Sam into the seat. The climbers stood

in a sombre circle, lifting their hands in farewell. George was still in the communications tent.

'I'll see you back in the US, buddy,' Adam said. The pilot started up his engines again and for the second time carefully lifted his machine off the glacier.

Without powerful friends or family to make decisions for him, Sam was only bound for the hospital in Kathmandu. By the time he reached it, Finch was already on her way out to Hong Kong.

Twelve

Other climbers' wives had told her that they always knew that this one was the call, when it came.

Jen opened her eyes on the first ring. The bedside clock read 5.15. It was already light outside and the birds were singing in the old lilac tree that lay unpruned against the back of the house.

She lifted the receiver and listened to the Mountain People's expedition director, relaying news from the foot of Everest. The room was full of liquid birdsong.

'I see,' Jen said quietly at the end. 'Thank you for telling me.'

'I'm so sorry,' George replied.

'Thank you. Al and I are divorced, you know.'

Why did I need to say that now? she wondered.

'Al made a brave decision, right there at the end. A young climber survived the night because Al covered him with his body and protected him from the worst of the weather.'

Jen inclined her head, thinking about it. The voice at the other end had to ask if she was still there. She thanked it again, politely. Now the man was saying that he would call her again, later in the day when she had had some time to collect herself, to talk about arrangements. 'I will be here,' she told him, as if she were not always here.

Jen got out of bed, and put on her robe and slippers. She crept past the door of Molly's room. She would leave her to sleep, for now. To store up some rest against the onslaught of grief. Jen's heart twisted with pity for her daughter. It was the first reaction she felt to the call she had always known would come, sooner or later.

The kitchen was chilly with early light. Two cats thudded off the sofa and wound around her ankles, demanding food. She opened the refrigerator and spooned some into their bowls, then filled the kettle and switched it on. She made herself a mug of tea and stood at the back window, breathing in the scent of the rose geraniums on the windowsill. Al had never lived in this house so the corners and recesses of it were empty of memories.

She thought about his body instead, the remembered contours of it and the sacrifice he had made for the other climber. Covering him against the cold.

Al had always been brave and generous in the large things. And every decision he had ever made, in all the years she had known him, had been considered.

Jen drank her tea, watching the birds and the garden. Even today, within a day of his death, she was angry with him. Especially today.

At 7.30 she made a fresh pot of tea and carried a cup up the steep stairs. It was a rare stroke of luck that there had been no paying guests in the house tonight. She knocked on Molly's door and opened it, breathing in her child's smell and the overlying scents of perfume, joss sticks and training shoes. She sat upright, fully awake, as soon as Jen touched her shoulder. Jen put down the cup of tea very carefully on the bedside table.

'It's Dad, isn't it?'

'Yes.'

'When?'

'In a storm, yesterday night. He reached the summit and the weather came in on the way down. They waited to tell us until they knew for sure, when the people he was with came back down again.'

Molly's face seemed to dissolve. The smooth flesh wrinkled and her mouth fell open. Jen took her in her arms and let her bury herself against her shoulder. Molly wept as if sorrow would turn her inside out, and her daughter's grief touched Jen in the depths where Al himself no longer could and drew her own burning tears. The tea in its flowered cup went cold under a pellucid skin.

'What can we do?' Molly howled, in the ravages of loss. 'I want him back. I want my dad.'

'I know,' Jen whispered. She considered the dimensions of her own bankruptcy, without the wherewithal even to grieve at first hand. Al had always been Molly's special one, she thought. Just as Molly had always been hers, from the day of her birth.

How lucky I am to have her. Her arms tightened fiercely and she wound her fingers in the black spirals of her hair.

The first storm blew itself out and Molly hung limply in her arms. 'Where is he?'

'Above the South Col somewhere.' Jen explained

what had happened. Molly wasn't able, yet, to take in the significance of what he had done.

'What will happen to him?'

'That's what we have to decide. Whether we want them to . . . try to bring him down and fly his body back home. Or whether to leave him there because he is in a place he loved.'

Molly tore herself out of her arms and ran to the window. She wrenched the curtains open and shouted through the glass, as if Everest reared itself directly outside. 'No. I don't want him there. He didn't love it really, he did it for money. Bloody mountains. Fucking mountains. I hate them. I don't want them to keep him.'

'All right.' It was better to let her believe what she wanted. But just as Al never made an unconsidered decision, so he never did anything he didn't want to.

The girl turned back to the bed. 'Mum, I'm so sorry for you too. He said this was going to be the last time. You ran after him when he was going, do you remember?'

'Yes, I remember.'

They put their arms around each other and lay down, in the shelter of Molly's quilt that still had nursery rhyme characters on the faded cover.

Thirteen

The hospital was familiar to Finch. It was where she, Suzy and Dennis had trained, and she knew the worn tiles on the back stairs that led down to the med students' coffee room in the sub-basement, and the stuffy little bedrooms where interns tried to doze between night calls, and the alcove in the A & E department where the crash trolley was parked when not in use. She didn't even register the polish-and-antiseptic scent of the main halls because she had lived with it so long.

She had been dozing, so when she woke up to see Dennis sitting beside her it didn't surprise her because he belonged here. It took a second or two longer for the shreds of awareness to knit together and for her to realise that there was an unfamiliar element that twisted everything else askew.

She was in a bed, in an acute med ward. She was a patient.

With the memory of that all the other recollections started up and stacked around her, and the small exhalation that sounded like a sob escaped her before she could suppress it. She hated waking up and having to inhabit her grief all over again. The pain from her wrecked feet was considerable, but it was nothing compared with the agony of remembering over and over again.

Dennis's hand tightened over hers. 'Hi,' he said quietly. 'I'd have come before, but it was family only for a couple of days.'

Finch recovered herself and smiled at him. 'You are family. Thank you for the flowers.'

He looked at the rank of vases. 'You could set up in the floristry business.'

'Dennis, I am so pleased to see you,' Finch whispered.

He lifted her hand and rubbed the knuckles against his cheek. The affection of it almost undid her again.

'What about the feet?'

'Too soon to say,' she answered simply. The fear was gangrene and her own estimation was that she would be lucky to keep the toes on her left foot and lucky to keep the right foot at all. She was able to think dispassionately about this, just as she could bear the physical pain of it. It was much easier than to deal with the memories of summit day and after.

'Can I take a look?'

She moved her legs under the cage that held off the weight of the bedcovers. 'Are you sure you want to?'

'I guess I can handle it.'

They removed the cage and unwrapped the dressings to expose the feet. Dennis took off his ordinary spectacles and replaced them with his clinical pair, a routine she had witnessed a million times, and the minute normality of it helped her again as his affection had done earlier. They studied the damage together.

The left foot had been covered in huge blisters, now deflating. Each toe was a swollen pad of dark, discoloured tissue. The right one was completely black and the flesh was shrivelled. The toes were hooked like an animal's claws.

'My darling,' Dennis said at last.

Finch could deal with the practicalities of her injury, but she couldn't absorb his sympathy. Ever since she had come home her mind had been a swirl of guilt as well as grief. 'There are fresh dressings in the cupboard, there,' she pointed.

They covered the blackened feet in layers of antiseptic white. When the job was complete Dennis walked to the window and looked out. 'It's a fine day. Do you want me to take you out for some air?'

Her smile rewarded him. 'Yes, please.'

He found a wheelchair, and together they shuffled her into it and wrapped a blanket over her legs. He pushed her down the hall and into the lift. Half of the people they passed on the way knew Finch, and although she responded to each of them he saw how she flinched under the constant stream of concerned questions and good wishes.

It was a clear afternoon, warm for the middle of May. Dennis chose a path through the hospital gardens that led past rose bushes and beds of verbena. Finch sighed with relief and let her head fall back so that the sun hammered copper discs behind her closed eyelids. The heavy air smelled of grass clippings and flowers, laced with the sharp reek of the tide. At the end of the path there was a bench, set in an angle of the boundary wall with a view of the Berrard inlet and the glittering walls and windows of north Vancouver on the opposite shoreline. Dennis positioned the chair and put on the brake, then sat down on the bench beside it. They watched the race of the water and the red-and-white sails of dinghies flying across it.

It was so sure and safe here, Finch thought. It was so precious and beautiful to be alive, an undeserved gift, and it was empty because Al was dead. She found herself wondering, as she had done plenty of times while she lay in her hospital bed, how Jen and Molly Hood were dealing with their loss. Tears weighted her eyelashes and dropped on her cheeks, and she tiredly brushed them away.

Dennis saw that she was crying. 'I believe that decisions about amputation should be delayed as long as possible,' he said. 'Not that I'm any kind of expert. I'm sure Amos Faulkner has plenty of ideas.'

Faulkner was the doctor looking after Finch. His main speciality was dermatology and his private enthusiasm was golf. He regarded mountaineers with disapproval and incredulity.

Finch rubbed her eyes with the heels of her hands. 'It isn't my feet. Except that I feel lucky it isn't far worse. I feel lucky to be alive at all and entirely undeserving. In all the time I've had to think about it, the only conclusion I can come up with is that it was an act of selfishness to try to climb Everest in the first place. An act of indulgence. And the loss . . .'

Dennis said, 'You are grieving. Denial and then anger. Anger directed at yourself, in this instance.'

'Grief,' Finch repeated. It seemed such a small

word for the enormity of loss. For the battalions of memories that wheeled in her head and the blank drill field of the future. 'Yes. Not for my feet.'

'I talked to Suzy last night. When I knew I could come to see you today. And she told me that you were in love with the man who died.'

'One of them,' she said. 'Two people died. One of them was a young man from Australia. The other was Al.'

'Why didn't you tell any of us about this before you went out there? Do Clare and Angus know, even now? The Dream Team?'

The Dream Team was Dennis's term for the Buchanan brothers. Finch's face contracted. 'No.'

'Finch, why not?'

He was persistent – she knew how Dennis could wheedle the truth out of the most defensive patient.

She frowned and let her hands rest, empty and palms upwards, on the blanket that covered her knees. How wrong everything had been, she thought. How determined she had been to prove herself, and separate herself from the weight of family concern by being strong and successful in her own right.

Al had been part of that determination. He was apart, and secret, and hers alone, and the escalation of her mountaineering ambitions had been her private conduit to him. She had guarded the secret of him, keeping it even from Suzy, and she had used Ralf as a mask. Perhaps, Finch thought, she had even deliberately allowed their separation to lengthen to five years, as a means of preserving him for herself alone.

And then, in a matter of days he was dead.

Death's finality was beyond her control and loss was her exposure. Her face contracted again, this time with a spasm that was almost a laugh at her own wrongness. Al, I am so sorry. For my vanity and stupidity. For the waste.

But then, Al had not come to search her out either. Perhaps for similar reasons, to do with the need for privacy and the demonstration of control. How alike we are, she thought.

'Why didn't I tell you and Suzy? He was married when I met him. He didn't ask me to . . . to continue anything with him. We went in separate directions.'

But that wasn't true. We both knew there would be another chapter, when we were ready for it.

Dennis was looking at her, waiting.

She took a breath. 'No. All right. I thought I was . . . powerful. That I didn't need any of you. You would have given me advice, told me to forget or advised me to act differently.'

Maybe to admit all this made the beginning of amends.

She covered her face with her hands and began to cry, proper tears, the first she had shed since coming home. The crying escalated into huge, racking sobs.

Dennis went on waiting, watching the boats on the inlet water and letting her weep. Finch sobbed and wiped her eyes on the blanket, and he took a clean handkerchief out of his pocket and passed it to her.

He knew the mechanics of it all too well. When Stephen died, who had been living with another gay man and had not even been Dennis's partner, even though Dennis had loved him entirely, Finch had been there to help him. She had been strong, as she always was.

'Get her to talk,' Suzy had told him last night. 'She'll resist it, of course, but she needs it.'

'I can't imagine what it was like,' he said, as the weeping subsided.

'Death?' she asked incredulously.

'The mountain.'

She inhaled, a bubbly breath and then another, fixing her face to speak again. 'I hated it. The implacability. The way we all hurled ourselves against it.'

He smiled faintly. 'I thought it would challenge you, rather than stir your detestation.'

'Oh, it did that. All the men. No, not just the men, me too. Puffed up, seething, transfixed with the desire for conquest.'

'Hm. And what about Al?'

'He wanted to climb it. But he was doing a job. A really difficult and dangerous job. It was his responsibility to help us up and down again, and that was his main focus. It was what he did and it was how he died.'

Wastefully, with mistakes compounded by mistakes, but still in spite of and also because of the mistakes he was doing his job right until the end.

It had been, Finch thought, part of her own misjudgement that made her believe he would stop doing it and turn his back on the mountains just because she wanted him to. Or even because his daughter wanted him to. That was what Jen Hood had understood after the years of marriage and she had been unable to endure it any longer.

A question came back to Finch, the one she had turned away from in her hours in the hospital bed and which continually resurfaced to stalk her uneasy dreams. Had Al known that he would never divorce the mountains and had he even unwittingly pushed himself and his clients too far on Everest? So that he could make one sacrifice instead of another?

I don't know, she answered herself. I can't ever know.

'How did it happen?' Dennis asked quietly.

She told him in bald, unadorned language that gave the bones of the story and none of the terror of the storm or the pathos of their battle against it.

'Sam was different from the other climbers. He came out there by accident, but he ended up as fixed on it as the rest of them. Just as his father would have wanted him to be. Isn't that ironic?'

'He sounds interesting,' Dennis said, looking at her.

'Does he? It was Al who was interesting to me. I wish you could have known him.'

'I wish I could, too. Tell me one more thing, if you are not too tired. How does it feel, how did it feel, not to have got to the summit yourself?'

She saw again the long curved spine breaking away above her, white with snow spume. And the rock gash of the Hillary Step. She gave the question proper consideration. 'I knew I couldn't go any further. I've never been certain of that before, about anything in my life. Never even come close to it. I said *I can't* and it was the truth. Everyone else went on somehow, the two Americans, Rix and Sandy, Sam. Following Al. He said to me, come with me, I love you, and I still couldn't do it. Even for him, if not for myself. You want to know what it felt like? It wasn't disappointment or loss or defeat. It was bigger than that. I felt humbled.'

Finch looked down at the blanket covering her ruined feet. A breeze had started blowing off the inlet and it plastered a strand of hair across her mouth. Removing it she said, 'I've never been a humble person, have I?'

'No,' Dennis agreed. 'Many things, but not that.'

'Well, then, that's what it felt like, all the same,' she said quietly.

The breeze made the afternoon feel suddenly cool and she drew the blanket closer around her.

'I'll wheel you back inside.'

When they reached her room, more flowers had been delivered. She read the card. They were from Ralf, with best wishes for a full recovery. Dennis fussed with vases and she sat watching him. The waxy curve of a petal, the serrated edges of leaves and pollen-heavy stamen were lent a crystalline brilliance by her awareness of life's fragility. There was this perfection and it was so transient. There were layers of affection and concern surrounding her, and she was isolated by grief. She fumbled with the equation in her mind, trying to balance it.

Al was dead. What they had briefly been was all that was left to her.

What followed on could be all negative, or she could try to find some way to turn it.

It was too difficult. Her spirit failed in her. Love gaped like an open wound and the pain was more vicious than anything physical. She hunched her shoulders to contain it, not wanting Dennis to see.

Dennis finished arranging the flowers and stood back to admire his handiwork.

Finch said, 'Evening surgery beckons, I know. I'm sorry I'm not there. Will you come again soon?'

'Don't worry about the practice. And of course I will.'

Finch smiled. 'You can tell Suzy that you made me talk. That was the mission, wasn't it?'

'Yeah. She wishes she were here.'

'I know.'

Dennis helped her from the chair and back on to the bed.

She put her arms round his neck as if this simple connection would help her to make other more complicated ones. 'And, Dennis? Thank you.'

'You helped me, remember. When Steve died.'

Of course that was how it was, the theory, Finch understood. She also would have agreed theoretically that it was much harder to accept help than to bestow it. How much more difficult, though, was only becoming apparent to her now that her life's equation was reversed.

What kind of a doctor have I been, all this time? she wondered. What kind of a daughter and sister since I was old enough to think for myself?

She let Dennis go with a kiss on his forehead and leaned back against the pillows. Clare would be here soon to visit her and Marcus had promised to look in. She submitted herself consciously to the prospect, trying to work her awakening insight around it.

'You think I should tell my mother and father and the boys about Al and me?'

'You think I should answer that, or should you?'

They laughed at each other.

'Go on. Look after our patients.'

'And you look after yourself.'

Left alone, Finch studied the flowers that he had left on her bed table. The profligacy of scent and texture and the intricacy of each blossom amazed her.

She felt as if she had never looked properly at anything in her life before.

Michael nosed his ten-year-old Pontiac Sunbird into the airport parking lot, not far from where Finch had left her rental car on the night of Suzy's and Jeff's wedding. He battled his way awkwardly out of his specially adapted driver's seat, using the lip of the door as a lever, balanced and hoisted his stick out after him. He didn't often drive places nowadays, it was too much damned trouble. But he wanted to come and meet Sam off the plane. He nudged the car door shut and left without locking it. Nothing in the old heap to steal, he thought with satisfaction.

The arrivals concourse was crowded. Who were all these people and where were they headed, in such a rush and flurry? He hobbled along the wall, the flat of one hand sliding to steady his progress. He reached the arrivals board and scanned it suspiciously. Sam was coming in on a flight from San Francisco that connected with his Nepal flight. In taking down the details when Sam telephoned from the hospital in Kathmandu, Michael hadn't tried to ask questions about why his son was coming back to Oregon, instead of going straight to Seattle. If there was something to know, Michael thought, he would learn it in good time. He made his way across open space to a row of chairs and sat down, hands clasped over the head of his stick.

He was looking the wrong way when Sam emerged in a crowd of passengers. Sam saw him first; a man with a head too big for his twisted body and a frown that pulled his features into a knot. He felt the familiar chafe of irritation and affection at the sight. It was a surprise that nothing had changed, even though his own world had tilted into a new orbit. Did you actually expect the old man to be different? he asked himself, as he rolled his luggage trolley forward in the laggardly stream of travellers.

Michael looked up at his son. 'Here you are.'

'Here I am.'

Sam reached out his hand and helped his father to stand.

Michael accepted his help and retained the hand. He looked down for a moment at the long cracks driven by the cold into his son's fingertips, then at the white patches on his cheeks left by the removal of his mountain beard, which only emphasised the hollowness of his cheeks. He had seen plenty of men who looked like Sam did, emaciated and other-worldly, coming back from the big climbs. He had been jealous then; now he felt a simple quickening of relief that the boy was here. 'So you did it,' he said.

'At a price.'

'There is always a price. Shall we get on home?'

'Yes, please.'

The house was an oasis of silence, for once. Michael left the television switched off as Sam put his small grip down on the bed in his old room. The rest of his belongings were being packed up at Base Camp and would be flown home by the Mountain People.

Adam Vries was in charge of that. 'Most of this shit is *mine*,' he had told Sam on the telephone.

Sam came out of his bedroom and sat down in the armchair next to his father's. Mike gave him a cup of bad coffee and he drank it. A car passed on the road in front of the house and disappeared towards town.

'I am glad to be here,' Sam said.

Michael nodded. He meditatively drank his coffee and gazed at the pictures on the mantelpiece. Sam liked it that he didn't demand an immediate account of the expedition, or even seem to expect talk. He let the quiet sink through him, easing his bones.

After four days in the hospital in Kathmandu it wasn't Seattle he had thought of, or Fran and their shared apartment and disjointed lives, but his father. The days on Everest and his friendship with Al had brought subterranean layers of himself to the surface and had buried others, like the freak effects of an earthquake.

After a while Michael said, 'This is the first time in I can't remember how long that you've just sat still. Usually you're running around getting to the store and laying in provisions and answering your phone messages and telling me I should get about more.'

'I'm tired,' Sam said. Not just physically, although he was that too.

'Go and sleep for a few hours.'

Sam slept the night through, dreamlessly, as he had not done for weeks. The next day he sat in the sunshine at the front of the house, and in the evening he and Michael watched the television soaps and an old Clint Eastwood movie.

Another day came and Michael drove the Sunbird into town for some groceries. When he came back Sam carried in the bags, and put the packets and jars away in the peeling cupboards. He remembered his mother moving in the same space, neat in her movements. A thick weight of emotion rose in his throat and found its way out in words. 'I said your names, on the summit. I think I shouted them and the wind ripped them away into Tibet.'

Michael folded the used brown bags and put them in an old canvas sack that hung behind the yard door, just as Mary always had done. There is so much of her still here, Sam thought. He must miss her every day. And he wondered what it would be like to live in the same way with Finch, sharing days creased with routine, two parts of the same organism, as he and Frannie had never been.

'I like to think of that. Your mother would have been proud.'

Sam turned around from the yard door, still with the weight in his mouth, and demanded, 'Can't you say that *you* are proud?'

Michael steadied himself again, fingers kneading the laminate edge of the kitchen table. 'Do you think that I am not?'

There was such surprise in his voice that Sam couldn't doubt it. I am the one who has the gifts of education and articulacy, he thought in sudden shame. I am guilty of not using them. 'No. I did, all the time I was growing up, but I don't now.'

He pulled out one of the straight-backed wooden

chairs that tucked under the flap of the table and guided Michael into it. He positioned himself opposite and at once Michael began to talk. They had both been waiting for the moment and now it opened around them, catchy with attention, dense with listening pauses.

'I'm proud, all right. My son and Everest. My son the mountaineer.' He gave his unreformed chuckle and then turned serious again. 'I know there was a tragedy, made it difficult for you to celebrate your own achievement. It's there, though, just the same. No one can take it away or say you didn't do it. Still, you didn't go out there to climb because I wanted you to, did you? You didn't say to yourself, hey, I'll just go and climb the big one because I want my daddy to be proud of me.'

'No. I went because of a woman.' Sam held up his hand to indicate that that wasn't what was important in this opening between them. 'I followed her and worked my way on to the expedition. But once I was there I was taken up. By lust for the summit.'

Michael's mouth made a curve, brief and knowing, acknowledging the accuracy of the word.

'And I was also taken up by Al Hood and finally by a version of you. The higher I got and the harder everything became, the closer together you and Al drew in my mind. He was exacting in the way that you once were but I could meet his expectations in the way that I never seemed able to do with you, when I was a kid. He was generous with his approval, too, once we understood each other. I think we did understand. We were in love with the same woman; it was a rivalry and one night he hit me, but it was a bond as well. On the last day he gave her to me to look after. Not that I made a great job of it.'

'And then?'

'There was just him and me left on the mountain. And you, in the way that you fitted between us. You were with me as well as Al, when I was climbing, just as if you were at my shoulder. I talked to you. Rambling conversations that I wished we'd had for real. I still wish it. Maybe like we're having now.

'It was late, after the summit, and the weather turned bad. A guy lost his way and walked off the face. Al and I searched pretty hopelessly for him, then we were lost ourselves. We were out of oxygen. Things got pretty sketchy. I don't remember all of it. But we hollowed out a shelter, of sorts, and huddled up to wait it out. Some time in the night, Al rolled himself on top of me. I stayed warm, because of his warmth. When it got light again I was conscious and able to move on down the mountain. But Al was dead. That was what he did for me.'

'An act of will. Himself for you.'

'If you like. An act of great generosity, anyway.'

Michael rubbed his nose with the back of his hand and glared away through the ribbed-glass panel in the yard door. Sam hadn't seen him even close to tears since Mary died. Breaking the taboos and barriers that they had created between themselves, he took hold of his father's hand and to his great satisfaction he didn't try to remove it. Sam studied the tributaries of blue veins and stretched tendons under the freckled skin. His injury and the years of disability made Michael seem older than his real age.

Michael said, 'You know something? I'm jealous of

him. He did that for my son. I wish I could have done it.'

'No.'

'Instead of the piece of crap I did inflict on you.' He glanced down at his lower body. 'Piece of solo arrogance. Thinking I was bigger than the problem. So I fall off and break my back, and screw up life for you as well as myself.'

'Al was arrogant. He did what he wanted to do. Whereas you stayed here and provided for Mom and me. Maybe if you had taken off, gone out to the Himalayas, you would have been less . . .'

'Bitter.' Mike formed the word easily, as if it had been often in his mind.

'I was going to say disappointed. In me, as well as in the way things turned out.'

The kitchen was full of afternoon warmth and the humming of the refrigerator, and the buzz of a failing tube in the old-fashioned neon strip light.

'I'm not disappointed in you, son.'

The small domestic noises didn't alter their pitch and the sun continued its travel across the pale sky. The two men sat for a moment longer, then Sam released his father's hand.

'You didn't screw up life for me, either.'

They shifted the alignment of their chairs, moving their shoulders and feet. They weren't practised at intimacy and they both understood the signal to move on, tidying up in the wake of their confessions.

This was how it probably always would be between Michael and himself, Sam understood. But today had touched them both. He had come back to Wilding in the hope of exchanging exactly these few words.

'What are you going to do now?' Mike asked.

'Big question.'

'Back to Seattle?'

He couldn't stay here for ever, hiding in his boyhood bedroom, trying to come to terms with death and sacrifice. 'I'll have to go back, but I won't stay. I think I may sell out the business to my partners and just pull out, go travelling for a while.'

Michael nodded. 'What about the woman you were chasing?'

'I don't know.' Although he did.

In the early evening, after he had cooked some food and they had eaten and Michael had cleared it away, Sam went into his bedroom. He sat down at his cramped desk to write two letters. It was a long time since he had tried to write anything without a screen and a keyboard, and the pen and paper that Mike gave him felt cumbersome in his hands and set up a block in his head, reminding him of being a kid again and wrestling with a term paper on a summer's evening.

Before he began the first letter, he took a photograph out of his wallet and propped it against the wall in front of him. Molly Hood on a long-ago beach smiled into the camera.

'Dear Jen and Molly,' he wrote. 'Al talked about you, and I wanted to write and tell you exactly what happened, and what he did. I owe him my life, as you already know.'

He told the story, spilling it out in racing sentences, without construct, just as he remembered it. The photograph had been in Al's inner pocket, he explained. He found it when he was searching for the radio.

At the end, when he had related all the facts, he wrote that he had never known anyone like Al and that their brief friendship had affected him deeply. He said that he was sorry for their great loss and that he hoped in time to come and see them in person. Then he shuffled the sheets of paper together and laid them to one side.

The second letter came less easily. 'Dear Finch' looked so bare on the little blue sheet of paper, but anything more intimate struck him as overbearing. He wrote that he had had news of her from George Heywood and from Adam Vries, and that he had heard there could sometimes be miraculous recoveries from the worst cases of frostbite. He would be thinking of her, he said, and if he only knew how to pray he would be doing that too. 'I can't know how you will be suffering Al's death. I can only guess, and send you my love and sympathy. He was remarkable, and he saved my life, and his generosity is incalculable.'

After that Sam sat for several minutes, biting the pen. There were a thousand things he wanted to say to her but he stopped himself. He had found a delicacy now that had evaded him before. In the end, he just wrote that he didn't know what he would be doing, exactly, for the next few months, but that she would be in his mind. And that he would see her again.

'With love always, Sam.'

Michael came and knocked on the door. 'You want a beer?' he called.

'Yeah, please.'

He popped the ring from the can that Michael handed him and tasted the silvery froth. The letters were separately folded in front of him. The addresses had been dictated to him by George Heywood.

'Do you have envelopes?'

'Someplace.' He came closer and peered at the photograph. 'Who is this?'

'Al Hood's daughter. I'm sending it back to her.'

Mike rested his weight on the corner of the desk and examined the picture. His face softened as if he was looking at someone he knew. 'Nice little kid.'

'It was taken a long time ago. She's nearly grown, now, I think.'

'Must have been a memory for him, some particular day, that made him choose to take this one picture with him. I remember a day, too.'

Sam waited, looking at him.

'We were at the boulders together. You were halfway through a nice little problem and you suddenly called up to me and said that you wouldn't go any further. Sure and certain. And you down-climbed and untied yourself, and ran off into the woods. I knew then you'd got a mind of your own and whatever you did you'd make something right of it.'

'I remember that day too,' Sam said.

They spent another evening watching the soaps together.

The next morning Sam found an old pair of sneakers in his closet and went running. He took the route around the lake again, and now the bushes were fat with leaf and ducks were busy in the reeds at the water's edge. He caught himself watching the birds and the tiny ripples spreading in their wake, and his pace slowed and his stride turned ragged. The light glittering on the water was so intense that it dazzled him.

He ran on for two more miles, forcibly turning his concentration inwards. He was surprised by how strong he felt, considering the weight loss and the part-healed frostnip damage to his feet, and all the other depredations of Everest, but he still couldn't make himself move properly. The machine that had once turned over with minute precision now seemed cranky. He slowed again to a walk. The dirt path was pleasantly gritty and firm underfoot, and little puffs of dust rose as he trod. At the head of the lake was a little group of Douglas firs and when he reached them he turned off the path, and sat down in the purplish shade under the trees.

Immediately he began thinking of Al. He would have liked to be able to talk to him now, here where the late spring muzziness of green and gold was in such contrast to the harsh high places. He thought they might have lounged on the grass and talked about childhood and first loves, and exchanged the details of their lives in the way that they had never had time to do. He would have liked to hear how he had met Finch and what it had felt like. But none of this would ever pass between them now. Sam felt the place that their friendship would have occupied empty inside him. It was the most intricate fold of grief, the mourning for what would now never be.

He bent his head and studied the blades of grass.

The words formed soundlessly in his head: thank you. He had tried often enough since coming down from the mountain to make sense of what Al had done for him. The grandeur of his generosity made Sam constantly awed and incredulous. It also weighted him with the need to be somehow worthy of such a gift, another man's present of his life and future. If Al had done this for him, how could he allow his existence to go on being stagnant and so devoid of meaning?

As he sat in the aromatic shade he made a promise to Al: I don't deserve what you did for me. I don't deserve to be here when you are not, but if I am, if I must be, then I will try to do it right. Without compromise, because you were an uncompromising man.

The first thing, Sam thought, was to extricate himself from the web of his old life. He had done his job badly, making a mess of half-hearted decisions. He had made Frannie unhappy, who didn't deserve to be.

After that, what would happen would be better and clearer because he would make it so.

He scrambled to his feet and interlocked his fingers, stretching his arms and shoulders. He began to run again, slowly up the steep rise through more fir trees to the crest of the ridge and faster out on to the blacktop that led to his father's house.

He didn't feel the desire in his chest and gut any longer. Running was just running, a man pounding along at the roadside with the occasional car or pick-up truck incuriously sweeping past and bringing a little buffet of wind in its wake. He had been running for so long because he wanted to prove something, but there was nothing to prove here after all.

Mike had made another pot of foul coffee. He handed Sam a cup as he came in through the door. 'Good one?'

'Run? I dunno.' Sam flexed his shoulders, keeping an eye on the scummy brown meniscus in his coffee cup to ensure that it didn't slop over the rim. 'I think maybe I grew out of it.'

Mike gave a cough of laughter. 'Always thought you would.'

After a second Sam laughed too. Nothing to prove, he thought.

'Yeah. So you did. Listen, I think I may call the airport and see if there's a flight this evening.'

It was time to get back to Seattle, to think about making an end in order for there to be another beginning.

The old man nodded. 'I'm glad you came down here first,' he said. 'I appreciate it.'

Sam told him, 'I wanted to. I wanted to say what we did.'

'Yeah. Well, then. And you climbed Everest first.'

'Not on my own,' Sam said quietly.

Mike made a struggling movement that resolved itself as a hitch of his shoulders, drawing them up to his ears and letting them drop again. 'I'm proud of you whichever way you did it. And I guess you know I love you,' he mumbled.

'I do know. And I also love you.'

His father took up his stick and prodded with it at thin air. 'Yup. All right, then. You better make that call.'

Fourteen

At the end of May, Finch sent an e-mail to Suzy from her hospital bed, detailing the latest medical developments: 'Gangrenous progression now arrested but circulation to the impaired areas not improved. Surgery to remove dead tissue apparently inevitable. Orthopaedic team includes Taylor Buckaby, of course. I should have stayed at home, like Maddie. I know that's what he's thinking.'

And Suzy responded: 'You shouldn't have stayed home. You don't really think that. You knew what you wanted to do and you did it, and that's admirable. I know how brave you are – if amputation is what has to be done, then thank God you are alive and that it isn't any worse. We didn't choose to marry him, but Taylor's a good surgeon. I'm coming up as soon as I can to be with you for a couple of days. Expect me when you see me.'

Finch read the message.

Only I'm not brave, she thought.

I don't know how to live without Al. I don't even know what every other patient in this hospital knows, like how to bear the prospect of sickness and disability.

All the years she had lived until now seemed coloured with unexamined privilege and powered by her assumption that she would always be strong and in the right. Now she wept, dismayed by the scale of grief and helplessness.

Two days later, Taylor and his colleagues removed three toes from her left foot and the entire right foot from above the ankle. She submitted finally to the medical procedure because she knew there was no alternative, and she fought to accept the loss of her flesh and bone with the sense that this was punishment for having been careless of herself, even helpless at the most crucial moment. She had made a small mistake with fastening her boots on the Lhotse face and a much graver error at the Col when she didn't reckon what wet boots would mean. It was true that she had been exhausted and hypoxic, but better mountaineers would not have made the same error in the same conditions. She had failed herself, she thought, and put other climbers at risk as well. And she had been arrogant enough at the beginning of the expedition to imagine she could provide care for other people. Now the fine threads of interconnected cause and responsibility seemed to radiate from her and to stretch all the way through the storm to the catastrophe of two deaths.

Not all the fault was hers, she didn't believe that much – Rix had speeded the momentum of the tragedy, and Sandy, and maybe even Al himself – but she had made her contribution.

In one light, to lose toes and a foot seemed no more than just for having been such an embodiment of weakness and pride. And at the deepest level of herself Finch struggled with her loss as inadequate payment for living at all, even crippled, while Al was dead.

Arriving at the hospital on the day of the operation, Suzy found Clare and Angus Buchanan waiting in a side room for Finch to be brought down from theatre. Of course they would be here – Finch's parents were always on hand. They made the family into their own art form. But when Angus kissed her and Clare folded Suzy's hands between both of hers, Suzy felt ashamed of her cynicism. Clare was trying not to cry and Angus kept a protective arm round her shoulders. Their faces were drawn with anxiety and Clare was unmade-up and carelessly dressed, as Suzy had never seen her before. They sat down on three upright chairs, with a low table and a fading bowl of flowers between them. It was another bright afternoon and shafts of sunlight striped the floor.

'Finch will be glad you are here. So am I. She won't ever tell us anything, but I know she'll talk to you,' Clare said.

Suzy covertly rested the flat of her hand over her thirteen-week pregnancy. How did you stop this happening to your children, the drift from umbilical connection to resentful distance?

A nurse looked in at them. 'Dr Buchanan is awake. Just a short visit.'

'You go. I'll wait,' Suzy said.

A few moments later Clare and Angus came back again.

'How is she?'

'The operation went well. She's asking for you.'

Suzy hadn't expected to feel sorry for Finch's parents, but she did now. The glamour had gone thin and they looked bewildered, and sad and old.

Finch was propped up in her cubicle with an IV tube taped to her arm. There wasn't much contrast between her face and the pillows. She attempted a smile when she saw Suzy and nodded at the cage over her lower limbs. 'Feet of clay,' she murmured.

'Will of iron,' Suzy countered. 'You know that prosthetic athletes, for example, can run as fast and jump as far as non-amputees?'

Wordlessly Finch lifted her arms up to her friend and Suzy held her. They pressed their faces together and Suzy whispered, 'You are alive. I am so thankful.'

'I don't deserve to be.'

Finch drew a breath, trying to maintain control, then the defences cracked and she gave way first to anger, blindly shouting at Suzy, 'I don't deserve it,' followed by a paroxysm of tears. Suzy held her, stroking her hair and making soothing noises as if she were a child. Over Finch's head through the cubicle window she saw Taylor Buckaby hesitating and she waved him away with a little movement of her fingers. She pulled a handful of tissues from the box on the bed table and began to dry her friend's face.

'I haven't cried properly for him yet,' Finch blurted.

'Cry, then.'

'Not just for Al,' she added. 'For Sandy Jackson and all the people.'

The dead man in his tattered clothes. The stone cairns on the windswept Khumbu plateau, each one a lost life. Spider. And the people who were left behind, Al's wife and child, Ang and the others and Mingma with his *puja* fire.

Suzy thought as she held her tight that if her friend had a fault, it was the brazen quality of her strength up until now. She had never known her weep like this before, for the sadness of everything. She stroked her shoulder and under the blue theatre gown her fingers touched a frayed and faded red silk thread that was tied round her neck.

'Don't go away. I need you to be here,' Finch pleaded.

'I'm not going. Taylor would have to drag me,' Suzy answered. She couldn't remember Finch ever having confessed to needing anyone. No wonder, she thought, that she had fallen in love with a man like this Alyn Hood who belonged nowhere, with nobody, and whose dislocated strength of will had presumably matched her own.

In the end Finch fell asleep, with her hand locked in Suzy's. Suzy gently disengaged her fingers and stepped out into the corridor, where she met Taylor.

'You stayed far too long,' he reprimanded.

Suzy ignored this. 'What's the story?'

He gave her the medical details. The surgical procedures had gone smoothly, they would work on rehab, there had been major advancements in prosthetic technology.

'She will be all right,' Suzy said.

'Of course,' Taylor agreed with a touch of heat, misunderstanding her by assuming she was referring to Finch's physical recovery.

*

Two days later Finch was taken for her first session with the hospital physiotherapists. She was shown the heated pool where she would learn to swim again and the parallel bars where new amputees practised shuffling steps. The gym was full of people with transtibial prostheses, metal springs and hydraulic joints strapped to residual limbs, busy on the treadmills, and she watched in fascination from her wheelchair. This was different from the tour of the same places they had made as impatient students, bored with this apparent backwater. Now the sight of it was like being thrown a lifeline in the ocean.

'When do I start?' she asked the therapist.

'On crutches, a few steps, in a day or so.'

It was a relief to realise exactly how this physical restructuring was waiting for her. Before the operation the prospect of amputation had threatened to crush her. She had been so strong and had always taken her strength for granted, and now she would shuffle and balk, and be forced to rely on the help of others. But suddenly, from the sight of these people in the gym she understood that she too could work on disability. It was measurable.

The empty expanses of loss had seemed infinite, ready to drown her, and now there was a line to cling on to.

When she was wheeled back to her room she found that Dennis had called in with a sheaf of mail collected from her apartment. There was one letter sealed in a creased brown envelope and written on small sheets of blue lined paper, and as soon as she saw it she knew that it was from Sam. She read it eagerly.

It was very short. The three sentences he wrote about Al made her lift her head and straighten her back, and look beyond the squared-off covers of her hospital bed to the window and the outside air. She sat poised with her memories, clear-eyed today instead of foggy with tears.

She folded the letter in its creases again and put it away, wondering where Sam was going for the next few months and why. He didn't mention it but she knew he was recovering from his superficial frostbite and the effects of the summit bid. George Heywood had told her that much.

It would have been an ordeal to talk to him about the mountain and Al, but there was also a pressure for it inside her. She realised now that she had been half expecting Sam to appear in Vancouver, or at least to telephone her, and the idea of his absence made her understand that she would miss him. There wasn't even an address at the top of the blue sheet. If she wanted to write in return, she would have to do it via George and the Mountain People.

'You look so much better tonight,' Clare said when she came in to visit her. She put the latest *Vanity Fair* on the bed next to Finch, together with a new silk nightdress that she didn't need. It was dark-blue, lustrous, and Finch stroked it with her fingertips and saw how the light rippled on the fabric.

'It's beautiful. You mustn't keep bringing me things every day.'

'I want to,' Clare said. The twist in her voice made Finch understand that she didn't know what else to do for her.

'I feel better. They took me down to look at the gym and the pool. There were rooms full of people with no legs or no arms, walking and bicycling and running and pumping iron, and all I've lost is a foot and some toes. I'll get the artificial foot and start walking again.'

'Yes, you will. If anyone will, it's you.'

Finch held up the nightdress against herself. 'How does it look? Does it suit me?'

'It's your colour.'

I am here, talking about nightdresses, and Al is dead. But we had the truck and the metal well between the seats, and the barn at Deboche. He told me that he loved me. And I am not the only person he left behind.

She smiled at Clare. 'Thank you.'

Her mother smiled back, surprised and pleased to be.

After Clare left, Suzy came. She kicked off her shoes and padded around the room, hands on her hips, leaving moist barefoot prints on the tile floor. 'I can't do my skirt up.'

'Maybe you're pregnant, have you thought of that? Perhaps you should see a doctor.'

'Hey.' Suzy saw the nightdress and whistled. 'Look at this.'

'Clare brought it.'

'Spoiled kid, you are. Always have been.'

'I know.'

Suzy paused in her circuit and looked at her, and Finch met her eyes.

'You look better.'

'Exactly what my mother said.'

'Has something happened?'

'A couple of things. Rehab. And a letter from Sam. He said that Al saved his life and that his generosity was incalculable.' Pride lit up her face like a light switched on in a dim room, and knowing that it did made Finch look down to where her fingers pleated the bedcover, in case even Suzy saw too much.

'I wish I'd known him. He must have been remarkable.'

'He was. Sam said that, too.'

Suzy sat down on the edge of the bed. She opened a box of Finch's chocolates after absently reading the card attached and began a two-fingered rifling of the contents.

'Sam is the same guy you met on the plane from the wedding, right, who followed you out there and went all the way to the top?'

'Yes.'

'Uh, okay. I see.' She ate another chocolate and sighed. 'Finch, listen. I've got to go home tomorrow. Work, Jeff. All that. You know I'd stay longer if I could.'

'You've been here four days. I don't know how I'd have got through them without you.'

It was the truth. Finch thought how much she loved this woman and missed her every day they didn't see one another. 'Thank you for coming. It meant everything. Just stay a bit longer now and talk to me.'

Suzy knitted her fingers to keep them out of the chocolates.

'Did you think about having a baby with Al? When

you thought about what it would be like between you when the climbing was all over?'

Suzy was smiling as she asked the question, amused by self-recognition. As womb-centred as every pregnant woman she had ever encountered, no different. The world was suddenly all to do with babies and bringing them into it.

How beautiful she looks and how happy, Finch thought.

'I didn't think about it, no,' she answered, after a long moment. 'Al didn't belong with . . . houses and fixtures. He was too wild and too uncompromising. You couldn't fix him with a family. And he had a daughter of his own, almost grown.'

'So he must have been fixed at some stage.'

'No. I don't think so. I think that was the trouble.'

'I see,' Suzy said doubtfully. To be fixed, where she was now, the way she was with Jeff, seemed the essence of perfection.

Finch put her hand over Suzy's. 'I wasn't dreaming of a ring, and a home and a baby stroller. Al wasn't a man you could do that with.'

'What did you want?'

Finch looked through her, at something Suzy couldn't see, that made her face change and her eyes glitter. 'What we had was enough.'

It was sad only to realise it now. She had been asking him to change, to give up his life to fit into a tighter mould, because she hadn't properly understood the mountaineer's mechanism. Maybe he would have tried to give it up, to please her or to reassure Molly, and it wouldn't have worked. How could she have believed that it would?

'Hey.' Suzy was shaking her hand. 'Where are you?'

'Here. I'm here. Let's talk about something else.'

Obligingly, Suzy launched into some gossip she had picked up in a visit to the doctors' dining-room with Taylor Buckaby and his colleagues. They talked about old friends and medicine until it was time for Suzy to leave.

They hugged each other.

'Come and stay with me as soon as you're out of here. We'll test the wheelchair access in all Jeff's bars.'

'Screw the wheelchair. I intend to be ambulant. Did I tell you, I had a welcome message from an amputee support group called Stumps R Us?'

'I want to be there. Take me along as your date.'

After Suzy had gone, in the space left by her departure, Finch unfolded Sam's letter and read it one more time. But there was nothing else she could glean from it.

'Man, you took some finding. Ever heard of a forwarding address? I thought your ex was going to withhold all information as to your whereabouts.'

Sam held the door open. Adam Vries hoisted the holdall that Sam didn't want to see again and swung it into the hallway of the borrowed apartment.

'Frannie's angry with me. I don't blame her.'

'No shit. Hey, good to see you, dude. You look better than last time. What is this place?'

Sam glanced backwards over his shoulder and shrugged. The rooms were piled with lumber and decorators' supplies. The only sign of occupation was a divan bed pushed into one corner with a rumpled quilt and a paperback face down on the floor beside it. 'Belongs to a guy I know who's supposed to be fixing it up, but he's somewhere else right now. I just needed a place to sleep while I sort myself out. Thanks for bringing my stuff.'

The bag stood between them with the Mountain People label curled around the handle. There was a silence while Sam unwillingly looked at it, then he took a step closer and touched the zipper. He pulled it open and put his hand inside. There was a mess of dirty clothes and the smell that came out was kerosene and smoke and sweat, and the reek went straight to a place inside his skull. Remembered cold and pain reared up at him, stinging his mouth and feet, and crushing his chest, and his ears roared with the wind.

'Christ,' he whispered. He knelt down with his hands in the bag's open mouth, turning over the memories, dropping them in a gritty heap on the floor. Everything he touched brought back the mountains and the people he had left there.

'Packing's not my strong suit,' Adam apologised. 'I just shovelled up everything from your tent. Your camera's in there. You left it inside my down suit.'

Sam found it. The film was still inside, pictures from the summit. He put it aside without comment. He stood up and pushed the spilled heap of belongings aside with his foot. 'Let's get out of here. Let's go and have a beer.'

'Sure thing,' Adam said.

They went to a bar. The neighbourhood was a long way from where he had lived with Frannie and Sam knew no one. They took an outside table under an awning, and a waitress brought them drinks and a dish of olives. There was a group of women at the next table, in office clothes, with bags and briefcases at their feet, and Adam looked appreciatively at them.

'I love the city in summertime.'

'Seattle?'

'Any city. Bare calves and exposed elbows, sexier than the beach.'

Sam drank his beer and Adam signalled for two more. They began to talk about the expedition, edging into the subject, out of the ordinariness of the bar and their surroundings.

Adam said that George had heard from Ted and Vern, and from Rix, all of whom were greatly pleased to have achieved their objective. 'I wonder how much responsibility that bastard Rix feels for Al's death?' he mused.

Sam considered. 'Rix was possessed up there, that's for sure. He was going to go and nothing would hinder him. Al should have stopped him, but I haven't a clue how he could have done it and I was there watching. So Al did the only thing he could, which was go on up with him. We knew it was too late. And so it turned out that Rix got away with it and Al was left with me. So is it my fault that he died? What's fault, anyway, divided between Rix and me and Sandy?

'My dad always used to say that climbing is about purity and there was nothing that day but muddle and misfortune and greed. Al said that above the South Col, it's every man for himself. And that was true, except for him. If you're looking for purity, it's what he had. And there's a kind of purity in fate as well – the storm, the lateness, Sandy just wandering away. I wouldn't think Rix blames himself. Would you?'

Adam shook his head and tilted his glass to look at the lace of froth down the side of it.

Sandy Jackson's father had written to say that his son had died doing what he loved and that his family were proud he had reached the summit.

'I wish I'd done it,' Adam said.

'Do you?' Sam could feel the beer buzz. He didn't drink much, but now it was in him he found that he wanted more, to dull the questions and the memories. 'Given what happened?'

'Yes. Even given what happened.'

'I think that's our answer,' Sam said quietly.

It was a silky, scented evening. The women at the next table were laughing and tilting their chairs, and the traffic at the end of the block rolled in a slow column, and lights were coming on in the apartments over the street. There had been a hundred evenings like this, in bars and at restaurants with Frannie and other friends, here and in other cities, and there would be hundreds more, if he chose, if that was the direction he chose. The world was intricate and coherent, and even though he felt dislocated from it tonight, Sam thought, he was still embedded in the grain of it, still living and absorbing the detail, and dimly trying to comprehend the wider pattern. He knew that he was at a turning point and what he did with every day from now on mattered, because of what he had been given on Everest. Was this, he wondered, the onset of adulthood, or had he been adult for years and just exceptionally slow to understand what it meant?

He heard Finch's low voice in his ear. *Yes*, she said. She was always in his head, her face and her voice.

'What now?' Adam was asking. 'Are you going to go on running?'

His glass was empty again.

'I have run, once or twice, since I got thawed out. But I can't locate the motive any more. It's as if a stopper was pulled and everything that I've kept bottled up under pressure just went flat and leaked away into the sand. Maybe reaching the top of Everest did what I didn't expect it to. Maybe after all it was complete as an achievement in itself – I did that, climbed it, went as far and as high as I could go, and having done it I can let it go. It meant something but not everything. It's an answer to one question, a very simple one, *can I?*, but there are many more subtle ones I've no idea how to solve. I just know that I can't do it by climbing any more mountains, or by running faster. Maybe that's what I learned from being around Al. Do you know what he did for me?'

Adam said, 'Tell me.'

Sam described the last night again. He needed to talk about it, the pressure of need deep in the pit of his stomach. As he talked he felt the weight of warmth resting on top of him, and he flexed his feet and fingers repeatedly as if to keep the blood circulating. One of the group of women noticed and glanced half curiously at him, but Sam didn't see it.

'Why, do you think?' Sam asked at length. 'Why the sacrifice for me?'

Instead of dulling his senses the beer was sharpening them. The bowl of olive pits discarded by Adam, the lettering on the bar awning, the weave of Adam's sweater, all seemed hallucinatorily clear. Turning point.

'No one can answer that. Only Al himself. But I think you can be sure that he did it because he believed it was right.'

'Finch was in love with him. He had everything. All he had to do was take the people up there and down again, and then it went wrong.'

'Maybe,' Adam said slowly, frowning through the beer haze. 'Maybe the promise of *everything* was too much for a man like Al.'

Too rich, too plentiful, too enticing. Too accessible for Al, who lived by what was difficult and dangerous, his strength that was also his failure.

I wish I had known him longer, Sam thought. Or maybe I did know him, and all the better because the time was so short and so raw. I wish I could let him know that I'm not going to fuck up now. He said that once, *I don't need you to fuck up out there . . .*

'I think there might be something in what you say,' Sam murmured at length.

The eerie clarity of perception was fading at last, falling down like a theatre curtain obliterating a stage set. He looked out for oblivion, with relief.

The evening was changing gear around them, shifting from early into late. The after-work drinkers were drifting away, leaving the groups of stayers who moved inside to the lit-up magnet of the bar. One of the women looked back over her shoulder at Adam and smiled as she moved off. He watched her go, with an echo of a smile.

'Did you talk to Finch?' he asked, turning back to the table again.

'I wrote her a letter, that's all. About Al. What else could I do? The guy she loves is dead. I was there, I was part of the reason.' He shrugged, finding words inadequate. 'I should call her and ask her to dinner?'

'George says she's had a rough time. One foot amputated.'

'A foot?'

He didn't intend to diminish the loss, but it seemed insignificant measured against the sum of her. She was alive, just as he was alive. Adam was watching him, waiting for something. They had acquired two more beers.

'Look. I followed her out to Kathmandu, I forced my company on her, I was crass and embarrassing.'

'Yup. You were.'

'So I'm going to leave her to recover in peace.' It was chilly now and the other tables under the awning were all empty. He tried to remember what it was that his mother used to say. If you love something, let it go; was that it?

'Okay, buddy.'

Sam sighed, then lifted his glass and drained it. It was lonely without her. It was lonely without both of them. 'What're you doing now? You want to make a night of this?'

'You have to ask?'

In the morning, Sam opened his eyes very carefully. There was a weight crushing his skull and a desert lining the inside of his mouth. Beer followed by whisky hadn't wiped out any consciousness in the end, all it had done was make him feel like throwing up. He got out of bed, went to the sink and drank a half-pint of water. He rubbed his mouth with the back of his hand, winced, then crossed to the table where his laptop sat among paint pots and pizza boxes. He tapped at the keys to log on.

Frannie could sell the apartment, or buy him out if she preferred. His share of the business was for sale too. All that mattered was that he got out and moved on, and it came to him now what he should do. He stared bleary-eyed at the Net pages.

'Cheap flights,' he muttered to himself. 'Let's see.'

The Buchanans' glorious living-room overlooking the water was long enough to serve as a practice walk. Her own apartment was too small to permit more than a few consecutive steps without the need to negotiate a turn or a corner. Finch placed one careful foot in front of the other all down the expanse of polished maple.

It was August and she was breaking in her new prosthetic foot. Except for the constraints of space it was much easier to work on it indoors, because the loss of the toes on the other foot made it harder still to hold her balance and the smallest unevenness of the ground could cause her to stumble. Triumphantly she reached the far end of the room, clasped her hands around the waist of a primitive stone statue to steady herself and swung her hips round for another lap.

To be without crutches at last, walking under her own power, felt like being given a pair of wings.

The foot was excruciatingly uncomfortable, but that was the point. She was supposed to walk as far as she could manage so that her prosthetist could evaluate the fit of the socket. It was too tight now and the pressure points on her flesh would indicate where the plastic cup should be heat moulded to ease the pinch. Finch glanced down at the foot. It was a functional structure of metal and composite, with a plastic leaf spring to mimic the spring of a real foot, but with no attempt to resemble the appearance of what had gone. She had been given the choice of flesh-coloured rubber and plastic with moulded toes and blank nails like a huge doll's, but she had refused it. She liked the polished steeliness of this one. Once she had mastered it, she was sure that it would feel strong and solid.

Glancing down even for a second was a mistake. She was supposed to keep her chin up and her eyes fixed on where she was heading. Her new foot wandered away and she overbalanced on the real one and fell over sideways, adding a fresh bruise to the multicoloured collection on her hip. It was an effort to haul herself upright again, with the aid of a chair back, and she was panting and splay-legged as she held on.

Clare came in from the terrace overlooking the sea. She let her daughter recover her balance and take another free step, instead of running to help her, and Finch gave her a half-smile of acknowledgement. When she first came out of the hospital she had spent several weeks living back at her parents' home because she couldn't manage on her own in the city. She had had to learn patience with their protectiveness. It was like thinking herself back into childhood, remembering how it was to be vulnerable and to accept their physical ministrations. Her mother dressed her stump and pushed her wheelchair, and talked about Finch and her brothers when they were children. Finch listened to the stories, even finding that she was interested in them now.

In return for her submissiveness, by some unspoken exchange Clare recognised her longing for independence. Like a child again, growing up and away.

'You learned to walk the first time right where you are now. It was a complete surprise. Up on your feet and three tottering steps before your father caught you.'

'A surprise? That's why there's no video footage? I've always wondered.'

Clare laughed, after a second. It was acceptable, now, for Finch to tease her about the adoring documentation of every milestone in their lives. Today was another milestone, although a small one. It was her thirty-third birthday. Caleb was in town from San Diego, to give a lecture, and Marcus and James and their wives were also expected. It would be the first time all the Buchanans had been together since Finch left for Nepal.

'You could do the table for me, darling,' Clare suggested, and Finch at once moved with her tentative gait to the drawers where the cutlery and glassware were kept. Even the balance of expectation around the most banal domestic chores had shifted. Now she was grateful that Clare wanted her to do this, instead of suggesting that her disability disqualified her. She took out her mother's ivory-handled knives and the beautiful heavy glasses, and laid them in their places, moving behind each chair. She had to do everything very slowly because hurry was beyond her. She found an unfamiliar satisfaction in this deliberate concentration on the simple task.

Clare came back as she was finishing. She had often complained in the past that Finch never had time to do anything properly, it was always a rush. She'd eat off a sheet of newspaper on the kitchen table if she could. And because they always rose to one another's bait Finch would answer briskly that it was exactly what she did do, in her own home. Now Clare said simply, 'That looks nice.' The space of mild evening air between them seemed to stretch and glimmer with altering perceptions.

Marcus and Tanya arrived with Angus, and Finch demonstrated the new walk for them all. The prosthesis hurt even more viciously now, but she walked anyway.

'Look. No stick.'

Six steps across the polished maple. Marcus was interested in the system of springs and bumpers that were designed to replace lost muscle function and he knelt to watch the action.

'In time, I'll have a set of different feet for different activities. I can have one made to fit a ski boot.'

'One for driving?'

'And one for dancing.'

Angus opened a bottle of champagne. James and Kitty came with Caleb from the airport, and the family gathered round her to drink a toast.

'Best foot forward, Bunny,' Angus said. 'Many happy returns.'

Finch drank her champagne, looking around the circle of faces. She saw sympathy for her injuries and relief that she was safely with them. 'Thank you,' she said. She accepted her place among them gratefully and without the need to push at the boundaries. 'I'm so glad to be here.'

They ate dinner at the long oak table and Clare sat serenely at the foot of it, facing her husband at the head. Finch remembered the last one, the farewell dinner, and how her mother had needled her about getting engaged. She could recall her irritation, but the underlying reason for it seemed to have broken up. Of course Clare would want her to be married, why wouldn't she? Her own marriage had been successful, here was the evidence of it around the table in the candlelight. Suzy had mocked the family idyll, but she was now immersed in creating her own version. Thinking of her, Finch felt an unfamiliar contraction in her belly and she minutely curved her spine to suppress it. It was the first pang, she realised. The first twist of yearning for a baby.

Suzy: Hallelujah.

Finch: Hallelujah nothing. I'm thirty-three, I'm one-footed and I'm alone.

She looked again at Kitty and Tanya, and saw how they had been absorbed into the family. How our families define us, she thought, whether we wish it or otherwise.

She tried to imagine Al sitting here among them and she could not.

After dinner Finch sat out with Caleb on the

terrace. There were huge salt-glazed pots out here, groups of them presenting voluptuous curves against the navy-blue sky and sea. Finch had taken off the metal foot and Caleb cradled her lower leg on his lap while they listened to the distant murmur of the surf.

'Are you finding it very hard?' Caleb asked after a while. He was rarely in Vancouver and Finch had seen much less of him than of the rest of the Dream Team.

'Not so hard, I suppose. I see plenty of people who have worse things to deal with. And it was my choice to go, wasn't it?'

'Sometimes in a dream, or when I'm just waking up, I think that you didn't come back. I grapple with the loss, you know, shifting it around like a weight to be carried. I find that I'm angry with you, and jealous that you are gone and it's me who's left here without you. And then I wake up properly and it's like putting the weight down, and everything is bright with relief.' He rested his hand on her knee and laughed. 'How selfish.'

'I feel a version of the same thing. Grief, for the people who died and relief that I survived. Anger at . . . their absence. It is selfish, but I think it's normal.'

Her favourite brother was looking at her and she knew that he was waiting for her to tell him something more. She moved her mouth, experimentally, but nothing came out. If she told Caleb that she had loved Al and he had died, then it wouldn't be fair not to tell the others. Maybe some time she would talk about it to Clare, and her father and brothers, but not now. She would keep him for a while, keep him from being absorbed by them.

And that is truly selfish, she thought.

'Does it matter that you didn't get up there?'

'Yes. But I couldn't go any further. Not just because of the feet, maybe that only happened after I knew in my heart that I wasn't going to make it. The blood not pumping round fast enough and the extremities protesting. I didn't have the determination that the others did. Not quite the will of steel.' She added, very quietly, 'It was a valuable thing to discover about myself.'

Caleb said, 'I think that in the past, philosophical is the last word I would have reached for to describe my sister. But you seem to have become so.'

'Maybe.'

James came out to join them and stood leaning against the tallest of the pots. 'What are you two talking about?'

'Matters of life and death,' Caleb answered.

When Finch was in bed, sitting up in the blue silk nightdress, Clare knocked on her door. She was in a bathrobe and had taken off her make-up. Her face looked soft and lined, disarmed. She came in when Finch invited her and sat on the side of the bed, as she hadn't done in this room since Finch was a schoolgirl. They talked a little about the evening and Finch thanked her for the celebration of her birthday.

'Thirty-three years,' Clare said. 'I wanted a daughter more than I have ever wanted anything. I thought if I had a girl, she would be just like me. An ally, a friend in a house full of men.'

'And then you got me.'

'I'm sorry it hasn't been easier between us. I

suppose it was wrong of me to assume you would want all the things I believed in.'

There was no need to enumerate them. It was as if Finch had made a list, as soon as she could write, and worked out the ways to make her life the opposite of her mother's. 'I never understood that I was lucky to have you. I certainly never told you, so I'm saying it now. You were staunch for Dad and for all of us in a way that I didn't let myself see because I rejected what you stood for. What wives and mothers stood for, I mean, not just you. I thought women should work and fight.'

'And climb mountains.'

'In the purest sense, if you like. A mountain is a metaphor.'

Clare looked straight into her eyes. At the margin of Finch's mind a resemblance tugged and when she shifted her attention to it, it was of course between the two of them. The bone under the flesh, the will, were so similar as to be almost the same. The aspects were different and so the likeness had never struck her properly before.

'I'm proud of you,' Clare said abruptly. 'Your work, your place in the world. And your friendships. I wish I had friends like yours.'

Clare was partisan. Her husband and children came first and their interests were to be promoted above everything else. The fierce determination didn't make her easy to befriend.

Finch put her hand over her mother's. 'You've got us.' It was a child's blinkered assurance, she knew that. Everything about this talk, even about all the time she had spent with her family since Everest, was like being a child trying to grow up. Making a better job of it this time, she hoped.

'Thank you.' Clare let go of her hand and stood up. She was always poised, in the end, with her motherly dignity. 'Do you want me to drive you to the city in the morning?'

Finch was working full-time again. It was a relief to be back in her surgery and to look after her patients after the long weeks of recuperation and physical therapy. But she couldn't drive her own car yet.

'Yes, please. If you've got time.'

'Of course I have,' Clare said quickly, as they both knew she was bound to. She bent down and kissed Finch on the cheek. Not quite tucking her up, but almost. 'Happy birthday.'

Autumn came, and days of rain and wind. The city slowly battened itself down for the long winter. Finch worked hard, covering for Dennis who went to India to travel for a month, and in the rest of her time she lived a measured existence between her apartment and the rehab clinic, and her circle of friends. The practice nurses and Dennis helped her out with procedures that were physically awkward for her to manage, and her patients were mostly obliging and accommodating.

Her walking steadily improved, and the artificial foot was altered and adapted until it became comfortable. She spent more time wearing it and discarded her crutches. A stick was usually necessary, especially when she was tired or on treacherous ground, and she used it even when she could just have managed without. She made the effort not to push herself beyond reasonable physical limits, trying instead to accept her disability. She thought of Al in all the spaces and silences of her days, and at night when she lay staring up into the darkness. After the one letter from Sam, she heard no more.

On 14 December the telephone call came when she was eating breakfast and sliding half an eye over the newspaper.

'Suzy?'

'Ten past three this morning. A boy.'

'Oh, darling. How wonderful. How *wonderful*. How was it?'

'Total nightmare. Agony beyond belief, as a matter of fact.'

'Who does he look like?'

'Short straw. Jeff's dad, the living image.'

Finch laughed delightedly. 'Don't tell me any more. I'm on the next flight, it's all worked out with Dennis.'

When she arrived in Oregon Suzy and the baby were already home. There were Christmas lights in the trees in front of all the houses down the Suttons' road and a Father Christmas in a sleigh drawn by four miniature reindeer sat on a neighbouring front lawn. Jeff came to the door when Finch made her way carefully up the path from the airport taxi. He was wearing an apron and carrying an armful of laundry.

'Hey, Dad.'

'Come in and see them. They're amazing, you won't believe it.'

The house looked like the aftermath of an explosion. Flowers still in their delivery wrapping were lined up on the stairs, carrier bags of shopping spilled their contents across the hallway and an undecorated Christmas tree leaned against the kitchen door. Finch barely even noticed: Suzy had been her room-mate for years and mess was her milieu. In the bedroom Suzy was propped up against cushions with the baby in her arms. Her gappy smile was a blaze of triumph. Jeff hovered tactfully in the doorway to give them their moment together.

'Here he is. James Shepherd Sutton.'

Finch bent over him. There was a tiny, wrinkled fist pressing against a smooth crimson cheek with a fuzz like the skin of a peach and two damp crescents of dark eyelashes. She had seen dozens of newborns including her own nephews and nieces, and they were invariably affecting, but this one was different. He was Suzy's. Closer to being her own than anyone else's baby ever could be. Her hands instinctively reached out for him and Suzy's grin widened still further. She lifted up her son and gave him to Finch.

The weight was nothing. He fitted in the curve of her elbow and as she shifted him his tiny mouth opened in a yawn, an expression of ancient and infinite wisdom flitting across his crumpled face.

'My God,' Finch whispered. His head was damp and pungent with newborn scent. The road outside lay silent and empty in the failing light, and the tiny lanterns twinkled in the branches of the trees.

'He is perfect,' she said.

Jeff had come in to sit by Suzy on the bed and he put his arm round her so that she nestled against him.

'Suzy was just great,' he told Finch proudly. 'Did it all straight out of the textbook.'

'What about the cursing and yelling?'

'Isn't that what you're supposed to do?'

'Of course it is.' Finch smiled. She lifted the baby with one hand cradling his damp head and kissed the tiny forehead. Then, reluctantly, as if she was peeling away a layer of her own skin, she handed him back to his mother and her empty fists dropped to her side. The parents bent their heads over him, murmuring and incredulously touching their fingertips to the curves of nose and cheek. It was a nativity scene, touched with the comedy of the fibreglass reindeer, and the fluted beard and Disney leer of the Father Christmas on the opposite lawn. But the rightness of it and the purity, that was elemental.

Finch stood at the margin of the circle, looking inwards.

I wish he were mine, she thought.

Fifteen

There were no guests in the house, of course, because it was Christmas Eve. All the fishermen who came and the climbers and the rest of them were presumably at home with their families, doing family things. Molly sat in the dark at the top of the stairs, listening to the small clicks and creaks of resting woodwork and the swish of cars passing outside in the steady rain. She was aware of the underlying threads of silence, looping in filaments through the rooms, and the unspoken words caught in them.

It was hard, nowadays, to talk about anything in this house, beyond the everyday exchange of information about chores and mealtimes. Al had never lived here, it wasn't that some physical thing had gone out of the place when he died. It was more that when he was alive she and Jen had shared their separation from him. They had made a partnership of surviving together and mostly they had allowed each other their different shades of feeling about him. Now that he was gone, and gone so absolutely, they seemed to have moved apart rather than coming closer together.

Molly folded her arms on her knees and rested her

forehead on them. She squeezed her eyes shut until blooms of colour burst behind her eyelids and briefly distracted her from the pressure of missing him. She wondered what to do with the evening. Most of her friends had put in money to rent a minibus and a driver for the night, and had themselves taken to a club in Llandudno. If that wasn't a contradiction in terms, she thought. Jen was busy in the kitchen; she could hear the rush of water in the pipes when she turned on the sink taps. She had offered to help but her mother had turned from the table with a mixing spoon in her hand and a perplexed look. It's Christmas Eve, don't you want to go out somewhere? I might, later, Molly had answered vaguely. She had gone up to her room and then come out again to sit on the stairs. The telephone ringing made her open her eyes and stand up in one movement that gave her a swoop of giddiness. She hung on to the banister and waited for Jen to call her to the phone, but her mother's voice murmured in the kitchen and broke into low laughter.

When she was sure the conversation was over Molly went slowly down the stairs and put her head around the door. There was the Christmas tree in its usual place behind the cluttered sofa and two small piles of presents beneath it. Only the permanence was different. Last year, Al had been away for three weeks over Christmas, taking a group of businessmen to Argentina to climb Aconcagua.

'I might go down to the Dragon for a drink,' Molly said. 'If you're sure there's nothing that needs doing.'

Jen smiled at her. 'Good idea.'

There was one other person coming tomorrow to

share their Christmas dinner: Al's much older sister Cath. Molly didn't like her particularly, but Jen said it was Christmas and Cath had had a sad life.

'See you later,' Molly said. She took a slicker jacket off the peg in the hall and let herself out of the front door.

Rain made pallid haloes around the street lights and laid shiny tracks on the tarmac. There was a slaty smell, spiked with cats and wet evergreen. Al's old Audi was parked in Jen's usual place. It represented the major part of their inheritance, Jen had once remarked. Tyn-y-Caeau had only been rented and there had been very little in the bank. There was a small insurance policy but most of that went, Jen said, on bringing his body back home and the party for a mob of climbers after the funeral.

Molly put her hands in her pockets and started walking towards the pub, without any sense of anticipation. It was just a relief to get out of the house.

A car was coming towards her, spraying a glitter of puddle water across the pavement. She was retreating towards the hedge as it braked and the front passenger wound down his window. It was Dave from her class at school.

'Hey, Moll. We're going to Hoot's place. Want to come?'

The rear door swung open, scraping the kerbstone. 'We've got draw, we've got drink, we're going to have a party.' In the back seat was Phil Williams, who had been her boyfriend in the fifth form.

Molly shrugged. 'Okay.' She squeezed in beside Phil who immediately draped a heavy arm over her shoulders and began nuzzling her ear. They drove on, back past Molly's home and away from the ribbon of other houses. Hoot lived in an isolated farm out on the Capel Curig road. Phil smelled very strongly of beer and Eternity for Men, neither of which did much for her.

She twisted herself away from him.

'Dave, stop here. I'm not coming. I'll walk back, thanks.'

There was a murmur of dissent, but nothing vociferous. The car slithered to a halt and Molly extricated herself. Happy Christmas she agreed to the chorus of voices, happy Christmas.

There was a low stone tower ahead and a curved stone wall under a black yew tree. Molly walked slowly, following the bend of the road, until she came to the lych-gate under its little slate roof. There was a wooden seat beside the gate, covered with coarse graffiti. Younger kids came here to smoke and get off with each other, because there was nowhere much else to go. But there was no one here tonight.

Al's grave was in the new part of the cemetery, over to the far side beyond the Victorian angels and marble monuments. He had a plain slab of local slate, just engraved with his name and dates. Molly didn't visit it that often and she didn't creak the lych-gate open tonight. Instead, she sat down out of the rain on the bench and fished a pack of cigarettes out of the pocket of her jeans. She lit one and smoked, watching the dribble of rain off the roof. It wasn't really cold, just raw and wet.

He had broken his promise, that was the point. He had promised he would come back and he hadn't.

Except in a box, if you could count that, and that was only because she had insisted on it herself. He had once told her that dead people sometimes lay on the mountain for years and other people went by them on their way up and down. Molly didn't think she would have been able to close her eyes ever again, without the sight of him lying there in the snow. Maybe he would have preferred to be left where he was. But he couldn't always have what he wanted, could he?

They had to get him back down from the mountains, the greedy, cruel, white, killing mountains. Everest and the rest couldn't have the last say. Jen had understood that, anyway, because she hated them too.

Brave men, the Sherpas who admired him, had gone back up and rescued his body. They brought him down and sent him home, and Jen and she had been able to have a funeral on a bright May afternoon with the hawthorn hedges foamy with blossom. Aunt Cath had stood by the grave crying like a kid, her mouth wide open and her eyes squeezed shut. She was old, sixteen years older than her brother, and she had always been strange. Molly was proud of the fact that she and Jen had kept control of themselves. She had cried enough herself, enough to make her feel that her tear ducts were drained and her eyelids lined with sandpaper, but not in front of all those people in their dim black clothes.

How Al would have hated it, she thought.

The party afterwards, or as much of it as she could remember, would have been more to his taste because he could be sociable, when it suited him, with his own kind of people. She had drunk a full mug of whisky and had gone away to be sick on her own, with the sound of shouting and singing rising through the floorboards.

Molly finished her cigarette and the drip of rainwater gradually lessened. She was glad she hadn't gone with Phil and the rest to hang out at Hoot's place. It was better to be alone. The fact was that you couldn't count on promises. Even Al's. Especially Al's. Only the ones you made to yourself, you could make sure that you stuck to those. She stared down at the paving stones and their greasy film of wetness, and promised herself that she would be all right. She was marking time now, in a place on her own, but she didn't think she would always be lonely, or at odds with her mother, or left sidling between the seizures of grief. She would leave here and go to university, and life would move forwards again.

I won't be angry, either, about what has happened. If I can help it.

The man who had sent her back the picture of herself had written a lot about how brave Al had been, and how generous, to save his life.

Maybe, Molly thought. Of course he had been brave, no one could ever say otherwise about her father. If he had made a mistake in taking those men on up when it was too late, then the mistake was all wound up with courage and obligation, and he had put it right as far as he could. It was more that it seemed a brassy, temporary kind of bravery, summoned up in the pumping of adrenalin and sadly extinguished by the storm. There were quieter kinds, that had to be kept up for longer in humdrum places and without applause, and maybe these were worth more. Jen's kind of bitter, stoical bravery, that was one of them.

'I don't know,' Molly said aloud. 'Could be I'm wrong about you. I won't know now, will I?'

She didn't expect an answer. Her father was gone, completely, and nothing of him lingered here. If there was some ghost, some print of him in the membrane dividing two worlds, then it was up on the south-east ridge of Everest.

Al always did what he wanted in the important things. That was what Jen said.

Molly stood up. She had been sitting too long and the damp made her shiver. She turned her back on the graveyard and began walking home.

As soon as she turned her key in the front door she knew there was someone else in the house other than Jen. She padded down the hallway to the kitchen door and twisted the handle. Jen was leaning against the Rayburn, nursing a glass of wine and laughing with her head on one side and her face collapsed into creases of happiness. It gave Molly a shock because she hadn't seen her look that way for so long. The man was sitting on the edge of the sofa with cats wound around him and his hands loose between his knees. He was Tim someone, he did Jen's accounts and VAT for her. An ordinary man with corduroy trousers, thinning hair and sandy skin.

'Hi, Molly. Who was in the pub?'

Tim was trying to get to his feet, impeded by cats and cushions.

'No one, really.'

'On Christmas Eve? You remember Tim, don't you?'

'Yes.'

They smiled at each other, mouth-smiles.

'Hello, Molly. Happy Christmas.'

'You're all wet. Do you want a drink?'

She didn't. She made excuses and wished them happy Christmas, and Jen embarrassingly reminded her to hang up her stocking – a red felt thing with a bell on the toe she had had since she was five. She backed out of the kitchen and left them to themselves.

There was a small silence after she had gone.

'She misses her father, they were very close. She took it very badly,' Jen said at length. 'I worry about her.'

'Don't worry. Everything will be all right,' the man said, which was exactly what she longed to be told.

Sam worked a long shift in the kitchen under the bamboo and canvas shelter. He enjoyed the rhythms of manual work and the routines of preparing large quantities of food, and regularly volunteered for this rather than the administrative work he was supposed to do. He started at first light, and scrubbed and chopped mounds of potatoes. He consigned them to the big pans to make soup, then he boiled rice and stirred up curried vegetables. A stream of people came and went, looking for hot tea and Tibetan bread, or a talk and a comfortable place to sit, and he and his two cook assistants attended to them and kept the food preparation going at the same time. When midday arrived three hundred people crowded under the canvas mess shelter. There were street children who lived on the filthy waste ground next to the refuge, and beggars and cripples, and women with tiny, sick babies, and all the crowds of Kathmandu's poorest and most desperate inhabitants. They came past the big metal vats of hot food, and Sam and his helpers ladled out the servings. The canvas sides of the shelter were rolled up and sunshine sliced in and lit up dusty slabs of air. The children spilled outside and played in the dirt with the dogs. It was late March and the bitter winter was over. Kathmandu lay under its awning of pollution and steamed in the warmth.

'Sam, visitor for you,' Linda, the Australian volunteer, shouted to him from the open doorway that led to the charity office. The office and communications centre was supposed to be his domain, although he spent little time in it. Sam was still serving food to the last people in the line and he called back over his shoulder, 'Send whoever it is in here.'

Visitors were a regular feature at the project. Supporters, travellers and short-stay volunteer workers dropped in all the time because it was a sociable place. When Sam looked up a minute later from another plateful of food he saw a Mountain People uniform jacket in front of him. Immediately the steamy clamour of the food tent dropped away, and the sunshine faded and he was back on the ridge with the wind howling in his head.

'*Namaste*, Mr Sam.'

'Mingma?'

Mingma stirring his *puja* fire with a juniper branch.

Then high on the mountain, turning back to lead Finch down to the South Col.

Sam put down the soup ladle and held out his hand. 'I'm so pleased to see you. How did you know I was here?'

The little man laughed at him. 'Kathmandu a very small place, you know that. Soup any good as Dorje's?'

'Try some.'

'Ang here with me too, outside.'

Sam filled two platefuls and left his assistants to finish off the queue. They ducked under the canvas side wall and passed by a group of the smallest street children who were rolling in a game with two puppies.

Ang was sitting cross-legged with his back against a wooden post but he scrambled up at the sight of Sam. '*Namaste*.'

There was a shiny pucker of scar tissue running up into Ang's hairline, but no other visible sign of his injuries. They took their places in a row, with the soup and the view of scrambling children.

Mingma carefully tasted a spoonful. 'Not so good as Dorje's, I think.'

'What do you mean? I made it.'

The two Sherpas roared with laughter. 'Just as I say.' But Mingma added seriously, 'Very good work, here. Everyone speaks of it.'

It was Adam Vries on their evening together back in Seattle who had mentioned Netta Gould and her work with the homeless in Kathmandu. Sam had listened to him talking about her and, through the fog of whisky and loss and indecision, had decided immediately to come back out here and offer his help. He had fixed on the idea of doing something for someone else, for once, and he had clung on to it like a lifeline.

He had been here now for almost eight months. He had worked for Netta for a tiny wage, dealing with the accounts and administration of the soup kitchen and children's shelter. He had designed and set up a website for the charity, and rationalised their chaotic communications system and drawn up fund-raising projections. And he had enjoyed making countless gallons of potato soup, and playing with the little kids who lived with Netta and regarded her as their mother, because they had no one else.

'Netta does it,' Sam said simply. 'What are you both doing here?'

Ang finished his soup and took a single cigarette out of his pocket. He offered it to Sam with a lift of his eyebrows but Sam shook his head.

'Work,' Ang said.

Mingma went on, 'Everest climb again. We meet clients here in two days, then we go up.'

Of course, it was that time of year. A year since George, Al, Finch and the others had assembled full of anticipation at the Buddha's Garden. It seemed much longer.

'Another company. Not Mr George this time. He does not come with clients this year.' Mingma flashed a gold tooth in a smile. 'But he gave me the coat to keep. I like it.'

'Seeing it brings back memories,' Sam said.

They nodded at him. He knew that there was not the same weight of regret and sadness balled up with the memories for them. Not because they cared less, but because risk and death in the high places were what they lived with, and the means by which they fed their families. It was everyday for them. They had less choice in the matter than Al had done.

Then Mingma said, 'We went for him. Me and Pemba and the others. Bring him down for his family.'

'Al?'

'Yes. The other man, gone for ever. In Tibet.'

'I know. But that was a good thing you did for Al,' Sam said and Ang laughed.

'Not telling us what to do, that time.'

Sam laughed too. There was nothing else to do and it was a fact.

'Sad for the boy who fell, you know, but not Al. He die in the best place for him,' Mingma concluded. 'This is the way.'

'This is the way,' Sam echoed.

It was true. The pain that jarred his movements and memories was easing. He had been carrying the burden of Al's death and trying to make some amends for it out here in Netta's extended family. He wouldn't forget what Al had done, but he could begin to fit it into his understanding of Al's life and his own, and the way to live from now on.

He sat for a while longer in the sun, watching the children and the puppies, and chatting with Mingma about the new expedition and the new season's work.

After the Sherpas had gone Sam went to look for Netta. He found her in her house, where she kept a tiny room for herself and gave the rest over to the children. She was in her fifties, a grey-haired woman with a lined face and a bulky body. In the months after Sam had turned up at the project and demanded to be given work, Sam and Netta had become close friends.

'What's happened?' she asked when she saw him.

'Can I have some tea?'

'Pour some for me too.'

When they had their glasses of *chai* Sam said, 'It's time for me to think about going home.'

She looked at him, sharp-eyed behind her spectacles. 'I'll be sorry to lose you, Sam. Not just because of what you do here, but because I'll miss you. But I think it's time, too.'

He told her about the visit from Mingma and Ang. He hadn't run away to the project and he hadn't been hiding from anything in his time here. If there had been self-interest in what he had done, it had been in using it to deal with Al's death and what it meant to him. He had needed to make himself useful, to be a contributor, instead of a competitor and a consumer. And he knew that he had been useful because Netta told him so, and Netta never coloured the truth. But he had been waiting for a sign from outside that would remind him and stir him up, and tell him that it was time to start moving again. The Sherpas had done that, talking about Al and others, and bringing Finch alive in his head again.

'You have things to do. But stay as long as you like and go when you are ready,' Netta said.

He put his arms round her meaty shoulders. 'Thank you. Who'll do what I've been doing?'

'Someone will come,' she said, in her composed Buddhist way.

Maybe, he thought, some of this remarkable woman's composure had even rubbed off on him.

Sixteen

The receptionist buzzed through to tell her that there was one more patient, a new registration. Finch looked at her watch as she clicked off the intercom button. It was seven in the evening, the beginning of May, another springtime with blossom on the back-yard trees, and voices and music drifting through open windows into the city streets.

The day's last patient knocked on the door. She called come in and the man who walked in was Sam McGrath.

She stood up awkwardly and caught at the edge of her desk to steady herself. There was pleasure at the sight of him definitely and, warmly slicked in with her surprise, a startled happiness that caught under her breastbone and gave her voice a breathless edge. 'Sam? Do you always turn up when you're least expected?'

'I won't do it again, if it bothers you too much.'

They took a step closer, examining each other's faces. Sam's had lost the puppyish, insinuating grin. He looked older and tougher.

'Why didn't you write to me? Or call? In a whole year.'

'I did write.'

'Once.'

'I've been away until last week. And I thought you needed some time.'

He put his hand very lightly on her shoulder and kissed the hollow of skin beneath her cheekbone. A blind softened the light from the window and standing against it she was thinner and more beautiful than he remembered. In spite of the smile that lit up her face she looked solemn.

'I did,' she said quietly. She moved away and back to her desk, as if seeking its security. 'So, my last patient of the day. Are you here for a consultation?'

'I have no new symptoms.' Sam smiled as he watched her. She walked slowly, looking as if she might be tired, but there were no other signs of her injury. She was wearing loose trousers and high-cut shoes. 'I wondered if you might have dinner with me, though.'

Climb Everest first. They both heard her saying it but Finch winced at the memory. 'I am ashamed I ever said that.'

'It was a joke. You didn't expect me to go and do it. I didn't expect myself to. It seemed like a good idea at the time.'

An idea that had rooted and branched, then withered.

The time they had spent climbing together and everything that they had seen and done in that time seemed to have developed a shorthand between them; each knew what the other meant without the need to say it. That was such a luxury, Finch thought.

'I'm sorry you lost him,' Sam said.

'You lost him too.'

'Yes. I did.'

It was true; his brief connection with Al had offered more than a friendship, more than the example of a mentor. It was only in retrospect that Sam understood what a space Al might have filled in his life. His absence still snagged in the small hours when he woke for no reason and in the unguarded intervals of the day. He could only imagine how the same feeling must be amplified for Finch. They hesitated now, a metre apart, in the diffused light of Finch's consulting room. Their shorthand cut and elided the exchange so the words were almost unnecessary.

'How are your feet?'

She stood upright and took three steps, then sidestepped, sinking into a little bob as the left foot crossed behind the right before she raised herself on to tiptoe like a ballerina on points. She spread her arms, palms out, and took three more tiny steps, her face creased in concentration. It was only on the third point step that she lost her balance and dropped to flatfoot again.

'What do you think? Not bad?' she demanded, lowering her hands to her sides.

She had looked to Sam like a little girl rehearsing a variety turn. He was touched by her serious intentness. It must have taken so much effort to achieve these movements. 'Impeccable. Would you like to dance?'

He began to hum the 'Blue Danube' and Finch inclined her head in mock-polite acceptance like a debutante at a party. He took her in his arms and they circled in a slow waltz step, singing together, *da* da da, *da* da da. They covered the space between the door and the desk, and turned in front of the examination couch and the trolley loaded with wrapped speculums and latex gloves. They were lost in the humming intricacy of another turn when Dennis tapped at the door and eased it open. He saw Finch's head held up and the curve of her arm resting on the man's shoulder before they realised they were being watched and stopped dancing, almost guiltily.

'Excuse me. I didn't mean to interrupt.'

'You aren't interrupting,' Finch said quickly.

Yes you are, Sam mentally contradicted.

Finch introduced them and they shook hands.

As she stood between them Finch was thinking that meeting Dennis was Sam's first small exposure to her life, the real life that was lived between city streets, busy surgeries and her silent apartment. Nothing to do with the glitter and bare-bones urgency of the mountains. She was comfortable with his being here. It was odd that Al had never been any part of this world, but she was grateful for that now because it made his absolute absence easier to bear.

'Finch was showing me her paces.'

Dennis beamed through his round glasses. 'She has been amazing. More determined than any amputee I've ever known.'

She answered seriously, 'It's only one foot and three toes, Sam. It's been difficult sometimes, but I've had it much easier than some of the people I'm in rehab with. People who have lost whole limbs. And did you know that a man with an artificial leg just climbed Everest?'

Sam said, 'I read about that. Do you feel another challenge coming on?'

She met his question full on. 'No. I couldn't go back there again. It died, that bit of me, at the same time. Would you?'

He shook his head. 'No.'

'You got to the top, didn't you? Finch told me,' said Dennis.

'It isn't that, exactly. Not the business of did I step up there or not,' Sam answered. 'The truth is that I'm not a mountaineer. I don't have that need in me. Not the craving in my veins to go back and back, without which everything else is dry and peripheral. Didn't someone write about how life is poorer when the highest stake in the game, which is life itself, can't be risked?'

'Freud,' Dennis remarked.

'Yeah. Well, I don't want to play at the high-stakes table. Life is rich and varied and promising enough for me without needing to . . .' he cast around for another suitable metaphor and grinned because of his waltz with Finch '. . . keep dancing with death just to improve the rhythm.'

Finch murmured, 'I don't want to play either. I only thought I did.'

Dennis pursed his lips and said, 'I'm glad to hear it.' The light shone on the shields of his spectacles, making his face unreadable. He changed the subject deliberately. 'What do you do, Sam? Are you in town on business?'

He laughed. 'I'm between businesses. Finch has heard that before. I'm just visiting Vancouver.'

'Sam and I are going out to dinner,' Finch said.

Sam didn't turn his head to look at her because he didn't dare. It was too important, this trivial social announcement. It opened a door on a view that was so wide it made him breathless, but was also suddenly treacherous with invisible crevasses. If he had misread her, he thought, if after so much she turned out to be not what he had imagined, but something smaller. If they sat across a table from one another and found a desert instead of a fountain.

He made himself look. She was waiting, calm in profile.

'Then I won't keep you,' Dennis said quietly.

They walked out into the hall together. Sam and Dennis shook hands once more as Finch pressed the elevator button and they listened to the whine of the machinery responding. When the doors opened Sam and Finch stepped in together, and Dennis lifted his hand – an ironic blessing and a real salute.

'Enjoy yourselves,' he said, as the doors slid together and cut him off.

They rode down through the emptying building. The foyer was a space of shining tiles and the street outside was a blue-grey canyon with a river of evening traffic. They hesitated between the glass pinnacles of downtown office blocks.

'Shall we walk a bit?' Finch asked.

'Can you manage?'

'Pretty well.'

They took a direction at random. There was the slightest hesitation in Finch's gait and Sam tried to match his step to hers. She took his arm, sliding her hand to link them together, and they found a comfortable pace.

'I've got used to depending on people,' she said, without adding that before the mountain she had been defensive of her self-reliance. Sam nodded. The shorthand again.

The city street smelled of the warm dust of subways and corner-stand hotdogs, and the rubber and plastic and fume exhalation of clogged traffic, but the scent of summer always seemed stronger because the strip of clear sky overhead was lavender-grey and there were white wooden tubs of canna lilies outside the doors of a smart hotel. Finch and Sam walked arm-in-arm through the tide of passers-by as if they were the only two people in Vancouver.

'Are you tired?' Sam asked. 'How far do you want to go?'

She tilted a look at him. 'How far do you think?'

They were fencing with each other still.

Maybe this is all we can do, Sam thought, on a sluice of pessimism.

I don't know how to be with a man any more, Finch was thinking. Everything with Al was so fierce and with everyone else I have known so colourless by comparison. This is neither fierce nor colourless and I'm stumbling, as if I've lost the toes and feet of my feelings as well.

They came to an uneven kerbstone and it threatened her balance. Sam held her more firmly and they crossed the road, under the metal snouts of the impatient cars.

Everest and everything that clung around it had been so huge, and now they were walking composedly through the safe and familiar city as if the smooth seas had closed over and obliterated it.

I don't want that, Finch realised. I want to talk about it. The need swelled inside her and firmed her step. She nudged her shoulder against Sam's to alter their direction and he stopped in immediate response. Looking into his face she tried to fix it in her mind. The features were familiar but he seemed to be changing even as she stared at him. It was as if she were looking straight through the skin, and the net of nerve and muscle underneath it, into his head.

'There's a place near here. We could eat something. If you still want to, if we've walked far enough . . .' She broke off, confused.

'Which way?'

She pointed at an awning on a corner a block away.

'Good,' Sam said.

They reached the restaurant, an old-fashioned Italian place with red tablecloths and high-backed wooden chairs. A waiter in a white shirt and a dicky bow led them to a table in an alcove and made a show of unfurling napkins and presenting menus. Sam looked at the list of dishes with a pucker of memory chafing the corner of his mind. When he glanced across the angle of the room he remembered. He had come here once with Frannie, when they were killing time before catching a bus up to Whistler and a week's skiing. They had been tired and tetchy with each other, he recalled. The holiday that followed had not been a big success, either.

Tonight he read the menu, ordered food and chose wine. The other tables were occupied by couples and families, and loose groups of friends, a neighbourhood crowd in a good humour on an ordinary evening. With the red tablecloth, and the oversized pepper mill and the olive oil bottle between them, Finch and Sam warily let themselves be absorbed. It was only dinner. It wasn't a contract or a commitment.

Finch told him about her recuperation. She described the terrible helplessness of the first days when she was unable to walk at all, and the sense of inadequacy and the fear of a lifetime's dependence that had snapped at her.

Once the rehabilitation started, she said, learning to take her first steps had seemed to parallel other lessons, mostly in how to accept help from other people. She had needed emotional as well as physical support, and everyone around her had given generously. 'Dennis and my family were always there. My mother was the best of all. I never really valued her much before. I was forever defying her, without any particular reason, because I wanted to be different from her. And she always rose to my bait. But she looked after me and I let her, so I don't think either of us needs to prove anything any more.

'I hate being slow, and needing to look where I'm going and working out whether I can do something that I would never have given a thought to before.' She glanced at him now, amused and considering. 'But maybe it makes me a kinder person.'

Sam thought of her shoe, under the tablecloth, and the foot contraption sheathed inside it. He felt a soft weight of tenderness that made him want to cup the metal heel spring in his hands and kiss the steely arch.

'It's a clumsy kind of parable, isn't it?' Finch asked. 'Losing a foot in order to find your feet in the world?'

She was playing with a chunk of bread. Sam watched her hands, square with neat short nails; doctor's hands. On Everest, he remembered, they had been torn and chapped, and the fingertips split and seamed with cold. As had his own. The whorled skin stung with the memory. Fingerprints, marked with what had happened. It was as if Al and Sandy were there, faces under his hands, features to be traced with damaged fingers.

'Clumsy? Harsh, maybe. There must be things you can't do, things you used to enjoy.'

She dismembered the bread crust, bending her head over it. Look at me, he wanted to say. He hadn't come here to set her a test or to face one himself, but he still found himself edgy with apprehension. What if, after so much? What if the certainty was an illusion?

'I can bear that quite well,' Finch said. 'I would be a poor specimen if I couldn't. If I lost sight of how lucky I am.'

'Both of us.'

The waiter brought veal piccata and grilled swordfish, and set them down with murmurings about *la bella signora*. Finch raised her eyebrows minutely and Sam suddenly laughed, just from the simple pleasure of finding himself sitting here opposite her. Not too complicated, he warned himself. Don't make everything so complicated.

'I liked Dennis. And I'd like to meet the Dream Team.'

'You will,' she said. The space of table between them lost its geometric definition; it was a hair's breadth and a continent, both at the same time. How,

Sam wondered, am I going to stop myself just putting my hands on her?

Not yet. This would definitely be the wrong time. She was wary of him and he wouldn't give her any more reason than he had done already.

He sliced up veal and ate a couple of mouthfuls without tasting anything. He talked about his months in Kathmandu. Finch was knowledgeable about aid work and asked informed questions about the charity's medical programme. The table became just a table again.

Plates were removed and puddings declined. Some of the places nearby were empty now. Sam realised that time must be passing with hallucinatory speed. He had told her about Michael and the time he had spent recovering in Wilding after the climb. Now she knew about the partial truce he had reached with his father, making a kind of symmetry with hers. But he hadn't asked the question he had intended.

Little cups of espresso were put down in front of them. He didn't remember ordering them; if he hadn't known otherwise he might have believed he was drunk. Time and distances seemed to be contorting in just the same way. Finch wasn't twiddling with her food any longer or pushing the foot of her wineglass among the crumbs on the tablecloth. She was looking at him, straight-faced and clear-eyed. Waiting, he thought, for what he was going to say.

'I wanted to ask you something,' he began.

'Yes.' A statement, not a question.

'I'm going to Wales, to see Al's wife and daughter. I want to tell them face to face what he did and how he died.'

She continued to look at him.

'Do you want to come with me?'

He picked up his cup while he waited for her answer. It was hot and the tiny handle was too small for his fingers; somehow it slipped and a trickle of coffee ran down his chin. Sam choked and put down the cup with a clatter. *Am* I drunk? he wondered.

Finch reached out with her napkin and dried the corner of his mouth. 'Yes,' she said.

'Why?' He couldn't help asking, without intending it.

Sombrely, she considered. Sam tried to follow her thoughts. To meet Molly, who was a part of him. To see where he had belonged, if he had truly belonged anywhere except in the high mountains. To salve some kind of guilt, a difficulty of conscience, perhaps, by seeing Al's wife. All these things and others he probably shouldn't guess at. Her private goodbye that still cut him with jealousy, even of a dead man.

'I wanted to go too. I wouldn't have had the courage without you.'

The waiter brought the bill in its saucer.

'We'll go together,' Sam said.

The next thing, they were standing outside the restaurant under the little awning. They were almost the last to leave. The sky had clouded and light rain was falling, drawing acrid scent out of the street dust. Only a few cars swished by. One of them was a cab and Sam whistled for it. When it drew in at the kerb he opened the door and helped Finch into it.

He stood back. 'I'll call you.'

'Do you have my home number?'

'I've had it for a year. Adam Vries got it for me from the Mountain People's files.'

Finch laughed and closed the cab door. He stood in the rain and watched the tail lights until they turned out of sight. He thought of himself coming out of this same door with Frannie and making his way with her to the bus station. Now there was the pointed end of happiness here, the fragile and brittle tip of a great solid wedge that lay waiting to be excavated.

When she let herself into it, the small space of her apartment was stuffy and silent. Finch moved slowly, looking at the bare walls and the precise alignment of the few pieces of furniture. No ornaments, no keepsakes, nothing extraneous at all. It was a colourless shell, kept for the bare motions of a bare life.

What am I denying, she wondered, and for whom? What have I been afraid of for so long? Was it just of encumbering myself?

I thought I was so fearless and I was nothing but a coward.

For that reason, did I choose to love Al? And did I love the man, or what he stood for?

She went into her bedroom. The covers on the bed were smooth and flat. There were no photographs on the bureau, no clutter of mementoes on shelves. That had always been Suzy's way. Long ago when they had been room-mates Suzy would exclaim, You've got no *stuff*. Where are all your *things*?

She found herself wishing for a picture of Al. Something that she could hold on to, now, just to talk to. Since the early days she had hardly cried for him. She walked to the window intending to draw the blinds and shut out the night's eye, but she leaned against the glass instead and stared out at the tiers of windows shuttering other people's lives. She let the tears slide down her face, thinking of going to Wales and saying goodbye.

Seventeen

They rented a car in London and drove north-westwards. Finch had been to England before, but this was Sam's first visit. She took the wheel and left him to look at the scenery. She was almost adept at driving again now, accustomed to the numb interposition of the prosthesis between her leg and the pedals.

Sam exclaimed about everything.

'It's so small. There's no space between the houses. It's like a toy place. You feel like you should put it all down in the rumpus room and run model trains through it. Look at that church. How old do you think it is?'

'Do you know that you sound exactly like an American tourist?'

'Of course I do.'

He was full of energy and curiosity; she liked that. He bought a guidebook, and insisted during their twenty-four hours in London that they went to see Westminster Abbey and the Tower. He took her to tea at the Ritz and, under the gilded and cerulean ceiling, enquired tenderly about whether her leg was hurting after so much walking and sightseeing. He handed her a pale cup of china tea and offered a silver tier of tiny triangular sandwiches. His behaviour was such a study of properness among the Japanese families and the pairs of British matrons with their Harrods parcels that Finch coughed with laughter into her starched linen napkin.

His behaviour was just as proper in other directions. He walked her to the door of her hotel room, took her key and opened it for her, and said goodnight. It was like going on holiday with a more amusing version of one of her brothers' well-behaved friends. She was intrigued by him, after the irritation his earlier pursuit of her had generated.

'What did you expect?' he asked, raising his eyebrows when she mentioned how decorous everything was. 'Beavis and Butthead?'

'How far is it now?' she asked, as they headed towards North Wales. There was a flat, fertile landscape that made her look around in surprise. She couldn't imagine that Al came from anywhere near here.

He examined the map. 'About an inch and a half, according to this. We'll be there in a couple of minutes, maybe less. Be careful not to accelerate or you'll overshoot.'

They passed a huge petrochemical works with everlasting torches of flame turned pallid by the afternoon light and a modern bridge over a broad, invisible river. They could have been approaching Detroit, Finch thought. Or anywhere urban and industrial and ordinary.

Sam had made all the arrangements for their journey. He had chosen an overnight stop in Chester, and they entered the maze of a traffic one-way system and eventually found their hotel in a double-decker layer of old shops and walkways.

At least this place was old. The window of Finch's room looked out on a steep jumble of timbered eaves and unevenly pitched roofs. She hung a pair of trousers uncertainly in the wardrobe and hesitated in the space between the door and the bed. It was only two hours' drive from here. Now that she was close to Al's home, a place filled with people and busy with domestic details that they had never shared with each other in the greed of their passion, she wondered why she had been rash enough to come here. She felt like an intruder, almost a spy. It was selfish of her to want to meet his daughter and to look at the views and the horizons that would have been familiar to him.

The soft knock at the door briefly startled her.

'Finch?'

'It's open.'

Sam stood in the doorway. He was big and broad in the confined room, and he stood sideways on as if he felt himself to be too large and wanted to diminish himself as far as possible. His grey eyes briefly held hers and flicked away again. The studied brotherly-friendly atmosphere of this strange non-holiday had suddenly dissipated, leaving an awkward edge. Sam also clearly felt the uncertainty of what they were doing and was concerned for her. She was glad of his company and the unspoken sympathy.

'Shall we go out and have a look around?' she asked as brightly as she could.

It was a grey, humid afternoon. They wandered

along the arcades of shops and peered in at the window displays, and then came to a section of the city wall with a wide, smooth walkway between raised battlements of stone. The paving of stone blocks was shiny and dimpled with centuries of wear. On either side of them the streets and houses and traffic glimmered in the thick heat.

'It's Roman. A Roman garrison town,' Sam said wonderingly.

The perspective of history made their concerns seem miniature. After a while they came to the bank of a river, with willow branches tilting over the water and a wide view of a racecourse beyond it. The path was busy with strolling couples and families trailing little children on wobbly bicycles. Sam and Finch continued among them, aware of how they looked like any other couple and silently conscious of their uncoupled status. A thin and constant slice of air remained between their adjacent arms and shoulders.

'Do they know we are coming tomorrow?' Finch asked.

'I telephoned before I came to your room this afternoon. I spoke to Jen and explained that we are . . . here, and asked if we could call in and talk to her. She said yes, of course we could, but we must understand that she's running a guest house and it's the busy season, so she might not have a lot of time to spare.'

'How did she sound?' Finch couldn't help asking.

'She sounded surprised. And maybe a little wary,' Sam answered after a moment's considering.

They walked back the way they had come, more

slowly because Finch had got tired before bothering to realise it. They stopped for a drink in a dark pub that smelled of beer and smoke, and later they found a bistro with checked tablecloths and ordered food that they didn't really want. When they came out again it was dark, with a threatening weight in the air. They had only walked a few steps before lightning flickered above the orangey glare of the street lights. There was a growl of thunder and the pavement was suddenly blotched with raindrops. By the time they reached the revolving doors of the hotel it was raining in solid sheets and they were both soaked. They scuttled across the lobby and into the lift, and Sam hurried Finch to the door of her room. He took the key from her, according to custom, and unlocked it. Then without warning he took her face in his hands and thumbed back strands of wet hair that were plastered to her cheeks. He kissed her, a quarter of an inch from the corner of her mouth and stood back.

'Goodnight,' he said. With her empty room behind her Finch watched him walk away and resisted the impulse to call him back again.

The thunder overnight left the air clearer and lighter. In the morning, as they drove further west into Wales, a line of purple hills swelled against the horizon ahead of them. They watched them coming closer, not saying much. Finch played with the buttons of the car's tinny radio, then flicked the off knob. The road was quiet and they covered the distance quickly. Suddenly they were in the mountains.

The place where Al's wife and daughter lived was a ribbon of dark stone and slate houses interspersed with gift shops, cafés and climbers' outfitters. Behind the buildings were sweeps of conifers and hills buttressed by crags and black slopes of scree. Even on a summer's midday there was a suggestion of darkness. It would come quickly, wrapping the rocks.

Finch thought, I can imagine him here.

A ponytailed boy in cut-off jeans and flipflops worn to thin crescents under grimy heels, stood with his back to them reading the cards in a newsagent's window. He carried a coil of perlon rope shrugged over one shoulder and the sight made Finch and Sam glance at each other. Finch eased her foot out of the car and awkwardly stood up, supporting herself on the door lintel before letting the prosthesis take her weight. Sam came round to her and she leaned on his arm.

'That's the first time I've seen you really falter,' he said. 'Is it hurting?'

She shook her head. 'He reminded me of Adam Vries.' Meaning that there were many other memories to be glimpsed over the shoulder of a long-haired boy with a rope. She shivered. 'I was afraid of something.'

'This is a climbing town, I guess. And I have never seen you afraid, either.'

'You haven't been watching very closely.'

'I think I have. Look, that's the house.'

Al's widow lived in a big, blank-faced house behind a line of spear-topped railings. There was a short path of coloured tiles leading to the front door.

'Are you ready?'

When she hesitated he stood in front of her with

his hands cupping her elbows. 'You wanted to come.'

'I know I did.'

They walked together to the door and rang the bell, hearing the sound of it somewhere deep in the recesses of the house. There was a long wait. Finch frowned at her two feet placed on the step. Then the door suddenly opened.

'Mr McGrath, Dr Buchanan,' the woman said.

Al's wife was small and thin, with shiny eyes and the creases of frown marks showing between her brows.

'Sam, and Finch,' Sam said. Jen's glance shifted to Finch's face. Behind her, framed against a door beyond which there was a glimpse of tables set with cloths and cups, stood a young woman. She was holding a bunch of cutlery in one hand like a spiky posy and she was the image of Al.

'This is my daughter Molly. Come in for a few minutes.' Jen defined the extent of the welcome and they followed her down a passage past the residents' dining- and sitting-rooms to a big room at the back of the house. Finch's attention was riveted on Molly and she had only the briefest impression of shabby functional furniture and a clutter of papers, laundry, knick-knacks and cats. There was the sound of hoovering from upstairs.

'Would you like a cup of coffee?'

They accepted politely and sat down where they could find space. Molly went to the big filter machine and slid a half-filled jug off the hotplate. Where Al's hair had been roughly cut short and was faded with grey, Molly's was a mass of dense dark curls. Her features were smaller and neater, but otherwise the resemblance was remarkable. Even her hands, setting out flowered mugs and pouring the coffee, were the same shape. Finch felt an equal longing to reach out and hold her in her arms, and to hide her face in her own hands from this image of the girl's father.

They took their mugs of coffee and sipped at them. Jen sat at the table and pulled a package of paper napkins towards her. She began folding them into tidy triangles, one after the other, as if she couldn't afford ever to sit still without doing something useful. She looked as if she was used to working hard. Finch thought of Al's life, by comparison, against a backdrop of remote and beautiful places. What he did was hard work too, but with a balm as well as a challenge in it that seemed absent from this mundane and industrious house.

There was a small silence. Overhead, the hoovering continued. A strong sense lay between them all of the man who had brought them together. His presence was almost palpable and yet, at the same time, he was so completely gone.

It was Molly who spoke first, to Sam. She sat on the sofa between two cats, with her hands clasped between her knees. The same posture, even, as her father. 'Thank you for sending back the picture of me. I'm sorry I never wrote.'

Sam nodded. He sat calmly, without fidgeting. Finch realised that she had never properly noticed the way that he could keep still. 'I didn't expect you to. I wrote to you when I sent it because I wanted you to know straight away that your dad took your photograph all the way with him to the top of the mountain and I found it in the pocket of his windproof after he died. I – Finch and I – came here because we wanted to tell you that Al was brave and very good at what he did. You know that, of course.'

'Yes,' Molly said fiercely.

'And I wanted to tell you as well, in person, what he did for me. He knew exactly what he was doing at the end up there, and he made a decision and it saved my life. I would surely have frozen to death if he hadn't protected me from the wind by lying on top of me. I don't know why he did it except out of nobility. I was only a guy on a mountain expedition, not even really a friend. Although I admired and respected him more than anyone I have ever met.' Sam paused and reflected for a moment. 'Except maybe my father.'

Finch thought that this was a remarkable speech. It was unaffected and honest, and she was moved by it. Molly's eyes were full of tears and Jen was looking straight back at Finch.

She knows exactly who I am, she realised, even if Al never gave her a word or a sign.

This was what she had feared, while hovering on the doorstep, and now she understood that, in fact, fear and even guilt were misplaced. Jen Hood didn't deserve or require either.

'Maybe it was what he wanted to do,' Jen said. Her voice was dry and cool. Finch remembered Sam's line from Freud, about the impoverishment of life if life itself could not be staked. The mountaineer's creed.

Molly rubbed the skin beneath her eyes with the heels of her hands, wiping away the trace of tears. 'Did you climb it?' she asked Finch suddenly.

'No. I turned back at the Hillary Step. My feet were frozen.'

They glanced automatically at her shoes. Finch didn't offer any more information.

'I'm proud my dad did it,' Molly said. 'It was really good that he did. I'm sorry the other climber died, you know, and if him dying was anything to do with Dad's leading. But maybe he was doing what he wanted as well.'

'I think he was,' Sam said.

Molly asked some more questions about the expedition and the part they had played in it. Finch and Sam took turns to tell her and Jen went on folding and stacking napkins, listening without speaking. In the end the talk faded out.

'Thank you for coming.' Jen slid her pile of napkins aside, indicating that the visit was over.

'There's one more thing,' Sam said, reaching into his inside pocket. He brought out a yellow envelope and put it on the table next to her. Jen looked at it, her frown deepening. Then she quickly opened the folder and took out the little sheaf of photographs. She laid the glossy rectangles in a grid on the table and gazed at them. They were of bearded men, their heads outlined against a lurid blue-green sky.

Al and Rix on the summit, snapped by Sam in the short minutes when they stood at the top of the world.

Molly leaned over her mother's shoulder and picked up one of the pictures to look at it more closely, and Finch watched them both hungrily. For some reason she had never thought that of course there would be photographs. And of course Sam would have thought it right for Jen and Molly to see them first.

'Yes,' Jen murmured. 'I'm glad he did it too. Have you seen them?'

She was asking Finch, who silently shook her head. The other woman held out three of the pictures while Molly still studied the fourth.

The hood of Al's wind suit ballooned behind him in the rip of the wind and his hair was torn back from his forehead in icy spikes. He had taken off his goggles and his eyes were narrowed to slits against the light. After enduring so much he was smiling, his lips pulled back to bare his teeth, a wild grin of pure triumph.

I didn't know it was like that, Finch was thinking. I thought it was all effort and suffering. Like it was for me up there.

There was his face, utterly familiar and with the same features as his daughter's, and the sound of his voice in her head, and still it occurred to her now looking at his picture that perhaps she had never known him. She shuffled the other photographs quickly, noting the small variations of the same image, then handed them back to Jen. Jen calmly looked at her.

'Can we keep them?' Molly asked.

'They are for you,' Sam told her.

The telephone rang and Jen walked across the room to answer it, jotting down the details of a booking in a big diary. When she replaced the receiver she looked at her watch.

Sam and Finch politely stood up and they found themselves filing back to the front door, past the room with the tables that Molly had been laying up ready for the next day's guest breakfasts.

'Molly's exams are finished. She's helping me with the work for the summer, until she goes to university,' Jen explained. Finch was at the door now. Her hand was groping uncertainly for the latch when Jen added, 'We had his body brought down and flown home, you know. You could go and see the grave, if you wanted to. Molly will show you where it is.'

Finch said, 'Thank you.' She was much taller than Al's wife but their eyes squarely met as they shook hands and said goodbye. Molly sloped out in front of them and headed for the street.

'Wait,' Jen said abruptly. 'I . . . maybe . . . perhaps you'd like to come back later? I don't do dinners for the residents. Once the rooms are cleaned and the breakfasts laid up there isn't much else to do before the morning. You've come a long way. I could give you both something to eat and we could talk some more, if you like? My partner will be here. You could meet him . . .'

Her voice was uncertain, interrogative.

'Yes,' Finch said. 'Or, wait a minute, Sam, is that all right with you?'

'Of course it is. We can get back to Chester a bit later.'

'About half six, then,' Jen said.

They followed Molly along the street. After a few hundred yards they came to a lych-gate with a pitched roof of purple slate and a bench in the shelter beneath it. Molly unlatched the heavy gate that gave access to the churchyard and pushed it open. There was a square stone church surrounded by partially clipped grass, and marble and slate headstones, and Molly took a path diagonally between the graves and through another small gate into a new enclosure. This quiet space was shaded by oak trees and it was only half full of new graves. The grass was unmown in the empty part, and it was thick with clumps of cow parsley and buttercups. In the sloping field beyond there were sheep gnawing the short turf.

Molly walked nearly to the end of the line and stopped at the foot of one of the graves.

'This is it. It cost a lot of money and it was difficult for the Sherpas who used to work for him to bring him back but I'm glad we did. I couldn't bear to think of him lying up there in the ice with nobody.'

Back before Finch's eyes swam the image of the dead climber she had seen and his forever frozen body. A sob came out of her mouth before she could swallow it down and tears started up in her eyes. Molly turned her head, with black spirals of hair whipping her cheeks, and reached out a hand in an instinct to comfort. Finch took it, then she put her arms around this smaller and vulnerable version of Al and held her tight.

'I loved him too,' Finch said.

'Yeah. I thought so. Mum and I thought that must be why you were coming.'

Sam stood a little to one side, looking at the inscription on the plain slate slab.

Molly disengaged herself quickly, shaking her arms and shoulders free from Finch's grasp like a cat slipping out of an armhold. 'Look. I'd better get back to help Mum, right? I'll see you later.' She sped round the corner of the field and disappeared past the church.

'Why didn't you tell me you had the pictures?' Finch asked.

'I guess I wanted everyone to see them at the same time.'

Al belonged to Sam too, she thought. How strongly we are all affected by him and by his absence. The sun shone on the purple-grey slate and sharpened the new incisions of the lettering with heavy shadows. It was warm and scented in this buttercup meadow, but she still had the sense of how quickly it would get dark in the valley when the sun slid behind the mountains. She remembered the sun setting behind Pumori and the icy still twilight of Base Camp. Sam walked slowly away past the last row of graves and left her to herself.

The last time Al tried to kiss her and her face was insulated by her oxygen mask.

The last words he spoke to her. She thought she had forgotten them, that pain and hypoxia and exhaustion had wiped them away, but they were still there: 'Wait just a few more hours for me. Then we'll never have to be apart again. I promise you.'

Finch thought of Jen Hood's bright eyes and the way she seemed to see so clearly.

Maybe Al had meant what he promised. Maybe when the time came he had understood that he must do better than that. The last gesture had been an act of great heroism and maybe that outreached a future of ordinary love. Maybe he always did what he wanted.

She said aloud, 'I thought I knew you. I know I loved you. And I will keep you in my heart.'

There was no sound except the hum of bees in the

wildflowers and the cars passing beyond the church. Finch looked again at the name on the gravestone and at the view past the big old trees and the meadow, towards the Welsh mountains. Then she slowly walked away. She found Sam waiting for her on the bench under the lych-gate, with his long legs at an angle in the gritty dust.

At 6.30 they were ringing Jen Hood's doorbell again. She opened the door and led the way to the cluttered living-room at the back of the house where the table had been cleared and laid with five places. There was one of the folded paper napkins on each side plate. Jen had changed into a skirt and applied a thin slick of lipstick.

She poured surprisingly large measures of gin into three tumblers. 'Molly's having a bath. My partner Tim will be joining us later.' She gave them their drinks and tilted her own glass before taking a substantial gulp and coughing a little as the alcohol hit her stomach. 'Cheers. Thank you for coming all this way to see us. Thank you for the pictures of him.' One of them was propped on the mantelpiece next to a vase of dried flowers. The lurid pre-storm sky and the wind-suit hoods made a dot of colour next to the sere blooms.

Finch and Sam drank deeply too. There was a tense interval of silence while they all looked around the room and tried to gauge the temperature of it, before Finch gently asked, 'Are you and Molly all right?'

Jen considered, swirling the gin over its ice cubes and taking another mouthful before she answered.

'Yes. I am. I believe Molly will be. And are you?'

'Me?'

'You were in love with him, weren't you?'

The sudden intake of alcohol lowered Finch's control by a single degree. 'Yes.'

'And he loved you.'

'I think so. In his way.'

A smile tucked the lipsticked corners of Jen's mouth. It looked involuntary and she tried to suppress her amusement but then laughter suddenly took hold of her. The sound of her laughing was incongruous in the quiet room, but the brightness in her face compensated for the oddity. 'That sounds like him.'

Sam was smiling too. Finch threw back the rest of her drink, disconcerted, then looked from one face to the other. Jen leaned forward with the warmth of her amusement still in her face. She looked pretty and, suddenly, as if she would be very easy to like.

'Let's drink to him. You missed the wake, you Americans, so let's drink to him now.'

The gin bottle was applied again and Sam briefly caught Finch's eye. He returned his gaze immediately to the middle distance. When her glass was full Jen stood up in the centre of the room and raised it. This was not, it was now becoming clear, only her second drink of the evening.

'Here's to Alyn Hood. Big-time mountaineer, small-time husband. Friend and father, and fucking nightmare. The best friend I ever had, the best company, the worst bloody proposition for marriage and security. I loved him all right. I'm not surprised you loved him too, Doctor Whatsit. I don't mind, either, I don't want you thinking I do, because Al and I were finished as soon as Spider died on K2 and we both knew it. Anyway, let's have a drink in his memory.' Jen turned on a wobbly heel and nodded to the photograph on the mantelpiece. 'Here's to you, mate. My love.'

'The bravest man I know,' Sam said and followed suit.

'Al,' was all Finch could manage. She stood up as unsteadily as Jen, with gin setting up a warm, dazed sluice in her gut. A slice of westerly light lay across a dusty rug and revealed the cat hairs threaded among the tufts.

Molly pushed open the door and stared at the three of them. 'Christ,' she muttered. 'Give me some of that, please.'

Molly took a drink as enthusiastically as her mother. Finch wasn't used to more than a couple of glasses of wine at a time while Sam had spent years of marathon training without ever touching alcohol, and it was evident that they were out of their league here.

Finch knew that she was already well on the way to being drunk. 'Wait a minute,' she protested as Jen topped up her glass.

'I'm just hoping you won't notice the food too much.'

'I'm afraid I can probably promise that already.'

By the time the third guest arrived the room had gone hazy. Jen was telling a story about the time Spider and Al hid in the empty guard's van of a Chester-to-Llandudno Junction train, hoping for a free ride to go climbing, only to be locked inside it, uncoupled and shunted into a remote siding for a whole weekend.

'They were always ravenous, needed food every two hours. Can you imagine what they were like after two days?'

Molly still smiled at the story even after many retellings. 'They had some beer, that was all. Spider tried to eat his climbing shoes. They were the only pair he'd ever had, and he'd worked a paper round to buy them and they stank. That was how hungry they were.'

Jen's partner turned out to be a mild man with a shy smile. He carried three bottles of Rioja in the crook of his arm. He kissed Jen and shook hands with Finch and Sam, and uncorked the first of the bottles. Molly gave him a cool nod.

'Oh, God, it's incinerated,' Jen shouted as she retrieved the dinner from the Rayburn.

'It's fine,' Tim reassured her.

They ate shepherd's pie and drank wine. Sam told them about Pemba and Mingma and the other Sherpas who had brought Al's body down, and about the members of Al's last expedition, and Finch supplied the details that he forgot. The room grew warm as darkness fell outside, and Molly lit candles that were reflected in glimmering ovals from the navy-blue window glass. Jen was interested in everything they told her, an open-eyed, alcohol-softened interest that held its own sadness but no trace of bitterness. She turned her glance to Tim once in a while and he rested his arm over the back of her chair or touched his fingers to her wrist. Jen was plainly loved, Finch thought. Maybe that was what had smoothed her frown and left only the creases as evidence that it had once been habitual. Envy prickled her and she suppressed it with a shiver.

Jen made coffee. They had drunk all the Rioja and begun a bottle of something else, and Sam was laughing at a joke Molly told him. Molly had watched them all, all evening, with a dark, cynical flicker of amusement and appraisal in her eyes, but it was Sam who captured her interest. He asked her questions about her life and her plans, and she became suddenly animated, talking about what it had been like to go out in the hills with Al when she was a little girl. Then, almost in the space of a minute, between starting the joke and delivering the punchline, she had had too much to drink. Her words began to slur and she sprawled back in her chair.

'That's enough, love,' Jen warned.

'I'll have another glass.'

'You heard what your mum said,' Tim murmured.

Molly sprang to her feet and her chair overbalanced with an ugly clatter. 'Don't tell me what I can't do. You're not my *dad*.'

Tears blurred her eyes and overflowed down her cheeks.

She yelled at him, angry with herself for crying as much as at his intervention. 'You're not my fucking father and don't you forget it.'

She turned and stumbled out of the room.

Jen said quietly, 'I'm sorry about that. She misses Al. It's hardest for her and she won't really talk to me about it.'

'It's time we went,' Finch offered.

'Don't go yet. I want to talk some more, if I'm not too sloshed.'

It was Tim who stood up. 'I think I'll get back home. I'll give you a call in the morning, Jen.' He kissed her on the top of her head and took his jacket from beneath one of the cats on the sofa. Sam eased himself out of his chair as well, standing up and wincing.

'I'll walk out with you. Get a breath of air.'

Jen and Finch were left alone. From upstairs they could hear the sound of footsteps, doors opening and closing, a lavatory flushing. The guests were returning from their evenings out.

'What time do you have to get up?' Finch asked.

Jen sighed. 'Half six, tomorrow. I've got some fishermen who want to be out early.'

Finch rested her head on her hand. 'How will you manage that? I don't know about you, but I seem to have had a lot to drink.'

'I think you *do* know. I saw you looking at me earlier on, thinking here's an old soak. But I just had a drink or two beforehand because I was nervous about you coming back here, sitting down to dinner with Molly and me and Tim, and taking mental snapshots of us to put in the background to Al. I didn't know why I'd asked you once I'd done it, to be quite honest. Al never told me properly about you, but I knew. You can't live with someone as long as I did with him without being able to read him clearly enough. After Spider died, wasn't it? That was when everything fell to bits between Al and me although it had been going wrong for a long time. A *long* time. He had the need in him, just like Spider did, to go on and on climbing. There was always another expedition, another peak singing its fucking siren song.'

Jen's head dropped back, exposing her pale throat so that Finch saw the column of her trachea and the wings of her clavicles. Jen gave another huge sigh, letting her shoulders loosen, then sat upright again. 'I wanted him to live here with Molly and me, like an ordinary man, but he refused to be ordinary. I thought he owed it to us to be and he thought that the only real reason to be alive was to climb mountains.'

She had been talking quickly, her tongue loosened by the drink. Now she stopped and saw that Finch was staring at her. 'What did I say? Why are you looking at me like that? You knew him, you were his lover, none of this'll be news to you.'

Still Finch didn't say anything and Jen shrugged. She tilted the bottle again and a chain of dribbles marked the tablecloth between them.

'Let's have one more drink before you go. Come on, sit on the sofa and talk to me.'

Out of her mind's blurry confusion one piece of understanding stood out diamond-sharp to Finch. She had been chasing it through the recesses of her mind for months and now she saw it with perfect clarity. Her concentration on it meant that she stood up obediently and absently, and forgot about her foot. She lost her balance immediately and crashed over in a heap, her head just missing the corner of the table. The next thing she saw was Jen crouching over her, her face a pucker of concern and dismay. A wave of humiliation broke over Finch and made her launch into a babble of excuses. 'It's not that, I'm not that drunk, I lost my footing. I lost my *foot*. It got frostbitten and gangrenous, and they had to amputate. Look, you see?' She pulled aside the cuff of her trousers and her sock to show Al's ex-wife the glimmer of steel.

'Oh, God. I didn't know. Are you all right? Can I help you? What can I do?'

'Help me up.'

Jen put her hands under Finch's arms and with a joint effort they managed to haul Finch to her feet. Once she was upright they kept their balance by clinging together, swaying like a pair of pantomime drunks.

'Oh, God, I'm sorry,' Jen repeated.

'Let's sit down.' Finch pointed to the sofa and they shuffled to it with their arms round each other.

Jen lowered her to the cushions. 'Are you okay?'

Finch explored her limbs. 'A couple of bruises. Nothing new.'

'Tea. Let me make a cup of tea. The Welsh cure for all ills.'

She boiled the kettle, poured hot water and gave Finch her cup. Then she brought hers and sat down beside her.

Sam walked with Tim to his car parked a little way down the street. They might have exchanged some observations about the evening, or about the women they had spent it with, but they chose a kind of meditative silence. Beside Tim's car they shook hands and wished each other goodnight. As he walked back towards Jen's house, slightly dizzy with the exposure to night air, Sam saw Molly sitting on the low wall beside a neighbouring house. He stopped in front of her, standing easily with his hands in his pockets.

'I suppose you think I was a creep, back there,' she challenged him.

'No.'

'I just got a bit large, that's all. I wish my Dad was still here.'

'We all wish that.'

'Not as much as I do.' Even in the dark he could see her glowering at him. The angle of her jaw and the miserable heat in her eyes set up a shiver of association in him and he realised that Molly reminded him of the way he had been himself after Mary died.

'That's true. You may not think it but I do understand how you feel.'

'Why?'

He told her briefly, without emphasis, then asked, 'Do you fancy a little walk? Help me sober up a bit? I can't stand the Welsh pace.'

Molly hopped off the wall. 'There's fuck all else to do here but drink.'

They began to walk. Molly pushed her arm through Sam's and skipped a couple of paces to fall into step with him, her hip glued to his.

Sam surveyed the deserted and silent street. 'You won't have to live here for ever. When do you go to college?'

'October. If I get the grades.'

'There you are.'

'Yeah. You know, you're okay? I like you a lot.'

'Thank you,' Sam said seriously.

'I haven't got a boyfriend at the moment.'

'Are you kidding? As gorgeous as you are?'

She swung round to check his expression, almost overbalancing them. 'Do you mean that?'

They had walked the same route as this afternoon and now they stood beside the church lych-gate. On the other side of it the graveyard was a dense wall of darkness.

Sam stopped and looked down into her face. He lifted one of her springy curls away from her cheek and twisted it around his forefinger. 'Yes, I do. You are beautiful to look at, for a start. Plus I think you have your father's fire and will and singularity, and your mother's good heart. All that makes you quite a rare young woman.'

Molly's mouth opened a little now and she breathed harder. Her eyes were luminously fixed on Sam's. Uh-oh, he thought. She took his hand and drew him under the shelter of the gate. 'We used to come here to sit on the bench and snog each other when we were kids. I'm surprised there's no one here tonight. Bit late, I suppose.'

She pressed herself closely against him and wound her arm round his neck. She kissed him with a wet mouth and tongue that tasted of stale wine and extreme hunger, and her body felt very young and smooth and urgent along the length of his.

With a distinct effort Sam made himself reach backwards for her arm and disengage it, and turned the kiss from an eager exploration into an affectionate nuzzle. 'That's enough,' he murmured. He steered her to the bench where he had sat and waited for Finch to finish whatever she needed to do at Al's grave.

'I suppose you're with *her*?'
'Her?'
'Doctor Finch Buchanan. First my Dad, now you.'
'No, I'm not with her. I wanted to be. But she was in love with Al, too much in love with him even to notice that I was on the same planet. I think she still is, still feels the same, and I think it's time for me to leave her in peace and get back to my own life. I wanted to come with her to see you and Jen and, now we've done that together, I guess we'll go back and go our separate ways. So now you know.'
Molly sat sideways, gazing at him in the darkness. 'I don't want her to have you, but if I can't . . .'
'I'm flattered, but I'm way too old for you.'
'It all sounds a bit sad.'
'Yeah. Life's a bitch and then you die.'
There was a silence. A car passed somewhere in the distance.
'I'm sorry, Molly. That was a dumb, clumsy thing to say.'
'He was always going to die. I always knew.'
Sam reached for her hand and held it.
'I *am* proud of him, though.'
'You should be.'

Finch and Jen sat on the sofa and drank their tea. Finch told her about her first encounter with Al when he came crazily down from K2 with Spider's death in his eyes. She described the truck ride they had taken through Pakistan down to Stuart Frost's house in Karachi.
'Stu.' Jen smiled. 'We were all friends, twenty-five years ago. Al and Spider and Stuart and me, and half

a dozen others. Never any money, nothing much to worry about, just climbing days. Long before the demons of mid-life started snapping at all of us. I should have married Stu. He wanted me to, way back then.'

Finch remembered the man living alone in the dusty villa behind the eucalyptus trees. 'I wonder what would have happened if you had done?'

'Who knows? Stu wasn't one of the ones who thought the only reason to be alive was to climb mountains. He might have been here now in his slippers, asleep in front of the television.'

'Al talked a lot about those early days,' Finch said.

'Oh, did he? And what did he tell you, exactly?'

The other woman's tone changed. She wanted to know how much of himself and of his past Al had given her. Even death couldn't silence jealousy. Be careful, Finch warned herself, knowing at the same time that the effects of drink, and the confusion of barriers coming down and going up again, had probably already made care impossible.

'Did he talk about Cath, for example?'

In the barn at Deboche, with the night sky outside the window hole, Al telling her about his childhood in Liverpool, his much older sister and his brother's antics . . . 'Yes, he did.'

Jen's eyebrows made a sharp, questioning arch. 'So then you knew she was his mother?'

'What?'

'Cath was really his mother. Not an unfamiliar story hereabouts, or anywhere else in those days I suppose. Fifteen-year-old girl gets pregnant, has the baby, the parents keep quiet and bring it up as their own. Are you shocked?'

'Was that the intention? To shock me? I'm a doctor, remember. I work in a big city, I've lived in Asia. I have heard of more terrible things.'

Jen reddened, a faint flush washing over her cheekbones. 'Okay, I deserved that. I meant, were you surprised that he didn't tell you something so fundamental about himself.'

After a moment Finch said, 'Yes.'

'Well, Cath and me are the only ones left who do know. Molly doesn't. Cath spilled it out to him when he was a teenager, when she'd had one too many. It was something that did affect him. Don't worry, Al was full of secrets. He had a core of them. A white, cold seam like snow in a gully.'

'Yes,' Finch said again, sadly, acknowledging it as a truth. She lifted her head. 'Is there any more wine in that bottle?'

'Nope, we finished it. *But* here's another full one. Tomorrow's another day, eh?'

That was certainly true, Finch thought. And the other truth was that she had only known a version of Al Hood. That version was all she had and all she had to remember.

When Sam and Molly came back Jen and Finch were still sitting there, talking, chasing their memories of Al back into the separate past.

Molly was grinning in delight. 'Sam's wasted. He just tried to back his car up to the front door so you didn't have too far to walk, but he rammed it in the back of Dai Davies's Volvo.'

'Not rammed,' Sam protested. 'A small miscalculation. An even smaller bump. I'll be owning up to the Volvo man, of course, and to the Hertz rental company. But I don't think driving all the way back tonight's a great plan. Sorry.'

'Me neither,' Finch said hastily.

They looked at each other. 'Is there somewhere local we can stay?' It was well past midnight.

'No. But I've got one room here, the couple left unexpectedly this afternoon. You're welcome to it. It's a double bed.'

'Done,' Sam said. And added to Finch, 'You've got nothing to worry about tonight, the state I'm in.'

Molly laughed.

Finch washed her face and dried it on the towel Jen had given her, then brushed her teeth with the new toothbrush Jen had also provided. The night was taking on a faintly surreal quality but when she peered in the mirror she saw the same old features. Nothing changed. She undressed to her T-shirt, wound the towel around her waist and tiptoed across the landing. Behind the other doors Jen's bed-and-breakfasters were presumably fast asleep. In the last room was a double bed, with Sam lying on his back under a pink-covered quilt. She edged around the bed and sat down with her back to him. She undid her foot and removed it, placing it neatly beside the bed. Finally she hopped and slid under the covers, retrieved the towel by an awkward contortion and dropped it on the floor.

'I was with you on Everest,' Sam said softly.

'Do you think I've forgotten?'

'So I've seen you at your worst, and your best. I know you, I know who you are and what you're like.'

'What does this mean?'

'It means you don't have to squirm around me wearing a towel like a comedy virgin in a frat house movie. Have I given you any reason on this trip to be afraid that I'll jump on you?'

'No, none.'

'Finch. I'm beginning to wonder if you're not an uptight, over-defensive, somewhat self-concerned girl. Not the woman I believed you were.'

He had never said a critical word to her. The shock was considerable.

'I don't have to walk about naked just to demonstrate how well we know each other.'

'No, you don't. Shall I turn the light out now?'

'Yes please.'

They lay on their backs in the darkness, separated by a width of Jen's pink flowered sheet. When Finch closed her eyes the room whirled unpleasantly so she snapped them open again. Quite soon Sam's breathing slowed and deepened. He sighed once, then shifted on to his side, settling himself with his back to her. As far as she could tell he was asleep. Finch lay awake for so long that the birds were singing and there were grey margins around the curtains before she finally drifted into a doze. She dreamed unilluminatingly about Cath, the mother-sister she would never meet.

When she woke up the bed was empty and the opposite side already cool. There was no one on the landing, or in the bathroom where she splashed her bleary face with cold water and ran her hands through her hair. The smell of frying bacon rising from downstairs was completely unwelcome.

Going downstairs she met Molly on her way to the guests' dining-room with a tray loaded with plates of eggs and bacon. Finch averted her eyes from the food.

'Afternoon.' Molly grinned. It was 9.30.

Sam was sitting at the kitchen table with a neatly cleaned plate still in front of him and a mug of coffee at his elbow. He was reading a newspaper and Jen was standing at the stove manipulating a frying pan. Sam gave her a non-committal good morning and Jen offered her breakfast, which she declined, pouring herself a cup of coffee instead.

Molly came back with her tray for the last batch of full plates. Jen dispatched them and wiped her hands on her apron.

'Another day, another fifteen fry-ups.' She came to Finch and put her arm round her shoulders. 'Okay? Sleep well?'

'Thank you.' Finch smiled at her. She knew that she liked Jen Hood very much indeed. The long journey to North Wales had been crucial and she owed it to Sam. She would have to find the right time to thank him.

'Back home, then?' Jen said.

A short, square woman in an apron came in at the same moment and took a carrier of polishes and dusters out of a cupboard. 'I'll get started,' she announced to the room at large.

'Thanks, Menna.' There was work to be done.

'Yeah,' Finch agreed. 'Back home.'

Jen and Molly came out to the street to see them off. They inspected the damage to the rear bumper of the hire car and the corresponding dent in the Volvo.

'Totally hammered.' Molly laughed.

'Thank you for coming.'

Jen kissed Sam on both cheeks, then folded her arms around Finch. Finch bowed her head, to bring it level with hers, and embraced her in return. She was reluctant to detach herself and they stood for a long moment with the sense of connection strong between them.

'Thank you for bringing the photographs and filling in some of the things we didn't know. It means a lot to Molly and me. And I think we all understand that you can't know everything about anyone. Only some of the things, some of the motives. Some of the time.'

'Yes,' Finch said.

'Can I come and visit you in Seattle?' Molly was asking Sam.

'Sure you can. Any time.'

'Be happy. You can choose to be, you know.' It was Jen's advice to Finch.

'I'll remember that. I'll remember you told me.'

Looking around at the long street, at the square tower of the church just visible over the roofs and chimneys, Finch thought, *he's gone*. The sadness and silence fell away, leaving a wide expanse of clear white, like untracked snow. Molly was enthusiastically kissing Sam goodbye.

Then they were in the car. Sam took the driving seat. Molly and Jen stood back on the pavement, lifting their hands to wave in an identical gesture.

Finch had only seen the resemblance to Al, but now she realised that the two women were also alike.

Sam reversed and then the car rolled forward. Jen and Molly stood waving until it was out of sight.

They drove a long way without speaking. Sam broke the silence. 'I'm sorry I said what I did last night. I'd had too much to drink and I felt angry.'

'It's all right. You're probably right about me.'

There was another interval of silence. It lengthened and grew weighty, and neither of them could find the right words to break it because they knew that they were on the point of a decision about each other that was much too important to blur with the wrong language.

They were probably heading back separately and permanently to their individual lives, whereas only a matter of hours ago there had been other fragile possibilities. It now seemed that without there even being a moment of actual decision, the choice had already been made.

They returned to the Chester hotel and checked out, then drove on south towards London and the airport. Finch had a flight to Vancouver the same day; Sam's Seattle flight was not until the next morning.

Staring unseeingly at the motorway traffic, Finch thought about last night's moment of insight. Jen had said that the only real reason to be alive, for Al, was to climb mountains. Finch had always understood that too, on one level, but in the flush and glory of love she had missed the obvious point. He had promised her that Everest would be the last peak and that when it was done they would be together always. This was what she had demanded of him and he had been willing to try it for her even though he must have known that he could not keep the promise. Her relationship with Al had been defined by impossibility and their only destiny was to be disappointed. She had tried to make Al what she wanted, instead of allowing him to be himself.

The oldest mistake in the book. No wonder she had felt a sense of kinship with Jen.

Al knew all this, she understood, when he set out for the summit. He had offered himself up for Sam because the most difficult choice was the easiest.

Then there was Sam himself, Al's gift. Finch did know him and now that it was clear it was also too late; matters already seemed soured between them. She turned over the possibilities in her mind. She could still put out her hand to Sam and tell him that she didn't want him to go anywhere else without her, but she was afraid to do it. It might not be the truth and the last thing that she wanted was to offer him anything less than the whole truth.

Finch had always been sure of herself and now the certainties had collapsed. She had been blazingly certain of Al and all that seemed to be left of that was the white, the fresh snow obliterating past tracks and robbing the world of perspective. She took stock of all the implications of this. They were inextricably linked, Al and she and Sam. While Al had been insolubly riven and Sam's only mistake had been to be there, it seemed that she had made all the remaining blind and greedy assumptions. Silence enveloped her and the miles slid away. She couldn't talk even to Sam.

*

Sam looked two or three times at her profile. She was immersed in her own thoughts, and whatever they were they gave her a cold and bleak expression. He remembered the night they had had dinner together back in Vancouver and the tremor of misgiving he had felt at the beginning of it – that she might, after so long and so much, turn out to be less than he had imagined and longed for.

Say something, he willed her now. Tell me what you feel, give me a sign that you know who I am. Don't be the small and defensive person who crept into bed last night. Don't be a *fridge* – hadn't that been Adam Vries's joking definition, long ago?

But she didn't speak. Her remote expression became set. They made a few remarks about the distance and the route, and a mutual decision not to stop anywhere on the way. Within four hours they were approaching London from the west and the first road sign with an aeroplane graphic whirled up and dropped behind them.

'Nearly there,' Sam said.

'Plenty of time for the flight,' Finch answered, consulting her watch. 'Where will you stay tonight?'

'Airport hotel, I guess. After I've taken my medicine from the car people.'

He wanted her to say that she would change her flight, stay over with him, but a distance had opened between them that now seemed impossible to bridge and he knew that she wouldn't say anything of the kind.

They took the turning for the airport and crawled through a tunnel clogged with traffic. The terminal building loomed ahead, with signs for short-term parking. Sam negotiated the route with a mechanical efficiency that took up only just enough of his attention to stop him shouting aloud. Disbelief hammered in his head – they couldn't have come all this way together and be about to part like this, but the first move *must* come from Finch. Even the smallest inclination towards him would have been enough, but there was nothing. She sat frozen, her expression a mask that he couldn't penetrate.

They went through the mechanical business of parking, unloading luggage, finding a trolley and trundling it to the check-in. Sam stood patiently to one side while Finch went to the desk and he remembered his first glimpse of her at another airport, long-legged and blazing in a ski parka with a bridal bouquet in her arms. A long way, he thought, a very long way that had in the end led nowhere. Disappointment in her lodged beneath his diaphragm like nausea.

The moment came. She had a boarding card and a gate number. The departures avenue led behind screens into airside and a separation of much more than a few thousand miles.

'I'm glad we came. It was important,' Finch acknowledged. 'Thank you.'

He waited, watching the tension of the tiny muscles around her eyes. She hesitated, seemingly on the point of saying something, then changed her mind. She waited instead for Sam to speak and when he didn't she nodded.

'I had better go.'

She reached up, lopsided on her stronger side, and kissed his cheek. It was a small, dry peck of her lips that was amplified in his inner ear into the rending tear of final separation.

He straightened and briefly rested one hand on her shoulder. 'Good luck.'

'And to you.'

There were no meaningless promises to write, or telephone, or meet again.

She was already walking away through the departures channel. He noticed that she was limping, as if the effort to mask her disability had become too much for her. He watched her until she was out of sight but she never looked back.

Sam stood in the tide of passengers, with a stream of pointless obscenities coursing through his head.

Eighteen

Finch waited for the day's e-mail message from Suzy to download. It took several minutes so she knew that it must contain pictures. When it was finally complete and she clicked it open, the first thing she saw was the baby standing naked and unsupported, his solemn gaze directed straight at the camera. James's tiny feet were splayed between heaps of cushions and his bandy legs were plump, creased columns.

'Look what he can do on his own!!!!' Suzy had written underneath. 'Not exactly a world record in developmental terms, but he's so perfect!'

Finch examined the pictures. They were good; Jeff must have taken them. Suzy was notorious for her lack of talent as a photographer. The baby's skin was pearled with light and his dark eyes seemed to hold the wisdom of ages. He was beautiful. Finch could almost smell the musky sweetness of his head under the spikes of black hair and she felt again the involuntary tightening of her muscles in a spasm of longing to hold a child of her own. Her fingers lifted off the keyboard and clenched into fists.

Stop it, she admonished herself again, *stop* it. It is a purely hormonal function, you know that.

She was able to convince herself for most of the hours of most of the days that she could match her own artificial foot for efficiency of function and absence of feeling. She attended to her work and went through the motions of play, and three months had already passed since the visit to Wales. The short summer in Vancouver was fading into grey, foggy mornings and evenings that brought rain sweeping in from the ocean. Soon the mountains to the north of the city would reveal themselves in mantles of snow.

The twist of her inner muscles gradually loosened into nothing more than a dull, dismissable ache. Breathing evenly, Finch flexed her fingers and cupped her right hand over the mouse to scroll down through the remainder of Suzy's message. After the pictures it was the day's news and gossip – comment on an article on cognition she had read in one of the medical journals and wanted Finch's opinion about, a gripe about Jeff's tidiness when after all there was plenty else in life to get worked up around – Finch smiled at that, knowing well that a mild desire for occasional domestic order counted as obsessive-compulsive in Suzy's book – and an update on the development of James's language skills. He had just said 'tac' not once but *twice* at the sight of the neighbours' morose Maine Coon cat crossing the yard.

The usual affectionate shorthand jottings of friends separated only by distance. But today there was an unusual coda: 'I've been thinking about you since yesterday, did you know, could you feel it? Your last message was so sad.'

Was it? Finch wondered. I didn't think so, I

certainly didn't mean it to be. And she hadn't felt anything out of the ordinary, telepathic or otherwise, because she was so careful not to. She clicked open the out box and reread what she had written. It was only an account of her day's work and, if there was any sadness in it, it was indecipherable to her.

She went back to Suzy and read the coda again: 'When are you going to stop marking time like this and start living for real? I never thought you were afraid of anything, Finch, but maybe you are just frightened to be ordinary and happy. Don't be – just go and do it. Whatever it is. Before it's too late. Love always, S.'

You can choose, Jen Hood had said.

Finch sat and looked at the blank wall of her apartment. No picture of Al. She hadn't asked Sam for one and he hadn't offered it.

Then she clicked on Reply and tapped out a response. Real affection and admiration for Junior and his achievements, a reminder that some people including Jeff liked to hang up clothes and towels. And a disclaimer: 'I don't know what you mean about being ordinary and happy. I'm both. What else is there? Don't worry about me. F.'

She sent the message and closed down her laptop with a series of sharp clicks. It wasn't the truth and she was lying to Suzy about happiness because she wasn't being honest with herself either.

The apartment intercom buzzed, startling her. It was only Dennis, she remembered, and she went to press the button and let him in. They sat at her kitchen table and drank a glass of wine, then she griddled some chicken with chillies, which was right at the frontier of Finch's cooking skills. They ate companionably and talked about the possibility of buying new surgery premises and taking on an extra nurse. After she had cleared the plates Finch suddenly leaned over his shoulder and rested her cheek against his head.

'What's wrong?' he asked.

'Dennis, I can hug you without something being wrong, can't I?'

She kissed him before standing upright again. His hair was cut short almost to the bone and she felt the shy prickle of it against her lips. It was so long since she had kissed anyone at all and the shock of intimate contact was like being burned. And it wasn't the barn at Deboche that came into her mind now, but the pink bed in Jen's house where nothing had happened at all.

Dennis remembered two people in the barred light of the surgery, between the desk and the steel trolley with its cargo of gloves and disposable spatulas, two people dancing. He put his hand on her wrist. 'You don't need me to tell you what to do.'

'It would be too little and too late, whatever I did.'

Dennis didn't say anything to that, but she could see that he was disappointed in her.

In the last few weeks Finch had taken to driving across to her parents' house to spend Sunday evenings with them. It was as if the empty space of a weekend was tolerable up until the last hours and then became suddenly unbearable. The first one or two Sundays she had pretended that she was passing and had dropped in, or needed to collect something, but now the routine was fully established. Clare laid a third place at the big table and Angus sat in his chair on the terrace watching the sea and waiting for her car to turn off the road.

There was no smell of cooking, but the absence of it only touched the periphery of her consciousness as she climbed the stairs to the big room.

'Finch?'

Her father was calling her, with a terrible sharp note in his voice she had never heard before.

'Where are you? I'm coming.' Her gait was suddenly awkward as she tried to run up the wide steps.

At first glance the magnificent room was empty. A newspaper lay fanned out on the floor with the top sheet stirring in the draught from the open terrace windows.

Then her father's grey head rose up from behind the nearest sofa. His face was blanched with shock. 'Thank God. She's here.'

Clare lay on the floor in a heap with one leg twisted beneath her. Finch took in the scene with a glance and knelt over her mother. Somehow she stayed calm and went through the routine.

Airway, breathing, pulse. Not a cardiac arrest then. But her skin was white as paper, drained of blood.

She jerked her head up at Angus. 'Here's the keys. Can you get my medical bag out of the car?'

While he was out of the room Clare opened her eyes and moaned softly, 'Finch? Help me. What happened?'

Conscious and coherent, thank God, thank God.

Not a stroke either. Clare's colour was changing as

blood swept through the vascular system. Bright rosy pink washed over her face and throat.

I know, Finch thought, I know what it must be.

'Don't worry. Lie still for a few minutes.' Finch made her comfortable with a cushion and a cashmere throw from the sofa, then held her hand until Angus burst into the room again.

'She's come round. Tell me what happened to her.'

'She complained of feeling tired, so she lay down on the sofa for an hour. Then she got up because she wanted to fix dinner. She walked six steps and just fell. Are you going to get her to the hospital?'

'No, I don't want to go,' Clare whispered.

Finch folded away her stethoscope and smiled at her. Her mother's vital signs were all steady now. If it was a Stokes-Adams attack, as she was almost certain it must be, it didn't require emergency treatment.

'Tomorrow, for a proper checking over. Let's wait and see, but I don't think it's going to be necessary this minute. I'll stay here and make sure.'

Clare closed her eyes in relief. Her eyelids were coloured with shadow and her mouth was made up. Always the high standards and the duty of dinner. But under the steel will and despite the pink flush that was now gradually fading, Finch saw that she was suddenly frail. She leaned over and held her mother in her arms. Angus's hands were shaking with shock. They were two old people.

'Listen, Mummy, can you hear me? You blacked out for a few seconds, that's all. You haven't had a heart attack or a stroke or even a fit and you don't have a fever so it isn't a catastrophic infection. You haven't taken any interesting drugs, have you? I thought not. I think we'll just let you have a rest and keep a careful eye on you.'

Between them, once she was ready to be moved, father and daughter put Clare to bed. Finch sponged her face and hands, and smoothed moisturiser into her fine skin, then combed her hair and drew the covers around her shoulders. Her face was a tiny triangle against the pillows. Finch checked her pulse again and kissed her forehead.

The roles reversing, as inevitably as the passing of time itself.

'I love you,' Finch said, sitting on the bedside with her mother's hand folded between both of hers. It was simple to say. The spectrum of meaning was less easy to encompass.

'I know,' Clare answered. 'Always such an angry girl, you were, but bursting with love too. Full of passion and looking for something to bestow it on.'

'Was I?'

'You were always determined to beat your brothers and show Angus and me what you were made of. Maybe you'll grow up now.'

'Shh. That's enough for tonight.'

'Thank you for looking after me. Will you be here in the night?' She was as anxious and trusting as a child.

'Of course I will.'

Angus came in to say goodnight and Finch left them together.

She occupied herself with putting up a rough meal for herself and her father, and they sat at the kitchen table to eat, absently picking food off the plates with their fingers and spreading a fine mat of crumbs.

'Are you all right?' she asked. There was still a tremor in his hands.

'What do you think really happened?' His eyes implored her. The scale of this successful man's dependence on his wife was evident.

Finch answered thoughtfully, 'I'm pretty certain she had a transient ischaemic attack, a Stokes-Adams. The total pallor and then the vascular flush are characteristic. The heart's natural pacemaker falters briefly and the sufferer blacks out. Then in a matter of seconds another pacemaker further down the system clocks in, the circulation is restored and full consciousness returns. It's a benign condition, unless you fall under a bus as you black out.'

'She won't die?'

'Not of the condition itself. I'm not a cardiologist, so I'll make sure Neal Fletcher sees her tomorrow. But I would think they'll want to monitor her heart rhythm for twenty-four hours and depending on what that reveals maybe fit her with a pacemaker.'

Her father sombrely absorbed this information.

'Do you want a Scotch?' Angus asked when they had finished eating. Finch knew that he rarely drank spirits, but she nodded now. She went to check on Clare again and found her quietly asleep, and when she came back Angus had moved out on to the terrace. He gave her a heavy tumbler of whisky and they leaned on the balustrade in the darkness to listen to the invisible sea.

'She has been the best wife in the world,' he said.

'She's only sixty-nine,' Finch gently reminded him.

'We're both getting old.'

'There's a lot of time for you yet.'

Finch told herself, we should use it. We should all do everything we can in the time we have, instead of hiding and turning our backs and being full of fear. *I* should.

She rested the cold tumbler against her cheek. Concern and love filled her in equal measure. 'She is very strong-willed.'

'And so are you, my darling.' Angus put his arms round her and she caught the fatherly scent of cologne and good clothes, and clean sweat in the folds of skin around his neck.

'We are alike, aren't we?'

'Yes. You have the perspectives and expectations of a different generation, that's all. Clare thought it was more than enough to be a wife and a mother, while you needed to prove that you didn't have to be. I wonder now, maybe, whether you might not regret that absolute rejection of what she stood for.'

'I might.'

'And so?'

'I don't know, yet. I promise I will think about it.'

After Angus had gone inside to bed, Finch sat alone on the terrace among the fat silhouettes of the salt-glazed pots. If it was cold she didn't notice it, or even hear the mournful rustle of the sea. The lights of the opulent room blazed behind the screen of glass and Finch's eyes slid over the huge masks, the native American carvings, the blond wood and limestone, and the pale fabrics. A lifetime of rejecting her mother's values hadn't led her very far from home. She was thirty-three years old and she had crept back here to be nursed out of her injuries, and she came by choice to eat dinner every Sunday evening.

A little bubble of laughter squeezed itself out of her chest.

It was funny and when she recognised that much she knew she didn't feel angry any more. Whatever it had meant, to be the girl, the last, the best-loved and least demanded-from, no longer mattered. What was there to prove to anyone but herself? Clare and Angus were getting old and they loved each other. Her brothers' lives took their separate courses and she had her own to lead.

She thought of Al with tenderness, then of Sam who was still alive and had never disappointed her, and had accepted everything she dealt him with grace and good humour.

She missed him deeply but if she had thought it was already too late when they left Wales together, it was surely much too late now.

Finch bent her head and struggled with her demons of pride and independence. Sam wouldn't come looking for her again. If she went to try and find him, now and at last, it would be a capitulation on her part. But he would understand that too and the giving way itself would be something she could offer him.

Finch jumped up with the impetuous determination of a decision suddenly made. She forgot to balance and almost toppled against one of the big jars, and her hand slithered over the salt-gritty stone. She knew what she was going to do now and a great wash of impatience to be doing it coursed through her. In her old bedroom she lay sleepless for most of the night, looking at the ceiling's pallor, willing the morning to come.

When daylight and a civilised hour finally arrived

she drove Clare to the hospital and left her in the care of the cardiac team. Then, in the brief interval before her day's surgery, she rushed back to the apartment and sent an e-mail message. She didn't even know where Sam was living now, but she was sure that Adam Vries would.

At the other end of the day the cardiologist Neal Fletcher confirmed that Mrs Buchanan had indeed suffered a Stokes-Adams attack. They would monitor her heart rhythm over the next twenty-four hours and make a decision on the basis of their findings. Finch sat with Clare for half an hour, then left her alone with Angus. She drove through the end-of-day traffic back to her apartment and opened the e-mail programme. adamvries@compuserve.com was waiting in the in box.

There, amid the expected nudges and winks of the message, was an address and telephone number. Still in Seattle.

Finch sat back hard in her chair. She could pick up the telephone right now. Or she could do better than that, as Sam himself would do, had done. She could get on a plane and go to him.

'Of course. Take as long as you like,' Dennis said. 'So long as it isn't more than three days.'

'I'm in no hurry to intervene,' Neal Fletcher announced. 'It depends on what your mother will feel most comfortable with.'

'I'm going to Seattle, just for a couple of nights,' Finch told everyone. Nothing else.

*

She took an afternoon flight, and it made her think of their first encounter and the storm, and John Belushi swallowing Sam's story about being newlyweds. She remembered all the details of that and deliberately didn't think about what might be about to happen in case he was friendly, only friendly, or in case he didn't want to see her at all.

Once she was on the ground at SEATAC, she consulted a city map. Sam's latest address was in the Magnolia district, not far from Elliot Bay. A bus would take her downtown, where she could find a cab to deliver her to the door. She made her way along halls and down walkways with mechanical concentration, only now admitting to herself that this was an absurd undertaking. Sam had the style to carry off dramatic appearances and she did not. He could be anywhere, working, travelling, wrapped up in a new love.

She should have called.

She found the bus and boarded it. The doors closed with a hydraulic hiss and it rolled into the cloudy afternoon.

Sam and Frannie had been sorting books. When the old shared apartment was finally sold, during Sam's stay in Kathmandu, Frannie had moved in with a girlfriend and the books had been packed into boxes and stored. Now Sam finally had a new place to live, nothing fancy and bought with the last of his savings, and so did Frannie, and the packing cases had been brought out of storage. Frannie's art books were easy to separate from Sam's travel and biography, but the creased paperbacks of poetry and classic fiction, and the weight of association that went with them, were less straightforward.

'That copy of *archy & mehitabel* is mine. Look, I've written in it.'

'I'm sure I remember buying it in Boston.'

'No. Definitely mine.' Frannie placed it in her pile.

'My *Bright Lights, Big City*. I got it at a bookstore signing.'

'Really? Okay, then.'

They were being considerate to each other and minimising the awkwardness of this ritual dismemberment. Sam packed Frannie's piles back into the boxes ready to be ferried out to her car. It was dusty work.

'Do you want a glass of wine or something?'

Frannie looked around at the new space, heaped with Sam's familiar possessions, not yet properly arranged and probably destined never to be, at least by her standards. 'Um, no thanks. I think I'll just get back. Have we finished?'

'Yeah. I'll carry this lot down for you.'

He made three journeys down the single flight of stairs, through the shared hallway and out into the street, to Frannie's Toyota. The boxes were heavy but they stacked up neatly. The dividing was melancholy but he was glad that it was done. Soon there were only two boxes left. Frannie took one and he took the other, and they filed down the stairs once more.

Finch sat in the window of the bar, behind a dingy half-curtain over which she could just see the door of Sam's building. It wasn't a smart city bar or even a popular local one; it was a tired place, and only half full of tired and muted people at the end of a working day. She sat watching the street with a glass of Coke in front of her that she didn't really want, giving herself time to collect up her thoughts and her courage before she rang his doorbell. She played with the idea of going to the payphone at the back of the bar and giving him at least this much warning, but then she remembered how he had materialised at the Buddha's Garden, then at her surgery, and decided again that she would match him with this reciprocal total surprise.

If he was in, that is. If this was even where he really lived.

While she was still thinking this the door across the way opened and Sam himself came out. He looked exactly as he always did but more so, as if before now she had only partly registered his height and the way he moved, and the colour of his hair. He was carrying a heavy-looking box that he stowed in the trunk of a car. Finch found that her mouth was dry, and she was red in the face and breathless as if she were back in high school. Except that she had never felt like this in high school and only once in her life since then. And that had been so distorted by urgency and tragedy and distance and danger whereas this was – she searched for the word – level.

Sam went back inside and closed the door. Finch sat with her untasted drink and a minute later he was back with another box, and yet another after that. Was he moving again? Had she been lucky to catch him, before he drove off into the traffic a block away?

That must have been the last box of whatever it was, she thought, as the minutes slid by and he didn't re-emerge. She should go across now. She couldn't sit here blushing and procrastinating for ever.

The door opened once more. A woman came out, in khakis and a baseball cap that hid her face. A ponytail of fair hair was caught under the strap at the back and she, too, had a box in her arms. Sam came behind with another. They stood shoulder to shoulder at the rear of the car, clearly used to touching one another, evidently debating how to place this new load on top of the others. Sam rested his box on one hip while he made more space, then shoved it into the trunk and took the woman's from her and stowed that. She flipped the car keys in one hand while he did it. Then they walked round to the driver's door and Sam opened it for her.

Finch watched without blinking. Her eyes felt hot.

He put his hands on the woman's shoulders and tilted his head sideways to avoid the peak of her cap as he kissed her upturned face. One cheek and then the other. She said something, smiling, and Sam answered. They were lovers, briefly separating for a whole hour or so.

The woman got into the car and reversed out of the parking space. She slid past with her hand raised and Sam watched her, standing on the kerb until she was gone. Then he walked calmly back into his building, a nondescript low-rise in an ordinary city street, and closed the door on Finch. Too late, much too late, she thought, and bound to be.

I have been a fool and I resisted what I should have given everything to hold on to.

Upstairs, Sam skirted the furniture that was still

awkwardly herded instead of arranged in patterns. There was work on his desk; a new Net-based company in which his partner offered a range of personal financial services and Sam provided the technical and sales support from a series of linked websites. It looked promising, but it didn't capture his interest right now. He went across the room instead and looked out at a view of windows and fire escapes and balconies, and small domestic tableaux. Other people's lives, maybe no fuller or any more satisfactory than his own. Although at this moment that seemed hard to believe.

'C'n I get you anything?' A waiter in a grubby apron leaned across Finch to swab spills off the table.

'No, thanks, I'm just leaving,' she said dully. She stood up and counted money into a saucer. Where now? What to do now?

Cross the road and ring the bell. Make up some story about being in town. Wish him luck and then escape. She could just walk away without ever letting him know that she had been here, of course she could do that instead, but the longing to see him and talk to him even just for a minute was stronger than the instinct of self-preservation.

There was no intercom and walk-up buzzer, just a bell-push with his name in a little illuminated box. It seemed to take a long time for him to descend and check out his latest visitor.

At last she heard the lock draw back. He pulled the door open and immediately, faster than she could have even have wished in her most longing moment, joy filled his face.

'It's you. It's *you*.'

'I was . . . I was in town and I thought . . .'

'I didn't think you were going to come. What's the matter? You look unhappy. Why?'

'I nearly didn't come, I saw . . .' and she gestured across the sidewalk to where the car had been parked. 'Your girlfriend.'

He laughed then. A pure shout of it and his face told her more than the most eloquent words.

'Frannie. That was Frannie, I told you about her. She came to take her belongings away.'

They looked at each other, allowing the possibility that after all, after so much, they might finally be in the right place together at the right time.

'Can I come in, then?'

'Oh, God, yes. Come in, come in and stay for ever. I won't let you go.'

He took her hand and led her up a flight of stairs into his apartment. She had a confused impression of spread-out papers, two computer screens, hasty arrangements and impermanence. He was here because he had to be somewhere, not because he cared about it. Then the door closed behind them and in two steps Sam was holding her in his arms.

'I can't believe it's you.'

'It's me. Look.'

He lifted his hands and cupped her face, minutely examining it. He kissed her then, at first as if she might break, then their mouths opened to each other with a year and more of hunger in them.

'Why did you come now, rather than at any other time?'

'My mother had a heart block. She's all right now.

But she has always been so strong and when I saw she was fragile I thought how precious everything is.' Finch paused, unused to saying such things, then said it so softly that he had to strain to hear. 'I thought how you are the most precious of all.'

'Why didn't you tell me you were coming?' he murmured.

'You never used to tell me.'

'I was afraid of being forbidden.'

'So you know why.'

'Is this all right?' he asked, taking her hand again. 'Now?'

'Yes.'

He led her through into another room. There was a bed and a skylight in the beamed roof above.

They lay down on the bed, still hand in hand. Finch looked briefly upwards and saw a rectangle of perfect evening sky, clear and fathomless, framed and floating over her head. Then she closed her eyes as his mouth found hers.

In her head she heard Suzy's voice: 'About time, too. And good luck to you both.'